SMITHY
By Amanda Desiree

Published by Inkshares, Inc., Oakland, California
www.inkshares.com

Edited by Adam Gomolin & Avalon Radys
Cover design by Tim Barber, Dissect Designs
Interior design by Kevin G. Summers

ISBN: 9781950301218
e-ISBN: 9781950301225
LCCN: 2021932268

First edition

Printed in the United States of America

For my cousins from England

PART ONE

EXCERPT FROM
SMITHY: A TWENTY-YEAR COMPENDIUM
BY REID BENNETT, PHD

INTRODUCTION

Are we alone in the universe? Are human beings the sole source of intelligence, the only ones capable of rational thought and self-reflection in all of existence?

These questions have dogged Homo sapiens since the species walked out of Africa. The search for answers has taken many forms. Some turn wondering eyes to the stars in search of alien life-forms. Others pursue worlds beyond this one, reaching into the void to connect with spirits of the afterlife. And at one time, the quest for nonhuman intelligence focused on man's nearest neighbor in the animal kingdom.

In 1972, an ambitious psychologist from Yale University launched a revelatory study designed to bridge the gap between man and animal, proving chimpanzees could master the art of communication. Believing high-functioning primates could learn words and syntax, Dr. Piers Preis-Herald acquired a newborn chimpanzee and taught him American Sign Language, hoping to establish that longed-for link with another intelligent being, and thereby unlocking the secrets of a previously unplumbed mind.

What followed has since inspired decades of speculation and embroiled psychologists, linguists, ethologists, primatologists, parapsychologists, historians, animal rights activists, teachers, attorneys, clergymen, and other curious minds around the world in controversy.

When Chimpanzee #710642 was born at the Kohlberg Center for Primate Research on an autumn morning in 1972, his destiny was undetermined. He could have been sold to a traveling circus and taught to tap dance like Daisy, born one week earlier. He might have become a guinea pig for the cosmetics industry like Avery, born three weeks later. And if the chimp called Webster and later known to the world as Smithy had been born a mere five hours sooner, he would have spent his childhood before Hollywood cameras, as did Goofy, instead of starring in the incredible real-life drama that ensued.

The Kohlberg Center was then one of five facilities in the United States that bred chimpanzees for distribution throughout the world. Most of the offspring were designated for zoos and laboratories, with a small fraction bought by the entertainment industry, and a more miniscule portion ending up in the exotic pet trade. Applicants desiring a chimpanzee were placed on a lengthy waiting list; barring special requests for characteristics like sex or birth weight, orders were filled on a first-come, first-serve basis. Therefore, it was entirely by chance that Smithy entered Dr. Preis-Herald's orbit.

Considering the incredible outcome of this turn of fortune, many have questioned whether any chimpanzee in his position would have behaved the same way, or whether Smithy himself possessed unique abilities.

Historians always ask whether the man makes the situation or the situation makes the man. So it is with man's nearest relation. Did Smithy's intellect and other purported gifts trigger the unbelievable and sometimes tragic events of his young life, or was he shaped into an unlikely prophet by a potent and chaotic environment? Since it's impossible to separate Smithy from his surroundings or to engage in counterfactual thinking, what remains is to investigate the actual data.

Was Smithy a hoax? A clever mimic? A helpless animal caught in the machinations of selfish humans and nearly crushed by them? Was he the harbinger of a new era of interspecies—and possibly interdimensional—relations? Was he an illusion? A Rorschach projection of humanity's greatest hopes and fears? Or was he indeed what devotees of metaphysics have claimed for so long: a link between our world and the next?

In the following chapters, I review the most complete collection to date of primary source documents: letters, journals, interviews, video and court transcripts, and related media. Included publicly for the first time are first-hand accounts by the principals in the case and details of never-before-released film footage. In addition, I present insights gleaned from my own minor part in what came to be the greatest mystery of the modern age.

The world may never know the truth about Smithy, but as it is human nature to seek answers, we must boldly sally forth into the unknown with open eyes and open minds. Let the journey of inquiry commence!

Reid Bennett, PhD
Newport, RI
May 10, 1995

WCCT NEWS BROADCAST

Date: December 8, 1972
Location: Local News Studio

A female newscaster sits behind a desk. She smiles and says, "Now we turn to Art Delafield, who earlier today visited Yale University's Primate Studies Center to investigate a groundbreaking new experiment."

The scene cuts to a male reporter standing in a laboratory with whitewashed walls. Behind him are a sink and empty countertops. He says, "Good evening, ladies and gentlemen. My beat is usually the human-interest story, and while this particular story is sure to interest humans, it features another animal entirely. Let me show you what I mean."

Delafield walks to a workbench and sits beside a man approximately forty-five to fifty-five years old with a receding hairline, dark eyebrows, and piercing eyes. He smokes a pipe and wears a collared shirt with the top button open. A dark-haired, bearded young man in his mid-twenties stands behind him. The young man is wearing a lab coat and is stirring something in a bowl.

Delafield introduces the older gentleman. "This is Dr. Piers Preis-Herald, formerly of Cambridge University, currently a professor of psychology here at Yale and the voice of radio's syndicated *Secrets of the Mind in 60 Minutes*. Dr. Preis-Herald, I understand you've long been interested in the process of language acquisition. Can you explain what that involves?"

Preis-Herald smiles. "Please, Art, call me Piers. It's so much less unwieldy. As to your question, my research deals with how humans learn novel words and acquire the rules of language or syntax. Further, how does one learn to use language in a more sophisticated manner, developing metaphors, similes, or idiomatic expressions? How does one discern shades of meaning in sarcasm or veiled threats?"

Delafield remarks, "That all sounds complex."

Preis-Herald says, "Indeed. In fact, some of my peers claim language is so complicated that only the human brain is equipped to handle it. I disagree. Higher mammals such as porpoises and primates—and even certain breeds of bird—have shown an aptitude for advanced understanding of language. I've wondered at what stage of development language can be learnt. By 'development,' I mean the development of mankind, not merely the development of a single human. For instance, can language develop in man's biological coevals? Are certain components of the brain required to perform the magic of communication? To investigate these questions, I will look closely at how an infant acquires language. The infant I've selected for my new experiment is a young chimpanzee. My wish is for this little chimp to show me if the brain is, in fact, hard-wired with a mechanism for arranging and applying words, or whether these skills can be taught."

Delafield begins, "Doctor—"

Preis-Herald interrupts. "*Piers*, I insist. My hypothesis is that language is a transmittable skill, much like cooking or tying a shoe, a consequence of culture and socialization. Chimpanzees in the wild lack a society such as we're accustomed to defining it. Although apes can communicate the presence of dangerous predators in the area or the location of a food source, they don't use language as you and I do to share our thoughts or to bond. Chimpanzees don't debate or pour out their hearts to an analyst. But if an ape were raised from birth in a context in which communication for communication's sake was the norm, it might adopt this norm. I believe if an animal with a high intellectual capacity were immersed in language from birth and taught to use words, it would demonstrate mastery at least on par with a young human child or a retarded adult."

Preis-Herald reloads his pipe. As he speaks, he gestures to the bearded young man behind him.

"My research assistants and I have acquired an infant chimpanzee—about two months old now—that we've kept here at our lab in anticipation of placing it with a human family to be reared just like an ordinary child. You see, Art, a human infant grows up constantly absorbing language through observation and direct coaching. To better transmit language to our chimpanzee, we shall relate to him as one human being to another. He will be exposed to every milestone of a human child, including dressing, feeding, and toilet training. He will be fully embedded in every aspect of human culture to stimulate his intellectual growth."

As Piers smokes, the reporter's eyes water. Delafield averts his face to cough discreetly several times. He says, "That's amazing. Will you be raising the chimp yourself?"

Preis-Herald says, "Ah, dear me, no. The faculty housing isn't spacious enough for a youngster, and besides, a baby needs a mother. I, alas, as a bachelor, am unsuited for the role. Fortunately, I've maintained contact with a promising former graduate student who is now married and rearing her own family. She and her husband have agreed to take our little chimpanzee into their home as a surrogate son. He will have every advantage a good American family can provide, and he'll be drilled in language every single day. I shall periodically visit the family and their protégé to observe, record, and measure his progress."

Delafield asks, "How do you plan to test this chimp for language, Doc—Piers? Do you expect it to talk to you?"

Preis-Herald answers, "To vocalize as you and I do, no. Instead, we shall use the method the Deaf use. Our chimp's host family happens to have a Deaf child, and so the family uses American Sign Language, or Ameslan, alongside spoken English. They will teach the chimp to recognize and produce these signs. To document his progress, we'll have registered Ameslan interpreters independently judge his use of sign language."

Delafield asks, "Piers, aren't you concerned some of your colleagues might accuse you of, er, simply monkeying around? This is a very unconventional study."

An amused smile creeps across Preis-Herald's face. "It's high time scientists broke out of the box created by the current paradigms in psychology and linguistics! After all, we would never have reached the moon if everyone continued to parrot Aristotle. Scientists must question and be daring. They must launch new ventures with detailed plans in place. In our language study, everything will be thoroughly documented. The data concerning the introduction of new words into the chimpanzee's vocabulary, the accuracy of their usage, and the frequency and pattern of presentation will be made available for any interested party to review. I'm confident the results will speak for themselves. Now, would you care to meet our subject?"

Delafield and the camera follow Piers as he crosses the room and stands behind a highchair in which sits a baby chimpanzee wearing a bib. The bearded young man feeds him with a spoon.

Preis-Herald continues, "This is the young man of the hour. At the facility where he was born, he was known as Chimpanzee #710642. However, I have decided to call him 'Webster.' An affectation, or rather, an augury."

The bearded man lifts the chimpanzee out of the highchair and paces in the background of the shot, patting Webster's back to burp him as Piers speaks.

Delafield asks, "How so?"

Preis-Herald says, "We'll teach our Webster a wide vocabulary, the likes of which would impress his illustrious namesake, who demonstrated his own mastery of language by creating a dictionary. Our goal is to fashion him into a proper wordsmith."

In the background of the shot, the chimp spits. The bearded man wipes his mouth with a towel.

Delafield says, "That's a most ambitious goal, er, Piers. We look forward to learning from both you and little Webster all about the mysteries of this most precious—and up till now, most human—talent: language!"

The camera picks up the young man's words as he murmurs to Webster: "You hear that? You've got your work cut out for you, little Smithy."

LETTER FROM GAIL EHRLICH
TO EHRLICH FAMILY

May 22, 1974

Dear Mom, Dad, Vanessa, and Snoopy:
I hope this letter finds you all safe and sound. I arrived in Newport three days ago and I'm having the time of my life! I sat down to write to you all about it on my first day, got distracted, started over, then the same thing happened, and here I am now. The third time is the charm!

My flight was good and got in right on time. Descending was like traveling through another world! When I looked out the window, all I could see was wispy white. It felt magical. When we came out of the cloud, I still felt like I was in some other world. I never saw so much water before! It was all silver and shiny like a mirror with little bits of green grass sprinkled over it. When I think of an <u>island</u>, I think of sand and beaches with palm trees. We do have beaches but no palm trees.

On the plane, I sat next to a very nice man who was going to Newport for a business meeting. He realized we were going in the same direction and offered to give me a lift in his rental car. We went over a big bridge and were so high above the water. I was a little afraid driving over it and held on to the door handle until we reached the other side, but I still couldn't take my eyes off the view. I saw sailboats, motorboats, row boats, big yatts. I waved to them when we went by even though I knew they couldn't see me and Mr. Peters laughed and patted my knee and told me I was a cute kid.

When we got back on land, I saw the cutest little cottages everywhere. They all look like little dollhouses. Mr. Peters told me there called salt boxes because the roofs look like lids. There long and steep like the flap on a box. I must of looked pretty silly pointing and squealing at everything because he laughed at me again, but he kindly drove me all through town, even the parts that weren't on our way so I could see the shops and the warf. We drove by the big church where John and Jackie Kennedy got married! Mr. Peters said you can even go inside on certain days to see it.

Then we started up Bellevue Avenue, the major street where all the rich people built their summer houses. That's when I really felt like I was in a fantasyland. All the houses here are enormous! They look like palaces or Roman temples. Most are three and four stories tall and there covered with little statues and carvings. You won't find a salt box on Bellevue Avenue!

These houses were built by some of the richest people in America. In fact there's a house just up the road from where I am right now that belongs to a famous herress! But here's the crazy thing. They only lived in them for a couple of months at a time. Mr. Peters says people only built these houses to show off. They would have a bunch of parties in the summer and the rest of the time the houses would just be shut up with maybe a caretaker living there.

If I had a big house like that I'd want to spend my whole life there. But he said the rich families probably had other houses that were just as big and fancy in places like New York or Boston or wherever they came from. And then after the tax laws changed, it got harder to keep the big summer houses so a lot of them were left empty longer or even abandoned.

Mr. Peters drove me right to the door of Trevor Hall. When I saw the house, I thought, "It looks like a castle!" It has a big tower with a pointy roof just like the castle at Disneyland. It has some statues, too, but not as many as I saw on a house called the Breakers. Trevor Hall is a mansion that got left abandoned for a long time, so its not as fancy as it's neighbors, but its still the most glamorous house I've ever been in. Its got old tapestries on the walls and a fancy carpet in the hall and a carved banister on the stairs and lots of windows. Sure the carpet is old and stained and starting to wear out, but you can still see the original design. In some places, you can still see gold thread winking up at you. Can you imagine it? Me walking on a <u>gold carpet</u>! Me living in a real honest to goodness <u>mansion</u>!

Mr. Peters dropped me off and wished me luck. He comes to town alot and said he'd look me up on his next visit. Even though he was *practically a stranger I still felt nervous after he drove away. He was the closest thing to a friend I had in Newport.*

Dr. Preis-Herald isn't here yet, but his assistant Wanda's been getting everything ready for us, and she came out to meet me. I thought Wanda would be an old teacher like Dr. Preis-Herald, but she's just a few years older than me. She's still a student, too, (a graduate student) but she looked so glamorous standing in front of the big mansion just like she was a rich herress inviting me into her palace. She has shiny dark hair that curls around her shoulders and blue eyes, and she looked like someone from TV. Maybe Marlo Thomas or Marie Osmond. She wore a dress like the one on the cover of the Vogue magazine I had on the plane. I bet she could be a model if she wanted. I was nervous until she started to speak to me. She's very nice and didn't mind answering my questions. Alot of what I wanted to know will have to wait until the big meting we'll have after everyone else has arrived.

Wanda showed me around the first floor of the mansion to the kitchen, the library, and the solarium, then she took me to my room on the second floor. Trevor Hall has three floors in all. The chimp is going to have a room on the top floor. Wanda's staying on the second floor in a part of the tower, just like a princess!

My room is the size of two rooms. The part you first walk into is huge! It has space for a couch, a desk, a bed, and a wardrobe. Wanda said we'll have to use wardrobes instead of closets because that's how it was done in the olden days. There's a bathroom attached on one side of the room, so I don't have to go down the hall in the middle of the night, and there's another smaller room connected on the other side with its own bed, a desk, an easy chair, a chest of drawers, and a lamp. Best of all, I have a balcony and a view of the back garden with roses growing close to the house and a big lawn and lots of trees all around. No one was taking care of the flowers while the house was empty, but you can tell how pretty everything once was.

I ended up in such a big room because I have a roommate! She arrived by train the same evening I did. Her name is Tammy, and she's from New York. She goes to school at Columbia and she's a graduate student in psychology so she's Wanda's age. Tammy isn't as glamorous as Wanda, but she's still cool. She dresses like a hippie in long skirts and blouses, but she's not dirty at all. She wears glasses so she looks like she's smarter than everyone else. She talks like it, too.

Tammy asked Wanda tons of questions, mostly about the house and Newport. Wanda told us the house was built after the Civil War by a man named Curtis Trevor who made his money selling goods to the army (just like Rhett Butler!) He invested it in a gold mine and when he struck it rich, he built a house in Newport with all the other wealthy families. After he died, the house was a boarding school, but it closed after the Depression, and private families have rented it off and on ever since. And now we have it!

It was already getting late by the time Tammy arrived, so we ordered a pizza delivered to the house so we wouldn't have to cook. Can you imagine a pizza boy delivering food to a mansion? I wish we could have had a butler to open the door and pay the delivery guy. How funny would that be?

We sat at the big dining room table to eat, just the three of us. Its a beautiful room with big windows that open into the backyard and clouds painted on the ceiling with gold angel faces carved in wood smiling down on us. I said it looks like Heaven! Well, we were getting along great but when dinner was over, Wanda told Tammy she would show her to her room, and Tammy would be staying with me. Tammy started arguing that the house was so big she shouldn't have to have a roommate. I thought she was being rude not wanting to room with me. I know Vanessa complains about me sometimes, but I'm not really a slob, and I don't snore or sleepwalk or anything.

Later I found out Tammy has _five_ sisters! Her family lives in a small apartment, and she's always had to share a room all her life. Even when she got to college. So its not anything against me, after all. I tried to make her feel better by offering her the big room with the balcony, but she said she'd rather have the little one because if she wants privacy, she can just close the door and not have to worry about me walking through to go to the bathroom. I hope she doesn't close her door too often. I think she's really neat, and I'd like to talk with her about life in the Big Apple...

LETTER FROM TAMMY COHEN
TO THE COHEN FAMILY

May 23, 1974

Dear Family,
I hope this letter finds you all well. Here at Trevor Hall, we're all of us excited about becoming the vanguard of a new field and settling into our new home.

I arrived Monday night, just in time for dinner. The train was punctual, and my taxi driver brought me directly from the station. The only people at the house were Wanda Karlewicz, Dr. Preis-Herald's second-in-command, and a very young undergraduate named Gail. Wanda is capable, astute, and organized while Gail's enthusiasms—for Newport, Trevor Hall, the ocean, and Preis-Herald's reputation—outweigh her knowledge of either psychology or linguistics. Luckily, Wanda is majoring in the latter and I'm studying the former, so we've a chance to pull off some decent work together.

One hitch marred my arrival: Wanda assigned me to share a room with Gail. I was so flustered by the announcement, I'm afraid I was rather sharp with both of them. Isn't it reasonable to assume, with an entire mansion at our disposal, I might have a room all to myself for once? Gail pouted and Wanda frowned, so I realized my faux pas and backed down. I really haven't grounds for complaint; our shared room is the size of three dorms at the college, and my side has a connecting door I can close for privacy.

I'm almost tempted to hand-letter a "Keep Out" sign for it, too—not that that ever kept the little no-neck monsters out of my and Ellie's room, but after griping over the room assignment, I'm ashamed to be any more discourteous to Gail. The kid's never been away from home before; she might as well have "sheltered" stenciled across her face. Gail desperately

15

wants a friend here, and it looks like I'm it. Doesn't it just figure I would end up playing caregiver again?

At least I don't have to teach Gail to talk and observe basic decorum. Young master Webster has yet to materialize, though rumor has it tomorrow is the big day.

Two other researchers have arrived: Ruby Cardini is a transfer student from a community college in Pennsylvania, while Eric Kaninchen is a graduate student of education and child development at Harvard. I'm curious to see how his experience with kids translates to working with a non-human. Ruby is a pleasant surprise. When she introduced herself as a junior, I braced myself for another sorority-type like Gail, but she's much more mature. Ruby has completed some undergraduate projects in psychology and compensates for her limited hands-on experience by reading widely in the field. Moreover, she's curious. Where Gail points and exclaims, Ruby asks "who" and "why." I'm looking forward to working with her, and I think we're going to be friends.

I wish Ruby were my roommate, if I must have one. We're closer in age and temperament. But I don't want to hurt Gail's feelings by suggesting it. Nor do I think Wanda would take kindly to the idea. Though it shouldn't make any difference in the grand scheme of things, she bridles when her authority is challenged in any superficial way. Incidentally, Ruby has her own little room a few doors down. It hasn't got a balcony or a bathroom, only a tiny washstand, but it's all her own. I don't know why I couldn't have one just like it...

LETTER FROM GAIL EHRLICH

(CONTINUED)

...The next day, I went for a walk to see Newport up close. Wanda recommended I take the Cliff Walk, a scenic path that wraps around the coast. In some places you have to climb over rocks or cross the beach. You can see the ocean on one side of the path, and on the other you can see the backs of all the fancy mansions (at least the roofs and towers and chimneys). I'd love to walk into the backyard and keep going right to the ocean, but Trevor Hall is on the other side of the street and pretty far back from the water. I wish I had the room in the tower. It has windows facing all directions. I bet you could see the ocean from there.

On the way back, I went down Bellevue Avenue. Most houses have signs out front that tell you it's name and it's history. The house down the road from us is called Herbert Terrace, and its a real Italian villa built from genuine Carrera marble! The house originally was situated in Tuscany where Jonathan Herbert spotted it while on a post-nuptial tour of Europe with his bride Leticia. The couple fell in love with the property, purchased it, and had it moved to Newport piece by piece via steamer. (I copied that from the sign.) You can peek through the gate and see the house, even though its at the end of a long driveway. It looks just like a palace and has cupids over the windows and gold ornaments on the corners of the roof. Just now, the sun was setting, and all the walls were glowing pink. It was so beautiful!

By the time I got back, more of our team had arrived. There's a girl, Ruby, who took the bus in from Scranton and a boy, Eric, who goes to Harvard. He hitchhiked here, and his last driver took him to Herbert Terrace by mistake because he didn't know anyone was staying at Trevor Hall. I must of just missed seeing him. Eric said the guy who answered the door wasn't very happy to see him. I guess the neighbors didn't know we were moving in. Eric said he wasn't sure if the owner (Wanda says his name is Mr. Belancourt) was more upset about living next to a bunch of college students or a chimp.

The chimp and Dr. Preis-Herald won't get here for a couple more days. Another guy is coming with them, but for now its just us five.

Ruby's very nice. She was transferring to Yale from junior college for her third year and hasn't been away from home before either. I felt better after talking with her. Even though she's older than me, its like we're in the same boat and we're both trying to find our sea legs. I told Ruby about the Cliff Walk and the mansions, and she wants to see all of it, so maybe we'll go sightseeing together soon. I think the Cowsills live around here somewhere. I'll have to look for they're house next.

I really wish you could see this place. Maybe Vanessa can come for a visit at Christmastime during school break.

LETTER FROM RUBY CARDINI
TO SARAH-BETH ANDREWS

May 23, 1974

Dear Sarah-Beth,

I'm here! I can hardly believe it, even as I sit writing to you from the desk of the library at Trevor Hall. Yes, we have a real, wood-paneled library with wingback chairs and wall sconces, though most of the books are moldering away now. I feel like I've been named Queen for a Day, every day, and I have to keep pinching myself every few minutes to prove it's not a dream. I'm really here! I know I'm in the right place, I made the right decision, and it was all worth it.

I won't pretend my rift with Dad doesn't still hurt, but I won't let it drag me down. I never could have been content to spend my days slaving over a stove or cleaning up after some meathead from the old neighborhood. I just have to put that bitterness aside for now and hope in time, he'll talk to me again.

Maybe I can win him over with my stunning findings. Can you just see me on "Johnny Carson" conversing with Webster? That's what I'll aim for now: something to make my parents take notice and want to claim me and my accomplishments. If I wasn't fully motivated before, I'll have that little dream tickling the back of my mind now.

I have so much to tell you, yet I'll try to be brief. I'll start with Trevor Hall.

I had no idea what to expect coming out here. I tried to find some information about the house in advance, but neither the school nor public libraries had any articles, photos, or etchings to prepare me. I guess our mansion (boy, I never imagined I would someday be writing those words!) is just too obscure. I saw pictures of some of the other Newport estates though, and in my head, I'd constructed a turn-of-the-century chimera with hundreds of windows, sculptures, gables, gingerbread trim, a coat of arms over the door, a timbered roof, and a massive gate with spiked tips surrounding verdant rolling lawns—maybe even a moat and a drawbridge. I'm kidding about that last one, but I did fantasize about every other possible architectural configuration.

The real thing is both more sedate and more elegant than I envisioned. For one thing, the gate is not spiked; it just has little rusty curlicues along the top. The house itself is huge (seventy rooms!) but not exquisitely fancy. Trevor Hall has three stories. It's built of stone with cornices around the windows and the edges of the roof; tiny carvings are interspersed above or between windows. The images are mostly of angels and birds, though I saw one that looked like a dragon or gargoyle.

I was right about the many windows; some are even made of stained glass! Every room of the house has a window, although some are large and multi-paned, and others are small and round. I counted at least seven gables in total. A flat roof with a walkway wraps all around the building. A large tower makes the house look more like a castle than a lowly mansion. Maybe that drawbridge wasn't so far-fetched, after all! No herald perches above the front door, but it is crowned by a porte cochere with ivy-covered pillars.

The grounds are large, but the lawns are overgrown and interspersed with clusters of towering trees that look like willows. Immense roots twist out of the ground, just waiting for someone to trip. As I approached, I saw a weed-straggled rose garden and a cracked flagstone path with more weeds spurting up through the plaster. Between the weeds and the ivy, nature is trying to reassert its hold over the place. I started walking along that weather-beaten path and got just far enough to spot a statue of Mercury beside a chipped marble bench, a large spreading tree, and another little outbuilding, when a sharp voice yelled, "Excuse me, this is private property! No tourists allowed here!"

Oh, that made me jump! And that was my introduction to the project manager, Wanda Karlewicz.

I should have knocked on the front door and officially presented myself instead of exploring on my own, but I was nervous and wanted a few minutes to cool down. Literally. I had been cooped up in a hot, stuffy bus for hours before trekking all the way up Bellevue Avenue from the *bus depot (probably about three or four miles) carrying my backpack, so my clothes were sticky and smelling none too rosy. The jeans and blouse I had on are among the nicer things I brought, but they felt shabby in the shadow of the great estate, and especially next to Wanda's tailored pantsuit.*

Meekly, I introduced myself as one of Dr. Preis-Herald's researchers, and her hostility melted. Wanda is also a Yalie. She's been Dr. Preis-Herald's graduate assistant for the past two years, helping in his classroom and even in drafting some of his "Secrets of the Mind" broadcasts. When I asked her about that, she demurred: "All I did was gather the research and arrange it into bullet points for reference. Piers speaks off the cuff. He's a natural." She's on a first name basis with him and says that's how he prefers to be addressed by his colleagues. I guess that's what I am now, but I can't imagine calling a professor by his first name, let alone anyone so well-regarded.

We didn't have that conversation standing under the porte cochere, *of course. Once I established my identity, Wanda invited me inside, and I got my second eyeful. We entered a spacious foyer half-furnished with antiquated chairs and tables. I know nothing about old furniture, though now I'm inspired to learn. They could be Chippendales or Heppelwhites for all I know, but I fear they would have little value in their current condition. The marble-topped side table by the door looked like a penknife had attacked it! An old tic-tac-toe game defaced one corner, and various initials were gouged up and down its legs. The chair cushions were also stained and torn. Bits of stuffing protruded from the backs.*

The carpet shielding the entryway must have once been vivid with cobalt and cochineal, but now it's a faded mud-and-dun pattern through which you can glimpse the hardwood floor. The walls are pockmarked with shadows from where paintings used to hang, and the now-way-off-white paint is peeling. Chipped imitation classical statues stand in nooks and corners. When I looked up at the highest ceiling I've ever seen before, I saw a faded fresco of ethereal figures painted among the rafters. To the left of the doorway is a sweeping staircase with carved wood banisters, sadly also scuffed and graffitied and missing a newel post.

I had difficulty reconciling the grandeur of that room with the house in all its disrepair. On one hand, my excitement gave way to disappointment over the sorry state of our accommodations. On the other, I felt I was standing in a museum, that I was only being given a tour, and there was no way I would ever actually sit in any of those grand, aging chairs, or grip that scuffed banister on my way upstairs. Either way, I felt disquieted. I thought, "This is my new home. I'm going to be living here," but I couldn't wrap my head around the idea. I just didn't see myself fitting in at the mansion or filling a role in the project. For one critical moment, I almost told Wanda, "Thank you very much for showing me around, but I think I'll be going back now." Luckily, my other housemates appeared and put a stop to that.

Wanda introduced me to the two other girls and one of the two guys with whom I'll be working. Tammy Cohen is a first-year grad student from Columbia; Eric Kenonsha (sp?) is a second-year grad student from Harvard; Gail Ehrlich is the youngest of us, a freshman who just moved from Missouri to attend UConn, but like me, is taking a detour through Newport. Everyone was welcoming and all shared that they, too, had initially felt overwhelmed by the scope of Trevor Hall.

Tammy and I have hit it off. I've learned she comes from a big family, so she never had a lot of money for fancy things either. Most of her clothes come from second-hand stores ("shabby chic," Tammy calls them), so I feel less self-conscious about my own wardrobe. She worked to earn enough money for college, too, but she got two scholarships. I'm not surprised. Tammy sounds brilliant when she talks. With her glasses, long hair, and confidence, she reminds me of Gloria Steinem. Tammy doesn't seem to care about not having stylish clothes and doesn't even wear make-up. I should learn to be more like her.

Before going upstairs (or into the beautiful glass-walled solarium, or the surprisingly modern kitchen, or the dining room with the carved angel faces on the ceiling, or even this comfy old library), we spent some time examining the foyer and corridors. The paintings spread onto the hall ceilings, too. They seem to depict the seasons, or maybe specific months of the year, but they've deteriorated so much I can't tell. I would love to be able to spend a week—or more likely, a month—just fixing up the house: touching up the paintings, polishing that banister, powdering the carpet with tea leaves or whatever has to be done to clean it. Maybe I can make myself useful as the maid in case the ASL-instructor/zookeeper gig doesn't work out.

Tammy also praised the beauty of Trevor Hall and denounced the vandals who'd marred it. Evidently, the house was once a boarding school, and the students abused the place. What ingrates! If I had been lucky enough to attend school in such a palace, I would have done everything I could to prove myself worthy of the privilege.

Another reason why the mansion looks forlorn is that Trevor Hall has been unoccupied for almost ten years. Tammy speculated: "From what Wanda says, the owners have had a hard time renting out the place. Given its size, I guess the living expenses are a lot for anyone to manage, even with a silver spoon in their mouths. I don't know how Preis-Herald was able to afford it, even with endowments. Maybe he got a discount on the lease."

I wanted to see the entire house, but Wanda said that was impossible. That's when I found out it has seventy rooms! "But they're small by modern standards, and not all of them are habitable," she warned. "Some sections of Trevor Hall are pretty dilapidated, so for safety reasons, and in hopes of scaling down our utility bills, we've decided to close off the rear wing and most of the third floor." (With the exception of the tower, where Dr. Preis-Herald will stay when he's in residence, and Webster's quarters.) Then she walked me through the main rooms on the first floor and promised we'd get a more in-depth tour during orientation.

All of us are staying on the second floor, which is how I've always supposed a college dorm would feel. I have my own little room with a bed, a wardrobe, a built-in bookcase, a window facing the garden, and a sink so I can wash my face and brush my teeth. The toilets and showers are down the hall. There are two bathrooms: one for the guys and one for the girls. I'll only have to share with Wanda, since Tammy and Gail have their own bathroom inside their suite. That room is twice the size of mine and came with a lot of its own furniture, whereas I'm going to have to find someplace to buy a cheap nightstand and a lamp, at the very least.

To listen to Tammy, you'd think staying there was a punishment. She counted on having her own room after years of sharing with sisters and other college students. When we were checking out my new digs, she looked so longingly at the narrow space between the bare walls that I asked if she wanted to switch. I wouldn't mind having a balcony and my own shower. But after a moment's consideration, she said she didn't want Gail to feel abandoned. I think that was sweet. Gail's fresh out of high school, after all. For all her sighing and eye-rolling, Tammy is nurturing and protective; I think she's the perfect roommate for Gail. Maybe later on, after we're all settled in, Wanda will let us spread out and take individual rooms.

After putting away my clothes and other belongings as best I could, I decided to explore the mansion. I figured I'd just walk around the second level, the safe part, and get a feel for the layout of the house. I wanted to peek into the other rooms and see what the view looked like from different windows.

The second floor is like a maze; I can't imagine what the third floor must be like! Once you reach the end of our corridor, the hall dog-legs down a smaller hall that branches off into two other corridors. One of the corridors was short and ended in a small suite of four rooms. Sadly, they were all locked.

Many of the doors I tried in my exploration were locked (or stuck). The unlocked doors merely opened into empty, dorm-style rooms with only the occasional bedstead or cot for adornment. I spotted a little side table in one and made a mental note to ask Wanda if I could move it into my room. Of course, then I'd have to admit I'd been prowling. (Is it still prowling if you're snooping around in your own new home?)

I was lured by a nice big picture window down the left-hand branch of the corridor that would have given a lovely view of the front lawn if it hadn't been partially obscured by ivy. Also, the threshold of that corridor was carved with grape leaves, but the carvings were broken, splintered, or engraved with initials. It's a real shame! Beyond the window, the rest of that section was dark and drab. I could feel how disused it was, and that's when I really began to feel like a trespasser.

I opted to get out of the maze and found a second staircase running from the kitchen (it must have been for the servants' use) up to the top floor. Eric's head was in the fridge when I walked down the stairs behind him, and he jumped. Then we joked about my return to "civilization."

Sightseeing in Newport was more enjoyable. Gail, Tammy, and I walked down to the wharf, then decided to tour one of the grand mansions that are now open to the public as museums...

LETTER FROM TAMMY COHEN
TO THE COHEN FAMILY

(CONTINUED)

...*Yesterday, we explored our environs. The town is charming but very EXPEN$IVE. Newport gained fame as a retreat for the wealthiest families in the country, and it has retained its power as a major tourist attraction. Unfortunately for us, we've arrived at the opening of the tourist season, just in time to encounter inflated prices in the grocery, restaurants, and museums. Wanda has advised us to shop for our daily necessities in neighboring Middletown.*

Speaking of tourist attractions, I visited the vaunted Breakers, the grandest mansion in Newport, a Vanderbilt "summer cottage." It's certainly the biggest, showiest, most ostentatious, overgrown pile. Everywhere I looked, I saw luxury: three floors of marble, gold-coated walls and ceilings, carved banisters and lintels, crystal chandeliers, mosaics in the bathrooms and on the balconies. Everyone in my tour group walked around with their mouths hanging open. But while they gawped in appreciation, I gagged at the tremendous frivolity.

The "Gilded Age" was a phrase surely coined for the Breakers. Everything that could be dipped in aurum was. Did you know that family even ate with gold utensils? Who on Earth needs gold dining utensils? Also, the giant, elaborate carved chairs were formed from bronze, not wood. The tour guide said the furniture was almost too heavy for the footmen to move. Nothing was practical. It was all for show. How could anyone live comfortably amid so much decadence? The house isn't even beautiful once you look closely at the excess.

As I said to Ruby, I'm glad to be living in a house that's shabby-genteel. Next to true wealth, chipped paint and nicked fireplaces don't seem so bad. I didn't even mind when the water in the shower came out cold and brown. According to Wanda, the pipes will flush all the rust with regular usage. In a couple of weeks, we won't notice anything amiss. I begin to think Wanda should be selling fixer-uppers to newlyweds.

But I exaggerate. She's been very accommodating. On Arrival Day, Wanda gave us a brief tour and history lesson. Trevor Hall's relative modesty is due to its founder's humble origins. No captain of industry, Curtis Trevor was a scalawag who cast his lot with the winning side in the last days of the Civil War. The lucky stiff then made money from operating a coal mine. My roommate somehow heard "gold mine" and is convinced Trevor struck the mother lode. I haven't had the heart to disillusion her.

Gail puts the most exalted spin on everything to do with Trevor Hall. On our first night, I listened to her rave about the dining room ceiling, a trompe l'oeil *painted to look like the sky and interspersed with carved angels. These angels haven't quite fallen, but I wouldn't want to encounter one in a dark alley. Their halos have lost their sheen. One sad cherub is missing his chin and lips. Yet to Gail, this is the image of paradise. The poor kid deserves to look up to a better heaven than one covered in cracks and grime, populated by angels with broken noses and broken wings.*

Truthfully, Trevor Hall is a lovely place. This afternoon, I stood on the front lawn, gazing at the façade of the house and mentally comparing it to the Breakers. I suddenly realized how much I could <u>hear</u>! The air buzzed with the sounds of insects in the grass and birds chirping in the trees. It was almost like listening to the hum of telephone wires, except these noises had rhythm and life to them. I stood on the lawn like a dummy for I don't know how long just marveling that all the little critters could make themselves heard at all. But in a world without traffic or el-trains, where the homes are farther than arm's length apart, quiet is something tangible—so much so that you can notice the slightest deviation caused by a mere cricket. This is true luxury, and I look forward to getting used to it...

LETTER FROM RUBY CARDINI
TO SARAH-BETH ANDREWS

(CONTINUED)

... The admission at the Breakers was a little steep for me, so I went down the road a pace to what must have belonged to Cornelius Vanderbilt's slightly poorer cousin. Alva Vanderbilt, an early 20th century firebrand who had the gall to divorce her husband and become a suffragette, owned Marble House. What a hoot she must have been! From the outside, her home looks like a miniature White House; on the inside, precious marble in slightly different shades lines every room. It was the most beautiful house I've ever seen.

The house was powerful in other ways, too. Our guide told us vivid stories about its history that brought the home and the occupants alive in our minds. For instance, Alva had a daughter, Consuelo, whom she was determined to marry into European royalty. Back then, it was common for impoverished aristocrats from England to wed American heiresses. They could gain a fortune through the bride's dowry, and the women would acquire titles and access to a blue-blooded family. Ambitious Alva arranged to wed Consuelo to an English count, even though she already had an attachment to an American commoner. Her mother delivered the news to Consuelo in the drawing room, a funereal chapel sunk in dark reds and blues from the stained-glass windows. The gloomy room made the grim announcement feel even more dire. Our guide pointed to the sofa and told us that was where poor Consuelo Vanderbilt sat and cried after her mother had decreed her fate.

I stayed in the room, even as my tour group moved on, and looked at that sofa, imagining this woman, who would have been just a little younger than I am now but was born almost a hundred years before me, pampered and wealthy but not so different from me. She'd had her own hopes for her life. She hadn't wanted to get married and settle down either, at least not with someone she barely knew and didn't love. I considered what I would do and how I would feel if I had no choices about my future. I imagined Consuelo curled up on the cushion with her head buried against the armrest. I felt like I could reach across the years and touch a real flesh-and-blood human being, not just a name and a date on the page of a history book. It was as though her story were unfolding again, right in the room where I stood, just on the other side of a wispy curtain. The hair on my arms began to prickle, and I exited the room, grateful to be just a working-class girl from a family of no note whatsoever, living in the 1970s, with the power to seek my own destiny.

Taking that tour made me wish I had majored in history instead of psychology. As you know, I struggled to narrow my focus, and that was also a sore spot with my folks. First, Dad couldn't figure out what use a college degree would be for a woman; then he couldn't understand why I was wasting so much time exploring the humanities. Literature was tempting, and history even more so, but I figured psychology would give me the opportunity to make a mark in the world. Marble House reminded me how much I still love the sense of connecting to something older and greater than myself, something real but just beyond my reach. I want to point to photos of long-gone days and people and say, "Look, they lived! This happened! It was so!" and bring them all to life again for others. Then again, if I were getting a history degree, no way would I ever have crossed paths with Dr. Preis-Herald and Webster. Maybe living in Newport will give me a chance to get my history fix _and_ gain fame through psychology.

After my tour, I walked around town for a bit. Newport is such a rich source of history. Many houses have little plaques on the wall testifying to when they were built. I saw 1792, 1686, 1704, and 1771. Most of the larger houses also have names: Seacliff, Mid-Cliff, Bennett House, Chateau Sur Mer. There's so much heritage everywhere you look! I can't believe this is where I'm going to be living. Am I the luckiest girl or what?

There's no telling how much more time we'll have for fun and sightseeing. I gather we'll have our hands full teaching Webster. According to Wanda, Dr. Preis-Herald and "the menagerie" (whatever that means) will be driving up two days from now. Thinking about it makes me excited and nervous. I hope once the study is under way, I'll stop feeling like a pretender. I want to pull my weight and prove my worth. I want to show I deserve to have a position alongside scientists like Tammy, Wanda, and Eric. You'll see: in one of my letters someday, I'll enclose a journal article with my name as co-author.

At the very least, I'll be able to tell you what Webster is like and what's ahead for us...

MEMO FROM WANDA KARLEWICZ

May 25, 1974

Dear Team:

Please note I've posted on the bulletin board in the solarium a list of ten target words for Webster's lessons this week. I'll review these vocabulary signs after breakfast tomorrow (8:30 AM).

Please do your best to expose Webster to every sign at least once during the next seven days. Above all, <u>document</u> his attempts or successes in reproducing the sign(s), including who initiated the sign (you or Webster), the circumstances/ environment of its use, the level of accuracy in producing the sign, and the context. Use the journals in each room to record your observations, questions, and thoughts in relation to the project. This data will be crucial in demonstrating the success of our endeavors.

Thank you!

—WK

LETTER FROM RUBY CARDINI
TO SARAH-BETH ANDREWS

May 25, 1974

Dear Sarah-Beth,

The menagerie finally arrived today: one professor, one graduate assistant, two cats, one dog, and, of course, one very special chimpanzee.

The five of us already present waited in front of the mansion to greet Piers Preis-Herald and his entourage. I felt like a servant welcoming back the master after a long absence. Wanda had a rough idea of when they would show up, with a buffer for traffic. Gail spotted them driving up the road from a window and sounded the alarm, so out we all trotted. I was nervous; I'd only seen Dr. Preis-Herald once before and wondered if he would even remember me. Part of me was convinced he'd hired me by mistake; he would take one look at me and announce I wasn't the right one, that he'd wanted a different, older, smarter, more capable co-ed, and I would be sent packing in disgrace.

Fortunately, that didn't happen.

Piers's car, an elegant blue sedan, pulled up first; then, a battered old station wagon, the windows obscured by junk piled up inside, sputtered in behind him. We all rushed to offer what help we could. Piers (I must remember to call him Piers; he insists) was jolly, calling out "Hullo!" and greeting each of us by name as he disembarked. That's how I realized I was in the right place.

Maisie put me at ease immediately. She's Piers's dog: a beautiful sleek Australian Shepherd with black-and-white patterning, a warm tongue, and a fluffy tail that never stops wagging. She bounded out of the sedan and ran right to me. When she jumped up, she came to my shoulders. I could have given her a hug and almost did. I've forgotten how much fun a dog can be.

And the fun continued. Piers handed Tammy a carrying case containing a black-and-white cat called Peter, then gave me a second case belonging to a lovely calico called Harriet. We'll have a house full of pets to play with! Technically, the cats are Wanda's, but they're on loan to the study for Webster's sake. Piers says they fascinate him. Webster gets to play with the pets as a reward when he performs well in his studies. "They'll also help to soothe him as he acclimates to his new accommodations. The more familiarity we can provide him, the more comfortable, and hence, the more productive he will be," Piers explained.

We were all dying to meet Webster. I was surprised he was riding in the station wagon instead of with Piers. We gathered around the vehicle, torn between wanting to get closer to see him and wanting to give Webster space so he wouldn't feel spooked. Finally, the driver emerged, cradling the most adorable little being. He is the size of a six- or nine-month-old child—small, covered in shiny black hair, and dressed in a toddler's shirt and pants. He held tightly to his keeper, though he did look up at the rest of us. He has a tiny, wrinkly face and big, silly-looking lips! His big, shiny eyes fill up most of the space on his face.

As soon as we set our own eyes on Webster, we girls began to coo over him. Gail asked right away if she could hold him, but the guy from the station wagon warned us off. "He acts up when he's scared. We'll just give him a chance to figure out who you all are before we let anyone else have him." He turned out to be another grad student named Jeff Dalton, the study's videographer. All the apparent junk piled up inside the car was his equipment: Super 8 cameras and still cameras, tripods, and rolls and canisters and boxes of film.

Listening to Jeff talk as we unpacked his car, I could tell he knows a lot about angles, close-ups, and lighting, but I wondered how much he knows about cognitive processes and what he might contribute to the study besides recording us. He's a little on the scruffy side, and more than a little irreverent. I wonder if he wouldn't be better off at film school. However, he does seem awfully attached to Webster, and Webster in turn clings to Jeff. Jeff chatted with him and showed him around the house as if they were a couple of good old buddies.

After we helped carry in all of Jeff's recording equipment and released the cats to walk about and make the house their own, Piers called us all together for the orientation…

FILM FOOTAGE ENTITLED
"PROJECT WEBSTER—ORIENTATION REEL"

Date: May 25, 1974
Location: The Library

Piers stands before a large, ornate fireplace, holding a pipe. He faces the camera, looking stern. Then, as if responding to a signal, he smiles and says, "Good afternoon, ladies and gentlemen! I'm so pleased you've all agreed to participate in this venture. I promise it will be a remarkable experience. I've asked Jeff here—" He gestures to the camera. "—to film this, our first meeting, to set the tone of our investigation."

Piers lights his pipe and continues. "I'll discuss with you an overview of our study's goals and procedures momentarily, but for now, I'd like you all to introduce yourselves. I know some of you have had the benefit of getting to know each other in recent days, but as we've all arrived at various times, this orientation will bring us to an equal footing. Wanda, dear, why don't you lead us?"

Wanda enters the frame. Wearing a white collared blouse, a lilac skirt, and a matching headband, she carries Webster, who clutches a teddy bear in one hand and wraps his other arm around her neck. Piers hooks an arm around Webster's middle, and Wanda turns away in a quick half-circle; Webster peels off her and lands in Piers's arms. Webster squawks.

Piers explains, "This is an effective way to transfer our subject from one person to another."

Webster squirms in Piers's grip, wrinkling his face. Wanda murmers, "Piers, you know he can't stand your pipe." Piers glances at the pipe in his free hand as Wanda continues, "If you want him to hold still—"

Jeff, off camera, says, "I can take him."

Gail, off camera, chimes in, "Oh, please, may I hold him?"

Piers says, "In time." He sets his pipe on the edge of the mantelpiece and walks off camera, carrying Webster.

Wanda folds her arms in front of her and smiles around the room; as she speaks, she addresses the audience instead of the camera. "Hello. I'm Wanda Karlewicz, a third-year graduate student at Yale University. My major is psychology and my specialty is linguistics. I've worked as a teaching and research assistant to Piers Preis-Herald for the past two years, so I was one of the first to learn of his plan to teach language to a chimpanzee. Naturally, that was right up my alley. I helped prepare the grant proposal to obtain approval and initial funding, and I later worked with Piers, Webster, and Webster's foster family to implement a program teaching him to sign. I've a younger brother who is hearing impaired. My entire family learned Ameslan to communicate with him, so I've been signing since I was nine years old." She looks directly into the camera and smiles. "That was a very long time ago."

Piers, off camera, says, "Pshaw!"

Wanda continues. "At first, our goal was to socialize Webster into a human family in the hopes he would absorb language organically. Initial results were promising. The second phase of our project will involve directed, formal teaching by a staff of researchers instead of laypeople. Ergo, we've come here—" She spreads her arms to take in the room. "—to Trevor Hall in beautiful Newport, Rhode Island. This house is large enough to accommodate our party and equipment and has privacy enough for a chimp to get some exercise without frightening the neighbors. Now, the place needs a little work. If your lights short out, or your ceiling leaks, or the shower takes too long to heat up, you can complain to this guy—" Wanda grins and points off camera to Piers. "—instead of coming to me. He holds the purse strings; he's got the authority to call a handyman."

Piers's nonchalant voice, off camera, calls out, "Jeff's our handyman for this term." Off-screen, everyone chuckles. Wanda smiles unsteadily, looks at the camera, then looks back in Piers's direction. She mouths, "Is that all?" Relief lights her face, and she crosses the room.

Piers meets her in the left frame of the camera and transfers Webster back to her. Piers continues to the fireplace and retrieves his pipe. "Thank you, Wanda. That was a splendid introduction. Gail, will you favor us next?"

Off-screen, Gail giggles. She enters the frame of the camera hesitantly, grinning. A petite girl, she wears false eyelashes and striking blue eye shadow, gold barrettes hold back her blonde hair. She pauses at an unseen direction, then steps back and asks, "Right here?" She shifts to the left, smoothes her colorful minidress, takes a deep breath, and smiles. "Hi, everyone! I'm Gail. Uh, Gail Ehrlich. Hi!"

She turns in a half-circle, waving to everybody in the room, then looks into the camera and clears her throat. "Um..." Gail laughs and turns toward Piers. "I don't know what to say! I haven't done anything important yet."

Piers, off camera, says, "Then just tell us about yourself and what you hope to accomplish."

"OK." Gail tosses her hair over her shoulder and faces the camera again. She grins, and although she appears to be on the verge of laughter, she reins herself in. "I'm Gail…I'm almost nineteen. I live with my parents and my little sister, Vanessa, who's fifteen. Oh, and our dog, Snoopy. She's not a beagle—she's a collie-shepherd mix or something—but we just call her Snoopy because I like the cartoon. Ummm…hmm…"

Gail screws up her eyes and looks up. "I'm originally from Lee's Summit…but I just started college at the University of Connecticut…because I wanted to see what life was like on the coast in the big Eastern cities…and I couldn't get into SUNY. Ah…I didn't have a major when I went in because I wasn't sure yet what I wanted to do. Lots of other girls I met felt the same way. But during my orientation week, Dr. Pr—Piers!—came to our school and did a presentation about his research. And I thought it just sounded like the most far out thing! Talking to animals? That's like Doctor Dolittle. I love that movie! So I stayed around to meet with him after the talk, and he told me he was recruiting for this study. And, um—and he picked me to work on it. So I'm here now! And, ah…I don't know any sign language—" Gail looks toward Wanda. "—but I'm hoping to learn. And…oh, I love animals, so I really want to work with Webster and teach him and, like, just blow people's minds with all the stuff we'll be doing. Talking apes! Only not like Planet of the Apes. I didn't like that movie. That was sad…"

Gail falls quiet. Off-screen, Tammy cheers softly and applauds. More applause follows. Gail beams and curtsies. Piers, off camera, says, "Lovely, Gail. Who's next? Ruby, how about you?"

Chairs scrape off-screen. Ruby, a pale brunette with a Roman nose and a pointy chin, in a blue sweater and jeans, walks to the center of the frame, adjusts her ponytail, and looks fixedly into the camera. Ruby says tentatively, "My name is Ruby Cardini. I'm in my first year at Yale, though I'm a junior. I transferred in the spring…" She lifts her eyes and sees something above the camera that makes her smile. Instantly, her posture loosens. "Thanks! It's easier to talk to a person than to a little flashing light. Though, I guess I'll have to get used to that. Ah…As I was saying, I transferred in the spring from junior college in Scranton, where I'm from. I was living there with my best friend since grade school, and she flipped out when I told her I would be working with Piers Preis-Herald. That came about through pure luck. I was going door to door, meeting faculty in my department, the psychology department. I didn't start by majoring in psychology. College was a candy store to me: I took English and history classes before I decided studying the mind would be more fulfilling. Anyway, Dr. Preis—"

Piers, off camera, calls, "Piers!"

Ruby blushes and grins briefly before continuing. "—happened to be in his office. You—he—made the time to talk with me about his study. I was fascinated like everyone else and said I hoped to observe some of his work while I was on campus. That's when he told me the study wouldn't be taking place on campus, and the next thing I know, I'm living in a mansion." She laughs. "Me, a little working-class kid from Scranton, living in the same city as robber barons and duchesses! This entire experience has been like a dream so far, and whatever happens next, I'm open to it. I'm going to work hard, especially since I don't know sign language either, and I'll do my best to help make this project a success. I'm the first girl in my family to go to college, and I want to make the most of that. I want to make my mark."

Piers, still off camera, remarks, "Your parents must be very proud of you."

Ruby grimaces. "Not quite. They weren't—my dad wasn't—thrilled about my going away to school." She straightens and tosses her head. "But I'm hoping he will be proud when he sees the work I do. I've tried to prep some for this research. When I was on the bus coming up, I read Robert La Fontaine's book about his work with Osage—"

Off camera, Jeff mocks her pronunciation. "Ooh la la, Row-bear!"

Piers off camera chimes in: "We say 'Ro-burt La Fon-tayn.'"

Jeff, off camera says, "Actually, we try not to say his name at all."

Ruby winces, closing her eyes and rubbing them with her thumb and forefinger. "Sorry, I didn't know. I've only ever seen his name in print, and I studied French in high school…I feel like a dummy right now."

Piers, off camera, says, "Not at all. You're an excellent ice breaker."

"Well, I think I've said everything I needed to. Who's next?" Ruby looks around.

The film cuts to Jeff standing in front of the fireplace. He wears a red T-shirt, jeans, and a full beard. He points and says, "Push the—there it goes!" He claps his hands and looks around the room, talking fast. "Hey there, I'm Jeff Dalton. None of you know me yet, except Wanda and Piers, because I've been down at Yale all week, so I'll bet you're wondering who the hell I am. I'm a third-year psych grad student like Wanda, only my focus is observational learning. Piers was on my thesis committee. I was planning to write about youth and violence, like: Does the age at which we are introduced to violent media make a difference in the severity of later behavior? Or does witnessing actual violence on the news—"

Jeff's eyebrows narrow, and his tone becomes harsher. "—like seeing your president get shot, or a bunch of university kids get gunned down by the military, have a more traumatic effect than fictive violence like in old Warner gangster movies. But then Piers told me about this work, and he emphasized the element of control and how much better it would be than looking at survey correlations and crunching through a bunch of regressions. And I said, 'Sure, I'm down for that.' Because…"

Jeff slumps faintly and his cadence slows. "… proving animals can communicate with humans is a lot more uplifting than any of that other stuff. And it's just as important. Maybe more so. But I think the real reason Piers brought me on board is that he's always known about my little hobby. I love movies. I love watching them, talking about them, taking them apart and analyzing all the minor elements that go into them. And of course, I've always thought about making them. I'm from Oakland, and when summer vacations rolled around, I'd always nag my parents to take us south to Hollywood. But they wanted to go to boring, educational places like Yellowstone or the Grand Canyon. As a compromise, and to shut me up, Dad got me a video camera and told me to make my own movies about the places we visited. He didn't know he was creating a monster. For the past ten years, I've been investing my money in video gear and my time in learning to use it. I'm not even thinking about Hollywood anymore, to be honest. I just like to film for its own sake. Who better to document this study, right? And my little wordsmith—"

Jeff turns, crouches, and waves off camera before continuing. "—loves mugging for the camera, so he's been the perfect subject. I was one of the first people to meet him when he came in from the primate center. For a while, he thought the camera was his mother because we were both right there all the time." Jeff straightens and his facial expression hardens. "I'm really looking forward to this new phase of the project, the challenges it brings, and seeing what discoveries develop. And that's enough out of me." Jeff walks toward the camera to the sound of applause.

The film cuts to Eric, a sandy-haired young man wearing a striped shirt, jeans, and sideburns, scratching the side of his freckled nose as he stares into space. He says, "Oh, it's on now? OK." He straightens up and clears his throat. "I'm Eric Kaninchen from Harvard. Second-year grad student in child development and education. I was recruited when, ah, Piers, came to campus to promote his study, and it intrigued me so much that I was willing to go work for the competition."

Off camera, Jeff boos teasingly.

Eric continues, "Actually, I never went in for that team rivalry stuff. I consider myself incredibly lucky to have been selected for this project. One thing that gives me an advantage, I think, is the teaching experience I have. I work part-time with special needs children. It's great, rewarding work. But it pushes me to think creatively and find new ways to get through to people who don't think and act like your typical student. I'm guessing I'll be doing a lot more of that with Webster as a pupil. I'm looking forward to it."

Eric pauses. The others in the room applaud. He beckons, and Tammy enters the frame. She has light brown hair pulled back in a ponytail, a paisley shirt, jeans, and glasses. He says, "And last but not least…"

Tammy says, "You mean save the best for last."

Eric steps aside, and the camera zooms in on Tammy. As she speaks, she addresses the camera, but occasionally glances at the audience. "I'm Tammy Cohen from Brooklyn, New York. I attend Columbia, where I'm a first-year graduate student majoring in cognition studies. My thesis project will be to compare learning styles between primates and humans. One thing that qualifies me to be part of this project is my extensive time spent rearing my younger siblings, of which I have five. I'm immune to begging, and I can shut down a tantrum quickly. Not that I'm expecting much trouble from this charge."

Piers, off camera, calls out, "Don't be fooled!"

Tammy says, "I'll be prepared." She pauses, nods, and says, "I think that covers it." She moves toward her seat, but Piers steps up behind her and sets a hand on her shoulder. Tammy glances back at him, and her face flickers in dislike.

Piers says, "Thank you, Tammy. Your introduction was charming, but it's not quite our last. Let me take this opportunity to more fully present myself."

Tammy exits the frame. Piers leans against the mantle, smoking his pipe as he talks. "You all know my name, and some of you have read my books or journal articles. I hope a few of you even tune in to hear me distill the latest in psychological research on Secrets of the Mind in Sixty Minutes."

Wanda calls from off-screen, "AM 710!"

Piers continues. "I consider myself a renaissance man in the field. After completing my studies at Eton and Cambridge, I turned to advertising, where I utilized my knowledge of persuasion and attitude change. However, applied psychology was less interesting to me than academic study. Fortunately, I was offered a teaching position here in America, which permitted me to conduct basic research. Recently, my focus has drawn toward exploring the traits and experiences that separate humans from animals. My review of extant research suggests we're far more similar than many scientists would care to admit. This study will detail, in part, the process of language acquisition in non-human primates compared to human beings."

His expression darkens, and he puffs aggressively on his pipe for a moment. "As you know, ours is not the first such study. Osage, and now Kiki, have both drawn attention for their purported use of language. However, those studies suffer weaknesses in design. The apes in question have learned a limited repertoire of signs they produce under the guidance of their teachers in artificial learning environments. My goal is to demonstrate that chimpanzees can communicate on a more sophisticated level, initiating interaction instead of merely responding to leading prompts, and even using grammar to form sentences spontaneously in a natural environment. In the coming months, we shall evaluate how our chimpanzee communicates with us, what words he adopts, and what processes underlie his communication. Naturally, everyone here will have to learn to sign, so we can properly understand what Webster chooses to tell us. Yes, Eric?"

Eric, off camera, asks, "Can we talk to Webster, or can we only communicate with him by signing?"

Piers says, "Nobody's under a vow of silence, Eric. Webster's certainly able to understand verbal commands or questions. However, because he can't speak back, we must engage with him on his own terms. For now, use Ameslan to enhance your speech. I strongly encourage you all to develop the habit of signing, so you can eventually use this language exclusively. Signing in your daily routines will normalize the behavior for Webster and encourage him to sign on his own. It will be arduous, but you're all tough, smart, determined people. The fact you've chosen to pursue higher education is evidence of your ambition. Apply that ambition to make this study a success, so when we present our work to the Annual Review Board, there will be no question of its authenticity, but only questions about which exciting directions we can explore next."

Piers extinguishes his pipe and surveys the room. "Now to review some ground rules for this study. Everyone will be required to sign, as I've said. You'll receive daily instruction and will in turn instruct Webster. Each week, a word list targeting a specific area of vocabulary will be posted in the solarium; these target words are what you shall teach and reinforce to Webster. The vocabulary will be practical, usually thematic, and can easily be used in daily interaction. You will learn a broader array of signs. If you feel it's appropriate, you may teach Webster a sign outside the parameters of the prescribed curriculum, if doing so facilitates communication, or if Webster prompts it himself. If he indicates a novel object and asks, "What is that?" for example, do please tell him.

"However, to guarantee the sign is presented correctly—that is, the motions are accurate, and the circumstances of usage are conventionally agreed-upon—you must inform the rest of the team and the research directors, who are yours truly and Wanda. In this way, other team members will recognize and assess when Webster uses your new sign. Secondly, you will document Webster's behavior—principally the number of times he uses a sign, the conditions under which production occurs, or any complications associated with production. However, we also want to obtain a general picture of his overall behavior patterns, so you ought to record his daily routines and other activities, including how he interacts with each of you. One means by which you will make these records—"

The camera tracks his movements as Piers steps over to a large roll-top desk across the room, against a wood-paneled wall, beneath a paned window, and lifts a hardcover journal. "—is through these journals. You will find one in each of the main rooms: this library, the solarium, the kitchen, the dining room, and Webster's quarters. These books are to stay in the rooms for convenient access. Please review them regularly to see what discoveries or challenges your peers have encountered and use them to further communicate amongst yourselves.

Piers passes the journal to Eric, sitting in the desk chair. He flips through it and sets it in his lap. Piers smiles into the camera and says, "Our other means of documenting our work will be by video camera. Jeff is adept with cameras and other recording equipment and will be filming our interactions with Webster to obtain visual proof of his behavior. Robert La Fontaine frequently stages interactions with Osage for documentarians. We may do the same, but I wish to capture Webster's naturalistic behavior. Therefore, we may have the cameras running freely throughout the course of the day to capture independently expressed communication. Gail? I see you waving your hand..."

The camera pans to a nervous Gail. She sits on a folding chair beside Wanda, who balances Webster in her lap. He stands upright and plucks at her hair, stealing cautious glances at Gail. She asks, "Are we going to have cameras in our rooms and be filmed all the time, like that family on PBS?"

Jeff, off camera, responds, "No. For one thing, I don't have enough gear to set up in every room, or enough film for that kind of surveillance, nor would I ever have the time to sort through it all after the fact. Maybe if I had half a dozen assistants at my disposal—

Wanda cuts in, "Also, Gail, we're not the ones being observed. Our goal is to record Webster's interactions. We'll run the camera when we're in the room with him and conducting a scheduled lesson, or if we're involved in structured playtime, but our own routines will not be filmed."

Piers says, "Jeff will make the gatehouse his base of operations, so he can periodically review the footage and cut reels for our record."

"Or to show the suits back at Yale," Jeff replies from off camera.

Ruby, off camera, says, "Oh, is that what that little building is going to become? Your workshop?"

Jeff, off camera, explains, "It's where I'll be living. I'm a night-owl. The gatehouse will give me freedom to move about when I want, and it has space enough for me to store my gear and screen the film. Oh, and it's got a TV. We can get together and watch 'M.A.S.H.' Smithy will like that."

Piers frowns. "Webster will have much more to do than watch telly, but you all deserve to watch an evening program occasionally. It's good of you to invite everyone, Jeff. Now, I'm sure you all have many questions at this point, but please hold them a bit longer until after we've taken our tour of Trevor Hall. Some of you have been here several days already, but I wager there are parts you haven't seen. I know Wanda has had sections of the upper floors locked up. What say you all to taking a peek at them?"

Voices off camera murmur approval. Wanda stands, shifting Webster to her hip as she approaches Piers and says sotto voce, "Piers, we didn't discuss—"

Piers whispers back, "Wanda, they're curious. We'll show them around and put it to rest. It'll be a fun interlude."

Wanda exits the room through a door bordered with floor-to-ceiling bookcases. Smiling, Piers swats her rear end. Ruby, rising from her wingback chair in the corner and standing in the frame, shoots a startled glance at Tammy beside her. Tammy spreads her hands as if to say, "What can you do?"

Ruby glances quickly over Tammy's shoulder toward the camera. Her eyes widen, apparently in response to Jeff, and she mouths "Really?" Shaking her head, Ruby turns away and walks beside Tammy. The camera follows behind them.

Tammy, aggrieved, whispers, "He gets his own house, and I have to share a room with Gail?"

Ruby whispers, "I thought you'd made your peace with that."

"I thought I had, too, but that was before I knew there was a whole house available."

Piers calls, "If you young people will just follow me. Jeff, bring the camera; we'll film our tour. We'll begin with the first floor, since you've already seen these rooms. We'll come back down after we've walked the rest of the house."

The group exits the library and walks down the hall toward the main stairs. The camera moves with them, bypassing Ruby and Tammy.

Eric says, "Uh, I'm sorry. Aren't we on the first floor?"

Wanda smiles at Piers as the group climbs the stairs. Webster hangs over her shoulder and makes faces at Eric. She says, "No, this is the ground floor, or it would be in England. The second floor is called the first floor, and the third floor is the second."

Eric looks nonplussed. Wanda laughs.

The mic pics up Ruby's whisper, off camera: "Well, Jeff has seniority, and he has all that camera stuff, so it makes sense he gets the gatehouse. Otherwise, Wanda would probably have to open the rear wing to give him enough storage space for it all. Besides, wouldn't you rather be in the big house with all of us? It's probably lonely staying in that little cottage all alone. And all the action will be here."

Wanda says, "You'll be confused before we're through. I think that's the real reason Piers wants to give us a tour; so we'll be able understand his obscure references to the various parts of the house."

Piers, still holding his pipe, slides an arm around her shoulder and jokes, "Guilty." Webster's face twists; he turns his head and sneezes.

The camera motion stops, and the frame rotates away from Piers and Wanda to focus on Ruby and Tammy lingering behind. Jeff's voice calls, "Hey, do you guys know this is an echoing corridor? It's constructed in such a way that even if you stand at the back-end whispering, people at the front of the hallway can still hear you."

Ruby looks up, eyes wide. "You could hear us talking?"

The camera bobs up and down as Jeff nods. Ruby looks stricken. Tammy looks annoyed and asks, "And you kept filming us?"

Jeff says, "Eh! This part is inessential since Piers isn't giving any instructions. I can always cut it out or loop music over it."

Tammy's face wrinkles. She guides Ruby by the arm until they're standing just behind Piers and Wanda.

The camera tracks their movement and focuses on Webster. He sneezes violently and tries to force Piers's hand with the pipe away from his face and off Wanda's shoulder. Piers suggests,

"Wanda, why don't you let…Eric here hold Webster for a bit?"

Eric's face lights up, but Wanda holds Webster more protectively. "I don't know. Eric is a stranger still, and Webster doesn't like other males very much as it is."

Eric points to the camera and says, "He likes Jeff."

Jeff, off camera, says, "Smithy and I are old buddies. But Wanda's got a point. He snapped at Wolf a few times; I wouldn't want your first impression of our boy to involve blood or bandages."

Gail asks, "What wolf?"

Jeff, off camera, says, "Smithy's step-father."

Piers, annoyed, says, "All right, we'll leave things as they are. And Jeff, what have I told you about not calling him that anymore? I don't want to confuse anyone reviewing our records."

As the group continues to ascend, Ruby lingers behind to talk to Jeff. Under her breath, she asks, "Why do you call Webster 'Smithy?'"

Jeff, still behind the camera, says, "It's my little joke. Piers called him a wordsmith in his first interview about the project. So that's what I nicknamed him. He likes it, even if Piers doesn't."

Piers remarks, "Note the lovely chandelier overhead; it was designed in Tiffany's workshop, though it may not look like much now." He pauses at the landing. "Observe: an intact newel post in the image of Newport's pineapple of hospitality!"

Gail asks, "Really?" She hangs over the railing, fascinated, and strokes the carved pineapple. "I didn't know pineapples had any association with Rhode Island. I always think of Hawaii when I see pineapples. Tropical islands, not New England."

Wanda says, "The symbol is particular to Newport. It signifies a welcome. The sailors of

Newport would bring pineapples back from their voyages in the tropics."

Piers resumes climbing. The others follow more slowly. He pauses, and when Gail draws closer, sets a hand on her shoulder and asks, "Do you find Trevor Hall welcoming, Gail?"

Gail says, "Yes, it's fabulous!"

Tammy comments, "It's a little battle-scarred, isn't it?"

Piers glances back at the group. "Alas, that is an apt description. The matching newel post from the ground floor has long since vanished, a victim of vandalism. From 1925 until 1939, this house served as a boarding school. I'm afraid the students living here failed to learn respect for property."

Tammy asks, "Say, Piers, where are the owners, since they don't live here?"

"They spend a lot of time abroad—Ah!" He enters the second-floor hallway. "This area should be familiar to most of you, as you have rooms here. Many of the rooms, however, are vacant." Piers opens the door of a random room. The interior is bare of furniture. A stained carpet stretches across the room, pulled up in the corners. Previous occupants or trespassers had carved initials into the wall, and canvas covers a broken windowpane.

He says, "Let's move into the rear wing. I know you've not seen that part yet. Because…" As he leads the group to a bend in the hall, Piers pulls a key out of his pocket and jangles it. "… it's been kept locked. This wing of the estate housed the male students of the Bradley School of which I spoke a moment ago. I'm afraid they were even more careless with their quarters than with the common rooms."

Piers unlocks the door to the unused wing, its hallway dark and dingy. Pale light slants through the few windows in the middle of the corridor. The floor is uncarpeted, and the wood floor displays visible scratches. The walls are mottled with torn paper. A large hole has been gouged into the plaster nearest the open door.

Tammy exclaims, "I'll say!"

The group proceeds wordlessly down the hall. Periodically, someone blurts or points out a new piece of destruction. Exposed walls are carved with lewd sayings or students' names, or they're stained with unknown matter. The wainscoting is chipped and broken. The mullioned windows are missing panes, which are taped over or tacked over with cloth. Webster kicks and squirms during this part of the tour, his face betraying discomfort.

Wanda asks, "Do you want to stand, Webster?" Wanda kneels and sets Webster on the floor. She signs, 'Walk give hand.' They hold hands as they walk. Webster continually glances up and behind him, slack-jawed.

Piers says, "I understand this wing was once richly furnished with antiques and valuable paintings, but over the years, it saw more wear and tear. Once the school closed after the Bradleys filed for bankruptcy in '39, departing students either snatched the valuables as souvenirs, or vagrants sneaking into the house made off with them, doubtlessly hoping to sell them. This section of the house is also somewhat hazardous. The flooring is weak…"

Piers turns a corner, and his voice becomes inaudible. Gail, Wanda, Webster, and Eric follow him closely, but Ruby hangs back and finally stops beside a carved wood panel depicting nymphs. The nymphs' eyes have been gouged out and their breasts Xed out. Tammy pauses beside her to survey the damage.

Ruby says, "Tammy, this is crazy. Why would anyone agree to let an ape stay here? He's only going to wreck this beautiful place."

Tammy says, "I doubt he can do much worse. The real apes have already come and gone. Look!" She points to a statue of Hercules installed in a nook beside the panel. Its genitalia have been broken off, initials carved into the pedestal. She points up to a darkened chandelier overhead. The camera zooms in on several broken, jagged globes. Tammy says, "They must have used a BB gun to do that; it's too high to reach."

Ruby exclaims, "Those brats! I hope they all end up on a cell block someplace dark and full of roaches!"

Jeff, off camera, says, "It's good you're pointing out the damage this place has sustained. I can document it now so the owners can't claim later that we did it."

Tammy spins around and puts her hands on her hips. She says, "You again?"

"Yup! Still here," he replies.

Gail's head appears around the corridor behind Tammy. "Guys, Piers wants you to stick with the group. It might be dangerous here. He doesn't want you to step in the wrong place and put your foot through the floor."

Ruby says, "I didn't know things were that bad."

Jeff, off camera, says, "Ah, he's just covering his ass. Liability." He calls to Gail, "We're coming!" She disappears, her retreating footsteps echoing down the hall.

Jeff grumbles, "Why did Piers have to recruit her?"

Ruby asks, "What's wrong with her?"

"She's a bimbo," Jeff replies. "She's got no credentials, no academic experience. All she's got is T&A."

Tammy whirls around; her face contorts, and she demands, "What did you just say?"

"I've known Piers for three years. I've seen this before. You should've seen some of the 'lab assistants' he hired. I ended up analyzing all the data while those girls 'worked'—" He coughs. "—one-on-one with Piers. She's just like them."

Tammy coldly remarks, "And you've decided this after knowing her for, what, two, three hours? What Gail lacks in experience, she can make up for in enthusiasm."

Ruby says, "That's right. Gail can learn on the job. This is a learning experience for us as much as it is for Webster. I have no academic experience either, you know. I just transferred in."

Jeff, off camera, says, "Oh, I never meant you—"

Tammy says, "You flat-out told us Piers hires women with looks and no brains. Is that why you think he brought us on board, too?"

Jeff, off camera, says, "No! I've read your papers. You're brilliant, Tammy! I'm glad to have you working with us. And Ruby, you might not have written papers or done a conference presentation, but Piers must have seen some spark in you to offer you a place on the team."

Ruby folds her arms and says, "Maybe he saw T&A."

Jeff takes a moment to compose himself. "No, you don't…Don't get me wrong, you're cute, but… you're not like Gail." Ruby turns her back and walks quickly around the corner. He calls after her: "You're classy!"

The camera moves quickly up the hallway, passing below a series of skylights, in pursuit of Ruby.

Tammy powerwalks beside it, her scornful face visible in the frame. "You're still taping!" She laughs and shakes her head. "I can't believe you're saying these things at all, but I really can't believe you're saying them on camera!"

Jeff, off camera, says, "I'll cut this part out."

Ruby pauses and asks, "What about what we said downstairs about room assignments?"

"Gone! I promise. And…I'm profoundly sorry. I never meant to antagonize you—either of you. And I was wrong to dismiss Gail. Piers is right: you all have smarts and ambition, or you wouldn't be here."

As they round another bend in the hallway and rejoin the group, Ruby exclaims. They are standing below an oculus opening onto the third floor. The upper room's walls have elaborate wainscoting, largely untouched. However, a couple of the balustrades on the oculus are missing. A small winding staircase leads from the second floor to the third level.

Piers gestures. "Here's a nice spot for a change of pace. This room used to be the lower ballroom where dances were held. The orchestra would be stationed above, so the music drifted down to the first floor while couples also danced on the second floor. A skylight on the third level just above us brings in most of the daylight."

As the group marvels at the design, Webster starts to pull away from Wanda; he leans out, straining against the tension of her grip as he looks all around the room. His gaze travels up the staircase and he grows increasingly agitated. When he finally looks up at the oculus, he whimpers and pulls at Wanda's arm.

Piers asks, "Shall we go up and see what used to be the servants' quarters?" He leads the group up to the upper ballroom, but Webster stays rooted in place, staring up at the third floor. Wanda tugs on his hand repeatedly, but he will not budge. Finally, she scoops him up and carries him up the stairs. Webster continues to whine, and his gaze tracks a particular spot on the landing. At the foot of the stairs, the camera pauses.

Jeff, off camera, says, "Hold up, Piers. I need to change film…"

The picture goes black.

EXCERPT FROM
SMITHY: A TWENTY-YEAR COMPENDIUM
BY REID BENNETT, PHD

Critics of the study frequently complained that Dr. Preis-Herald "cherry-picked" his evidence for Webster's communication skills, only publicizing film of the chimp's "good days" and his most cogent signing. In response, Dr. Preis-Herald made available over thirty hours of previously unseen recordings from the Trevor Hall days. Initially, news of the so-called "outtake reels" traveled only within academic circles, but word spread to the public within months of their release, which cynics observed was cleverly timed to coincide with the ten-year anniversary of the trial, though Preis-Herald denied any connection.

I have had the opportunity to view this footage. While some of it is uninformative, (e.g., experimental camera staging to determine the best perspective of a room for videotaping), many recordings do offer valuable insights into the chimpanzee's behavior and the interpersonal dynamics of the household, broadening our knowledge of the study beyond its mere academic aspects.

One may obtain copies by sending a check or money order for $1,000.00 (or choose four installment payments of $250.00) plus $25.00 S&H to Piers Preis-Herald, care of P.O. Box 20096 Stamford, CT 06092.

"OUTTAKE REEL" FOOTAGE

Date: May 25, 1974
Location: The Dining Room

The group stands inside a long room painted bright green on three sides; the third side features large floor-to-ceiling windows hung with green drapes and French doors opening onto a patio. A long table with seating for ten fills the center of the room. Webster walks beside Wanda, holding her hand. He balks when he looks at the ceiling, which is surrounded by three-dimensional, carved, gilded angel faces. Webster points and hoots at the faces.

Wanda pats his head and signs, "It's OK. Be good." She says out loud, "It's all right. They're not real."

Tammy regards Webster sympathetically and says, "Poor baby. It's no fun to have people staring at you like you're on display in a zoo, is it?"

Wanda says, "Oh, don't start thinking of him as a baby. We must resist the urge to anthropomorphize Webster, so we can accurately document his behavior. And never forget he's an animal, or you could find yourself at a disadvantage. He still bites from time to time."

Tammy says, "So did my sister Lydia, until she was three."

Wanda says tersely, "But I doubt your sister had jaws like a chimpanzee's. Just don't fool yourself that Webster is completely harmless. He's well-behaved most of the time, but he gets agitated around strangers, as you can see, and then he may act up. Piers, I think we may have to cover the ceiling."

Piers says, "He'll get used to it once he's been in the house a few days."

Ruby runs her hand over the wall and murmurs, "Acid green." Everyone stares at her. She looks embarrassed and explains, "It was one of the first artificial dyes produced during the Victorian age, along with mauve, so it was often used in decorating. They said so on the tour I took."

"That may be true," Piers says, gesturing to the walls. "But this coloring doesn't go back as far as the Victorians. This room was painted about ten to twelve years ago. Originally, the walls were covered with a unique, hand-painted wallpaper featuring forest scenes and animals to give diners the impression they were feasting among nature with the angels smiling over them, but…" He waves his hand.

Eric and Tammy together say, "The students."

"Brats!" Tammy finishes.

Eric says, "It's hard to have nice things with kids around. At the center where I work, we used to have cartoon characters painted on the walls: Casper and Wendy, Snoopy and Charlie Brown. But the kids would sometimes throw paint or kick holes in the walls during a tantrum, so we made one wall completely blank and left it as a space where they could express themselves."

Piers says, "I'll keep that in mind, but I'm counting on you all to keep a sharp eye on Webster, so he doesn't require such measures. Let's move on."

The group passes back into the hallway, covered with fading, flocked floral wallpaper. Gail rubs one of the flowers. "I love this. It's so pretty."

Wanda says, "Gail, please don't do that. The paper is fragile already; poking at it may cause more damage. We want to preserve what's left of the house and keep it from deteriorating further before we return it."

The researchers enter the solarium, a spacious, undecorated room with large casement windows and French doors leading to the rose garden on its long side; smaller windows let in light on the smaller exterior wall, but the wall adjacent to the library boasts a massive fireplace. Bench seats, lined with small potted plants, are built in next to the casement windows. The room is furnished with a small sofa, a coffee table, and several mismatched chairs.

In front of the fireplace, a border collie, Maisie, reclines but leaps up and runs to Piers, tail wagging. Webster signs, "dog," and tries to pull away from Wanda to go to Maisie. Piers takes Webster's free hand and leads the trio to a record player standing in the corner. Maisie follows behind Piers, sniffing the floor, then wanders out of the frame and starts barking. The researchers meander through the room.

Piers gestures toward a cardboard box atop a small stand beside the turntable and says, "I took the liberty of bringing up some of your records, Wanda. So at the end of a busy day, you all might relax and enjoy some music."

Wanda says, "They're my old albums from high school. Feel free to add to the collection."

In the background, Maisie barks. The camera tracks Gail as she breaks away from the group and approaches the large fireplace. She stands inside it and stretches her hands up, but cannot touch the top. Gail exclaims, "I love these big old fireplaces! Look, you can stand right in them! It's huge!" Ruby joins Gail at the fireplace, facing her. She also stretches out her arms, and though she is taller than Gail, she can't reach the top either. The girls laugh.

Meanwhile, Maisie turns in circles in the center of the room, agitated. She barks at the window, approaches it, then retreats, whining. Piers catches her by the collar and pulls her away; he makes her sit against the wall. Whining, Maisie lays her head on her paws. She continues looking at the window. Webster also faces the window and waves.

Piers says, "That's enough, Maisie." He addresses the room loudly. "All right, everyone. If you'll please take seats, I'd like to begin the next activity. Jeff, is your camera ready? Did you find your best angle?

Jeff, off camera, says, "Roger that! But I need to change reels again."

Piers asks, "Again?"

Jeff replies, "You talk a lot!"

Everyone in the room laughs. The film cuts to a blank screen.

LETTER FROM RUBY CARDINI
TO SARAH-BETH ANDREWS

(CONTINUED)

… The third floor was once the servants' quarters. All its rooms are tiny and clustered together. It's hard to believe two or three people used to pack into a single room. Many servants even had to share beds! That gave Tammy a new perspective. Then again, the help spent nearly all their waking hours working, so the rooms would have only been used for sleeping. I'll bet the mansion didn't seem so beautiful to those who had to clean it. As much as I love history, I'm grateful to be alive today when I have options and the agency to lead my own life. No one else owns my time or can tell me what to do!

Nevertheless, I wish we had some servants who could help us tidy up Trevor Hall. It made me ill to see how the house has either been left to decay or was purposefully damaged. How could anyone, even a vicious schoolboy, do such things to such a lovely place? Had I been a servant from the old days who spent my life on my hands and knees making the great house shine, I surely would have come back to haunt whoever defaced the fresco of the Graces.

Webster was well-behaved on the tour, though I think the dinginess of the closed wing put him off. He got fidgety, and Wanda continually had to put him down so he could walk, only to have to scoop him up again when he lagged and whined. I suspect he was tuckered out from traveling and all the excitement.

We tried playing a game to help Webster learn our names. It was a version of Monkey in the Middle, though Piers wasn't keen on Gail calling it that. I don't think he knew the American name of the game, or maybe they don't play it in England. He seemed to think Gail ignorant for calling Webster our "monkey." He reprimanded her: "No, no, my dear. Don't make that mistake. Webster is a chimpanzee—pan troglodytes—*an ape, a primate. Never a monkey!" Tammy set him straight, more sharply than the situation warranted. I think she was still feeling offended on Gail's behalf because of the ugly comments Jeff made.*

The game was great fun and a good teaching opportunity, though Webster seemed too distracted by his new surroundings to fully focus. He kept looking around the room instead of at us. Everyone sat in a circle around Webster and threw the ball to one another. However, we had to sign in advance to whom we would throw the ball so he could learn who we were.

Wanda instructed us to make name signs for ourselves, so Webster could learn our identities. First, you choose a sign that stands for something special to you or about you, and then you combine it with a letter from your name. For example, Piers's name is the letter "P" and the sign for smoking, since he's rarely without a pipe. Gail's is the letter G and the sign for yellow over her head because she's the only blonde in the house. Wanda suggested "T" and the sign for glasses for Tammy, since that's her distinct look. Wanda's own sign is a "W" and "think," to signify her intellect, I suppose. "There must not be a sign for 'bossy,'" Tammy kidded to me afterward. She was miffed that Wanda's symbol is for something she does while her own is based on her looks.

When Wanda asked for my sign, I went blank. I don't look distinct or have any special mannerisms. Jeff came to my rescue by asking me about my hobbies. Since I like to read, we went with "R" and "reading."

I think Jeff probably isn't as bad as he seemed on the tour. He helped me out twice today: once when I was taping, by getting me to look at him instead of at that awful, cyclopean, blinking camera light, and again when we named ourselves. Jeff also offered to sleep in Webster's room for the first night, so if he wakes up early in a strange place, he'll have someone familiar nearby. He really loves that little chimp. Jeff's a lot warmer with him than Piers or Wanda are; they treat Webster more like a possession. Maybe first impressions aren't to be trusted. I still can't believe I thought Jeff was just a film bum when it turns out he's one of the founding members of this study.

I want to trust him, even though Tammy thinks he's a jerk. We said some things during orientation that we shouldn't have, and Jeff caught them on camera. He promised he wouldn't use them in the final cut, and I hope he keeps his word.

Tomorrow will be our first day working with Webster! I'm already so nervous I can't sleep; hence, I'm up writing this letter to you instead. Looking at the stack of paper next to me, I see I've written a novel all about Orientation Day! Maybe I should copy it before I send the manuscript off to you. Piers might want my report as documentation for the study. Think of it: I'm writing historical documents for a history-making study! I am watching history unfold. No: I am <u>making</u> *history, Sarah-Beth...*

NOTE POSTED TO BULLETIN BOARD
BY WANDA KARLEWICZ

May 26, 1974

As we begin our study, let's all consider some questions from the field of linguistics:

1. How is language defined? Is it a fixed set of rules, or any method of communication? Are the two mutually exclusive?
2. If you can still understand a message that doesn't correctly follow the rules of syntax, does it count as language? Conversely, would a sentence that's grammatically correct but makes no sense qualify as language?
3. What characteristics are common to all languages? Do any exist?
4. How are children taught language? If language consists of rules, why are children taught vocabulary before syntax?
5. How do you confirm you've correctly understood the message someone is communicating to you? How do you confirm the other party has understood your message?
6. What's the best way to teach language to a chimpanzee? How will you verify the chimp is actually using language?

As an example, one critic of our study has argued that, while chimpanzees use vocal signals to communicate (e.g., citing the presence of food or a predator in the area), these "call signs" don't count as "chimp language." By extension, this critic argues that when Webster makes the Ameslan sign for "food" or "drink," he isn't using language either, just forming a new call sign. Do you agree? How would you prove otherwise?

NOTES POSTED TO BULLETIN BOARD

May 26-28, 1974

Re: Call signs and communication

The use of call signs, or pidgin, may be a precursor to language, and their usage doesn't preclude the development of more sophisticated communication. Toddlers make their wishes understood by using simple words: "cake" (for "I want cake"), "up" ("pick me up"), "poo poo" ("I need the toilet"). This doesn't mean they <u>cannot</u> learn grammar and syntax, only that their brains aren't equipped to deal with minute details at an early developmental stage. Even if Webster can only use "eat" and "drink" now, it doesn't mean he's restricted to simplistic call signs. With time and experience, he may be able to express more elaborate ideas. To dismiss his use of language now is premature.

Re: Grammar, syntax, and meaning making

It's more effective to teach words than rules because words are more easily recognizable, and because children, through exposure to language, can usually determine the rules themselves. Their tendency to bungle irregular plurals (e.g. "mouses") shows they at least realize adding an "s" to a word signifies more than one of it. Adults frequently make grammatical errors, but their meaning is still clear, especially with context.

Consequently, I prioritize the ability to communicate information over the form communication takes. To determine the meaning of a message, context is valuable. For instance, when my sister Dinah was learning to talk, she called bushes and plants "baby trees." Knowing small things often grow bigger, and knowing the word for "tree," she used her limited knowledge to describe the world around her. Even though her description was inaccurate, her intention was clear, especially given her background. I would evaluate Webster's surroundings and his level of exposure to the world when interpreting his messages. — **Tammy**

Writers often intentionally violate the conventions of language to make a point. Stream-of-consciousness writing doesn't follow proper grammatical structure. Lewis Carroll's "Jabberwocky," or the works of Dr. Seuss might not count as language under a strict definition because they use made-up words and play with syntax. Finally, an author may make factually incorrect statements through metaphor, such as "The eyes are windows to the soul," or "Juliet is the sun." Taken literally, these statements are confusing, but they convey an artistic concept or emotion. Such writings are celebrated, even though they abuse the rules of language. So I agree with Tammy; the rules aren't necessarily important.

It might be worth considering literary devices in this study. For example, if Webster calls a potted plant a "baby tree," it shouldn't necessarily be treated as an error. The chimp might honestly think the plant resembles a miniature tree, and could be expressing an opinion or using poetic license. — **Ruby**

Language can intentionally obscure meaning: Anyone remember "Who's on First?" — **Jeff**

Can we teach Webster that routine? —**Eric**

LETTER FROM GAIL EHRLICH
TO EHRLICH FAMILY

(EXCERPT FROM LETTER DATED MAY 27, 1974)

…Webster is adorable! He has big dark eyes that look like shiny beads, and he's got tiny hands with itty bitty fingers and fingernails, just like a real baby. His feet don't look like our feet though—they look like another pair of hands, only narrower. The toes are long and thin like fingers so he can grasp things and climb trees. He'll either go barefoot most of the time or wear sandals so his toes can stick out. Piers wants him to get used to living like a human so he's going to wear clothes, and one of our jobs will be to help him get dressed in the morning. I hope I get that job. It will be so much fun to dress up a little chimp.

Everybody fell in love with Webster, but I think he was a little scared of us at first. The only people he knew were Jeff, Piers, and Wanda, and he hung onto one of them the whole time. I kept hoping I'd get to hold Webster, but Piers says we have to let him get used to seeing us first.

But Webster's not the only animal we have to play with. Piers also brought Wanda's two cats Harriet and Peter and his own dog Maisie. We've all picked our own favorite pet to play with. I think Harriet is so pretty! She has white, brown, and red patches on her fur and brown and white spots on her nose. Ruby likes Peter best. He came right up to her and rubbed up against her ankles when he got out of his carrier. She had him on her lap this evening petting him, and he even followed her to bed. Even though the cats are Wanda's, she said they'll have the run of the house instead of staying in her room all the time, so sometimes they might end up sleeping in one of our rooms. But Piers wants Maisie to sleep in the Solarium or in the gatehouse where Jeff will sleep.

It turns out Jeff is really handy! He did a lot of the repairs and retrofitting in the house all by himself. He films, too. He's going to be taping our sessions with Webster and cutting them together at his studio in the gatehouse to make a movie to show to other scientists. I'm going to get to be a movie star (sort of)!

Jeff set up Webster's bedroom on the top floor weeks ago when he and Wanda were fixing the house for our arrival. It looks like a child's nursery. Webster sleeps in a little bed with a wooden gate around it and curtains hanging down that we can close to help him sleep. He's got a chest of drawers for his little baby clothes! Webster has alot of toys, too, like teddy bears and rubber balls and blocks. We have to teach him how to be responsible and put his toys away after he finishes playing with them. The people he was living with before didn't make him do it, so its one more job for our team.

Jeff put up special shelves for his picture books and some of his toys and anchored them to the wall, so they won't come off if Webster tries to climb them or pulls on them too hard. There are two little windows way up high, almost to the ceiling, that you'd either have to climb on a ladder to open or use a pole to flip the latch and push them out. Piers wants to keep them closed as much as possible, so Webster doesn't try to get out. I think their too high for him to reach, but maybe he can jump. The windows are across the room from the toy shelves, so Webster can't climb up those. But I guess he could climb onto his dresser and launch himself off.

The bedroom used to have carvings and fancy paneling all around the top of the walls, but Jeff covered it over with drywall to protect it. Piers and Wanda were afraid he might climb up the walls and scratch or bite the decorations off. (Webster not Jeff—oops!) I guess Webster can get pretty mischevious. Jeff painted the new fake walls with bright colors, and Eric, the other guy working with us, said we can put up posters of things we'd like Webster to learn about. Like if we want him to learn the words for different fruits, we can put up a picture of apples and oranges, and then when he's got those words down, we can replace it with pictures of animals or clothes or something. Wanda loved that idea.

Jeff also made a rope and tire swing for Webster in the tree outside and built a little tower like a jungle gym for the Solarium that either Webster or the cats can climb for fun. Webster can only play or eat or sleep in certain rooms. He has to learn a routine, so we have to be careful what we do, too, because Webster can learn bad habits from us. Piers says we have to remember there's a time and place for everything, and Webster can't have too many distractions.

Webster is asleep right now. Wanda or Jeff have been staying with him at night, until he gets used to being in a new place, and then he'll sleep on his own. Just like a little kid. I hope I get to babysit Webster sometime. I'm so excited he's here! I can't wait to see what tomorrow will bring. This is going to be so much fun!

WEEKLY WORD LIST
MAY 25, 1974

There
Here
Eat
Drink
Water
Sit
Please
Thank you
Man
Woman

LETTER FROM GAIL EHRLICH
TO EHRLICH FAMILY

(EXCERPT FROM LETTER DATED MAY 31, 1974)

...Wanda put up a list of words she wanted us to teach the very first day Webster arrived, and ever since we've been learning the signs and practicing them with each other and with Webster. Wanda and Jeff also showed us the signs he already knows. Some are signs Webster made up himself instead of what's in the dictionary (like when he's tired and wants to go to sleep, he'll cover his eyes with both hands), and Piers wants us to keep using those because their what's familiar to him—I mean Webster. They split us up to teach us better. Jeff worked with Ruby, while Tammy and Wanda taught me and Eric.

We spent about an hour the first day reviewing Webster's existing signs and then another hour learning new signs. It's super important we use the right signs with Webster, so he won't get confused or make any mistakes. Eric said he'll draw up some flash cards for us to share.

Finally, we got to start teaching him. Everyone sat in a circle. Wanda demonstrated all the signs, then assigned someone in the circle to teach one to Webster. Every time he got it right, we got to tickle or groom him, which means combing his hair like we're looking for lice. It's a funny way to teach good behavior, but it's better than giving him a treat every time. Webster must learn to like us and not just the food we give him.

The best part came yesterday. Piers wanted to meet with Wanda and Jeff after supper. That's usually the time Webster gets his bath and lies down for an evening nap. Wanda's the one who's always given Webster his bath, but she couldn't be in both places at once, and she didn't want to disrupt Webster's routine by putting bath time off. She thinks he would be making better progress by now if he'd followed a regular routine when he lived with the family in New York. She asked me if I would give Webster his bath while she was in the meeting. I thought if she'd ask anyone for help it would be Tammy. I bet she's given hundreds of baths to her little sisters. But of course I said yes, so Wanda took me up to Webster's room.

He has his own little bathroom connected to his bedroom. Jeff couldn't do much to chimp-proof it. He had to leave the big claw-foot bathtub where it was instead of putting in a baby bath. Webster's just a little too big to fit in the sink by now, so we had to put him in the big bathtub. Wanda only filled it up about two or three inches, just enough to get him wet and rinse him off after. We can't risk making the water too deep in case he slips underwater and drowns. Wanda told me I'd have to sit with Webster the entire time and be ready to hold him up. She made me nervous, but I said I'd do everything she wanted. Then she went to get Webster.

After a week in the house with all of us, he still clings to Wanda, but he wasn't afraid to come to me. He likes me. He always tries to grab for my hair. Maybe he thinks it tastes like a banana because its yellow. I try not to let him get it because I don't want him to pull on it, but I like that he's interested in me.

I splashed Webster, then used the washcloth to wipe him down. He wriggled a little but didn't put up a fight. I saw he had some bath toys on his shelf, including a rubber ducky. I asked Wanda the sign for Duck and then I tried to teach it to Webster. I squeezed the ducky to make it squeak and signed "duck." I made the ducky sneak up on him from behind and then I made it kiss his cheeks. When he reached for it, I took it away and showed him the sign again. I wanted him to be able to ask for it by name. Webster didn't get it at first. He did make the signs for "give me," so I did.

Wanda decided I wouldn't drown him, so she wished me luck and left. That was my first time being all alone with Webster and I was nervous! I know some babies cry when their mommies leave the room. I didn't want him to start howling after Wanda left. So I cheated a little. I ran some extra water in the bathtub—just a teensy bit—and added some soap to make bubbles. I don't know if Webster had ever had a bubble bath before, but he sure seemed to like this one. A couple of the bubbles floated away into the air and he tried to catch them. He looked so surprised when one of them popped! He kept staring at the air like he thought it might come back. I put bubbles on his foot, and bubbles on his head, and on the tip of his nose. I even put some bubbles on my nose and chin to keep his attention. If only I had asked Wanda the sign for "bubbles." I could have taught it to him. Instead, whenever Webster looked at me, I signed my name, "Gail," and "woman."

He was pretty good during most of his bath. Only once, he started to kick and make a lot of noise. I thought Wanda would come in and scold me, but she was still in her meeting. Webster splashed a lot of water over the side of the tub. I thought he was trying to wet me, but he wasn't even aiming at me, he was splashing at the door. Then I thought maybe he was trying to make more bubbles by stirring up the water, so I added a little more soap and made sure to blow the bubbles, so they flew in the air. Webster didn't pay much attention though. He kept looking at the door. I guess he was bored.

When I took him out of the bath to towel him off, he finally signed "woman" for me! I hoped he would do "Gail" or "ducky," something I could be sure he had learned from me, but at least he picked up one sign! I petted him and told him how smart he was and then he did it again! He signed "woman" and he pointed to the door. I guess he wanted me to take him to the bedroom for his nap, so I did. I had just tucked him in and gone back to the bathroom to dry up all the water on the ground when Wanda came back.

She was happy with the way I had taken care of Webster and said I could help with his bath again sometime. She was _really_ happy when I told her he signed for me and said she was going to put me in charge of feeding him, so I can teach him the signs for his silverware and his food.

Did you know Jeff has a nickname for Webster? He calls him Smithy and even made him a separate name sign. I'm not sure why, but I think it's cute anyway. Some of us have started to call him Smithy, too. He seems to like it, but Piers doesn't, so we do it in secret. Maybe I should make up my own nickname for him? How about Webby?

WEEKLY WORD LIST
JUNE 1, 1974

Chair
Table
Couch
Door
Window
Fork
Spoon
Knife
Plate
Bowl
Napkin
Cup

DIARY OF RUBY CARDINI

June 1, 1974

Wanda's turned up the heat on our lesson plans. This week's list is marginally longer than last week's, but that was enough to tip Jeff's scales. He inspired a minor argument at breakfast, telling Wanda she's piling on too many words too early in the study. He also complained about her choices: "Is it crucial for Smithy to know the difference between 'chair' and 'couch'?"

We'd started our meal in the dining room because it affords more space, but Webster kept squirming and snarling at the faces on the ceiling until Piers finally relented and let us take our breakfast on the patio, since it's warming up again. However, he warned us against humoring Webster's whims. "He'll manipulate you to no end if he thinks he can get away with it, and every time you give in to him, you teach him you'll do whatever he wants if he cries enough." I'd like to think the fuss about the relocation put Wanda in a bad mood before Jeff started in on her. I sided with Jeff at the start. Ameslan is all new to me, and it's a struggle. It startled me to think we might have to learn exponentially more words every week instead of a regular list of ten. Jeff is worried about the slippery slope, too. "Where will it end, Wanda? You give him twelve words now; will it be fifteen next week? Or twenty?" He told Piers, "We have to let Smithy get used to his new teachers and surroundings before you load up on him, or he'll get too stressed, and he won't perform at all."

"Now you sound like her," Wanda accused. I had no idea who she was talking about. "A little challenge won't hurt Webster. I'm not giving him an entire dictionary." She argued that Webster will encounter these words in his environment anyway, whether they're part of his target vocabulary or not, so it wouldn't hurt to err on the side of expanding his targets.

Eric tried to mediate. *I bet he's used to breaking up fights at his school.* "Giving a student a little more than he's used to handling can be a good thing. We call that 'scaffolding.' You build just a little more on top of what you know he can already handle. It keeps him from getting bored and shows you trust him to take on more. What's Webster's baseline for learning vocabulary? Is twelve a lot more than he can typically do?" He looked from Wanda to Piers, waiting for an answer, but they each just looked at their plates and chewed.

"We don't know," Jeff explained. Then he told us about 'her.' Lorna Bernard, now Mrs. Wolf McKenzie, used to be one of Piers's best students. They kept in touch long after she graduated, married, and divorced. A couple of years ago, Lorna married again and moved from New Haven with her three kids to live with her new husband and his four kids in New York. "One of her new stepchildren is Deaf. So when Piers got the green light for this study and was looking for a place for Smithy, he decided Lorna's would be perfect. They had a pretty cottage near the Hudson River where it's kind of pastoral. She had a background in psychology, plenty of experience with children, and by now, even some ASL under her belt. The idea was Smithy could grow up alongside her children in a bucolic oasis where he could run and play, and there would always be someone to keep an eye on him."

But the arrangement wasn't quite as perfect as Piers had planned. "For one thing, Lorna's scholarship got rusty. She didn't keep any notes, nothing like the journals we've got now. She also didn't establish any experiments to test Smithy's problem-solving skills or see which teaching method was most effective for him. We made house calls about once a month, and Wanda had more luck teaching him in the few hours we were there than Lorna had in the weeks between our visits."

Also, Lorna really didn't know much about signing. "She'd only been doing it for a little under a year and wasn't fluent. Her stepson spent most of his time with his real mother in the city, so Lorna's interaction with him was limited." Jeff thought Wolf would have been a better teacher, but he was always deeply involved in his writing and left the childcare to Lorna. "Besides, for some reason, Smithy couldn't stand him. He even bit Wolf a couple of times when they were 'playing.'" As for the kids, they were more interested in playing with Smithy than instructing him. "They indulged him—spoiled him, really—and made him the family mascot. This little devil used to get away with murder."

Lorna raised Smithy, bottle-fed him, and taught him to walk and climb. But, Jeff said, "She got too attached to him, as if she thought he was her own son. She got too involved, took everything personally." She started second-guessing Piers and challenging him when he tried to formalize how Smithy was reared. She wouldn't allow him to be punished when he acted poorly, for instance. Even when he climbed the walls, literally! "The McKenzies were pretty permissive, and if you think that's a problem with little kids, you don't want to find out how far a chimpanzee will take it." Tammy nodded along with Jeff's description. I guessed she had some stories of her own to tell.

The upshot is there's no conclusive evidence from Webster's first two years as to how rapidly he learns signs or even what signs he has definitively learned. He can sign "me," "you," "eat," "drink," "yes," "no," "good," "bad," and "more" unprompted. Wanda said she'd had good luck teaching him new signs in the short term, but Lorna hadn't reinforced them so that Webster would use them consistently. "Based on those trials, though, I'm confident Webster _can_ learn more than ten words in a week, and I think it's worth it to push him a little and see what he retains in the long term."

She emphasized that his signs must be "spontaneous, accurate, and consistent." Webster must make a sign on his own, it must clearly be the target sign and not half-way there, and he must use it every time. ("He has to sign 'couch' for a couch and 'chair' for a chair and not mix them up, even though they serve the same function. Introducing vocabulary with fine distinctions will test if he has that ability.") This is the crux of our study, and it's what all the other scientists will be looking for.

"We're in a different milieu, using different methodology than LaFontaine. Our results need to show that our procedure works because that will show support for primates learning language. We have to push ourselves and Webster to prove this field isn't a fluke, and that apes aren't just robotically responding to cues."

The whole time Wanda talked, Piers looked on and smiled. I waited for him to jump in, but he let her defend her methods and didn't rein her in. *She sure knows her stuff. Jeff still wasn't happy, but he no longer complained.*

So it's sink or swim now. I must be accurate and consistent with the new vocabulary, too, and be prepared to take on as much of it as possible to keep up with the pace of the study. I have doubters to silence and two years' delay to help mitigate.

Oh, boy!

Later, when we were playing with Smithy outside, Jeff shared more about the early days of the study and explained how Lorna's involvement had finally ended. "They decided to have a baby. Why not? They were still sort of newlyweds and wanted to have a family of their own, in addition to all the other kids they had between them. But Wolf had an ultimatum: a new baby or the new chimp. Even though Lorna was crazy about Smithy, she was willing to let him go to have a real baby of her own. She didn't think it would be safe to have an infant around a growing chimpanzee, either way. I guess she thought Smithy might get jealous. Plus, the more pregnant she got, the harder it would be to chase after Smithy."

I thought it sad Smithy lost his only family that way. I don't see how you could make a commitment to a child—or a chimp—and then turn from it when the going gets tough.

"It's really for the best," Jeff assured me. "The way things were going, he wasn't learning as many words as he should have, and he was getting to be way too manipulative."

I certainly think things worked out for the best. If Smithy still lived with the McKenzies, I wouldn't have the opportunity to get to know and work with him. I certainly wouldn't be living in luxury in Newport.

I just saw that I wrote "Smithy" instead of Webster. I'm starting to adopt Jeff's name for him. We're all picking up on the nickname, I've noticed. "Smithy" just feels friendlier. It's casual and fun. "Webster" sounds like a stuffy old man. "Smithy" sounds cute. And no matter what he's called, our chimp certainly is cute, even if he's also a little devil.

MEMO FROM WANDA KARLEWICZ
TO PIERS PREIS-HERALD

June 3, 1974

RE: Gail Ehrlich

I've been reviewing Gail's recent journal entries, and I'm impressed by the care she's taking with Webster. Gail provides a positive demeanor, warm reinforcement of the curriculum, and continuous encouragement. One of the tedious aspects of this work is the sheer amount of repetition needed to make the information stick. I've worried members of the team would grow weary, slack off, or give up before reaching the necessary threshold for retention. I was particularly concerned about our undergraduates, but those fears appear misplaced where Gail is concerned.

Gail constantly drills Webster on his assigned vocabulary. From time to time, she asks me for a sign that's not on our list just so she can address other aspects of Webster's environment. I wish her proactive approach would inspire her colleagues. Webster seems to like Gail's company, too, as evidenced by his learning her name sign ahead of any of the other new researchers', though he uses it inconsistently. Here is one example from the kitchen journal:

"This morning, I gave Webster his breakfast in the dining room because Eric burned bacon, and the kitchen smelled. I know he doesn't like it there much. I think the faces on the ceiling scare him because they watch him all the time but

don't speak or react to him. I spoke soothingly, and he was calm.

I put the spoon in his hand and made him hold it while he ate. I made sure he finished all his oatmeal. During breakfast, I signed to him "you eat" (1) "drink water" (4) and "good" (3). I also taught him the word for "spoon" (5). That is, I showed him the sign and the spoon, but he hasn't learned it just yet. I also showed him "table" (7) and "chair" (4) and said "give me" (6) regarding the spoon and some oranges that sat on the table. I asked for the spoon by name twice, but for the oranges, I just signed "give me that." Actually, I signed "give me that" (2), "give Gail that" (3), so he would get used to knowing my name, and "give the woman that" (2) after he wouldn't use my name.

Smithy was playful. He rolled the oranges to me when I asked for them, but a couple times, he rolled them past me to the other end of the table. He seemed surprised when they rolled off the table because he bounced in his seat and made little hooting noises.

I asked him "who give that?" (3), and he did my name right once, but the next two times, he just signed "woman." When he signed "Gail," I was standing right next to him, but when he signed "woman," I was standing at the far end of the table because I was picking up an orange. Maybe Webster doesn't recognize me when I'm far away, and he needs glasses?

Smithy did the same thing once when he wasn't looking at me and that was kind of weird. I was asking him, "what's that?" (5) and he knew "eat" for the bowl and "drink" and "water" (he used both one time each) for the cup, but when I pointed to a chair at the end of the table, he said it was a "woman." Do you think he was testing me? The sign for "chair" doesn't look a thing like "woman." I hope I didn't overdue the practice with him and confuse him.

LETTER FROM GAIL EHRLICH
TO EHRLICH FAMILY

(EXCERPT FROM LETTER DATED JUNE 4, 1974)

We had a big meeting today about what to call our chimp. See, Jeff always calls Webster "Smithy." It's a nickname he gave him when he was a baby, and a lot of us have picked it up, too. Except Wanda doesn't like it and keeps asking us not to call him "Smithy" or write it in the journals. She says it will confuse everyone (I guess she's referring to the people who read our study and Webster, too), and Piers wants us to stick to the name he's already chosen.

Jeff and Tammy got everyone together in the library to talk about it while Webster napped. Jeff said it doesn't make sense to think Webster might get confused. He already responds when you call him Smithy, so he knows we're talking to him. Ruby backed him up. Wanda looked surprised when Ruby went up against her. I don't know why. It's obvious she likes Jeff more.

Ruby said we should treat the nickname like a synonym for a word he already knows. If we teach Webster to respond to a new word or name, we're proving he can learn transitive properties. She said Piers refusing to let us use a nickname suggests he doubts his own experiment.

I thought that made sense. I told everyone how Snoopy used to be named Princess before we got her, but we changed her name because I always wanted a dog named Snoopy. I said it didn't take long for her to learn that was her name, and when we told her "Sit, Snoopy" or "Go fetch, Snoopy," she'd do it. Tammy thought that was a great example and gave us a demonstration. She brought Maisie inside and said: "Come here, girl," "Sit down, baby," and "Good dog." Maisie did everything she wanted, and Tammy never even used her name. Tammy said that's because context and tone of voice also helps in communication.

But Wanda said even though she and Piers agree Webster can learn to do complex things with language, we have to start him out with the basics and build a solid foundation for him. She said, "We want him to form sentences eventually, and maybe even use metaphors and puns, but it would be foolish to try anything that complicated this early."

Tammy accused Wanda and Piers of trying to have it both ways. She said Piers can't expect Webster to be smart enough to learn a language but not smart enough to respond to a nickname, and Wanda can't change the study whenever it suits her. Like she gives Webster extra words to learn but then she never lets us try our own spin on things to test what Webster can do. They went back and forth about it. Wanda said Piers can call him whatever he wants because it's his chimp and his experiment. Tammy said it's the university's chimp (I didn't know that), so everyone on the project should have a say, too. "Everybody deserves to have input. That's why we requested this meeting. So we can give our input," Tammy said.

Eric finally spoke up and said he's getting Smithy to use different words to mean the same thing. He showed him an apple yesterday and Smithy signed "food," "apple," and "good." All of those were acurate. Eric said a human would recognize that those are inter-changeable, and it looks like Smithy does, too. He agreed that using nicknames will show Smithy isn't just memorizing words.

So Wanda got overruled. She wasn't happy about it, but she said go ahead and call him Smithy, except when we're around Piers because that will really bug him. Then she said something like "at least we waited until he was out of the house on an errand, so he wouldn't have to witness our rebellion." Jeff told her we just want to be friendly with Smithy. We're not trying to hijack the study. I sure hope Piers doesn't think we're trying to take over. I don't want him to be mad at me.

But I do like the name Smithy…

DIARY OF RUBY CARDINI

June 8, 1974

Wanda posted another list today. I came downstairs for breakfast and quickly lost my appetite when I saw the paper tacked to the bulletin board. I only barely managed to learn the previous list, and now I must start on a new one already! This will be the way of the experiment going forward. It may get harder as Wanda adds more complex signs or expects us to start teaching Smithy actual phrases, or it may get easier as I slowly and painfully acquire mastery over ASL and pick up new material faster. Either way, must be done. I need lots of study and practice to tackle the official words and the signs Smithy already knows so I can recognize and document them—and reproduce them in conversation. Just thinking of all that work makes my head ache! I even took a pill with dinner.

But...the promise of <u>conversation</u> with an ape is so tantalizing! I can see myself, fingers flying, guiding Smithy through an actual discussion. I can't wait to reach that point. And so I practice, practice, practice. Luckily, I'm finding lots of partners ready to practice with me. ASL is totally new to most of the others, so I don't feel ignorant. Instead, I worry I'm not going to pick up the signs as quickly as everyone else, and I'll become a liability.

I studied the new signs with Jeff again today. He was very encouraging. He's been more supportive than I would have anticipated, given how he sneered at Gail and gossiped about Wanda on Orientation Day. Since then, he's always been friendly when I see him, always says hi and asks how things are going. Tammy says he does the same with her. So maybe he's trying to redeem himself. Maybe he really is a gentleman and just had a bad day that other time.

I also learned why Robert La Fontaine is persona non grata in this household. It turns out he released his book, <u>Conversations with Osage</u>, *just four months after Piers went on national TV to introduce his own study. La Fontaine never contacted Piers to mention he'd been conducting similar research with a chimpanzee of his own or to offer a preview of his book. He preempted Piers's discoveries and threatened to make his research redundant (or at least less groundbreaking).*

Piers was "pissed," in Jeff's words, but he's managed to maintain public interest in Webster/Smithy by stressing all the ways our study differs from La Fontaine's (e.g., our chimp will live with and learn directly from humans instead of through lab instruction) and by vowing we will go further ("Smithy will develop an understanding of language principles instead of regurgitating signs on command like a parrot," says Jeff).

I think La Fontaine's behavior was pretty low-down. Why can't scientists be more collaborative and pool their knowledge instead of trying to one-up each other? Look at Darwin and Wallace. I thought La Fontaine's book had some clever ideas; it's a shame he didn't reach out to Piers, so they could work together to build our collective knowledge of this topic. We'll just have to see what Piers comes up with now.

Correction: we shall see what <u>our team</u> does.

EXCERPT FROM
SMITHY: A TWENTY-YEAR COMPENDIUM
BY REID BENNETT, PHD

CHAPTER ONE, WEBSTER: THE EARLY DAYS

As one of the original researchers, Wanda Karlewicz's insights—into the methodology of the study, Webster's early accomplishments, the cooperation of the research team—are invaluable. Though she could easily fill a book with her memories and observations, she has never chosen to do so, which is regrettable for science.

Given her reticence and well-known reclusiveness, the few recorded interviews Karlewicz has provided, always back-lit in dim lighting to preserve her privacy, are noteworthy as much for their inherent informative value as for their rarity.

Watching the video footage never fails to raise a frisson up my neck. From the shadows of the darkened soundstage, her amorphous figure shifts. One can see only blackness where her face ought to fill the camera's frame and an occasional wavering tendril at the side of her cheek, perhaps the shadow of her hair or a billowing scarf. Yet her voice remains articulate and clear despite her obscured figure, and it is easy to envision her striding through the corridors of Trevor Hall, announcing the day's agenda and assigning tasks. Hers is the voice of knowledge and authority. It is the voice of the experiment.

What follows are combined, selected transcripts from Karlewicz's interviews with the BBC (1982) and PBS (1987), describing the formative stages of the study and the unusual hurdles it encountered:

On a darkened soundstage, Wanda's profile appears as a darker shadow against a darkened background. She shifts and brushes something over her shoulder.

From off-stage, the interviewer asks a series of questions:

Please introduce yourself and tell us how you became involved with the project.

I'm Wanda Karlewicz. From January of 1973 to May of 1975, I acted as Senior Research Assistant on the Preis-Herald Primate Language Project—the Webster Study.

I was then a graduate student concentrating on linguistics. Part of my curriculum included psychology courses under Piers Preis-Herald. We quickly developed a rapport: our academic interests overlapped, and we shared a strong work ethic and an ambition to blaze new trails in the fields of cognition and socialization. He became the primary advisor on my thesis, and I became his assistant. I taught his undergraduate introductory classes when he was out of town, proctored and graded exams, and analyzed data in his labs...

...Piers had always been fascinated by communication, which made him a natural fit to supervise my research. When we met, he was exploring language acquisition in young children, but soon after, he switched his focus to communication in animals. There are limits to how you can manipulate a human subject, whereas we could completely control an animal subject's environment. Additionally, to show that an animal could learn to communicate would be groundbreaking.

Primate studies were then in their infancy. Robert La Fontaine had just published his initial studies with Osage as we were launching our research, but Piers identified weaknesses in Fontaine's study he thought we could improve in our own. Osage had been taught to sign the same way seals are taught to perform by direct instruction and primary reinforcement. Webster would be motivated by a desire to communicate and reinforced by acceptance from his human family. To encourage the chimp's own initiative and reduce dependency on response-reinforcement, Piers chose to immerse him in a human lifestyle in which sign language communication was a natural and necessary feature. We believed that, in this way, the chimp could produce original statements that would reflect his internal thought processes, and we could learn what another species thought of the world, of us humans, of his own existence. The possibilities were dizzying...

...I'm fluent in sign language thanks to a lifetime spent interacting with a Deaf younger brother. I had the skill set and the theoretical knowledge, so I was a natural for the job. I developed lesson plans and selected the signs to introduce to the chimp. My lists were based on the ease of producing the sign and the frequency or relevance of the word. I had to include a mixture of nouns and verbs and introduce abstract concepts like "where" and "when," as well as concrete ideas such as "there" and "you."

Will you describe some of those lessons?

In the first sessions, I signed with another researcher so Webster could observe and imitate us. I worked with other volunteers from Piers's classes and with Webster's surrogate mother, Lorna McKenzie. Each participant had a varying degree of ability. Regrettably, I had to spend almost as much time instructing the other instructors as I did instructing Webster. It was important to get them to make clean signs for the sake of accuracy. We needed to verify that Webster's gestures were in fact true signs, and that one sign did not become confused for another. I expended a lot of effort on legibility and sacrificed quantity for quality. I've always regretted that and wondered how differently the study might have turned out if we had had more professional instructors during Webster's critical period.

Could you talk for a bit about Lorna McKenzie's role in the study?

Several volunteers from Yale and the surrounding institutions wanted to take in Webster. Some of them were distinguished cognitive scientists. Yet Piers insisted the best way for Webster to develop human traits was to have him grow up in a "normal" human family. I don't know if he had Lorna's family in mind when he began the experiment, or if he decided afterward that she would be the right person to pick up the slack. Lorna was accomplished, though she later proved to be a laissez-faire mother. The family lived in a large house with spacious fields and plenty of room to run and play. The nearest neighbors were over a mile away, which was another advantage. As we discovered after moving Webster to Newport, his vocalizing created a disturbance. In retrospect, we should have started him in a more populated area as an infant and moved him to the country once he approached adolescence and became more... assertive.

Lorna couldn't wait to "adopt" Webster. Her husband, Wolf, was easygoing, and he humored her in agreeing to take responsibility for the chimp. I think he imagined the experience would provide good fodder for one of his novels. That changed. Webster never adapted to Wolf. In fact, he was often hostile toward him. If I were a Freudian, I would speculate on the existence of an Oedipal complex in non-human mammals.

Can you elaborate?

Webster never was comfortable with Wolf as a caregiver. He wouldn't accept a bottle from him. He frequently became agitated in his presence, like a child left with a strange babysitter. At a couple of play sessions, he bit Wolf on the hand—nothing requiring medical attention, but enough to break the skin—and Webster would sometimes defecate in Wolf's study. This usually happened after tension had built between the two. The family ended up putting a bolt lock on the study door off the ground, so Webster couldn't reach it. That stopped him, though it never worked for us.

Did Webster resent any of the children?

Webster always liked to be the center of attention, and if he saw anyone of any age receiving more of it than him, he would act to redirect the focus his way, often by creating a disturbance. He showed no special affinity toward any of the kids. We hoped he would develop a bond with young Stephen, the boy who signed, but Webster's signing skills during this time never rose to the level that enabled him to reliably communicate with the little boy, and Stephen was more interested in sports than in animals, anyway. The other kids alternated between spoiling Webster like a special pet and complaining when he would mess up their rooms or monopolize Lorna.

How did you and Lorna McKenzie work together? Was there any rivalry between the two of you?

Because Piers had seen her first? No, we weren't in junior high school. Our interaction was… amicable. We didn't become friends, despite our similar academic backgrounds. Our personalities were so different. I'm very disciplined. It's one of my strengths as a researcher, though it hasn't always benefited me in casual interactions. Also, I saw Webster as raw material to shape; I was interested in seeing what he could learn and produce. Lorna was…well, more of a hippie. Her approach to the study was phenomenological. She wanted to experience the moment and go "with the flow." Lorna let Webster guide her instead of trying to guide Webster. I'd tell her that the curriculum called for him to obey certain rules, and she would say we needed to consider what he wanted. She wanted us to structure our lessons according to Webster's interests and Webster's desires, which varied from day to day and sometimes hour to hour. When he was inattentive and resistant to signing, Lorna shortened the lessons to let him play and "explore his own world." She constantly preached to us about how crucial it was to listen to Webster, but she never bothered to document anything he "told" her, so we only had her word to rely on regarding anything that went on in that house. It was absurd!

Piers tolerated her wishes to a certain extent. I think he worried that if he opposed her too openly, she would drop out of the study and he'd be left to care for Webster himself. Ultimately, Lorna's refusal to uphold a scientific approach only harmed the project. Webster didn't perform to his best potential. Our team periodically visited the home, and in a concentrated period devoted exclusively to signing, could teach him a great deal. But nothing we did was ever reinforced in our absence, so by the time of our next visit, Webster had forgotten so much that we'd have to spend about two-thirds of our time reteaching everything from the last session. We couldn't cover as much new ground as we needed.

The primate mind, like the human mind, is highly malleable for the first two to four years. Webster was nearly two years old and practically a little heathen. I worried we were squandering his best years. Jeff Dalton, the videographer for our sessions, also complained about the way Lorna spoiled Webster. He wanted to stage an intervention, to urge Piers to pull Webster from the McKenzie home temporarily. Jeff thought if we could keep the chimp for a week, a fortnight, in a more structured lab environment, we could make progress and prove Webster's limitations were imposed on him by his caretaker and didn't result from lack of ability. It was one of the few times we were in accord.

How did you convince Dr. Preis-Herald to end the McKenzies' involvement?

Actually, we didn't have to intervene. During all our fretting and plotting, Lorna announced she was expecting another baby and wouldn't be able to keep Webster. Piers, bless him, wasn't quite as blind as we'd feared. He'd sensed Lorna's phase in the study was playing itself out and had already begun arranging a contingency plan. With my help, he prepared another grant proposal to rent housing for Webster and a team of student researchers. This time, he would be raised within a fictive family group instead of a house full of children. The new plan allowed for a more controlled environment in which Webster could have regular lessons in a low-key, informal setting.

The infamous Trevor Hall.

Yes, it became that. I'd been looking at homes in rural Connecticut—not mansions, but farmhouses. I was seeking a countryside setting like the

McKenzies' when Piers suddenly announced he'd rented us a mansion in Newport. I was taken aback, but the romance of living and working in such a beautiful setting appealed to me. The house needed lots of work. I'm sure the lessors counted on us cleaning and making improvements for basic living arrangements when they worked out the rental agreement. Even so, it was still a bargain for us; a blessing, I thought.

Even with a new home secured, we still needed to accomplish a tremendous deal of work quickly. Lorna only gave us six weeks' notice. It had taken us almost six months to put together the initial phase of the study: three months build-up before we acquired Webster and another eight or nine weeks of prepping him in the lab and teaching the McKenzies a bit about chimp behavior. Now we had to prep the house, develop new lesson plans, and hire faculty.

Piers handled the hiring himself. He held interviews at Yale, but also toured other Eastern campuses and posted advertisements in academic journals to reach a wider audience. Jeff and I spent spring break working nonstop at the house. Between us, we fixed up Webster's quarters—hazard-proofed and furnished them—and Jeff got the plumbing and wiring in order.

I sealed off superfluous areas of the house. I also cleaned and furnished some of the bedrooms. I visited local yard sales and consignment shops and used my own money to get necessities like bedding, silverware, and a dining set. The house had been empty for so long. All that remained were some old, worn-out chairs and rusty bedsprings from the years it had been a boarding school. It was spartan, and I wanted Trevor Hall to seem welcoming to the people who would be giving their time and energy to the project.

I also purchased the journals and other supplies. Then I reworked some of the original lesson plans I'd developed for Lorna, interspersed with new ideas. I structured the play sessions and scheduled meal and nap times. I even designed menus so Webster could have a balanced diet to fuel his studies. As it turned out, I put in too much work...

...Once the new team assembled at the house, I encountered the same issues we'd faced with Lorna. Piers's recruits were talented and intelligent young scientists, but they were too easily enamored of the mansion and the excitement of working with a young chimp. Webster was charming and endeared himself to the ladies. Gail, in particular, fawned over him, though she was diligent in drilling him, too. I constantly had to remind everyone of the goals we had to reach. I'd hoped that working with other scientists would partner me with like-minded, equally motivated instructors. Instead, I felt like a kindergarten teacher trying to make the students settle down for a nap. I know I made myself an ogre, but it couldn't be helped.

I knew we couldn't afford to waste any more time as Webster's development progressed. His brain was wiring itself into its final configuration, and it was vital that language recognition and production be part of that configuration. Moreover, I understood then—even if Piers and Jeff hadn't considered it—that Webster's physical growth would put a "sell-by" date on our ability to work with him. As he got bigger, he was harder to carry. And as he grew stronger, he became harder to discipline. We couldn't make him sit still for a session. He began not to mind us. He learned he could push us around—literally. Somehow, that fact didn't register on anybody else.

Nor did they seriously appreciate that we had to submit data to the board that had approved our work. To continue receiving funding, we had to prove to the university we could achieve noteworthy results. You don't get results by clowning around; you need to be organized, controlled, consistent, and persistent. You need to record <u>everything</u> and interpret it. The Trevor Hall team acted as if we were in a Shangri-La where nothing would ever change, no one would ever grow old, and we could play forever without being accountable to anybody. It was up to me to tell them that wasn't so. Piers had so much on his plate: his own classes, his writing, his weekly broadcasts, more grant proposals. He couldn't be on site every day to manage the study himself. <u>I</u> had to do it. I did the best I could, but I didn't make any friends. They simply didn't want to hear it.

Why do you think there was such a lack of cooperation from your colleagues?

If I'm to be honest, much of the problem was my own doing. I guess I just don't know how to inspire cooperation. I worry too much about giving other people responsibility, especially when the outcome is important. Most of the time, I know I'll do a better job than anyone else, so why jeopardize the work by handing it off to someone inferior?

Early on, I read the profiles Piers gave me and tried to identify team members to whom I could delegate. Jeff Dalton would have been an obvious partner because of his longstanding involvement in the study, but I sensed that he, like Lorna, had a personal relationship with Webster. After all, <u>he</u> had given the chimp the nickname. I wanted a cooler head to pair with my own.

I was optimistic for Tammy Cohen. She was a good student; the undergraduate writing sample she submitted with her application was excellent.

She was the eldest child in a large family, so I imagined she had learned to be responsible and capable.

From the beginning, I expected Tammy to be more mature than the others. So when she showed up at Trevor Hall and immediately began whining about the rooming arrangements, of all things, it floored me. After that, I was less inclined to trust her. Tammy was one of the most serious and objective researchers in the group, but her petulance soured me. We got off on the wrong foot and never found our way back. It was unfortunate.

How soon after you moved into Trevor Hall did the unexplained incidents begin?

I said we weren't going to discuss that.

Our viewers want to know—

I don't care! This interview is over!

Wanda rises from her chair and removes her microphone. The camera shuts off.

DIARY OF RUBY CARDINI

June 9, 1974

We had a big scare last night—we almost lost Smithy!

In the wee hours of the morning, around three, all of us jolted awake by deafening, pealing bells and a blaring horn. I was disoriented—still not quite familiar with my surroundings and unsure of where I was when I first woke up. For a minute or two, I thought I was at school, about to be late for my next class. Then I focused on the siren and thought, "Oh, God, the Russians have done it! We're all going to die, and I'm here, over two hundred miles from home. I'll never have a chance to see my family again or make up with Dad!" I was shaking so badly I could hardly get out of bed, but I slipped on my sneakers without socks and staggered into the hall to face my fate.

Immediately, I was glad of the dorm-style living arrangements. I saw Tammy's light on. At least one of us was smart enough to try the electricity. She and Gail emerged into the hall just as I did. Just seeing them was a comfort.

"What's happening? What's that noise? Are we under attack?" We screamed questions at each other, and though we couldn't quite hear each other over the din, I could tell we were all asking the same thing. Tammy went down the hall to Wanda's room, but it was empty, save for Peter and Harriet, who burst out, yowling, and ran down the stairs before Gail and I could catch them. We had no idea what danger they were running into, nor where Wanda could have gone. What a time for us to be without authority!

Finally, a door at the end of the hall opened and Piers and Wanda came out together (?!) Piers was agitated, but I could see he was more annoyed than afraid, and that gave me hope. He explained to us that the fire alarm had been tripped. I was surprised such an old house would have anything so modern, but Wanda later explained the alarm had been installed when the house served as a boarding school. Thank goodness it was still connected!

My relief that the world wasn't ending gave way to a new wave of fear as I wondered where the fire could possibly be. Trevor Hall is a huge house with two wings. A blaze could have broken out anywhere. How would we know it?

By then, we had been joined by Eric, and even Jeff, who said he had been transcribing our orientation film when he heard the alarm all the way from the gatehouse. Gail asked if we needed to evacuate, but Piers told her to keep her head. "It's an old system with old wiring. Chances are the alarm was tripped accidentally and we're in no danger." He took a flashlight down to the basement to examine the breakers. Tammy suggested we take a quick walk-through of our floor, just to make sure there was no smoke.

In our fear for ourselves, we momentarily forgot our reason for being in the house in the first place: Smithy! Only Jeff had the presence of mind to think of him. "I'll go check on him. He's probably going bananas with all of this racket and being all by himself upstairs." I felt better hearing him joke like that. It was one more step toward normality and a release of tension from our rude awakening.

No sooner had Jeff disappeared upstairs than the honking and clattering ceased. We cheered, temporarily breaking the silence we were celebrating. "It's all better," called Piers, his voice faint from the lower level. "I think a circuit must have tripped. The stove is off in the kitchen. I can't detect any smoke."

Our relief was too short-lived, however, because even as Piers was reassuring us, Jeff began screaming for help.

"He's not breathing! Hurry! Hurry, Piers! Somebody call an ambulance!"

We ran up to Smithy's room, almost tripping over each other. Piers pushed his way into the lead, nearly knocking me over the banister. His face looked as pale as if it were carved from marble. He must have been so frightened for Smithy—and perhaps for his experiment, too.

We formed an anxious crowd outside Smithy's door. Poor Smithy was lying on the floor in Jeff's arms. His face was purple, and his eyes were black as buttons and just as dull. Jeff kept shaking him as if to wake him. "He was lying face-down on the floor," Jeff told us, "right below that."

At first, I couldn't see what Jeff was pointing to, but when Wanda exclaimed, "You mean _he_ set it off!" I realized he was indicating a button on the wall, about the height of a man. It looked like an old call bell for servants, but it dawned on me that this button must be connected to the fire alarm. Jeff meant that Smithy had somehow known to call for help with that bell. I marveled that he had even been able to reach it in his distress, but my awe was fleeting. Later, much later, over coffee, eggs, and bacon, we'd praise Smithy's ingenuity and sense of self-preservation, but at that terrible moment, I was still terrified that Smithy was dead.

"Does anybody know CPR? Besides me?" Eric asked. Gail and I didn't—and neither did Piers or Wanda. Tammy had read about life-saving techniques, what with all the babysitting she's had to do, but never actually practiced them. Since Eric appeared to be the most experienced, he went to work on Smithy. I think he was nervous about doing so; maybe he was afraid of making a mistake or scared we might blame him if he couldn't save Smithy, but I admire him for his willingness to try anyway.

Jeff tilted Smithy's head up so he would be able to breathe. Tammy called advice from the sidelines. "Swab his mouth out so he doesn't swallow his tongue. He could have had a seizure, you know."

"It looks to me like he choked," Eric said, but he followed Tammy's advice and pounded on Smithy's back, bending him forward. Our little chimp looked like a rag doll flopping around. It was terrible! I felt so helpless. I wanted to do something, anything, to help Eric and Smithy, but I hadn't a clue where to start.

Gail was crying, and I thought I had better get her out of the room before she made a scene or made Smithy's rescuers even more anxious. She didn't want to budge at first, but then we heard sirens. The fire alarm must have been connected to a fire station, or maybe the neighbors could hear the alarm, like Jeff had, and called for help.

I said, "We should let them in. Firemen know life-saving techniques." We had just turned to leave when an awful gargling made me look back. Eric was squeezing Smithy's chest. It looked to me like he was trying to crush him, but it had the opposite effect of starting his breathing again!

Smithy twitched, gagged, and finally spat out something hard. It bounced and rolled across the floor, and Piers picked it up.

I forgot all about the firemen and watched Smithy slowly come back to life. His face gradually faded to violet, then red, and the pink of a bawling child. And like a child, Smithy began to emit howling sobs. Jeff looked like he was crying, too, as he hugged Smithy and tried to comfort him. Gail ran over to hug Eric, shouting that he was a hero. For a moment, we all hugged and cried and rejoiced.

"But what made him collapse?" Wanda asked.

"It was this." Piers held up a tiny wooden ball. At first, none of us had any idea what it was or where it had come from, and we looked at one another with accusing eyes, as if one of our number had irresponsibly given Smithy a forbidden toy or deliberately tried to kill him. Wanda finally identified the ball as a knob from Smithy's chest of drawers. Had it been loose? Had he gotten hungry during the night and bit it off, thinking it was food?

We couldn't spend time trying to answer these questions because the firemen were pounding on the front door, ready to break it down.

They hadn't realized Trevor Hall had tenants. I think they saw the lights in the house and heard the animals howling and assumed we were squatters up to no good. I can't imagine what they thought when we finally opened the doors and revealed a gaggle of frightened co-eds and one very shaken chimpanzee. Wanda explained we'd had a false alarm in terms of a fire, but that we really did have an emergency. Sure enough, the firemen had first aid training and checked over Smithy. He seemed so startled and overwhelmed by the excitement that he let the lead firefighter examine him for wounds and take his pulse without protest. They gave him a clean bill of health. We even got a cute picture of Smithy wearing a fire helmet.

We invited the firemen to stay and have refreshments with us. Over coffee, Piers tried to explain the study to them, but he was so technical that Jeff had to interrupt every so often to translate into layman's terms. At least now they know a chimp has moved into Trevor Hall, and they'll be prepared in case of a future emergency—of which I hope we have none!

Jeff has taken all the knob handles off Smithy's furniture. From now on, we'll pull on the sides of the drawers to open them. He also volunteered to sleep in Smithy's room for the next few nights to avoid a repeat of this frantic nightmare. It was more excitement than any of us had bargained for, but definitely something to write home about.

LETTER FROM GAIL EHRLICH
TO EHRLICH FAMILY

(EXCERPT)

June 19, 1974

...Poor Smithy triggered the alarm because he was choking on something he had accidentally swallowed. It's a good thing he did, although none of us can figure out how he'd reached the emergency button. It's up pretty high on the wall. I'm surprised he even knew what that button was for. He's a smart little fellow.

He was so good, too, when the firemen came. I thought he'd get nervous with all the strange people around. Maisie kept barking at all the newcomers and crying because the sirens hurt her ears, but Smithy didn't make a peep. We took pictures of him with the firemen. One of them even let Smithy wear his fireman's hat. Piers said it will be a good memento for Smithy's scrapbook. It's too bad the firemen didn't bring their Dalmatian with them, but the new dog would probably have upset Maisie, too.

Since that accident, we've all been super careful with Smithy because we're afraid to lose him. Nobody likes to scold him now or punish him when he's naughty. Jeff's been staying in Smithy's room at night until after he falls asleep, just to keep an eye on him. He says Smithy has terrible nightmares that make him cry and howl at night. Sometimes, Smithy will even sort of sleepwalk. He sits up in bed and gazes into space as if he's looking at a person, and then <u>he'll start talking to them</u>. Well, he signs, anyway. I think it's far out! Our chimp signs in his sleep, just as a person talks in his sleep.

Tammy says it's not good because sleepwalking and sleeptalking are disorders that mean a child isn't developing properly. She's also worried he could get more boysterous and hard to handle when he's awake. So far so good, though. Smithy is keeping his normal bedtime, and he's not anymore ~~boyster~~ high-spirited than normal. During the day, he's still just as cute and smart as ever…

EXCERPT FROM
SMITHY: A TWENTY-YEAR COMPENDIUM
BY REID BENNETT, PHD

Curiously, these two accounts are the only references to the first of many remarkable occurrences under the roof of Trevor Hall. Neither Karlewicz nor Preis-Herald made any official record of the near-tragedy sustained by the priceless chimp, though they were likely eager to return to business as usual.

Indeed, that business resulted in some interesting developments...

LETTER FROM RUBY CARDINI
TO SARAH-BETH ANDREWS

June 13, 1974

(EXCERPT)

...That little chimp has the most devious intelligence I've seen in an animal! Last week, before Mother Nature decided to turn up the thermostat, Wanda baked brownies as a snack for us. She cut them and left them on a tray to cool while she went upstairs to meet with Piers about the study.

Gail and Tammy were working with Smithy in the refurbished library (Jeff put up screens to block off the books from him; it's almost like child-proofing the house!) Webster likes card games; he has an excellent visual memory, better than a human's. Gail sent him to the solarium to get a deck of cards so they could play Memory as a reward for his hard work. I was surprised they let him wander the house alone, but after today, it won't happen again.

In the afternoon, Wanda called us all together for a snack break. I smelled the brownies as we entered the kitchen and told Wanda how good they looked, piled on the platter in a tower formation, but she didn't seem to hear me. I noticed she was frowning.

"Did anyone come in the kitchen earlier?" she asked. No one had. Instantly, Wanda's eyebrows pulled together, and it looked as if an invisible antenna had shot forth from the back of her head. "I left these cooling on the cookie sheet. How did they get on the platter?"

"Maybe a good fairy did it," Piers suggested. "A brownie brownie. In any case, they look delicious." He reached for one, and I saw his face change. "What on Earth? Wanda, dear, I don't suppose you got peckish as you were baking? It looks like our good fairy has a sweet tooth."

Wanda exclaimed in distress, then Jeff began to laugh, and we all crowded around to see what was up. Except for the lone brownie atop the stack, each treat had a bite taken out of it! But they had been arranged in such a way that the bitten part was hidden: the solid ends pointed out, and each successive layer had been stacked to block the teeth marks beneath. At first glance, it was a perfectly lovely arrangement of brownies, and you wouldn't notice the desserts had been taste-tested until you actually picked one up.

I was flabbergasted at first. I think we all were. "Was it mice?" Gail asked, looking worried. Only Jeff continued to smile.

"Hey, Smithy," he called. For the first time, we realized that the little guy was hanging back and looking everywhere in the kitchen except at the delicious-smelling brownies. "Do you know anything about this?"

Smithy signed, "What that?"

Jeff laughed harder. "What do you mean, what's that? It's a sweet. You love sweets." Jeff held one out to him. "Do you want one?" he signed. Smithy looked away. "Hey, buddy, why don't you take it?" Jeff pressed. "You've never turned down dessert before. Is it because you've already spoiled your appetite?"

Wanda gasped. Piers looked from Smithy to the brownies, his face shrewd. Finally, Jeff turned to the girls. "Was he ever out of your sight?" he asked.

"Yeah," Gail admitted. "We sent him to get playing cards from the solarium. It took him a while to find them."

"That's because he took a detour!" Jeff announced, gleeful.

The way he figures it, Smithy smelled the brownies and came into the kitchen to get one. He must have sneaked sweets before from the McKenzies and knew one might be missed. So instead, he took one little bite out of every piece and tried to cover up his crime by artfully arranging them on the platter. He must have been familiar with the schema of brownies on a platter, or maybe he had even helped to stack cookies or brownies on a plate before; apparently, he enjoys being in the kitchen.

Smithy wouldn't admit to anything. When Jeff stuck the partially eaten brownie in his face, he just looked away guiltily. I couldn't believe how much intelligence he showed in playing that prank on us. Wanda forgave him in light of his ingenuity and even laughed along. Tammy began to disassemble the tower. She held the bitten-off ends up to her face and peeked through them as if they were glasses; we all started to laugh. Then she took a bite from the untouched end. "These are pretty good, Wanda. You can't blame him too much. Jeff, you've got to get photos of this before I pig out! We've got to document it for posterity!"

"We've got to document it for the board of review," Wanda added.

Only Gail still seemed amazed. "But how did he do it? Why?"

Eric explained, "He tried to hide his dirty work, just like a sneaky little kid. He could anticipate what we would do. This means he can plan. He has a theory of mind!"

This is a huge development, Sarah-Beth! To have a theory of mind— to be able to think about yourself in relation to other people and know that other people can think about you and anticipate how you might think or feel—is a major marker of higher intelligence and self-awareness. Until recently, it's been thought that only human beings have a theory of mind (and not all do—some autistic patients don't), but Piers told us about a study in which different animals had a mark put on their foreheads with makeup and were then made to look in a mirror. The less intelligent animals, the cats and dogs, reacted as if they were looking at another animal and attacked or barked, but the primates recognized themselves and rubbed the mark off. That was considered a breakthrough, but what Smithy did is infinitely bigger!

I used to wonder if my dog could understand me when I talked, or if she knew what I felt when I was sad. I liked to think so; she always seemed to be nearby when I needed cheering. Maybe she did, and maybe she didn't, but Smithy does. He may be the only chimp in the world who does. He may even be the only non-human <u>animal</u> who does. And he's ours!

Afterward, we celebrated by eating the rest of brownies (at last, the parts Smithy hadn't nibbled) and talked about what this finding implied and where we can take the study in the future. Piers was thrilled. You could tell from the way he kept touching us girls when he spoke. It was subtle: a hand on the arm or elbow—then on the waist or the back—all in the course of some casual remark. I half-wished he would light that stinky pipe, so he'd have something else to do with his hands.

Maybe I shouldn't be so annoyed by it, but I do think it's odd. After all, I'm pretty certain he and Wanda have a thing going. It would be weird for Piers to hit on the rest of us girls, too. And I'm certain he is flirting, not just being avuncular.

The other day, I was walking down the hall when Piers came up behind me, quite jovial. He asked me how I was and said something about it being a day for possibilities. While we walked and talked, he slipped his arm around my shoulder and let his hand rest there for a long time. He asked how I was enjoying my stay at Trevor Hall. Of course, I babbled I was having the time of my life. What else could I say? He told me he had every confidence in my ability and expected great things from me. He gave me a little squeeze when he said that. Then he added—and I remember this exactly—"I'm sorry we haven't seen much of each other lately. I so enjoyed our last meeting. You're a remarkable girl, Ruby, and I hope we can share more quality time together soon."

I tensed up; part of me was expecting him to try to kiss me, and the rest of my brain kept cycling through all the things I could do if he did: stand still, kiss him back, laugh it off, scream, kick him. Thankfully, he just smiled and winked at me (OK, maybe he was blinking, but it sure looked like a wink!) and walked on. I don't remember what I said back to him because I was so distracted. Probably, "Thanks a lot" or "Have a nice day." I had no idea how to respond.

I didn't confront him about touching me. In the first place, I wasn't sure what he meant by it. Maybe I imagined it to be more than it was. Secondly, even if he meant what I think, I couldn't do anything about it. I have to work with the guy! Even if he came right out and propositioned me, I couldn't say no, and I surely couldn't say yes, so I hope he doesn't try anything like that again. I'm a bit eager to avoid him now.

I like my job. I liked Piers when I met him, but not like that. He was charming and intelligent, and when he talked, it felt as if he was confiding in me—not talking down to me. I was flattered he saw something in me, a freshly transferred undergraduate, that made him want to talk to me in the first place. I thought he was brilliant, and I wanted to be on his team, but I sure as hell don't want to end up in his bed! I hope it doesn't come to that.

I don't know what to do. I hope this isn't why he brought me here. I keep thinking of what Jeff said about Gail. What if I don't really have any aptitude, and the only reason I'm here is because the guy in charge of the study wants to get into my pants?

He's done it to Tammy, too. I wanted to make sure I wasn't just imagining things, so I casually asked her yesterday what she thought of Piers, and if she'd had a chance to talk with him much since he arrived. "Not when I've been able to help it," she responded cheerfully. I asked what she meant. She rolled her eyes and said Piers was the biggest womanizer in New England academia, and that included some stiff competition.

She said that when she'd interviewed for this job, he kept trying to hold her hand—not just shaking, it but rubbing the back of it and actively taking her hand in his while he talked. He joked with her and asked a lot of personal questions, too.

"I reined myself in until I was sure I got the job. Oh, I was passive-aggressive. I fake-coughed a lot and blew my nose, thinking he'd keep his hands to himself if he thought I was sick, but no such luck. After we shook hands on the deal, he invited me to dine with him, 'to talk further about my career,' but I told him I was supposed to meet my girlfriend for drinks at the Stonewall Inn. I don't think he's familiar with its reputation. Then he started asking about my hobbies, trying to find out if I like sailing or long walks on the beach, I suppose. I said I usually spend my weekends running coffee klatches with the Daughters of Sappho. Ruby, you should have seen his face. He stared at me for a good twenty or thirty seconds. His mouth squeezed into a line, and he finally said that must be a very interesting use of my time, and he hoped that in Newport, I would discover even more activities to broaden my interests."

He's made a couple of other passes at her since, I take it, though she didn't elaborate on what exactly he's said or done. Tammy advised me to smile pleasantly and say something inconsequential so it seems as if his overture has gone over my head. "You'll be fine, Ruby. I think he wants adulation more than he wants sex. Just keep telling him he's a genius, and stick by me whenever you can." She doesn't think I should trust Jeff so much. "The assistant's spent too much time learning from the master."

I disagree. Jeff's never tried to give me a squeeze or slather me with innuendo. I think he feels bad about what he said on our first day. I've noticed him complimenting Gail on the way she handles Smithy, and he gives her useful (not condescending) tips. I think I underestimated Jeff. He's a serious researcher who knows the literature, yet he doesn't make me feel stupid when we talk.

And we don't just talk about work. I've found out Jeff and I have a lot in common. We're each the younger of two siblings (he's got an older sister, and I've got Vinny). We both love to read (historical fiction and the classics for me, fantasy and science fiction for him). We both like old black-and-white movies. Jeff even recommended a couple I'd never heard of. Talking to him about movies made me nostalgic; Mom and I used to always stay up late to catch those movies on TV.

Jeff does have some rough edges. We went on a grocery run yesterday. He asked if I wanted to stop somewhere for lunch. I agreed, and without further discussion, he drove us to an Italian restaurant. Jeff looked pleased with himself as we were seated and asked me if I felt at home. I informed him my family not only eats spaghetti and chicken cacciatore for our dinners, but we also enjoy pork chops, meatloaf, fish sticks, and occasionally enchilada casseroles.

His smile turned sheepish, and he apologized. "I shouldn't have assumed...Do you even like Italian food?" I assured him it was yummy, but for future reference, burgers and fries were just fine, too.

In short (goodness, six pages isn't very short, is it?), life is exciting, albeit sweltering, and I'm slowly starting to fit in. I hope I'll have more exciting adventures to share with you next time...

ARCHIVAL FILM FOOTAGE

Date: June 14, 1974
Location: The Solarium

Smithy sits on the floor near the turntable, playing with a set of toy cars. His head snaps up, and he looks at the door. The hair rises on his back, and he bares his teeth.

Eric calls from off camera, "What is it?"

Smithy backs away, clutching the cars to his chest. He hoots anxiously and signs, "No." He backs into the turntable and cries out. Then, he hurls one of the toys at the wall beside the door. It bounces off and clatters across the floor. Smithy recoils in surprise and throws another car. It also strikes the wall with a loud bang.

Eric runs into the frame, calling, "Hey, hey! Don't do that. That's not how we play."

He signs, "No." Smithy faces Eric, tilts his head, and throws his last two cars at Eric. One of them ricochets off Eric's belt buckle and strikes him in the chin. Eric raises his hands protectively over his face and exclaims, "Hey!"

Wanda bursts into the room and asks, "What's this?" She rushes over to Smithy and holds his hands. The chimp whimpers, looking from Wanda to the doorway, then to Eric.

Eric shrugs. "I dunno. One minute, he's playing quietly; the next, he's throwing a tantrum."

Wanda says, "I heard. No more, Webster. Bad." She lightly swats Smithy's hands, points to the cars, and signs, "No throw. Bad," and "Why." Smithy looks all around the solarium, blinking in surprise, and doesn't respond. Wanda picks him up and seats him on a chair, signing, "Stay."

Eric says, "I wanted to stop him before he threw anything at the windows. That could be messy."

Wanda replies, "I hear you. I've expected him to break something already, especially one of the plants." Eric picks up a small pot and studies it, still rubbing his jaw. Wanda asks, "Did he hit you?"

Eric says, "Aw, it won't leave a mark. He didn't hit me hard enough. I can tell. I'm used to getting beaten up. The big kids at school used to push me around all the time because I was short for my age. I used to worry they'd try to drag me around by my ankles like some caveman in a comic book. This was nothing in comparison."

He smiles weakly at Wanda, then looks down at the plant. "Hmm. It looks stunted. The plants aren't growing like I'd expected."

Wanda looks annoyed. "I did my best to make the rooms more hospitable."

Eric quickly says, "Oh, I appreciate them. It's just strange they're in a room designed to grow plants, but they're not flourishing. Maybe the season's not right, or they're getting too much light. These decorations are great, Wanda! They really make the Hall feel homey. You've got an artistic eye. I like your sweater, too." He smiles at Wanda, but she's picking up Smithy's toys and doesn't notice.

Wanda says, "I need one in here. The house is cold for summer. I'm thinking he shouldn't play with these anymore in here. Too risky."

Eric says, "I can pick up some stuffed toys for him in town, maybe some plush blocks. Those won't mark the walls or anybody's face. Something with bright colors should appeal to him." He laughs. "Here I'm talking like I'm an expert on kids when

I'm an only child. Tammy would have something to say about that if she could hear me."

Wanda says, "Don't let her intimidate you. Tammy doesn't know everything."

Eric says, "Aw, she doesn't mean it. She just likes to tease."

Wanda frowns. "Is that so?" She turns back to Smithy, who's still sitting quietly, looking around the solarium as if searching for something.

Eric says, "Hey, now that things have calmed down, would you like to get a soda and relax for a bit?"

Wanda says, "I have to finish a report. And you should give Webster some lunch before he gets crabby. But no sugar—he's already wound up."

"Got it." Eric helps Smithy down from the chair and leads him by the hand to the hallway. Wanda exits the room ahead of them, taking Smithy's cars with her.

WEEKLY WORD LIST
JUNE 16, 1974

Red

Blue

Yellow

Green

Purple

Orange

White

Black

Brown

Gray

SOLARIUM JOURNAL ENTRY
FROM JEFF DALTON

June 16, 1974

Spent a lengthy session with Smithy reviewing items of furniture one more time. He was hesitant to produce the signs when prompted. I modeled the first three words (table, chair, couch), then switched to asking him to identify items by pointing to the object and signing, "What's that?" In this way, I was able to get Smithy to spontaneously sign "floor" and "door" before he clammed up. I pointed to the carpet, and Smithy signed "floor" without first watching me make the sign. This suggests he possesses vocabulary but is selective about revealing it. After he signed "door," also without me modeling first, he asked me for the signs for "curtain" and "clock."

Two problems: First, Smithy confuses his question signs. When he pointed to the curtain, he signed "Who is that?" not "What is that?" He's done this before: once when pointing at a landscape picture on the wall, and once when pointing to a lamp. I don't know if this means he doesn't know which sign to use in the correct context, or if he can't tell the difference between a living thing and an inanimate object.

Second, Smithy made a big boo-boo when I asked him to make the sign for "window." After I made the sign three times (once for each window in the room) and asked him, "What is that?" while pointing to the center window, he made the sign for "woman." I can't imagine why he did this.

MEMO FROM WANDA KARLEWICZ

June 17, 1974

Re: Webster's identification error (window v. woman) ₍

People learning Ameslan often confuse similar signs. This is equivalent to a "false cognate" when learning a spoken language (e.g., "*étranger*" does not actually translate as "stranger;" it means "foreigner" or "outsider".)

Example: When I tutored a young high school student in Ameslan, the girl once mixed up the sign for "friend" (right finger hooked over left, then left finger hooked over right) with the sign for "fornicate" (left finger hooked over right, then right finger hooked over left). The visual appearance is similar, though the meaning is very different.

With pre-verbal children, such confusion can be overcome through heavy drilling and reinforcement of the correct sign, or through light punishment for incorrect responses, such as slapping the hand. The latter may be the best option to use with Webster.

In sum, I don't believe this error is cause for grave concern. Similar errors should be addressed in the future by repeated demonstration of the proper sign and consistent and immediate reinforcement of the appropriate sign, paired either with failure to reinforce or active punishment of incorrect signs.

—WK

SOLARIUM JOURNAL ENTRY
FROM ERIC KANINCHEN

June 18, 1974

Hey Wanda—
    Today, Smithy and I were practicing our signs, and I quizzed him on all the same words Jeff used. This time, he passed "window" with flying colors, but when I pointed to the door, he signed "woman." Why would he do this, since "door" and "woman" look nothing alike?
    –Eric

ARCHIVAL FILM FOOTAGE

Date: June 19, 1974
Location: The Solarium

Wanda, Ruby, Gail, and Eric sit on the floor surrounded by crayons, colored yarn, colored paper, magazine pictures, and different articles of clothing.

Ruby remarks, "It looks like a kindergarten class has run amok in here."

Wanda clears her throat and says, "We're on."

Ruby looks up and smiles. "Oh, hi! I'm Ruby. This is Wanda, Gail, and Eric, with Jeff on the video camera. We're preparing a new lesson for our chimp Smithy—AKA Webster."

Wanda begins, "Today's lesson will focus on the basic color spectrum. Good old Roy G. Biv. I've gathered different examples of colored objects to drive the lesson home." She looks up as Tammy carries Smithy into the room. "And it looks like our guest of honor has arrived."

Tammy says, "He's eaten, and he's becoming more alert. He kept fidgeting and playing with his food."

Wanda signs, "Come here." Smithy crawls to her. She signs, "Give me hug." The chimp embraces her. She signs, "Look," and points to all the items on the floor.

Wanda says, "These are colors, Webster."

She signs, "Color." Wanda points to a picture of an apple. Smithy points to it and signs, "Apple." Wanda signs, "Red," "color red," then "red apple." She places a piece of red construction paper on top of a sheet of blue paper and signs,

"Colors." She takes Smithy's hand and touches the blue paper, then molds his hand into the sign for "blue." She touches his hand to the red paper and makes the sign for "red."

Ruby holds up a yellow sweater. She signs, "Yellow." Gail holds up two yellow crayons and signs, "Yellow." Eric holds up a lemon and signs, "Yellow." As each person signs, Wanda forms Smithy's hands into the sign for "yellow."

Tammy holds up a skein of blue yarn and signs, "Blue." Ruby holds up a blue sneaker and signs, "Blue." Eric holds up a red crayon and signs, "Red." Gail holds up a red pump and signs, "Red."

Wanda says, "Now put the two shoes together."

Ruby and Gail set their shoes side by side. Wanda points and signs to Smithy, "What is that?"

He signs, "Shoe."

Wanda signs, "Good," and hugs him, rubbing his back.

Ruby taps the sneaker on the ground and signs, "Blue shoe."

Gail taps the pump on the floor and signs, "Red shoe." She laughs.

Wanda says, "Shhh! Don't distract him." She points to the red shoe and signs, "Red," then points to the red paper and signs, "Red." She makes Smithy point to the red paper and the red shoe in turn and molds his hand into the sign for "red." Wanda points to both of the pieces of paper and signs, "Colors."

Eric throws the crayons on top of the paper. He signs, "Color."

Wanda signs, "What color is that?" and points to the yellow crayon.

Eric touches it and signs, "Yellow."

Wanda points to the yarn in Tammy's hand and signs, "What color is that?"

Tammy signs, "Blue."

Wanda points to Gail and signs, "What color shoe?"

Gail signs, "Red."

Wanda points to Ruby and signs, "What color shoe?"

Ruby signs, "Blue."

Ruby picks up the sweater and signs, "What color sweater?"

Smithy stares at her then signs, "Yellow."

Eric cheers. "Huzzah!" Everyone applauds.

Ruby signs, "Good, Smithy," and reaches out to tickle his foot.

Wanda says, "Good work! He's learned a sign and he's learned to associate color with an object. Let's try another one. Eric, line up those objects on the tray."

Eric places Gail's red shoe, a banana, a green building block, and a blue crayon on a tray and shows the tray to Smithy.

Wanda signs, "Give me yellow." Smithy crawls over to examine the tray. Eric deliberately looks up over Smithy's head, toward the wall. Smithy picks up the banana.

Eric ruffles the fur on Smithy's head and praises him. "Yay! Good work, Smithy." Smithy crawls back to Wanda and shows her the banana. Before she can take it, he unpeels and starts to eat it. Wanda tries to grab the fruit out of his hand, but Smithy runs away and sits on Gail's lap.

Jeff, off camera, says, "Let him have it, Wanda. He learned his lesson; he deserves a reward."

Wanda grumbles, "I didn't tell him he could eat that. I told him to give it to me."

Tammy says, "Let's stay focused. We still have four more colors to go."

Eric corrects her. "*Seven* more. We're doing black, white, and gray, too."

Ruby looks surprised and asks, "All in one sitting, Wanda?"

Wanda says, "We'll expose him to every color so he gets an introduction. I don't expect him to learn each one today. The most important lesson is that he understands what a color is, so let's show him a few more."

Ruby picks up some purple yarn and holds it in her hands like a cat's cradle. Tammy tugs on it and signs, "Purple." She puts on a pair of heart-shaped sunglasses with purple frames, touches the glasses, and signs, "Purple."

Wanda molds Smithy's finger to make the sign for "purple" and touches his hand to a sheet of purple paper.

Eric shows Smithy a green crayon and signs, "Green." Eric holds up a magazine ad for a Volkswagen and signs, "Green." Wanda molds Smithy's hand to form "green."

Tammy unbuttons her gray cardigan; she is wearing a green blouse underneath. Wanda signs, "What color is Tammy shirt?" Smithy doesn't respond. Wanda signs the question again, and when he doesn't answer, she molds his hand to sign, "Green."

Ruby slides forward and stretches out her legs. She signs, "What color pants?" and pinches the fabric. This time Smithy signs, "Blue."

Wanda says, "Good. He can still follow the question. Maybe "green" was too hard for him."

Jeff, off camera, suggests, "Maybe you're overwhelming him with too many concepts at once."

Wanda says, "We'll see what he can do for now, and we'll practice extra on the words that give him trouble. Do we have a lime, Eric?"

Eric says, "No, but we have this storybook about a farm." He opens a picture book and shows Smithy a picture of some sheep and cows grazing in front of a barn. Eric points to the grass and signs, "What color?"

Smithy signs, "Green."

Gail says, "He got it that time!"

Eric moves his finger to the barn and signs, "What color?"

Smithy signs, "Red."

Eric points to the sky, and Smithy signs, "Blue."

Ruby notes, "He got them all that time."

Wanda says, "You see? He *can* handle it. He just needs to apply himself. Let's go on."

Eric asks, "What next? Do you want the brown shoe? The orange? The white sheet?"

Wanda suggests, "Let's do black."

Ruby puts on a black sweater, and Gail scribbles on a piece of paper with a black crayon. Wanda points to the scribble and signs, "Black." She points to Ruby's sweater and signs, "Black." Eric holds up black yarn, and Wanda signs, "Black." She molds Smithy's hands to make the sign "black." Smithy looks around the room and squirms.

Tammy remarks, "He's getting restless already."

Wanda urges, "Just a little bit longer."

Eric sticks out his feet and tugs on his socks. He signs, "White."

Gail holds up a white pillowcase and signs, "Color white."

Wanda molds Smithy's hands to make the new sign each time.

Eric puts on a fake Santa beard and tugs at it, then signs, "What color is this?"

Smithy signs, "White."

Eric signs, "Good," as he takes off the beard. He then puts on a black top hat. Pointing to it, Eric signs, "What color is this?"

Smithy covers his eyes. Wanda pulls his hands down and points to the top hat. She signs, "What color is this?" Smithy covers his eyes again. Wanda sounds exasperated. "No, you're not sleepy. You can't be; you just woke up."

She continues signing: "What is that?" as she points to the top hat again. Smithy squirms and tries to cover his eyes. Wanda takes his hand and forcibly makes the sign for "black." She picks up the black crayon and scribbles on the blank paper, then signs, "What color is this?" She holds up the crayon and taps the crayon on the scribble. Smithy covers his eyes. Wanda signs, "Bad."

"No," she scolds, "you know this. I just showed it to you. You're not going to worm out of this lesson so easily."

Jeff, off camera, sounds excited. "Wanda, hold on a second! I don't think he's trying to dodge. Look at what he's doing."

Wanda says, "He's signing 'sleep,' like he's ready to go to bed."

Jeff replies, "Yeah! What do you see when you close your eyes or cover them?"

Ruby says, "Darkness! When you shut your eyes, everything goes black."

Jeff says, "Exactly! I think he's making a connection. Sleep equals darkness or black!"

Wanda says, "That's a bit of a stretch."

Jeff argues, "Well, ask him something else, but don't mold him this time."

Wanda picks up a green crayon and scribbles with it. She holds up the crayon and taps the paper, then signs, "What color?"

Smithy signs, "Green."

Wanda says, "Got that one."

Gail shows him the lemon and asks, "What color?"

Smithy signs, "Yellow."

Ruby holds up her black sweater and signs, "What color?" Smithy covers his eyes.

Eric says, "He's associating that sign specifically with the color black, Wanda. I think Jeff may be on to something."

Tammy says, "He could be extrapolating, generalizing. Lots of small children do that at his age.

Jeff, off camera, says, "Let's stop for the day and test him later to see what he does. So far, "black" is the only sign he hasn't adopted. If that's because he's developed his own understanding of the meaning of "black," this could be big! Smithy's ability to spontaneously apply concepts and develop his own signs for words would be a *huge* step in favor of Piers's hypothesis.

Wanda protests. "We don't know that's what he's doing yet. You're guessing, making excuses for him."

Tammy says, "The ability to create new words is a hallmark of language. It's worth exploring. I'd rather follow Smithy's lead than try to force him into one particular kind of performance. I want to see what he does next."

Wanda says, "Letting the tail wag the dog isn't science, Tammy. If Eric is right that the only time other than bedtime when Webster covers his eyes is when he sees something black, then we'll have something to write about." She pauses, thoughtful. "It's possible. Signs can be used interchangeably. The sign for 'grow' is also the sign for the season 'spring,' and that's an intuitive connection."

Eric says, "Let's watch him for a while and see how he uses the sign. That's how we've decided in the past to accept a sign from him or not. If Smithy uses this gesture consistently, let's keep it."

In the background, Smithy crawls around, picking up the various objects. He scribbles on the paper with different crayons and hoots in excitement. Smithy takes a crayon and runs over to the wall. Gail catches him as he tries to scribble and says, "No, you don't, mister." She signs, "No."

Wanda says, "Fine. We'll call this recess. Cut the tape."

The scene cuts out.

MEMO FROM TAMMY COHEN

June 20, 1974

Generalization is the process of attributing characteristics of one object or agent to other objects or agents that share similar traits. Generalization is a heuristic frequently applied to never-before-seen targets on the assumption that prior experience with a similar target can successfully be extrapolated to the new, unknown target.

In adult humans, a common form of generalization is the stereotype wherein attributes of one representative are applied to all members of a race or gender. Generalization is also typical in the development of human toddlers. As children aged two to four gain more exposure to the world, they attempt to apply what they already know to novel experiences.

Here's an example: A family is at the zoo. Their young child points to a four-legged furry animal and says, "Doggie!" Mama says, "No, that's not a doggie. That's a lion."

Such generalizations may persist, even after the child has been taught the correct term for an object. In my example, a child's perseveration in calling the big cat a "dog" need not signify low intelligence or defiance in the child. Rather, the child may genuinely be unable to grasp the new idea of a "lion," and may derive more security from relating to this animal in already familiar terms.

Generalizations may be either broad or specific. My middle sister, Dinah, adored our neighbor's terrier, Sparky. Whenever three-year-old Dinah saw a terrier, she'd call it a "Sparky dog." She didn't call Labradors spaniels, or poodles "Sparky." Although these were also dogs, and some were even small and fluffy, none resembled the original model closely enough to qualify as "Sparky." Here, Dinah displayed <u>discrimination</u>, the ability to distinguish between similar targets.

On multiple occasions, Smithy has used an "incorrect" sign to identify an object or concept. These errors alternately suggest that Smithy is unable to use language correctly, is deliberately misbehaving to frustrate his teachers, or is generalizing broadly.

In support of the third possibility, I cite his use of the sign typically denoting "sleepy" or "sleep" (e.g., covering his eyes with both hands) to represent the color "black." "Sleep" and "black" or "darkness" are superficially similar. When preparing for sleep, one turns out the lights to darken the room. When closing one's eyes to sleep, one sees blackness. That Smithy persists in using this sign to represent the color "black," even after the "correct" sign has been modeled for him, demonstrates that he is generalizing his understanding of sleep to a similar, but new, concept. I don't believe this act is a true error or an indication of Smithy's failure to internalize the idea of "black." Rather, his behavior is more in line with a toddler calling a lion a "doggie," and should not be dismissed as a failure.

DIARY OF RUBY CARDINI

June 22, 1974

I'm writing here so I don't have to bother Sarah-Beth with everything that goes on in the study. I wonder sometimes if she gets annoyed or bored that my letters are almost entirely about Smithy. I don't want her to think I'm boasting about what we do here; it's simply that this study is my life. I don't just work with the chimp and Piers's team, I live with them 24/7. Sometimes, though, I wish I could go back to an apartment (or even a dorm room) and unwind without having to constantly worry about the experiment.

Case in point: this afternoon.

Wanda let Smithy play in the garden with Gail—under her own supervision, of course. I watched them as I rehearsed signs in the solarium, using some flashcards Eric kindly loaned me. He, Tammy, and Jeff were running errands, so I had no one to test me. Instead, I put the cards facedown on the bench seat and propped a mirror against the window so I could watch myself signing each word before I flipped over the card to check the answer. I thought it was a pretty clever system. The good news is that I'm improving.

Periodically, I glanced outside at my teammates. Smithy lost interest in gardening after a while, though Gail and Wanda continued. He wandered away, chasing a butterfly, but couldn't go far because Wanda had him in his harness with the free end tied around her wrist. Smithy looked adorable, jumping up to try to catch the butterfly in flight. I wondered if it was the first one he'd ever seen and what he thought it might be. The poor butterfly had difficulty staying aloft because it was awfully breezy, but it managed to keep just out of Smithy's reach.

Jeff had left a Polaroid camera by the record player where he'd been taking pictures of us dancing with Smithy a couple nights ago. I grabbed it so I could snap a couple shots of him trying to nab the butterfly. He got close a few times, but it kept bobbing away from him. Smithy even tried climbing up the statue to get closer to it, but the harness restrained him before he got all the way up. Wanda must have said something to him then because he looked back at her but stayed where he was and didn't return to her. Instead, he hopped down and started playing behind the statue, where I couldn't see him anymore.

I went back to my flashcards for a little while (I was on a roll: five signs in a row!). The next time I looked outside, Smithy was rolling on the grass, looking like he was having a wonderful time. I saw something dark fly past the window and strike the ground. It startled me at first, but then I realized it was a piece of tile from the roof. Wanda had warned us the roof was unstable, but I hadn't believed her until I saw it coming apart right before my eyes. I find little pieces of dark slate on the ground occasionally, but I didn't register that those were from our roof until the tile started to rain down. Three pieces in a row clattered past my view. They pinged against the window like hailstones but didn't break the glass. That wind must have picked them away like scabs.

I almost opened the window to warn Wanda and Gail to come inside. Those fallen tiles were sturdy pieces; I didn't want either of them to get beaned by one. Then I took stock of where they were working and figured they were far enough from the roof's edge that only a whirlwind would endanger them. So I returned to my studies.

A moment later, while trying to recall the sign for "toothbrush," I gazed out the window, the better to focus. The trees weren't dancing the hula anymore, and I figured the breeze must have stopped. Then the sign came back to me, and I checked my cards to see if I was right (I was).

I had no special reason for looking out the window again when I did. The view teased the corners of my vision, and I glanced out for just a millisecond. But that was long enough for me to see something dark swoop down on Gail like a malevolent raven. I heard her scream and saw her jump. She clutched at her shoulder, and Wanda rushed to attend to her.

The air felt charged, as in a storm; the skin on my cheek tingled. I turned toward that sensation in time to see Smithy launch himself in the air, arms outstretched, his expression intense. I see that same look *whenever he follows the plate of cake or cookies Wanda carries to the table for dessert. I followed his gaze, and the first thing I thought was, "He's going to catch one this time!" Because it looked for all the world as if Smithy was about to capture a shiny black butterfly. I blinked, and suddenly the funny-looking butterfly changed into a flat piece of slate spinning through the air. This time, I did cry out. I also grabbed the camera and snapped another picture, though I'm still not sure what made me do that. It was just something I felt compelled to do.*

Wanda may have heard me scream, or maybe she has a sixth sense about such things. She half-turned, then lunged aside in time to just miss getting smacked in the side of her head by the chunk of tile. I had difficulty fumbling the window open. By the time I had the casement out, Wanda was scolding Smithy. She took his hand and slapped it. I heard her shout "No" and "bad Smithy" while he cowered, covering his eyes with both hands. I asked if I could help, and she told me to take Gail inside.

Poor Gail kept rubbing her shoulder but seemed more surprised than hurt. She had a long, thin gash in her skin from where the edge of the first tile had sliced into her. I cleaned the cut with peroxide and put some gauze on it.

Meanwhile, Wanda took Smithy to his room for a lengthy time-out. She confiscated all his toys, too. He ended up eating dinner up there.

Wanda seems to think Smithy deliberately attacked them. She punished him for throwing tiles at her and Gail, on the assumption he was vexed with them for keeping him on a short leash. She used me as a witness to justify her actions when everyone else came back, and in an evening phone call to Piers (who's back at Yale for the day) that I overheard. She reminded me of a teacher calling a naughty student's parents to tattle on him. I protested to Jeff because I didn't think Smithy deserved to be punished. It looked to me like he was trying <u>catch</u> the tile, not throw it.

The photo is vague. You can see Smithy and a little black fleck that almost looks like a flaw in the image, both hovering in the air. Smithy's hands are extended; his teeth are showing. The tile is almost even with the position of his hands. It's ambiguous, I admit. It does look like he could have thrown it. But why? He wasn't annoyed in the moments before Gail was hurt. He was relaxed. He was playing.

I mentioned the other tiles I'd seen fall, but Wanda didn't believe the wind, powerful though it was, could have directed any debris in so targeted a fashion and so far from the house's edge. "The wind had stopped by then, Ruby," she argued. "And the tiles couldn't fly through the air by themselves."

Now, I keep replaying in my mind what I had truly seen. The tile that nearly knocked out Wanda had already been in the air when I looked. It was drifting at a horizontal angle to the ground. I don't know if the wind could have lifted and held a tile aloft like that for so long. The wind would have had to kick back up rather suddenly, because Wanda's right: I remember the wind had been still just a moment prior.

I remember the look on Smithy's face, too. He looked anxious, not angry. And was he also signing, "No"? Or was he trying to grasp the projectile before it could do damage?

If Smithy attacked them, why? Should we be worried?

MEMO FROM WANDA KARLEWICZ

June 23, 1974

Our subject's recent temper displays have interfered with our attempts to teach him. Yesterday, he almost injured Gail and me. Previously, he assaulted Eric. This cannot continue. I propose the following methods for improving our interactions with Smithy and our study's results.

First, Smithy's rewards must be regulated. Instead of giving him a cookie and letting him play a game, he should be offered a cookie or playtime. Specifically, his access to the pets must be scaled back to emphasize that playing with them is a special treat. Especially after he has been caught misbehaving (see Ruby's June 22nd solarium entry), a cooling-off period should be imposed when he's not to see the pets. I can keep Peter and Harriet in my room during the day. So far, Maisie has been given free run of the house, but she should also be restricted to certain ground floor rooms or kept to the gatehouse, as Piers originally requested.

We can work out a hierarchy of rewards to make primary rewards (e.g., food) contingent on low-level performance (e.g., sitting still, brushing his teeth) and secondary rewards (e.g., going for a walk) predicated on mastering more difficult tasks (e.g., learning a new word or producing a full sentence). We could even introduce a token system so Smithy can earn his way toward more desirable rewards by accumulating target behaviors.

Second, we can apply negative consequences when Smithy behaves poorly. By actively punishing unwanted behavior, we can extinguish it more rapidly than if we simply ignore or fail to reward it. For instance, after he was caught throwing tiles at his teachers, Smithy was confined to his room for a time-out. Mild physical punishment (e.g., a gentle swat to the bottom or a spray from a squirt gun) could also be employed to immediately curtail the undesirable behavior. Remember: not only does Smithy's poor behavior impede our study, but also it risks our safety.

I propose we enact both measures immediately. If anyone has questions about what constitutes appropriate punishment or what value to assign to a specific reward, please see me. We will meet on Monday at 3:00 PM in the library to formally prepare a schedule of rewards and punishments.

    —WK

MEMO FROM TAMMY COHEN
TO WANDA KARLEWICZ

June 24, 1974

Your recommendation re: punishment for Smithy surprises me. The volume of studies on its lack of effectiveness is hefty. Consequently, we now see more movement toward rehabilitation of criminals instead of incarceration in modern society. In your own senior project on classroom management, you and your co-authors, Judy Caswell and Roger Keene, noted 1) punishments have only a temporary effect on learning, 2) punishments don't reliably translate across settings, 3) punished subjects seldom internalize the intended lessons, and 4) unintended consequences (including, but not limited to, resentment of authority and future increased obstinacy) frequently occur.

Given these factors, I think it unproductive and even counterproductive to punish Smithy. Personally, I don't want to jeopardize our gains to date and end up with a chimp who hates me. Increasing our vigilance can limit his mischief; managing his reinforcements will improve his responses. Can't we stick with those strategies until they're proven ineffective?

DIARY OF RUBY CARDINI

June 26, 1974

More fuss and contention over how to govern Smithy. I've heard it said that disagreements over childrearing are a major cause of arguments between couples. Apply the same dilemma to a house of six (sometimes seven) people, and you have a recipe for discord.

We've spent so much time this morning debating what to do. That's almost an entire day of lessons out the window. I don't know why it hadn't occurred to me before I signed on to this study that discipline and child-rearing (chimp-rearing?) would be part of the job. I only thought about how we would teach Smithy sign language, but we may not even get to do that if we don't agree completely on how and when we're to reward or punish him.

Yes, punishment is on the table now. Wanda proposed we introduce mild discipline into Smithy's routine. I cringed when I read her memo. I don't want to be the bad guy, and I don't want to jeopardize my rapport with Smithy. It's hard enough to tell him "no" when he wants a second cookie or an extra snack at mealtimes. Moreover, Smithy is a higher mammal. He's capable of holding a grudge, unlike a rat or a pigeon. Suppose I must discipline him, he remembers it, and then won't cooperate with me later out of spite? Suppose Smithy stops taking direction from me because I've punished him in the past, even if I was only following Wanda's orders? If I can't teach him, will I be replaced? I don't want to betray his trust in me, nor undercut my own effectiveness in the study.

Luckily, Tammy has been a vocal opponent of the punishment tactic. She even used some of Wanda's own reasoning from an article she co-authored a few years ago against her.

I asked Tammy how she'd found Wanda's paper. She told me that when she received Wanda's letter welcoming her to the study and instructing her how to get to Trevor Hall, she had wanted to learn more about her. Tammy figured Wanda must be published if she were so highly placed in Piers's orbit, so she looked up Wanda's name in the recent publications at the library.

I wish I'd been that meticulous. It had never occurred to me to read up on Wanda ahead of time. I never even looked at Piers's articles; I just relied on what I knew about him from listening to the radio.

I felt very naïve at that moment. I want so badly to prove I am fit to work with the graduate students—that I grasp previous research, can hold my own, and can contribute meaningful ideas. But so far, I haven't done much. I've followed directions and practiced my own signing so I can be a better model for Smithy, but that's nothing extraordinary. Gail, without even an associate's degree to her name, has been singled out by Wanda for her diligence and persistence in teaching Smithy. So the team already has a designated grind. Who can I be?

I'm still trying to find my place. I can follow the discussions. I know the names and the terms bandied about. I just can't seem to innovate. How much longer will I be allowed to work on the study if I can't uplift the line of inquiry? Nobody has said anything about periodic reviews, but I wonder if Piers or Wanda won't pull me aside someday soon and tell me, "We appreciate your effort, but we need to give someone else a try now. Don't despair; you still have a fine future ahead of you, but not with this study." How humiliated I would feel if that ever were to happen!

I've got to speak up more. Even if what I have to say isn't groundbreaking, I need to establish a pattern of sharing what's on my mind. One day, I will have a promising idea, and I'll need to express it right away rather than second-guess whether it's worth sharing or not.

In today's meeting, I completely understood Tammy's arguments and even had some of the same concerns myself, but I didn't say so. If I'd spoken up first, it would have made me look like a potential leader.

Ultimately, Wanda was voted down. Nobody felt comfortable punishing Smithy unless he were to do something completely out of character or violent, like ripping up the furniture. Even then, we agreed a time-out would be better than a spanking. We've also tabled the token system for now. Eric says that strategy works well in an institution like the school where he works, but "the subject has to understand the value of the token first, and we're still trying to get Smithy to understand basic signs. I'm worried it would take too long to teach him that little colored chips are just as good as cookies and can be saved up for a big outing. I'd rather spend that time building Smithy's vocabulary or helping him finish his chores early so we can play."

So there.

Wanda seemed disgruntled and said Piers should have the final say—meaning if she can put her arguments to him the next time he comes to Trevor Hall and get him on her side, then he can overrule our five votes. It doesn't seem fair. It is Piers's study, and he can establish any rules that he pleases, but I wish we could restage our meeting for him so he can hear each person's point of view instead of relying solely on Wanda's. I hope she thinks better of going over the group to subvert our intent. If Smithy's learning his signs, does it really matter who's managing his education?

Wanda made one more threat—and I've no doubt it was a threat: "The board wants to see progress. We need to show that Smithy can do more than make a few signs. If we don't, the board may lose interest in funding our study. A new advancement—like the token system—would be a leg up over Osage and keep them invested. Think about that before you shoot down a suggestion out of hand next time."

Jeff griped about Wanda being a poor loser, but she drafted the study proposal, so she must know what the board wants. Have we sabotaged ourselves today? I'm impressed by everything Smithy does, but the board may not be, especially because his erroneous use of "woman" and the ambiguous "black/sleep" sign remain questionable. What if they focus on the uncertainties instead of the successes?

What if we get turned out of Trevor Hall? I couldn't bear to go back to Scranton now. Dad will find out. I'd have to get work, and if any jobs even existed, they'd have been snapped up long before this far into summer. I wonder if the economy in New Haven is any better. They probably wouldn't let me move into the dorm before fall semester starts though.

Calm down, Ruby. Disaster hasn't struck yet. It won't. We'll succeed.

DIARY OF RUBY CARDINI

June 27, 1974

Smithy was fussy at breakfast. He's too distracted by the faces in the dining room (I think they're a little creepy myself), so we're dining in the kitchen or on the patio as long as the weather holds. But even though Smithy usually behaves well in these places, this morning he acted strangely.

First, he wouldn't eat when I told him to. I gave him a cup of milk with his toast and fruit, and right away he signed, "More." I signed, "Drink," so he would finish the first cup, but Smithy got agitated. He banged his cup on the table and signed again, "More, more," then "Mine." Wanda was making herself breakfast, too, and she told him, "You drink." He obeyed her and drank all his milk, so Wanda refilled his cup. Smithy pushed it to the empty place beside him and signed, "Yours," still looking at the empty seat. Then he looked at me and signed, "Me drink. More milk. Give." That was the most he'd ever said to me, but it was also the first time I'd seen him sign anything when he wasn't addressing either an animal or a fellow researcher.

I asked Wanda, "Did you see that?"

"His syntax is off. We need to teach him to put the imperative before the objects." She pushed the cup back to him, but he picked it up and placed it back at the empty seat and signed, "You drink" to the chair. To us he signed, "More milk me." While we both watched, Smithy then took a piece of toast and held it out to the empty chair. He dropped it, and it fell on the floor.

"That's enough!" Wanda was getting mad, but I was intrigued. It looked like Smithy was talking to an imaginary friend, but I thought it would sound dumb if I suggested it. Instead, I asked if he had one of his toys on the chair. It still would have been cool if he'd been trying to

137

interact with a teddy bear, something inanimate that resembled a real person. Wanda checked, but the chair was empty.

"If we were in the dining room, I'd think he was signing to one of the faces, but he's just toying with us. Gail wrote about this. Earlier, he threw oranges off the table and made her fetch them."

Wanda signed, "Eat your food. You drink your milk," but Smithy kept looking behind her, even standing on his chair to see past her. She got annoyed, gave him back his milk, sat in the chair, and watched while he finished eating and drinking. Every time Smithy became distracted and looked around, she snapped her fingers or touched his hand to cast his attention back on her. To me, he seemed like a daydreaming child. I wanted to see what he would do next, but Wanda wasn't having it.

"We have to establish rules, or he'll walk all over us. He's got to eat his food, not throw it around. And we must be empirical, not fanciful. I know it's tempting to think Webster's playing a game, but we can't report that, or we'd just be projecting our fantasies onto him. If I described what I observed, I could only say, 'Webster was inattentive. He refused to eat and produced signs absent the presence of a target.' A neutral judge would rate that as a false positive. What's the use of Webster signing if he's not signing to communicate with anyone?

"Webster _is_ smart enough to communicate, _and_ he's smart enough to manipulate us. We've got to encourage the former and cut off the latter, or this study won't survive. If we let him fool around too much, we won't produce any useful data. Then we won't get spring funding, and you'll be looking for a roommate in New Haven for Christmas."

That shocked me. Piers had told me to request a year's leave from my coursework, so I'd understood he'd secured at least a year's funding already. It scared me to hear Wanda say otherwise. I don't want to quit early, even if I go back to Yale instead of all the way home. I've told too many people about this study: my friends back home, my brother, and through him, my parents. I wanted them to know I was part of something important, and if I'm not anymore, whether through my own failure or a failure of the study, that's still a failure. I hadn't realized the stakes were so high. I thought our goal was to observe Smithy's behavior in a home environment and determine how it contributed to his learning. I would have thought free play was part of that, but according to Wanda it's an obstacle. No wonder she's such a killjoy.

But she's not only considering the repercussions to the study itself. "As I see it, Ruby, we can knock the socks off the scientific community, both in regard to interspecies communication and women's role in the sciences. If we hit all our targets—or exceed them—within the first quarter, we'll earn more funding, but more importantly, we'll garner respect."

Wanda's eyes gleamed when she talked. It was the first time I'd seen her genuinely excited by something, as opposed to playing a role for the camera. I was spellbound. She was confiding in me, and she was saying the same things I've said in my own head.

"We have a team of very bright people, especially brilliant ladies. We can make our voices heard as we help Webster articulate his own. We'll break new ground—all of us. The concept of primate language is astounding, and this methodology of serving as a participant-observer in a human home environment is radical—but, Ruby, don't you think the most exciting thing is how many women are going to be making the discoveries? How many women get published in a scientific journal each year? Four of us are already lined up to do so!"

I hadn't thought about the work in that context before. Most of the time, Wanda seems so ~~full of hers~~ self-assured that I never doubt her confidence. But this study is probably a proving ground for her, too. We've only been able to attend Yale for a couple of years. We women have a lot of time to make up for and a lot to show everyone who wanted to keep us out. If Smithy doesn't learn to sign all he's supposed to, it could look bad for Piers—but it will definitely look bad for Wanda, since she's shepherding the study. Then, any time another woman tries to conduct research or lead a team—someone like Tammy, or even someone like me—the good ol' boys will roll their eyes and say, "Yeah, right. You remember how that chimp study went down with the dame in charge? No way!'

It occurred to me that Wanda and I have a lot in common, after all, and I felt badly about judging her so harshly. We both have the same goals. We're facing the same obstacles.

Wanda smiled at me. "You can see that's why it's so important to break Webster out of behaving badly. I'm sure you'll agree using the punishment system I proposed will be the most effective way to do that."

And just like that, she'd lost me. I wondered if everything she'd told me before was just to butter me up and try to win me to her faction. I smiled back and said something vague about keeping all our options open and testing which works best, like good scientists. Then I offered to write up the journal entry about Smithy's breakfast antics, but Wanda said she'd do it herself. So much for encouraging other women in the sciences!

I mentioned the incident to Jeff because I wanted to know what Smithy signs about when he gets up during the night. Maybe he's not really asleep; maybe he's playing around like he did at breakfast. Or maybe he's got too much energy and has to entertain himself because we're not doing enough to stimulate him? Tammy or Eric would probably have better insights into this.

Jeff says it's usually the same pattern. Smithy will say, "Hello woman what's your name?" He always addresses a woman. That's interesting, but then most of his caretakers are women, and the little guy seems to like girls best. Sometimes he signs his name first, then asks, "Who are you?" Sometimes he whines and signs, "No," "Bad," or "Go home." After a bit, Smithy will sign, "Sleep" or "Tired," covering his eyes and fussing the way he does when it's past his nap time. Jeff usually soothes him and tells him to go back to sleep.

"It sounds more to me like he's overstimulated. Like if he's having vivid nightmares, he could be telling the people in his dreams to buzz off and leave him alone," Jeff explained.

Piers thinks Smithy's going through a phase and says lots of children have night terrors around this age. I hope it doesn't get more serious. We can't afford to have our baby losing his beauty sleep; if he's grouchy, he'll take it out on us.

Jeff also wants to document Smithy's natural behavior: "We're supposed to see how he communicates naturally in a regular home environment. There's nothing natural about being pressured to meet a weekly word quota. I wish I could say Wanda will loosen up after we hit her targets, but she'll just keep moving the goal-post. And she'll make us sound like layabouts so she can take all the credit for Smithy's accomplishments by being 'the responsible one.'"

Jeff scoffed at what Wanda had said about renewing the grant. "The donors didn't give us a timetable. They love Piers, and they love this project. Wanda's pressuring herself—and us. She wants to make a huge breakthrough right away. She's a worrier and a perfectionist. Don't fall into her trap." I'm not sure the path is as smooth as Jeff seems to think, but I suppose he knows Wanda best after two years. Jeff said after Piers showed his classes a home movie that he and Jeff had made during one of their house calls, Wanda got all fired up to help teach the chimp. Clearly, she's good at it. Dealing with her demands is just something I'll have to get used to.

Jeff also told me not to let Wanda discourage me or to worry so much about my signing. "You'll trip yourself up if you overthink things. You're learning pretty quickly for an adult with no prior exposure, and you're holding your own in the study. I've seen your journal entries. They're exactly the kind of observations we need! You're detailed but not stilted, so we won't have to worry about the regents falling asleep while trying to read the reports—I've seen it happen with some thesis presentations. Were you ever in journalism? Creative writing?"

I never told Jeff I wanted to be a writer when I was in junior high. I never got accepted for the high school paper, so my reporting can't be <u>that</u> good. Maybe he was giving me an empty compliment. Or maybe I've improved since those days through all my journal writing. I care about this work much more than any assignment my teachers ever gave me. I'm consciously trying to write better than I normally do. I imagine what the graduate students must be observing and writing, and I try to match them. If Jeff is truthful, then my strategy is paying off. I hope I can believe him. I've decided I'd like to be his friend.

The sign for "friend": Hook the left and right index fingers together, release, turn your hands, and hook the right and left fingers together. There! Now back to work!

SOLARIUM JOURNAL ENTRY
FROM ERIC KANINCHEN

June 29, 1974

I never know what to write in these things. OK, here goes.

It's the afternoon. I'm in the solarium, observing Smithy through the window. Gail's now weeding the garden with Smithy's help. He pulls weeds and either hands them to her or puts them in the garbage pail. Smithy was playing with Jeff and Maisie before he approached Gail. She acknowledged him but didn't signal him to join her. He appeared to do so of his own free will. This indicates Smithy has an altruistic attitude. Furthermore, he can cooperate with others toward a common goal (i.e., gardening).

Wanda doesn't appear to want Smithy to engage in this work. She called out to Gail, scolding her. I wonder why. But Gail and Smithy are continuing their work, so it must not have been serious.

It's a nice day, not too warm and not too cold, and for a change, it's not gray. Maybe I'll take a stroll by the Cliffwalk later. I wonder if I should ask to take Smithy with me. Maybe he would enjoy the scenery. We do have a harness for him.

Question: Am I the only one who hears Jacques Cousteau's voice in my head reading these entries as I write them?

SOLARIUM JOURNAL ENTRY
FROM JEFF DALTON

June 30, 1974

Eric: I always hear Jacques Cousteau talking when I read your journal notes.

SOLARIUM JOURNAL ENTRY
FROM WANDA KARLEWICZ

June 30, 1974

To clarify, I don't object to Webster pulling weeds, per se. We've already seen that Webster has a problem with overgeneralization (e.g., "black" v. "sleep" and overusing the "woman" sign). I would hate for him to extrapolate from pulling weeds to pulling flowers. There are still some nice rose bushes on the property. I don't want Webster to uproot them or injure himself on the thorns.

I propose we meet at least once a week to set an agenda for Webster. We can review his target vocabulary and propose benchmark tasks (e.g., self-grooming, dressing, eating with utensils instead of with bare hands), as well as actions that should be regulated (e.g. not taking Webster to the Cliffwalk during peak tourist hours; people are liable to be frightened by unexpectedly meeting an ape. The crowds might agitate him, and the potential for injury is too high). I'll post memos to announce each meeting time and location.

DIARY OF RUBY CARDINI

July 1, 1974

Wanda's through buttering me up—no more bonding and confiding today; but I feel like I know her a little better, nevertheless.

I was observing Smithy practicing forming signs, just as I usually do. I didn't quiz him by making him identify objects; I wanted to see what he would do on his own. He ran through the recent vocabulary: red, blue, spoon, red, couch, stir, bread, green, window. It looked to me like he was playing with his words because he hooted over the combinations as he does when we're chasing or tickling him. I copied down his words, thinking I could post them on the bulletin board as "Smithy's First Blank Verses," and we'd all have a good laugh over them.

When Wanda came in to check on me, she did not laugh. "You can't treat this as a joke or make assumptions about his higher functioning. If you published this as a poem, you would be making a statement about Webster's abilities. A misleading statement. You must think like a scientist, Ruby. What do you observe? What can you demonstrate? Right now, you've just got Webster making random signs, divorced from any reference or meaning."

I tried for a scientific argument. "It could be a kind of babbling, like Tammy was talking about, in that he's playing with words to gain mastery over them."

Wanda still looked displeased. "Randomly producing words doesn't prove mastery. If Webster signs "red" in the absence of anything red, you can't speculate that he's speaking metaphorically. Even if you only treat it as a joke, you'll influence your expectations. You'll be more likely to imagine that Webster understands language better than he does. Our critics will say he doesn't know what he's talking about.

"These words are morphemes, the smallest units of meaning. We agreed meaning is more valuable than format, remember? We must demonstrate that Webster can use words appropriately before we can hope for anything more elaborate from him. Piers wants him to master syntax. If Webster can't even handle meaningfulness, you know what that will mean for us."

That chastened me. I've wondered if Wanda looks down on me because my background is in humanities instead of the sciences. Now I know.

She continued. "Have you seen The Miracle Worker? Or read the play?"

I had.

"There's something fundamental about the act of signing that even people with limitations can grasp. That's why Eric was chosen for the study. He told us he'd heard of some instructors successfully teaching Ameslan to non-verbal autistic children. Whatever prevents them from talking, they're able to use basic signs. Whatever basic mechanisms control humans' ability to understand language may be present in apes, too."

As she spoke, Wanda's voice rose, and her gaze sharpened. I speculated about what she was focused on: The paper she would write? The doubting faces of her colleagues? The problem itself?

"If we can establish that principle, we'll have established a major connection to our animal antecedents. We'll also have laid a foundation on which to build practical applications for people. If language is more basic than some researchers have claimed, communication may be easier than we think to master—and to transmit. Eric could apply what he learns from Webster in his classroom, and we could create interventions for stroke patients…

"But if we're not careful with how we approach our work, none of that will happen. Think about what our critics will say. Think about how you can foolproof your data, so they don't have room to challenge our work."

I promised not to let my imagination get the better of my observations and went back to drilling Smithy as usual. Her intensity humbled me. Wanda's brother uses sign language. Maybe communicating with him, or helping him communicate with the world, has been a personal challenge *for her. Maybe she's hoping insights from this project will ease the hardship for people in the same boat.*

Whenever Wanda does something to make me think she's too harsh, something else happens to make me see her humanity through her abrasiveness. I don't like her exactly, but I admire her.

LETTER FROM RUBY CARDINI
TO SARAH-BETH ANDREWS

July 2, 1974

Dear Sarah-Beth,

Big news: <u>I finally taught Smithy a new sign today!</u> I feel like I've won an Olympic medal. Wanda herself told me, "Good job!" Praise from her is probably harder to get than a gold medal. I know it's silly of me to want to impress Wanda when it's Piers's study, but so often it feels like it's really Wanda's experiment because of how closely she manages everything. So, yes, Wanda's acknowledgment meant even more than Piers's "Good girl" (which is also what he tells Maisie for retrieving her Frisbee).

Because Smithy's still studying colors, we've been using prisms to show him the spectrum. Smithy finds these toys fascinating, especially when you cast the rainbow onto someone's face or clothes, temporarily turning Eric's white T-shirt purple or Gail's golden hair green. I operated the prism today. Normally, we manipulate it to show one or two colors at a time, but Smithy seemed bored, so I decided to up the ante.

First, I revealed each color one at a time, signing them as they appeared. I went through the full spectrum, using a pointer to indicate each color in sequence. Then I waved my pointer up and down over the bars of color and formed the sign for "rainbow" itself, which I'd asked Jeff to show me when we first got the color assignment. I waved at the spectrum and signed rainbow three times, then I got one of Smithy's picture books about a circus. One of the characters wears a long gown displaying all the colors of the rainbow. I showed him the sign again while pointing to her, then I pointed to a different picture that shows all the characters marching beneath a spreading rainbow in the sky. He watched me, but held back, as if he couldn't figure me out.

We took a break, and after lunch, I ran through the colors again: red plate, white milk, green apple. I pulled out my prism and flashed the light through it. And Smithy spontaneously made the sign for rainbow! I nearly fell off my chair. I thought I was hallucinating, because I wished so much for Smithy to learn from me.

I showed him the full color spectrum again and asked, "What's that?" He signed, "rainbow" again! I gave him a big hug and rubbed his back and shoulders. I would have kissed him had Piers not walked in just then. Instead, I told him all about the new sign. He seemed amused but satisfied.

I wrote up our session in the journal and shared it with my friends at dinner. Jeff was delighted and applauded me afterward for teaching Smithy something new. "I knew you would do it," he told me. "Smithy likes you. You have a good rapport with him because you don't talk down to him."

He's right about that part; I'm a little in awe of Smithy and his abilities, so I defer rather than condescend to him. "He trusts you, and that's why he'll learn from you. Oh, he'll learn from Gail, too, just because she's relentless. I think he responds to her for the same reason Columbo's suspect always confesses: to get the pest off his back. With you, he feels comfortable. He'll work with you because he wants your approval. This sign will be the first of many. Watch and see!"

Jeff suggested a little party at his pad to celebrate. We made popcorn and threw most of it—in the air, at each other, at Smithy—instead of eating it, while we watched Carol Burnett. We laughed ourselves into fits, and Smithy hooted along with us. I don't think he understood a single joke, but he was having fun because we were. He's fascinated with the TV and the people who come and go in it. To him, it's better than a game of peek-a-boo (a game Smithy's strangely loathe to play; when you cover your eyes, he quickly pulls your hands back down and signals, "No." He struggles if you try to cover his eyes, even though he's used to us molding his hands to form words). A couple of times, I got him to sign about something on the TV, but mostly I just had fun. I'm ready to loosen up now and enjoy being in the study. It's still going to be a heck of a lot of work, but for the first time, I feel confident that I can do it. I _am_ going to do it. I'm doing it already.

Rainbow: Fold one arm in front of your chest. Extend the other overhead while holding up four fingers (keep the thumb tucked in). Slowly fold this arm down until your four fingers touch your elbow.

There, now you can do it, too, and if you ever get to meet Smithy, you can show it to him yourself, and he will know what you mean, thanks to me!

POSTCARD FROM GAIL EHRLICH
TO EHRLICH FAMILY

July 5, 1974
Front: Image of America's Cup Race, 1970

Dear Vanessa, Dad, Mom, and Snoopy,
  Happy July 4th!
  I hope you had a great holiday! This is a picture of the big race coming in September. They do fireworks in that harbor on July 4th. We went up on the roof to watch them. It was the best seat in the house! They were so pretty! Smithy came with us on his leash and loved it. He kept running around, trying to catch the fireworks like they were butterflies. So cute!
  Piers is going back to Yale soon, and we'll be on our own for a bit. Wish us luck!
  Love,
  Gail

ARCHIVAL FILM FOOTAGE

Date: July 6, 1974
Location: The Library

Eric kneels and plugs in a lava lamp on the small table. He says, "Can you please close those drapes? I want to make it as dark as we can." Gail walks behind him and the room darkens. The lava lamp glows a deep iridescent blue. Eric looks up at the camera. "OK. Today we're going to review colors with Smithy and see if he can learn to apply more than one word or concept to an object. So let's bring him inside…"

A knocking sounds at the door. Off camera, Jeff calls, "They're ready!"

The door opens, and Piers enters, holding Smithy's hand. The chimp hoots when he sees Eric and Gail. Eric waves and opens his arms. Smithy gives him a hug. Gail sits on the floor beside Eric. She signs, "Hug," and Smithy embraces her, too.

Piers says, "Let's limit our vocals today. I want to ensure he truly understands the sign and isn't reacting to our words. Remember, our goal is to teach comprehension and performance of sign language."

Piers signs to Smithy, "Who is that?"

Smithy signs, "Eric."

Piers points to Gail and signs, "Who is that?"

Smithy signs, "Gail."

Eric points to Smithy and signs, "Who are you?"

The chimp signs, "Me Webster Smithy me." Piers frowns when he sees the "Smithy" name sign.

Eric shifts his seat, and Smithy sees the lava lamp behind him. It glows a deep purple. He freezes and stands up straighter. He focuses his gaze on the lamp, and the hair on top of his head stands up.

Eric signs, "What is that?" Smithy runs over to the lamp and reaches out for it. Eric quickly signs, "Don't touch!"

Smithy hesitates, then reaches for the lamp again. Gail sits closest to him, and she swats his hand away. She also signs, "No touch."

Eric crawls closer to the lamp and signs, "What is this?"

Smithy signs, "Purple." As he signs, the color shifts to red. Smithy hoots and hops backward.

Eric says, "I wanted something that wouldn't be static, so he would have to constantly identify its changing properties instead of assigning only one sign to the object."

"How does it do that?" Gail asks.

Eric explains, "There's a small light underneath, kind of like at a disco. So the lava's always changing color slightly." Looking at Smithy, he signs, "What's this?"

Smithy stares at him. Eric points to the lamp and signs, "Water lamp."

Piers asks, "Why did you choose that sign?"

"Because the globs inside look like giant drops of water," Eric replies.

Frowning, Piers says, "My concern with 'water lamp' is Webster may try to drink from it."

Eric says, "We'll teach him that's a bad idea." He signs, "You no touch. Bad. What color?"

Smithy signs, "Red."

When the light changes to blue again, Eric signs, "What color? Hurry."

The revolving bubbles in the lamp distract Smithy. He crawls closer and peers up at the shifting liquids.

Piers snaps his fingers to draw the chimp's attention; he signs, "What color is this?"

Smithy signs, "Blue."

Eric points to the lamp and signs, "Pretty."

Gail signs, "Water lamp," then "blue water lamp," then "pretty."

"Right now, we're introducing him to various descriptors for this lava lamp. Later, we'll test his recall to see how many different signs for it he can spontaneously apply," Piers notes.

Smithy watches the lamp. Gail signs, "You like?"

Smithy signs, "Give me."

"What do you want?" Gail asks, signing.

Smithy signs, "Red". The lamp has just turned red again. He pauses and signs, "Red water lamp."

Jeff, off camera, exclaims, "He did it! He extrapolated from a previous sign!"

Piers grins. "It's too soon to assume that. We'll ask him about it again later."

Eric signs, "What is this?"

Smithy signs, "Pretty water lamp." Then, with greater agitation, he signs, "Give Smithy me pretty."

Eric signs, "No touch water lamp. Touch bad." He pauses, then signs, "Smithy touch water lamp hurt." He clarifies his signing for the humans in the room: "I don't want him to get fussy when he sees one of us handling it."

Eric continues signing. "Water lamp hot. Hurt. Eric touch water lamp good. You touch water lamp bad."

Piers asks, "What else can you ask him about its properties?"

Eric and Gail sit for a moment, watching the lamp, then Gail signs, "Water lamp light. Water lamp hot." She slides over to the wall socket and unplugs the lamp.

Eric asks, "Wait! What are you doing?"

Gail says, "I want to show him the difference."
She signs, "Where light? Water lamp cold. Water
lamp dark."

Smithy whines.

Eric says, "He wants it back on."

Gail plugs the lamp in. It glows a soft purple.
Eric points to it and signs, "Water lamp purple."
Smithy crawls toward the wall socket and picks
up the cord. Gail snatches it out of his hand.
Smithy grunts and signs, "No bad hot water lamp
me Smithy mine."

Eric asks, "What's that?" He signs, "What
do you want?" Smithy scoots backward suddenly,
snarling. The lava lamp tips over and breaks.
Glass and fluid spray across the table and carpet.

Eric exclaims, "Shit!"

Piers grabs Smithy and pulls him away from the
mess, toward the middle of the room. "You need to
clean this up right away!"

Eric says, "I'll get a towel." He jumps up and
runs out of the library. Gail opens the curtains
to let more light into the room as Jeff enters the
camera range and approaches the desk. He picks up
a newspaper from the desk and unfolds it; he sets
the papers down over the spill.

Piers faces Smithy and signs, "What happened?"
Smithy covers his eyes with both hands and rocks
back and forth. Piers pulls his hands free and
signs, "Look. You bad."

Gail says, "He must've tugged the cord when he
moved backward and pulled the lamp over."

Smithy continues to cover and uncover his eyes
rapidly, whining.

She remarks, "Look! He's crying. He's ashamed."

Piers says, "No, don't anthropomorphize him.
He's telling us something. Covering the eyes is
Webster's sign for 'sleep'…or 'night,' correct?"

Jeff says, "He also uses that sign to mean
"dark." He started using the signs interchangeably

about a week ago, and we all agreed to respond accordingly."

Piers says, "Hmm…I wish you had consulted me before adopting the sign as a synonym for another word. We risk opening ourselves to sloppiness and ambiguity if we allow him to overuse signs too generally. Now what meaning would make the most sense in this context?"

Gail says, "Nothing in the room is dark anymore. Maybe Smi—Webster wants us to turn the lights out and make the mess go away?"

Piers asks, "Isn't that a complicated message? Our boy usually uses simpler, more direct concepts."

Jeff says, "Gail could be on to something. Maybe he feels safer in the dark."

Piers says, "Webster could be reverting to the original meaning of this sign. Perhaps he's overtired. He may be asking for a nap. He's also signaled "sleep" in the past to extricate himself from unpleasant situations. Or maybe he recognizes he's about to be punished and is trying to escape a scolding."

Eric runs back into the library, his arms full of towels. He mops up the spill and says, "I'm so sorry about this. And about the delay. I had to get some cleaning rags from Wanda. She wouldn't let me use a regular towel."

Piers says, "That's all right, Eric. It was a good try. I'm going to take our boy up to bed. He needs a nap, or at least a time-out, for the breakage."

Piers scoops up Smithy and walks out of the library. The chimp is still agitated. He points to the lamp and signs, "Me no bad," then covers his eyes with his free hand. Jeff returns to the camera. The screen goes dark.

LIBRARY JOURNAL ENTRY
FROM JEFF DALTON

July 6, 1974

Today we explored both Smithy's use of equivalent concepts and his recall of colors from his vocabulary list. He displayed strong recognition of the colors red, blue, and purple. However, our target object was destroyed before we were able to explore transitional terms.

The results from this exercise are promising enough to warrant repeating, but I advise we don't use another lava lamp. I'm not sure they're safe. Gail thought Smithy might have knocked the lamp over by pulling on its cord, but I reviewed the film, and he's clearly scooting away from the cord. That lamp tipped over by itself.

LIBRARY JOURNAL ENTRY
FROM RUBY CARDINI

July 6, 1974

I have an idea of what Smithy was trying to sign just before the lamp broke. He had the cord in his hand. I think he was trying to unplug it so it would be off (e.g., "cold" not "bad" or "hot," but safe for him to handle).

LIBRARY JOURNAL ENTRY
FROM TAMMY COHEN

July 7, 1974

Re: Smithy covering his eyes after the accident with the lava lamp.

I've seen this behavior before with my sisters. At a young age, kids think if they can't see you, you must not be able to see them either. To me, it looked like Smithy was trying to weasel out of the situation, either by making it all go away or making himself go away from it.

LIBRARY JOURNAL ENTRY
FROM GAIL EHRLICH

July 7, 1974

That's what I said, too! Jeff, do you remember? I said he wanted to make the mess go black and go away.

JOURNAL ENTRY
FROM PIERS PREIS-HERALD

July 7, 1974

Gail,

Perhaps I owe you an apology for not considering your suggestion more carefully. I was reading the surface of Webster's statements, and you were delving into the psychology behind them. The next time Webster gets into trouble, we shall see if he uses the same sign. If "dark/sleep" becomes a pattern in response to his wrongdoing, we can further discuss how to interpret it.

LETTER FROM GAIL EHRLICH
TO EHRLICH FAMILY

July 9, 1974

We were playing Chase outside the other day. One of the words I helped teach him, "play," means you want any kind of game, and you make two fists with your pinky and your thumb pointing out, and then you shake them. We came up with a new sign for "Chase" referring to running games specifically. For that one, you make the "play" sign, then slap your knees with your fists.

Smithy was running outside with me, Ruby, and Tammy while Jeff filmed us. Smithy would chase one of us, and when we let him catch us, we'd chase him back. He had to sign first though, either "play" or "play" and "chase" together. That's Piers's new rule: if Smithy wants something, from now on he must ask for it if he knows the sign, so we can track his vocabulary. We're not to give in to him pointing or pouting or looking sad.

Poor Smithy had some bad luck. When it was my turn to chase after him, he ran right through a patch of flowers and got stung by a bee. He wailed so much. You probably could have heard him all the way back in Missouri. I saw him shaking his hand in the air, and at first, I thought he was making a sign I didn't know, but then he started to scream and suck on his thumb, so we knew he'd touched something bad. After that, he ran around the lawn crying and waving his hand. Jeff figured out what had happened and tried signing him to come here so we could treat his boo boo, but Smithy was too wound up to stop. We chased him for real then. I had gotten close to him when I stepped in a gopher hole and tripped and fell right on my face. It's a good thing <u>I</u> didn't land on any bees!

Smithy could tell something was wrong and looked back to see if I was still chasing him. I decided to act like I was hurt. I put my head in my arms and pretended to cry, and I didn't get up from the ground. Smithy is so sweet that he came running to me right away to see what the matter was. He forgot all about how much he was hurting, so he could see what was wrong with <u>me</u>. When he got close, I scooped him up and hugged and kissed him before he could get away. Smithy didn't mind. He likes me. I used tweezers to pick the sticker out and washed his hand and put ointment on it, and then I kissed his thumb to make it better. I wish kissing it had really worked. His poor hand is all swollen and red now, and we have to keep making sure he doesn't scratch at it.

Wanda was mad when she saw what had happened. She said we're not to play any games that could hurt his signing ability. Smithy doesn't want to sign while his hand is all puffed up. And he keeps trying to eat through the bandage we put on to keep him from picking at the wound. For now, he watches us signing to each other. It's good practice because most of us still don't know sign language too good, but I miss playing with him. I think Wanda is an old stick in the mud.

Tammy had a terrific idea. She suggested we make an educational film for Smithy that would help us all learn to sign better. She got the idea because her littlest sister liked to watch a show called Sesame Street. It has puppets who teach kids how to count and say their ABCs. They use games and songs to make learning more fun. Tammy thinks we should do our own version for Smithy. That way, he can watch the film while he's recooperating instead of always having us make signs for him in person. Then we can take a break, too, from time to time.

We're working on a script right now, and Jeff will start filming us tomorrow. I'm going to be one of the stars of the movie...

LETTER FROM RUBY CARDINI
TO SARAH-BETH ANDREWS

July 11, 1974

(EXCERPT)

... We've been making our own TV show for Smithy! OK, we're not really on TV, but we made a film of ourselves giving a sign language lesson as if we were characters on "Sesame Street." It was Tammy's brainchild. She'd read an article about the educational boost kids have gotten from watching the show, and she confirms her own little sisters have learned from it and enjoy it. "Why don't we make something like it for Smithy?" she'd suggested. "We can teach him a few basic signs, or maybe a process like cleaning his room or getting dressed. It will be fun!"

Everyone got on board with the idea. Even Wanda seemed to like it. She insisted on picking the vocabulary words we would use, and she, Tammy, and I wrote the script. Or rather, I made a few suggestions, Tammy wrote up the scenario, and Wanda made edits. We laughed a lot, and I enjoyed seeing how the material grew and changed as it took shape. I just wish I were more creative, so I could have made better contributions.

However, Eric proved to be our biggest asset. When we told him what we were planning, he went to the toy store in Middletown and came back with a bunch of hand puppets, including a monkey that will serve as the model for Smithy. It turns out Eric is a skilled puppeteer, <u>and</u> he can do cartoon voices! When I asked him about it, he said, "You'd be surprised how many kids at the center are willing to use their silverware or throw away their trash when Mickey Mouse or Donald Duck asks them to, but not when the teacher does it." Tammy asked if the kids ever wonder why

Mickey Mouse is stuck on their teacher's hand, but according to Eric, they talk directly to the puppet and don't notice the puppeteer.

Tammy was impressed with Eric's adaptability. She told him, "You'll make a great dad someday."

Eric got embarrassed by the compliment and said, "I'd need a girlfriend first." Then he seemed even more flustered. Poor guy. Eric's a sweetheart.

Our film stars are Eric (playing the monkey and a couple of other puppets) and Gail (the main human interacting with the puppet). We decided Gail should be the lead instead of Wanda because she used to act in plays in school and because Smithy has a little crush on her. He always approaches her to play first and watches her closely whenever she's in the room. Jeff calls her Smithy's "Golden Woman," in reference to King Kong. He took a snapshot of Gail holding Smithy, the two of them gazing into each other's eyes and smiling, that he labeled "Beauty and the Beast."

Jeff, of course, was the director (though Wanda had plenty more than two cents to add to every take) and cinematographer. And editor! He made us do three or four takes of each scene so he could pick the best cuts, but he didn't work us too hard. Piers supported us by taking Smithy to the beach (on his leash, of course), so we could have Trevor Hall to ourselves for filming.

We called our show "Smithy Street." Tammy wrote lyrics for the opening titles that everybody sang, and Wanda signed. The film is only thirty minutes long (an entire day of work and only half an hour to show for it)! Over three sequences, we humans teach skills and sign language to Eric's monkey (called "Smithy") and the monkey's friends. We shot one sequence in Smithy's room, one in the bathroom, and one in the backyard. I was a supporting player, but no matter. We all had a blast, and though we were serious while the camera was rolling, we joked between takes. Eric chased Gail, Tammy, and me with a dinosaur puppet. I think Jeff may have filmed that part, though he didn't show it to us.

When Jeff screened the finished piece for us, I couldn't believe how professional it looked. It was easy for me to be impressed because I had been "on set" and knew what everything truly looked like behind the scenes. Jeff zoomed in close on the puppets, so you can't see Eric at all. Eric even tried to operate the puppets' hands to make them sign, but alas, without fingers, the puppets couldn't quite master the words. Instead, most of the signing is accomplished via close-ups of Wanda's hands. Tammy assures us it's just like a real episode of "Sesame Street."

We showed the finished product to Smithy today. We had a big viewing at Jeff's pad with popcorn and soda, but while Smithy watched the screen, we watched him for his reactions.

Smithy loved it! He hooted all through the film, jumping and clapping and even trying to interact with it. When he saw Gail on the screen for the first time, he pointed at her and signed her name, then turned around to see her sitting on the couch. He looked astonished that she could be in two places at once. Best of all, he even attempted to sign some of the words Wanda and "Smithy" the puppet demonstrated in the film. We appear to have succeeded, both as educators and entertainers.

Piers is ecstatic. He told us to go ahead and make more films and include Smithy next time—either instead of, or with, the hand puppets. He's interested in selling our show to television to air on PBS or one of the local networks, both as an educational special that could teach children to sign, and as evidence of the success we've had with Smithy so far. Just think—soon, you might be able to watch me making a fool of myself on TV. Can you imagine?

SCENES FROM "SMITHY STREET #1"

Date: July 1974
Location: Smithy's Bedroom

Gail stands beside a bureau of drawers, holding an armful of clothes. She asks a monkey puppet perched on the edge of the bed, "Smithy, do you want to wear your *shirt—*"

The camera cuts to a close-up of hands signing "shirt." As Gail continues, "—or your *sweater*?" the camera cuts to a close-up of hands signing "sweater."

Gail sets the clothes on a chair and holds up a shirt and then a sweater. She says, "If it's *cold* outside, you should wear your *sweater*. But if the sun is out, it will be *hot* outside, and you would probably like a s*hirt* instead." After each stressed word, hands sign, "cold," "sweater," "hot," and "shirt."

Gail raises the window. Bars obstruct her from sticking her head outside, but she sticks her arm through the bars. She says, "The sun is out, Smithy. That means it's hot." The hands sign, "hot."

Gail says, "Here, Smithy. Put on your shirt." She holds up the shirt, and the camera cuts to it draped over the puppet's head. It shakes and squirms until it pokes its head through a sleeve. It looks from side to side, then sticks its arms over its head and waves them.

Gail says, "Oh, dear! That shirt is too *big*." The hands sign, "shirt" and "big."

Location: Outside Trevor Hall

Gail stands under a tree, looking down at the puppet. She asks, "What would you like to do, Smithy? What should we play?" When Gail signs, "play," the puppet points up. She asks, "You want to go *up*? Do you want to *fly*?" She signs, "up" and points to the sky, then signs, "fly."

The camera cuts to a seagull flying above the rooftop, then cuts to the puppet shaking its head no. It points to the tree.

Gail says, "Up there? Do you want to climb the tree?" She signs, "up," "climb," and "tree." The puppet nods enthusiastically.

The camera cuts to a shot of Tammy, Wanda, and Ruby in another tree. Tammy dangles upside down from a branch, waving. Ruby climbs up behind her, blowing a kiss toward the camera. Wanda sits on a high branch, beckoning. She calls, "Come, Smithy! Come and play up in the tree with us!" She signs, "come," "up," "tree," and "play" as she speaks.

The camera cuts to the puppet. It nods, claps, and makes a pleading motion to Gail. She says, "OK, you want to climb up the tree." She signs, "climb up tree." She says, "Let's go!"

Gail runs to the tree where the other women are already sitting or hanging from branches. Wanda, Tammy, and Ruby clap and chant rhythmically, "Up! Up! Up!"

Gail urges, "Go on, Smithy! Climb up!" She signs, "climb up." The puppet embraces the trunk and starts to make its way up the tree.

The camera cuts to the women in the tree, chanting and signing, "Up! Up! Up!" The camera cuts to the puppet sitting on the first branch. It wipes its head with his paw as if exhausted from the climb. The women clap and cheer. Wanda pats the puppet's head. Ruby gives it a high five.

Gail says, "You did it, Smithy! You learned how to climb! And you learned so many new words today! Let's review them all!"

The screen splits. On one side is a close-up of a pair of hands signing. On the other side is an image of Wanda, Gail, Ruby, Tammy, and the monkey puppet signing. All together, they recite, "Wash. Face. Hands. Clothes. Comb. Hair. Toothbrush..."

WEEKLY WORD LIST
JULY 15, 1974

Oven

Refrigerator

Egg

Milk

Butter

Jam

Sugar

Bread

Cake

Flour

Cut

Stir

VIDEO FOOTAGE: "20/20" INTERVIEW WITH GAIL BEVERIDGE

Broadcast Date: April 6, 1989
Location: Inside a Furnished Room

Gail, now in her 30s, sits in a chair, arms folded neatly in her lap. Her blonde hair is permed. She wears a blue pantsuit and a pearl necklace. A credit in the lower right corner of the screen names her as "Gail (Ehrlich) Beveridge." She begins to speak.

"When we first moved into that big house, every day felt like a party. Dr. Preis-Herald was still spending a lot of time at the university, getting ready for the next semester and working out a budget, so we were mostly on our own, and we wanted to play with Smithy. He was warm and loving and so enthusiastic. Whether we were teaching him a new word or a new game, he took to it like *that*."

Gail snaps her fingers.

"We used to play records and dance with him. He loved The Who and The Rolling Stones. 'Ruby Tuesday' was a favorite. He used to dance with Ruby Cardini for that one. It wasn't just for fun though; we used the music as a teaching tool. While the record played, we'd sign the lyrics for him. He picked up some of the words, but it was hard to say how much Smithy really understood. I mean, how can you teach an ape the meaning of 'Lucy in the Sky with Diamonds'? *I* never could figure that one out. And then there were times when he just wasn't up for a lesson…"

The screen cuts to archival film footage circa July 1974.

Location: **The Solarium**

"Ruby Tuesday" plays in the background. Ruby holds Smithy's hands and sways with him in the middle of the room. Smithy is docile and focused on Ruby. The other researchers are seated on the sofa or the floor. Tammy and Gail sing along with the chorus. When the song ends, everybody applauds.

Ruby curtsies and says, "Thank you, thank you. Come on. Take a bow, Smithy." Smithy bows to the audience. "She's a Rainbow" begins to play.

Gail coos, "Aww, so cute!"

Tammy says, "You know, we should try playing some songs with other people's names in them for a change. Debbie Reynolds has a song called 'Tammy.'"

Gail asks, "Are there any songs about Gail?"

Ruby protests, "But I like 'Ruby Tuesday.'" She sits beside Jeff on the sofa. Smithy totters over to Wanda, who grooms him.

Jeff puts his arm around Ruby and says, "We could try 'Ruby Don't Take Your Love to Town.'"

Ruby snuggles closer to him and says, "Nah. That one doesn't have a good beat you can dance to."

Wanda says, "Actually, folks, we *are* here to work. Play is fine and good when there's a time and place for it, but Trevor Hall isn't a resort. We're here to teach Smithy and to learn from him.

Jeff asks, "What do you suggest, Wanda?"

Wanda says, "As long as we're playing records, we can at least teach Smithy the words."

Eric studies a record jacket. He asks, "Do you propose to teach him 'Jumpin' Jack Flash'?"

"What's the sign for 'gas,' Wanda?" Tammy jokes.

Wanda sighs. "No, we'll start with something simple." She glides to the record player and moves the needle. The opening chords of "Paint It Black" begins. "This one should be easy enough. He already knows most of the words. Come here, Smithy. Look at me."

She sits cross-legged on the floor opposite Smithy and continues: "Listen and look at me. 'I see a red door… I want to paint it black.'"

She signs each word, finishing with covering her eyes on "black."

"No colors. I want black."

Smithy whimpers and backs away.

Eric says, "We haven't taught him 'summer' yet."

Wanda says, "Come on, Smithy! 'I have to turn my head until darkness goes.'" She signs, "Turn," "head," "darkness," and "leaves."

Smithy follows suit and signs, "Darkness leaves."

Wanda continues, "'I see cars and they're all black.'"

Smithy signs, "I see cars," but as Wanda signs, "Black," he jabbers loudly and sits on his hands.

Jeff says, "He's not in the mood right now, Wanda. Back off."

"Or try a different song. He doesn't seem to like this one," Ruby interjects.

Wanda says, "He can do this one! We must be firm with him. Don't let Smithy be in charge." She points to the camera. "And we need results we can show our sponsors, or our funding will dry up."

Jeff says, "You're exaggerating."

Wanda, ignoring him, signs, "I see my red door. Paint it black," concentrating her gaze on Smithy, who signs, "No black," then "black leaves."

Wanda says, "That's not right, Smithy. Pay attention." She reaches for Smithy's hands to mold them and sings, "I look into the sun…I see a red door, and I want to paint black."

Smithy resists and pulls away. He slaps at Wanda when she reaches for his hands a second time. She snaps, "Smithy!"

Jeff says, "Let's not have him throw a tantrum." He changes the record to "She's a Rainbow," and sings along, "She comes in. Colors everywhere…" He signs, "She enters," "colors everywhere," "she combs hair," "rainbow." Smithy watches and joins in at "combs hair." As the song progresses, he calms down and mirrors Jeff's signing.

Wanda says, "Thanks for your help, Jeff. Let me know when I can continue his lesson."

She leaves the room. Jeff and Smithy continue to sign the song together. Jeff doesn't recite the words, but he signs certain lyrics. Smithy also signs, "Blue," "sky," "white," colors," "everywhere," "combs hair," and "rainbow."

Jeff says, "Attaboy, Smithy." He tickles Smithy and continues, "We should buy some kids' albums. "The Farmer in the Dell" and "London Bridge" and "Mary Had a Little Lamb" are probably more his style. Smithy is just a kid, after all."

Gail says, "And then we can dance the Hokey Pokey with him."

"Yeah, that too." Jeff smiles.

The song finishes, and everybody claps. Jeff rubs his temples. "What else do we have to play?"

Eric shuffles through records and reads, "Ob-la-Di, Ob-La-Da."

Jeff says, "Wait. That has 'Penny Lane' on it, too. Give it here. Firemen, rain, and merry-go-rounds. I can handle that."

Ruby says, "You can also do "Here Comes the Sun" and "Fool on the Hill.""

Tammy says, "Don't forget the walrus!"

Eric teases, "Sign 'Coo coo ka-choo.'"
Jeff retorts, "Coo coo, screw you."

MEMO FROM WANDA KARLEWICZ

July 15, 1974

Dear Team:

Again, I've noticed most of the interaction with Webster involves play, tickling, and engaging with other animals. If you have a novel way to teach a sign using playtime or one of the pets, please write up your results in one of the journals so others may learn from your methods. However, I suspect most of these pursuits are purely recreational. It's not good for Webster to spend too much time in unstructured activities that don't contribute to his learning.

Remember: the university expects results in return for its substantial investment in our stay here at Trevor Hall. To that end, we _must_ direct more of our collective time and effort toward teaching, reinforcing, and documenting the use of sign language.

I know we all want to be the best teachers possible for Webster. I will be happy to work with any of you who would like additional tutoring. Feel free to come to me with any special needs or concerns you may have.

—WK

NOTE POSTED TO BULLETIN BOARD

July 15, 1974

Thought for the day:
Tempus fugit!

LIBRARY JOURNAL ENTRY
FROM WANDA KARLEWICZ

July 16, 1974

Webster has learned two new words <u>not on the weekly vocabulary list</u>, courtesy of Jeff: "Fuck" (middle finger extended straight up) and "Nixon" (waving the index and middle fingers of both hands in V-shape overhead).
    Thanks a lot, Jeff.

LIBRARY JOURNAL ENTRY
FROM JEFF DALTON

July 16, 1974

I will not teach Smithy to disrespect elected officials. I will not teach Smithy to disrespect elected officials. I will not teach Smithy to disrespect elected officials. [This message continues for three full pages.]

MEMO FROM WANDA KARLEWICZ

July 17, 1974

Reminder: the house journals are to be used to record serious scientific observations pertaining to Smithy's behavior and our interactions with him. They are not provided for private usage or to record jokes. Kindly observe this rule.
    -WK

LIBRARY JOURNAL ENTRY
FROM JEFF DALTON

July 17, 1974

I will not misuse the journals. I will not misuse the journals. I will not misuse the journals.
  Just kidding!

LETTER FROM RUBY CARDINI
TO SARAH-BETH ANDREWS

July 18, 1974

(EXCERPT)

. . . We do not spend all our time fooling around. On the contrary, we're working harder than usual now that Smithy has fully recovered from his bee sting. Wanda wants to make up for lost time by doubling up on Smithy's vocabulary. But even Piers has cautioned her not to overdo it, lest Smithy become overwhelmed and the lessons don't stick.

Having so many more words to learn is confusing. We met recently to discuss how Smithy keeps mixing up words (For example, he'll sometimes sign, "woman" when you point to a table or an empty chair). Wanda's particularly concerned that these negative results will prevent the board from funding us through the winter. I'd be crushed if that happened. We've tried different strategies to stave off the possibility: correcting mistakes, ignoring mistakes, reinforcing accuracy. Nothing yields a noticeable difference.

Smithy's not the only one struggling. Every time I see a new word list posted downstairs, my stomach plummets. By the fifth or sixth word, when I go back to review what I've learned, I'm already so mixed up. It's been a blow to my pride.

I used to think I was good at learning languages. I have a strong memory. I can even recall entire conversations up to a day or two later. But I've now realized my advantages came from hearing words pronounced and seeing them in print. I'd see "le garcon" next to "boy," and I'd remember the pair, the spelling, and the sound. Ameslan is different. It's more conceptual and procedural, which is tricky. You have to position your fingers just so, or you risk saying the wrong thing (just as Smithy does). I don't think my procedural memory is as good as my memory for facts. I can't memorize my way through this one, Sarah-Beth; I have to practice until the movements are part of me.

What if I can't do it? Wanda is fluent, and Jeff practically is, too, because of all the time he's spent with Smithy. I don't see Tammy struggling. Even Gail is making good progress. Though she may not grasp all the theoretical aspects of language acquisition, she's dedicated. She doesn't get frustrated when she makes mistakes, and when she's teaching Smithy, she'll go over the same exercise repeatedly without complaint. Gail may not be very imaginative in her techniques—she'll often ask Smithy directly to present a word rather than exploring more subtle ways to elicit a sign—but she gets the job done.

Eric is the only one I've talked to so far who admits to feeling challenged, and he gave me some advice: "When I'm learning a language, I'll translate everything I'm saying throughout the course of my day in my head. It's more practice for me. So if I'm ordering coffee at a restaurant, even if all I need to say is 'I'll take mine black,' I'll still think, 'Ich nehme ein Schwartz.'"

I guess I should get into the habit of talking with my hands whenever I'm talking out loud—or at least think about what hand movements to make before I open my mouth. Or maybe I should take Tammy's extreme suggestion and pretend I have laryngitis for a day, forcing myself to communicate only by sign language.

Eric and I discussed the experiment's chances of success. He brought up a good point: "Even assuming chimpanzees are able to acquire language, how can we be sure our *chimpanzee will? What if Smithy turns out to be, like, the Lenny of chimpanzees?" (You remember* Of Mice and Men? *Lenny was mentally impaired). "I know one kid at the school where I volunteer, who hasn't said more than a dozen words in the four years I've been there, but he's bright. If you put any mechanical gizmo in front of him, he'll have it dismantled and put back together in fifteen minutes. Now, if aliens picked this kid at random for a study like Piers's, they would think language was beyond human capacity. If language were their criteria for intelligence, Bruce would flunk."*

He's right. There's so much individual variation among people; why shouldn't there be just as much variation among chimps? From what I've observed, Smithy has high intelligence. He's certainly crafty, if that stunt with the brownies was a sample of his M.O. Maybe he won't be able to learn all the words Piers and Wanda want him to learn at the rate they hope (for that matter, maybe I won't either, but I don't think of myself as a Lenny), but I believe he _can_ learn. As I told Eric, "You found a way to teach that boy, even if speech wasn't the best tactic. We'll have to try different ways to reach Smithy until we find the one that gives us the best results." And I, too, will experiment on myself, be it with drills or films or signing in my head.

No word yet on whether "Smithy Street" will be airing any time soon. Wanda loved the idea of a teaching film so much she's decided to launch her own cooking show, or at least shoot a segment for the main show. Since Smithy always wants to be with her in the kitchen anyway, it made sense to have Jeff tape them preparing food and signing about what they're doing. Unfortunately, the initial demonstration didn't go quite as planned...

ARCHIVAL FILM FOOTAGE

Date: July 15, 1974
Location: The Kitchen

Wanda stands at the counter by the sink, while Smithy perches on the counter, rocking with excitement. She smiles and says, "Hello, everyone! My name is Wanda, and this is Webster, also called Smithy." She signs, "Hello" and each name.

"Tonight we will demonstrate how to prepare…" She holds up a pasta box and shows it to Smithy. She signs, "What's this?"

Smithy signs, "Spaghetti."

"Very good," Wanda says. "We've got spaghetti for dinner. To start, we'll fill the kettle with water. Smithy, turn on the water."

Wanda signs, "Open water." Smithy turns on the faucet. She signs, "Water inside bowl." He takes the kettle and fills it with water. When it is almost full, Wanda signs, "Stop."

"Very good. Now, I'll put the kettle on the stove and heat it. Stand back, Webster." She signs, "Back" and turns on the stove.

"We'll work on the sauce next. I won't let Smithy use a knife, but he can help with the vegetables. Webster, what are these?" Wanda signs the question and points to some tomatoes on a cutting board. He signs, "Red."

Wanda continues. "Yes, they are the color red. Red is the color, but what is the name?" She signs, "What this name?" Smithy signs, "Tomato."

"Yes, very good!" Wanda tickles Smithy's leg. She adds, "He can tell the difference between similar items. Observe."

Wanda sets a red apple on the cutting board and signs, "What's this?" Smithy looks at it up close, sniffs it, and signs, "Apple." Wanda says, "Good. This is an apple, and he knows it."

She signs, "What's this?" and picks up the tomato.

Smithy signs, "Tomato."

Wanda puts the two fruits behind her back and asks, "Now, what's this?" She holds up the apple.

Smithy correctly signs, "Apple." Behind her back, Wanda switches the tomato to the hand that previously held the apple and holds it up. Smithy correctly identifies the tomato. Wanda signs, "Good, Webster."

She continues, "Webster, give me a tomato." He hands her a tomato in response to her sign. Wanda slices it and gestures for another. Smithy complies.

"Webster, give me two tomatoes." Smithy picks up a tomato in each hand and gives them to her. Seven tomatoes remain.

The camera zooms in on Wanda's hands and the chopping knife. She signs, "Where tomato?" Smithy gives her a tomato.

Wanda signs, "More tomato," and says, "Give me one tomato." Smithy hands her one.

Wanda says, "Give me two tomatoes." When she signs, "Two tomatoes," Smithy hands them to her and watches her cut. She signs, "Give me a tomato. Give me a tomato." This time, Smithy doesn't hand her anything. Wanda signs, "Where tomato?" Smithy doesn't respond.

Wanda continues her questioning. "Webster, where is the tomato? Give me a tomato."

Smithy signs, "No tomato."

She says, "There should be one left. I counted. Did he eat the last one, Jeff?"

Off camera, Jeff says, "I'm sorry—I cut him out of the shot to better focus on your hands. I didn't see."

Wanda asks, "Webster, did you hide the last tomato?" She looks around to see if it's on the ground. She opens a drawer. "Webster, show me your hands."

He opens his hands. Wanda studies his face to see if he has juice around his mouth. She opens her mouth wide and sticks out her tongue. Smithy imitates her. Nothing is in his mouth.

Wanda says, "Well, we'll have less sauce then. OK, time to put the pasta in the water." She hands Smithy the spaghetti. He breaks the noodles and drops them into the boiling water. She continues to hand him fistfuls of spaghetti until it's all gone. Wanda stirs the pot with a wooden spoon and sets the spoon on the counter beside the stove.

Wanda continues. "Now we'll wait for it to boil. In the meantime, we can take a tour of the kitchen. Webster, what is this?" She points to a table.

He signs, "Table."

"Good. What's that?" She points to the refrigerator.

He signs, "Cold box."

Wanda points to the sink and asks, "What's this?"

Smithy signs, "Woman."

Wanda looks surprised. She laughs nervously and says, "No, that's not a woman." She faces the camera. "That's his favorite word suddenly. That's the *sink*, silly. You use it every day. Look, here's the water." She runs the water and holds up a bar of soap. "Come on, what's this?"

Smithy signs, "Wash soap."

"That's better." Wanda and Smithy wash their hands. Wanda fumbles for the cooking spoon but can't find it. She searches the stovetop and counter for it. She asks, "Webster, where is the spoon? The *spoon*. Do you have it?" She gestures for him to show his hands. They are empty.

Wanda looks around and says, "Well, it didn't walk away! Here, spoon!" She drops to her knees to look under the table and the appliances. "Jeff, did you see where I set the spoon?"

Jeff, off camera, says, "You left it on the counter."

"That's what I thought. Webster, where is the *spoon*?"

The chimp looks around and points to the rear of the kitchen. Wanda walks back to look. She calls, "Not here. Are you hiding it?"

She spots something on the counter and pounces on it. "Aha! Where did you have this?" Wanda looks at the camera and asks, "Was he sitting on it?"

Jeff, still off camera, replies, "I didn't see him move."

Wanda sighs. "Great. He's a sleight of hand artist. OK, Webster, come help stir." They stir the pasta. Wanda sets down the spoon. "Leave that there!" she directs. "Now we'll drain the water." She signs, "No touch" and "water gone." Smithy sits beside the sink and watches her pour the water into a large sieve.

Wanda says, "Next, we'll add the sauce." She signs, "Tomatoes in bowl." With Smithy's help, Wanda adds the chopped tomatoes to the pasta. "Now we'll mix it up. Not again!"

The camera pulls back to show the spoon is missing from the countertop.

Wanda says, "Webster, cut it out! This is not funny!" She signs, "Where spoon? Hurry." Smithy just gazes up at her. She signs for him to stand up. Wanda checks his hands and feet, sees they are empty, rolls up his shirt, then reaches along his pant legs. She opens her mouth and motions for Smithy to do the same.

Jeff calls from off camera, "Wanda, what's that on the table?"

Wanda turns around to see the spoon. "Now how did you do that? Ooohhh!"

Jeff jokes, "Maybe we should stage a magic show instead of a cooking show."

Wanda glowers at the camera and shakes her head as she stirs the pasta. Smithy glances over his shoulder at the rear of the kitchen.

The scene fades out.

LETTER FROM RUBY CARDINI
TO SARAH-BETH ANDREWS

July 18, 1974

(CONTINUED)

...Incidentally, Smithy is still experiencing troubled sleep. Jeff was falling behind in cutting footage due to all the nights he's had to spend bunking down with Smithy to keep him calm, so Wanda has started sleeping in Smithy's room on alternate nights.

I offered to take some shifts, too, but Wanda said, "No, thanks. He's known Jeff and me for most of his life and feels secure with us. Introducing a new face into the mix might only increase his stress." I didn't think I was a stranger after almost two months, but if Wanda wants the job to herself, I'll let her have it.

When he's not catching up on sleep during the day, Jeff and I have been spending more time together. We both had a day off yesterday while the others managed Smithy. I wanted to do more sightseeing, and he suggested we finally visit the Breakers. After listening to Tammy, I was prepared not to like it but couldn't help being impressed by the beauty of all the art objects. Even the ceilings and floors constituted art!

After our tour, we walked around the house to take some pictures. No photos were allowed indoors; otherwise, I would have enclosed some. Jeff told me to pose next to one of the statues. It was something Classical: a muse or a goddess. He said I looked like her, that we had the same nose. I've always hated my big Roman nose before. I couldn't see any resemblance in the photograph, but even if he was just being kind, it was still a sweet thing to say. As we were leaving, he snapped a flower off one of the bushes by the front gate and gave it to me because he said it matched my pink sweater. I wore that flower in my hair for the rest of the day. Right now, I have it pressed between the pages of my diary. Silly, isn't it?

MEMO FROM JEFF DALTON WITH ADVERTISEMENT FOR HARVEY H. MEYER SCHOOL FOR THE DEAF

July 18, 1974

Text: Reminder: Deadline to register for fall classes is July 31, 1974. Please contact our office to set up an appointment.

Please review the enclosed and let me know what you think about expanding our team. We could send Smithy to school a couple times a week to see how he functions in a different environment. I think Smithy would benefit from trained instructors for the deaf, and a professional setting with more discipline. We would also benefit from having additional data from extra observers (and more free time to take care of basics like repairs and housecleaning).

I've already talked with Piers, and he sounds eager to incorporate these instructors, provided they respect our goals and recognize we have the final say on how Smithy's training is handled. I don't want to decide anything unilaterally though. If the majority rules, I'll call the school tomorrow to gauge their faculty's interest, and hopefully arrange an appointment.

NOTES POSTED TO BULLETIN BOARD

July 18-19, 1974

The more the merrier! Maybe we can also learn from the Meyer School teachers. — **Eric**

I agree. If this goes forward, I'd like to sit in on some of the sessions to observe their teaching methods and pick up more ASL. — **Tammy**

It sounds good, but I'm concerned for the integrity of the experiment. We brought Smithy to this house instead of keeping him in a lab or a classroom to foster a sense of personhood. Will we be able to maintain that at the Meyer School? Feel free to override me if I'm off-base. I think it's a great idea otherwise. — **Ruby**

Ruby, you're absolutely right. We'll make sure the teachers treat Smithy as much like a regular pupil as possible. To ensure this happens, I think it will be necessary for one of us (Tammy?) to sit in on the lessons, at least at first. — **Jeff**

Far out! — **Gail**

(Scratched out, illegible) I see it doesn't matter what my objections are because I've been outvoted again. If the school consents, we'll sign up for a four-week trial period. I hope nothing goes wrong, given Webster's recent antics. — **WK**

SOLARIUM JOURNAL ENTRY
FROM ERIC KANINCHEN

July 19, 1974

I attempted to practice the new word list with Smithy this morning. Nothing doing. He threw a tantrum almost as soon as we sat down. Even Maisie started howling because of his screaming. I told Ruby to take her outside, and I tried to calm Smithy. He stopped crying but kept covering his eyes, so I figured he wanted to take a nap (or maybe he felt like playing hooky and decided feigning sleepiness was the way to do it). I took him to his room, and though he didn't sleep, he lay still and was quiet until lunchtime. Wanda says she'll give him a lesson later.

Good luck with that!

ARCHIVAL FILM FOOTAGE

Date: July 19, 1974
Location: The Kitchen

Wanda stands beside the counter, and Smithy sits on the edge. Around them are scattered bowls, spoons, and other cooking implements. Wanda smiles and says, "Good afternoon! Today, Webster and I are going to bake a cake using this delectable Betty Crocker lemon-flavored mix." She holds up a box of cake mix. "Then we'll frost it with delicious Betty Crocker vanilla icing that Webster keeps trying to eat." Wanda displays the canister and rotates it to show where the lid meets the can. "So I've taped the lid shut for now. To begin, we'll need a bowl. Webster, hand me the bowl."

She signs, "Give bowl." Smithy hands it to her. Wanda says, "Thank you! Open the cake mix. Pour it into the bowl." She hands him the mix and signs, "Powder inside bowl," and holds out the bowl. Smithy peers into the box and tries to reach inside with his fingers.

Wanda says, "No, don't eat it; pour it in the bowl. Just shake it in the bowl. That's it! Good! Now, can you pour the milk in the bowl?" She signs, "Milk in bowl." Smithy follows the instruction. She says, "Very good. Do you want to crack the egg? OK, pick an egg." She signs, "One egg." Smithy gingerly picks up an egg, cracks it on the side of the bowl, and dumps the yolk into the bowl.

Wanda says, "That's right. Good job. Now that egg is trash. All gone! Throw away the trash."

She signs, "Egg gone. Egg trash. Trash in can."
Smithy puts the broken shells in the trash can.

Wanda asks, "Webster, where is the spoon?"
Smithy hands her the spoon.

She continues. "Now we're going to mix it all
up." While she speaks, Smithy looks away from
Wanda to the back of the kitchen. Something has
caught his attention, but nothing is visible to
the camera.

Wanda asks, "Do you want to stir, Webster?"
She signs, "You stir spoon bowl." Smithy looks
at her but doesn't move. Wanda offers him the
bowl and spoon. She signs the question again, but
Smithy looks away.

Wanda says, "OK, not this time. So I will stir
the mix a little longer, and we'll pour it into
the cake pan."

Behind her, Smithy moves toward the rear of
the kitchen, still staring at the back wall. He
opens a drawer.

Wanda explains, "The oven has been pre-heated
already, and I've got the timer set for—"

Smithy pulls a handful of silverware out of the
drawer and hurls it across the kitchen, hooting
shrilly like a bird. Wanda spins around. She
cries, "Webster, no! Stop that!"

Smithy opens a second drawer and throws more
spoons and spatulas. He signs, "Gone." Wanda
grabs him by the arm to pull him back, preventing
him from reaching back into the drawer.

She says, "Yes, they're all gone now. Bad! Bad
Webster!"

He signs as she scolds. Looking up at her, he
hoots softly, using a free hand to sign, "Sorry."

"Yes, you're sorry, but it's too late now,
mister. Come on back to your room." She signs,
"Webster time out bed." Smithy whines and
struggles.

Wanda twists toward the camera and says, "Jeff, will you turn off the oven for me?"

Off camera, Jeff asks, "You're not going to finish?"

Wanda says, "No. This one doesn't deserve any cake." She wrestles the chimp out of the kitchen, and the camera goes dark.

KITCHEN JOURNAL ENTRY
FROM TAMMY COHEN

July 20, 1974

I see now why Wanda warned me Smithy has become a little mischief-maker. Throughout tonight's dinner preparation, little utensils and other items kept going missing. I tried to keep my eyes on Smithy, but I would have to be Argus to do that!

We were making a meatloaf using one of Wanda's recipes. I laid out all the ingredients and implements so Smithy could see them and sign them. I gave him two measuring cups to hold, a red one and a yellow one, so they would be easy to distinguish. I made him sit opposite me with both cups, yet when I asked for the red cup so I could add the chopped onion, he only had the yellow cup. Smithy tried to offer me ketchup when I asked him, "Where's the red?" That shows he's thinking about colors, but I can't fathom what he did with the other cup!

Finally, I had him use the yellow half-cup twice, and we continued preparations—until the salt and pepper shakers disappeared. This time, I made Smithy search with me. I held him by the hand and led him around the kitchen, opening cupboards and doors. I finally found the pepper on top of the refrigerator and the salt in the sink. The canister was wedged in the drain, just out of sight unless you stood over the basin and peered down into it.

Smithy must be passing objects from hand to foot and stretching back to place them (in which case, he's quite the contortionist), or he's hiding them where I can't see them during my examination (and I don't even want to think about where that could be) and bringing them out to place during my search.

We've long known he's deceptive, but he puts on a sincere, innocent act. When I asked him, "Where is the salt?" or "Where is the red cup?"

he looked at me pitifully and searched around the kitchen so earnestly, as if he really had no clue where they could have gone. A couple of times, he tried to weasel out of the situation by covering his eyes (trying to hide from me or make me take him to his room for a nap), but I let him know I wouldn't stand for it.

I finished preparing the meal, but in the future, I recommend we halt the cooking session, or even forbid Smithy from participating in food preparation, if his naughtiness continues. He should be taught his actions have consequences. Also, we should consider tiring him before dinner by making him play or run about to get the mischief out of his system.

As a final note, I counted three repetitions of the sign for "woman" in contexts that did not require it. Twice, Smithy produced the sign immediately after covering his eyes. The third time, he appeared to be referring to the refrigerator. Could it be a kind of instinctive drift? Maybe it's a self-calming behavior, akin to a child sucking her thumb?

ADDENDUM TO KITCHEN JOURNAL
FROM ERIC KANINCHEN

July 20, 1974

Tammy, I just found a red measuring cup in the freezer when I went to get some ice. I think it's yours, but I can't picture how Smithy could have stashed it there with the ice box all the way on the other side of the kitchen from where you were cooking.

SOLARIUM JOURNAL ENTRY
FROM ERIC KANINCHEN

July 21, 1974

Woke up last night circa 0230 when the fire alarm began screaming. Then the girls started screaming. I followed Maisie's barking to the solarium, where I smelled smoke and spotted a small blaze in the corner opposite the turntable. I put it out right away and called the fire department to tell them everything was under control so they wouldn't come knocking down our door again.

The fire was about two feet from the electrical socket, and only a patch of floor was burned (no records). I'm figuring we had a short and maybe a spark jumped and landed on the ground.

Anyhow, we're lucky it was small, and it was caught, and the alarm worked as it's supposed to this time. Let's keep an eye on the appliances and make sure not to plug too many things in one outlet.

LETTER BY RUBY CARDINI
TO SARAH-BETH ANDREWS

July 22, 1974

(EXCERPT)

... *The Meyer School agreed to take Smithy in September. In preparation for sending him to school, we've begun toilet training him; there are limits to what we can expect the Meyer teachers to do.*

Wanda's talked about getting Smithy out of diapers ever since Orientation, but the kicker came when Jeff went up to wake him on Monday. He found Smithy already out of bed and trying to climb the bookcase. He must have been awake for quite a while already because he had "decorated" the walls while waiting for one of us to show up. Wanda admits she's caught him doing such things before, but she had wanted to spare us the ickiness, so she just cleaned him up and changed the sheets herself. Poor Wanda! Now I wonder what other things she takes care of around here without telling us.

But now all of that will be Tammy's problem. She supervised every one of her younger sisters, so she's got the most experience. Jeff and Eric figured this out right away and bribed Tammy to take over their shifts with Smithy. They've each agreed to pay her a portion of their stipends if she'll clean up after him for them. Eric even sweetened the bargain by offering to buy her lunch once a week. I don't know if I would do it for any amount of money, but Tammy has a stronger stomach, and she's perfectly willing to profit from the boys' squeamishness. So she is the "designated diaperer." I pity Smithy a little; Tammy won't take any guff from him. If he pulls a trick, she'll rub his nose in it.

But enough about Smithy. I've got bigger news than him for once.

We—Gail, Jeff, Wanda, and I—had been playing outside with Smithy (all right, he factors into this a little). We put him on his longest leash and let him run around the yard until all of us were sweaty and breathless. Jeff announced, "It's gonna be three o'clock; UHF shows 'I Dream of Jeannie' reruns. Let's take Smithy to the gatehouse so he can watch TV, and we can cool off." We all loved that suggestion.

Then Jeff said, "Ruby, why don't you bring over your flashcards? I can drill you during the commercials." Unsuspecting, I went up to my room to fetch my deck.

As soon as I opened the door, I was hit by a flood of color. Rainbows dazzled my eyes, painted the walls, stained the comforter. After I blinked a few times, I realized this blaze of color was erupting through my window. Somebody had gathered the prisms we use to teach Smithy his colors and hung them there. The sun was at precisely the right height at that time of day for the light to strike my window and set the prisms ablaze. It turned my room into a funhouse, a living kaleidoscopic fairyland. It took my breath away, and for a long moment, I just stood in the center of the room, ogling the effect.

Finally, I heard footsteps behind me, but I didn't turn around until I heard Jeff's voice. "I wanted you to see what it's like for me whenever you walk into a room. You fill it up with light and color and beauty."

I still didn't turn around because by then I had started crying, and you know what I look like when that happens. Some beauty! Jeff didn't seem to care though. He looked a bit bashful as he tilted up my face. Then he asked me, "Is this OK?" I thought he meant was it OK he'd gone into my room to surprise me, and I was so overwhelmed I couldn't answer. Of course I didn't mind! Of course I liked the surprise! Then he kissed me! And I must have kissed him back, because the next thing I knew, we were making out in my doorway.

Finally, Jeff pulled away and laughed. "I told the others I'd see what was taking you so long. I wanted to see you away from them. Now I hope they don't come looking for me." We both went back to the gatehouse, without my flashcards and without trying to be too obvious. I'm sure I looked like an idiot with red eyes and a stupid grin on my face, but neither Wanda nor Gail remarked on it.

I cannot believe how romantic Jeff turned out to be. All the planning he went through: getting into my room, arranging the prisms, figuring out what time the sun would strike the window just so, making an excuse to get me into the room at the right time. That took effort! As soon as Tammy came back from shopping with Eric, I told her the whole story. Even she was impressed. I think she's finally ready to cut Jeff some slack.

Tomorrow is our first official date night. He's taking me out next week to celebrate my birthday, too, just the two of us, but we'll celebrate with the team on my actual birthday first. Piers will be back by then, and Wanda says they can handle Smithy, so she's giving us the night off. We're going to hit the town and check out the nightlife. Believe it or not, this will be our first time on the scene in Newport. We've been working that hard these past two months! We deserve a night out...

ARCHIVAL FILM FOOTAGE

Date: July 24, 1974
Location: On the Waterfront at Night

Eric, Tammy, Gail, and Ruby are walking along a pier. The camera focuses on Ruby in a wine-colored blouse with bell sleeves and a long dark skirt. Her hair, normally in a ponytail, has been set in soft waves around her face.

Jeff says from off camera, "Here we are celebrating a very important someone's birthday—"

Ruby turns around and grins at the camera, walking backward. She asks, "Are you really going to film this?"

Jeff, off camera, says, "Of course. It's our first adventure in town. And we wouldn't have this milestone at all if not for our birthday girl, the lovely and intelligent Ruby."

Tammy and Eric cheer. Gail applauds. The camera focuses on the entry to a pub. The sign beside it reads, "The Black Pearl."

Jeff's voice continues. "Tonight we're celebrating at the Black Pearl on Banister's Wharf. On Saturday, we'll celebrate again—or two of us will—at the White Horse Tavern."

Ruby's face lights up. She asks, "Really?"

Eric asks, "What's that place?"

Ruby replies, "It's the oldest operating tavern in America. A landmark!"

Jeff, still off camera, comments, "Perfect for a milestone birthday!"

Eric asks, "Shouldn't you take her to Atlantic City instead?"

"Someday. Maybe even Vegas," Jeff says as Ruby laughs and looks away, covering her face. The camera jiggles as Jeff runs to open the door. He asks, "Shall we go in?" Ruby passes him, smiling into the camera as she enters.

The camera cuts to the interior of a bar at night.

The dining room is packed with tables. Music plays in the background. Gail, Ruby, and Tammy sit on bar stools, but Eric stands at the edge of the bar beside Tammy, with his foot on the rail. He lifts his drink in a toast to the camera. The girls turn and wave.

The camera cuts to a crowded dance floor. From off camera, Jeff says, "Hey, Eric, hold this for me so I can dance with my girl?"

The camera cuts to Ruby and Jeff slow-dancing to "Let's Get It On." Ruby looks away as the camera dips in toward them and buries her face in Jeff's neck. Gail sways behind them. A young man in jeans and a polo shirt approaches and dances with her.

The camera swivels around to take in the full scene. A group of three men and two women stand at the opposite end of the bar. A skinny man with red hair and sideburns points toward the camera. A man in a vest and glasses standing beside him walks toward the camera, looking excited, but the red-haired man pulls him back. The third man steps over to Tammy and speaks to her, pointing to the dance floor. She shakes her head no.

The camera swivels rapidly away from the bar back to the crowd and lingers on Jeff and Ruby. As they become obscured by other dancers, the view drops to the floor and goes black.

The next moment, the camera focuses on Gail and Tammy dancing together to "Waterloo." Jeff's voice off camera gives instructions: "—can't spin it so fast or you'll make the viewer seasick."

Eric says, "Sorry, man. Filming is your specialty."

Jeff's voice says, "That's cool. Wanna try it again?"

"No thanks," Eric says as the song ends; "Crocodile Rock" begins, and the girls return to the bar. Eric approaches Gail and asks, "Want to dance?"

Gail says, "Oh, no thanks, Eric. My feet need a rest."

Ruby teases, "Isn't anybody going to ask me to dance? My partner's been stolen by a video camera."

Jeff, off camera, says, "In a minute. I thought we'd drink a toast to the birthday girl first." Gail cheers and whistles loudly. The group at the far end of the bar stares at her. Tammy notices and tugs on Gail's sleeve, shushing her. As the bartender passes, Jeff calls, "Hey, can we get a round of beers here? We've got a birthday to toast." Gail cheers again, shaking off Tammy's restraining hand.

Ruby says, "You're not going to sing, are you?"

"Of course!" Jeff calls out.

Ruby protests, "No! Don't do that; it'll be embarrassing!"

Jeff says, "Who's going to hear us in this racket?" The bartender sets down five glasses. Jeff lifts one and asks, "Are you with me?" The others pick up their drinks and raise them in a toast. Jeff begins to sing, "Happy birthday to you—"

Ruby covers her face. "Jeff, stop!"

Jeff sings louder, "Happy birthday to you!"

Ruby laughs. "Ack! Not a close-up! I'm all red!"

They all sing together, "Happy birthday, dear Ruby!" Ruby lowers her hands, blushing and shaking her head, but still smiling up at the camera. The singers finish. "Happy birthday to you!" The group applauds. Ruby blows a kiss to the camera, then turns to face her friends. Tammy and Gail each give her a hug, and Eric slaps her on the back. The young people from the other end of the bar approach behind him.

The red-haired man speaks. "Hey, you've got a birthday over here? Who's the lucky girl?"

Ruby raises her hand.

He says, "Hey, congratulations! Let me get your next drink?"

Ruby says, "I guess. I mean, thank you. I'm not used to such a fuss. I keep telling *him* that." She points to the camera.

Jeff, off camera, asks, "How can I help it? She is my jewel."

Ruby explains, "He's making fun of me. I'm Ruby."

The red-haired man shakes her hand and says, "Happy birthday, Ruby. I'm Fred Patterson. This is Shaun Hendricks." He points to the blond man who had previously asked Tammy to dance.

The man with glasses leans forward and shakes Ruby's hand. He says, "Hi! I'm Reid, Reid Bennett!"

Reid shakes hands with Tammy, but when he reaches for Gail's hand, she simply lifts it, waves, and says, "Hi there."

Fred gestures to a young woman with black hair tied in a kerchief; she wears large hoop earrings, a tank top, and jeans. "This is Jess, Jessica Soames, and this—" He points to a girl with a blonde braid and a purple pantsuit. "—is Trish Hartigan." The girls shake hands with Gail, Tammy, Ruby, and Eric.

Shaun asks, "You're the people staying at Trevor Hall, right?"

Tammy answers, "Yep."

Jess asks, "Is it true you're keeping a gorilla there?"

Tammy says, "No."

"No, it's a chimp," Eric chimes in.

Jess leans forward. "What?"

Eric repeats, "A chimpanzee. Smaller than a gorilla."

Gail explains, "His name is Smithy. He's cute."

Trish asks, "And you can talk to him somehow? That's what I heard at the diner."

Eric says, "We're teaching him sign language."

Ruby remarks, "Oh, you work at the diner? I thought you looked a little familiar."

Eric continues to explain: "He learns a few words at a time every week—"

Trish leans closer to Ruby and says, "Yeah, I wait tables. I've seen you before but not in a while."

"We don't get out much. Too much work to do. And the boss keeps us on a short leash," Tammy says.

Jess asks, "The English guy from the radio?"

Eric continues discussing Smithy's learning process over the others' hushed voices. "—and he combines them into short phrases. He really does understand! It's—"

Ruby says, "Dr. Preis-Herald. Yes."

"Actually, I meant his assistant," Tammy replies with a half-smile.

Eric finishes, "—incredible!"

Shaun, faintly, says, "Cool, man."

Fred says, "Hey, there're the Texeira twins!" He whistles sharply. The young man who had danced with Gail, and a young woman with dark hair, join the group. Gail smiles up at the boy and bats her eyelashes. Fred says, "This is Miguel and his sister Alicia. They're from Fall River. Y'know? Where Lizzie Borden lived?"

Gail shudders and says, "Ooh, I've heard of her. The ax murderer!"

Ruby chants, "Lizzie Borden took an ax..."

Tammy joins in. "And gave her mother forty whacks…"

Reid leans forward. "Actually that's supposed to be *sung*, not chanted. It goes to the tune of "Ta ra ra boom dee ay." He sings, "Lizzie Borden *took* an ax, Gave her mother *for*-ty whacks. When she saw what she had *done*, she gave her fa-ther for-ty-*one*. Ta ra ra *boom* dee ay, Ta ra ra *boom* dee ay…" He trails off as he realizes no one is paying attention. Tammy smiles sympathetically his way.

Eric asks, "Hey, isn't her house still there?"

Miguel says, "Yeah, and sometimes the owners can be persuaded to give a tour, if it's something you would like to see." He smiles at Gail. "It's not far. Perhaps an hour to drive."

"That could be an interesting day trip," Tammy remarks.

Gail protests, "Oh, not for me! I wouldn't want to go somewhere ghoulish like that. What if it's haunted?"

Trish, Jess, and Fred laugh. He says, "That's funny!"

"Uh, speaking of old houses," Trish interjects, "What do you think of Trevor Hall?"

Shaun asks, "Has anyone seen it yet?"

Jess shushes him.

Ruby says, "No, we don't really know anyone else in town. I was just telling, ah, Trish. Tonight is really our first chance to be in Newport socially, so no—we haven't had any guests over to the house yet.

Shaun and Fred laugh. Tammy tilts her head and looks at them quizzically.

Ruby offers, "You're welcome to visit, if you'd like a tour. Some parts of it are closed off—"

Jess crosses her arms as if cold and says, "No, thanks! Not me!"

Shaun says, "Maybe if, like, there was a thousand bucks in it for me."

Ruby looks around, curious. Alicia says quickly, "But you're all happy there? You like the house?"

Gail says, "Oh, yes, it's gorgeous! It's a little run down, and the boys have had to make a few repairs and some changes for Smithy's sake, but you can see how grand it must have looked in its heyday. I feel like a princess living there!

Ruby says, "Yes, I feel privileged to live there, too. We're probably the only college students in America who have our own mansion.

Alicia asks, "Do you live there by yourselves? Just the…five of you?"

Tammy says, "We're seven, actually. There are two more back home. See, Ruby—I'm calling it 'home' now. Yeah, another colleague of ours, Wanda, stayed behind, along with our professor, who's running the show, to care for our chimp."

"But the doc doesn't live there all the time," Eric explains. "He's in and out, going back to Yale or to other schools to speak. Plus he's got to tape his radio show once a week, so a lot of the time it feels like we've got the mansion to ourselves."

Shaun says, "You sure about that?" Jess elbows him, and Tammy frowns.

"But you don't mind being left on your own?" Fred asks.

Tammy asks, confrontationally, "Should we?"

The other men and women look at one another. Shaun laughs, and Reid shakes his head. "Did they tell you anything about the house when you moved in?" Fred asks.

Jeff, off camera, says, "Piers handled the lease. I wasn't on the initial walk-through. I know the place used to be a boarding school—"

Shaun says, "Didn't you wonder why the rent was so cheap?"

"Is there something you'd like to tell us?" Tammy asks, her tone still a bit confrontational.

Eric says, "Yeah, man. What's so funny? Why all the questions?"

"I apologize," Reid says. "Clearly, you're confused, and my friends should have been more discreet. You see…" He pauses. "How can I put this? Trevor Hall has a reputation in the community that you, being outsiders, are unlikely to know about."

Shaun yells, "It's haunted!" Reid glares at him, but Shaun gestures to Eric. "The man wanted us to cut to the chase."

"Are you serious?" Ruby asks.

Fred cuts his eyes to Gail. "That's why we thought it was funny when you didn't want to visit Lizzie Borden's house. Yours is just as bad."

Reid argues, "Now that isn't true! The Borden house was the site of a well-documented crime. Trevor Hall is a victim of innuendo."

Ruby looks around the circle of young people and asks, "You're serious about this? You all think the house is haunted?"

Fred says, "Look, I grew up here. I've heard things. Even when I was little, I knew not to go near that place. No one's lived there in years, and it's not because it's a fixer-upper, or because the taxes are too high, or any of the excuses you might have heard. People have seen things, felt things—"

Tammy asks, "Have you?"

"Like I said, I don't get too close to the house," Fred explains. "When I was a kid, we used to dare each other to go up and knock on the door or peek in the window, but the most I ever did was walk up to the gate. I admit it; I'm a coward. Sue me."

Eric asks, "So what's supposed to go on there? What's haunting the house?"

"Again, nothing is substantiated," Reid clarifies. "The haunting is founded on rumor. Most of the stories began about fifty years ago when Trevor Hall was a boarding school: The Bradley School for the Refinement of Young Ladies. It was a finishing school for the daughters of wealthy families. It did all right for itself until the stock market crashed, when it saw enrollment drop off."

Reid leans against the bar and pushes his glasses up the bridge of his nose; he looks from Gail to Tammy to ensure they are listening before continuing. "Now that's natural enough. The wealthy families who had lost their money could no longer afford the expense of sending their daughters away to learn dancing and art appreciation. But the decline coincided with stories of a mysterious figure who residents had seen walking the halls at night—a figure who walked without making a sound and who vanished when you turned the lights on. Some girls said this figure even sneaked up on them in daylight. While at her books or her music or her sewing, one would suddenly look up and see the figure of a woman in black, watching her from across the room—or standing right at her elbow. And as she watched, the figure would fade away. Needless to say, these stories didn't draw young ladies to the academy.

"In the 1930s, the Bradley School went co-ed to keep itself afloat. Trevor Hall was large enough that its proprietors could segment it out: one wing for the girls and another for the boys. Expanding enrollment temporarily stopped the school from sliding into the red, but it didn't stop the ghost stories."

"After the boys showed up, things got worse," Fred chimes in. "People didn't just say that they'd seen a ghost. *Accidents* started happening."

"Like what?" Gail asks, her eyes widening.

"One girl said she woke up and couldn't breathe because something was strangling her, but she couldn't see what. Her roommate was asleep in the next bed and didn't see a thing. Luckily, the girl kept a Bible on her nightstand to read before she fell asleep, and she reached out for it. When she touched the Bible, the hands released her, and she was free. Then she started crying and woke the roommate. Supposedly, she had bruises on her throat, but they'd faded away by morning."

Reid says, "That's one of the most lurid stories, and it was never substantiated. There *were*, however, small fires that broke out in various parts of the house without any discernible cause."

Ruby sits up and grabs Tammy's sleeve. Eric wipes his palm over his face. Shaun watches him and whispers to Fred.

Reid continues, oblivious. "It could be that one of the students was a fire bug. It could also have been a series of freak accidents. But townsfolk attributed it to the ghost. Also, students reported missing valuables, some of which later turned up in places the students swore they had already searched. Some items were never seen again."

Reid signals the bartender for a drink and continues. "Oh—and one boy fell down the stairs. He claimed a dark figure loomed up in front of him just as he got to the top step and spooked him. He threw up his arms to protect himself, lost his balance, toppled backward, broke an arm, and sprained an ankle."

Tammy says, "At least he didn't claim to be pushed."

Reid says, "*He* didn't, but a girl sleeping in the top floor tower room swore something tried to shove her out the window while she was admiring the view one evening. Now *this* tale does have some support. Boys playing baseball on the lawn below heard her screaming and saw her struggling in the window frame. One of the boys went to get help, and the teacher went up to the girl's room, where she found the student in hysterics. Naturally, she was alone in her room at the time; her roommate had gone home to be with her sick mother."

Tammy and Ruby look at each other.

Trish asks, "Is anyone sleeping there now?"

Gail says, "Piers is. Our professor."

"Better tell him to put a screen on the window, then. Or pick a new room," Jess says.

"It wasn't just the kids telling these tales either," Reid continues. "At least one teacher quit due to her experiences. Even after the Bradleys closed their school, later tenants continued to encounter eerie happenings. The house never stayed tenanted for long. I think the record stay was nearly nine months."

Fred says, "The last people packed up in 1962. They *said* they wanted to go to a warmer climate, like California or Florida, but my old man ran into the wife when he was in Boston on a business trip. Boston's weather ain't that different from ours. Pop said she just couldn't take it in that house anymore."

Jeff, off camera, says, "These are some cool stories, but does anyone know who this ghost is supposed to be? It had to come from somewhere. Was it somebody from the school? Someone who lost money in the stock market?"

Reid says, "Oh, no. Even though the richest period of reported sightings came after Black Thursday, the legend of Trevor Hall dates back much earlier. Now no one is *sure* of the ghost's identity, but there is a story."

"Well, let's hear it!" Jeff says.

"OK, you know how there's a walkway up on the roof?" Fred begins. "A widow's walk thing where you can see in all directions and down to the ocean?"

Eric says, hesitantly, "Yeah…"

Fred continues. "The servants used to go up there all the time. Their quarters were on the third level, so there were stairs that went up to the roof, easy. They could walk around, enjoy the view, and not have to worry about the master eavesdropping on their gossip."

"You also know that the U-shaped driveway is covered over with beech trees," Reid adds. "That was deliberate. The trees shade the stairs leading to the rear servants' entrance. Sometimes the maids and footmen would go out there on a break to take the air or talk. They could stand at the end of the drive, and the trees would block them from the view of anyone looking out a window. It was mutually advantageous. The servants got to have a little privacy, and the upper class didn't have to see any of the help, who were supposed to be invisible anyway."

The bartender sets down Reid's drink, and Reid takes a sip. His audience waits for him to continue. "According to legend, one of the servants, a woman, was up on the roof—taking a walk, watching the ships, or watching fireworks, depending on which variation you hear. Some say she had been stealing from her employers, and the housekeeper caught her. She was going to put the maid out without a reference. Back then, that would have been like a death sentence! Having no reference was a stain on your reputation. None of the other families in Newport—or in the tri-state area—would have hired her. In despair, the girl jumped off the roof and landed right smack on top of the canopy of beech trees. Her weight broke the branches, and she got impaled."

Fred says, "Yeah, she came right down on top of a couple of scullery maids who were out having a forbidden smoke. Scared the bejesus out of them! One girl had to go into a mental ward because she was so shaken."

Trish says, "I heard the housekeeper was having an affair with the master of the house, and she threw herself off the roof because he wouldn't marry her."

Jess adds, "And the way I heard it, the housekeeper *pushed* one of the maids off the roof because *she* was having an affair with him, too, and the housekeeper got jealous."

Reid protests, "No, no—what really happened was a housemaid from neighboring Herbert Terrace— what's now Belancourt Mansion—fell off Trevor Hall's rooftop, supposedly when 'a strong gust of wind caused her to lose her footing.' That's in the inquest report. The servants from both houses used to mingle at parties and on special occasions: Independence Day, New Year's Eve, and so forth. Some even courted. In fact, the carriage driver from Trevor Hall married the second parlormaid of Herbert Terrace…"

"Get on with it!" Shaun orders.

Reid continues. "Anyway, the servants were celebrating Independence Day on the roof. Maybe they were trying to watch fireworks from the harbor. This poor girl somehow fell to her death. I'll bet alcohol was involved."

Tammy asks, "Who was she?"

Reid says, "Her name was never recorded. The newspaper report just calls her 'a young housemaid of Herbert Terrace.'"

"Well, that's lousy!" Tammy says. "How would you like to be known only by your job function?

To be nothing but a nameless servant in death as well as life?"

Ruby asks, "Isn't there any way to research who she was?"

"There was no other identifying information in the news item, nothing about her age or survivors, or where she was from originally, and the rolls for Herbert Terrace show a high turnover that month. Almost a whole new slate of servants was at work by August, so you can't narrow down the dead woman's identity by seeing who was missing after the party. I guess a lot of the help must have been upset by her death and wanted to leave," Reid says.

"Or the Herberts sacked them to keep them from talking," Fred adds.

Eric says, "She was probably an Irish chick."

Tammy says, "That's mean!"

Eric says, "No, really! My ancestors were German and Irish, so I know about this stuff. The Irish were treated like trash in those days. Everybody hated them. 'No Irish Need Apply' signs in the windows, and servants working in lousy conditions. If an Irish maid croaked under mysterious circumstances, nobody would've cared."

Trish says, "Hold on, she did have a name. I remember my brother telling me the story when I was a kid and he called her…ah… Rock-something… Like the painter. Rockwell!"

"Imogene Rockwell?" Reid asks.

Trish snaps her fingers. "Yeah! Who was that, if not the maid?"

"Imogene Rockwell was the housekeeper at Trevor Hall during the 1880s, and she died there in March of 1890."

Jeff, off camera, asks, "Under mysterious circumstances?"

"According to the local doctor's report, Imogene Rockwell died of heart failure," Reid says.

"Yeah, her heart failed when a branch pierced through it," Eric remarks.

"The lord of the manor probably paid the doctor to write that report," Fred notes. "These people could afford to do anything. Hired help was a renewable resource to them. If a servant quit or died, there were hundreds more peasants clamoring for a job."

Reid says, "As it happens, I have some photographs of the house servants from that era, including an image of Imogene Rockwell. I'd be happy to show them to you sometime, if you like."

Fred says, "Yeah, we live in town. Stop by anytime. Reid'll tell you all about the servants. And anything else you want to know."

Trish covers her mouth to block a laugh.

Reid asks, "Did you know there are actually a few people still alive today who used to work as servants in the great mansions? I've taken their first-hand accounts. They're a bit dotty if you ask them what they had for breakfast, but they remember everything about what happened in the old days."

Ruby remarks, "Gosh, you're really into this!"

"I love history, especially Newport history," Reid says. "In fact, I'm doing my dissertation on Gilded Age living in America, from the side of both the haves and have-nots. I'm down from Harvard for the summer, volunteering with the Preservation Society to gather more research."

Eric smiles and says, "Heyyy!" He reaches across Shaun and Trish to shake Reid's hand. Jeff boos from off camera. Reid looks surprised, then stretches out his own hand to meet Eric's.

Gail asks Miguel, "Are you here doing research, too?"

"Ah, no. I take out fishing boats during the summer. My sister works in the café with Trish."

Tammy asks Reid, "Now are you a student of history in general or just ghost stories?"

"Oh, all history, certainly. The ghosts are incidental. Though ghost stories can provide a gateway to studying history. People who want to dig deeper into the local legends can find a great deal of legitimate information along the way. When investigating the background of a so-called haunting, you necessarily learn about the people and the events that fueled those tales. Now, it can be fun to delve into a ghost story to determine what, if anything, has a basis in fact—"

Eric interrupts, "Hey, are any of the other mansions around here haunted or is ours special?"

Reid straightens and adjusts his glasses. He says, "As a matter of fact, Newport has a rich lore—"

Ruby interrupts. "Oh, no! That's enough ghost talk for now. Weren't we going to dance?" She looks toward Jeff.

Reid bows to Ruby and asks, "May I have the honor, Miss Birthday Girl?"

Jeff, off camera, says, "Sorry, man. I'm next on her card. Just let me put this thing away." The camera view tilts as Jeff sets it down.

Eric approaches Gail and asks, "Gail, want to dance now?"

Gail says, "Oh, no thanks. Miguel is getting me a drink. I'm just going to sit here for a while."

Jeff says, "Good; keep an eye on this camera for me, will you?"

The screen goes dark.

ARCHIVAL FILM FOOTAGE

Date: July 25, 1974
Location: The Kitchen

Wanda peers into the camera. In the background, Smithy sits opposite Piers at the table. Piers asks, "Do you know how to operate that?"

Wanda smiles and says, "I've learned enough from watching Jeff to push 'start' and 'stop.'"

"Then I can let Jeff go and give the rest of us a raise from his wages?" Piers jokes.

Wanda laughs. "No, he has his value. All right, let's begin." She steps back, puts her hands behind her back, and smiles at the camera.

"Good morning. It's breakfast time at Trevor Hall. Dr. Preis-Herald and Webster will demonstrate their morning routine and associated vocabulary." Wanda steps out of the shot.

Piers signs, "Good morning." He waits. Smithy looks between Piers and the camera. Piers signs, "Good morning" again, and Smithy signs it back.

Wanda fills a cup and hands it to him. Piers taps the cup and signs, "What is that?"

Smithy signs, "Drink." Piers taps it again and repeats the question. Smithy signs, "Cup." Piers points to the empty dish. Smithy signs, "Plate." Piers points to each piece of cutlery and Smithy signs, "Fork," "spoon," and "napkin" in turn. As they proceed through the spread, Jeff, Eric, Ruby, Tammy, and Gail enter the kitchen, still in the same clothes from the Black Pearl.

Piers says, "Well, good morning. Or is this a continuation of last night? You look like you enjoyed yourselves."

Jeff says, "Oh, you're taping! Were you able to fix the settings?" He runs to the camera. The picture comes into clearer focus, and the lens zooms in on Smithy. He hoots and signs to the newcomers.

Wanda says, "I just set it on the tripod. We're not trying for anything fancy, just a candid breakfast and a demonstration of Webster's table manners."

Ruby walks over to the sideboard to fill her plate. "Yes. Thank you for giving us a chance to go out. We got to see more of the town and talk to its people."

Piers asks, "Did you have fun, Gail?"

Gail leans against the table and pokes at the food on her plate. She says, "I did…"

Piers teases, "Are you sure?"

"Well, at first, we were having a good time, eating and talking and getting to know some of the other young people, but then some of them started talking about Trevor Hall and…they said things I didn't like," Gail replies.

Jeff fills his plate, turns toward the camera, and says, "Oh, yeah! Piers, did you know this house was haunted when you booked it?"

"What?" Wanda exclaims.

"That's what we heard. Trevor Hall is haunted," Jeff explains. "That's why it's been empty for so long and why we got a break on the rent."

Wanda says, "You're pulling my leg!"

Eric says, "*We're* not. If it's a joke, it's at our expense. Everybody in town seemed to be weirdly well-informed about the ghost and all the sightings. Especially this one Harvard guy, Reid Bennett."

Jeff asks, "What was up with that guy and his singing? Ta ra ra *boom* de ay!"

He and Eric sing together, "Ta ra ra *boom* de ay! Ta ra ra *boom* de ay!"

Jeff jokes, "Was he drunk?"

Eric says, "Not drunk enough…"

"Give him a break, guys. He was trying." Tammy says as she hovers in the frame, eating while standing. Wanda passes Tammy a coffee cup and hands another to Gail. Piers fills his pipe.

Piers says, "It sounds like quite a night. And to answer your question, Jeff, no, I did not know we had the privilege of staying in a haunted house. With that in mind, I'm beginning to think I ought to have pushed for an additional discount."

Gail protests, "I don't think it's funny."

Piers asks, "No? I'm always intrigued by what people believe. It's amusing that a group of young adults, including one from *Harvard*, would endorse such primitive superstitions. Please don't tell me they convinced you of their silliness, Gail. You've been happy here so far. I'd hate to think some local gossip would turn you against Trevor Hall now."

Gail gazes into her coffee and says, "No, it won't. The whole thing just made me mad. First, they were laughing at us, making jokes without us understanding."

Tammy speaks through a full mouth. "Yeah, there were a lot of double entendres and ambiguities."

Gail says, "Then they told us all sorts of terrible stories to scare us. One girl even said you might be in danger in the tower room. It all gave me the creeps. Why would they treat us like that?"

"We're outsiders, for one thing. Insiders always circle the wagons," Tammy offers. "For another, through no achievement of our own, we're living in a mansion on a historic upscale street. I'll bet most of the students in town for the summer are living in hostels and working as dishwashers. Finally, we've brought a chimpanzee into the community. I doubt that's made us very popular. I've noticed people staring at Maisie and me on our jogs. I think they're curious about us, and maybe a little envious."

"You see, Gail. This was just a joke born of human envy and the desire for a bit of fun," Piers says, assuredly.

"I don't think our new acquaintances were all bad, and I don't think Reid was trying to scare us. It sounded more to me like he was practicing his spiel to become a tour guide. He kept qualifying everything he said with 'This story is undocumented' and 'Legend has it.' I hope we get to see more of them," Ruby says.

"Yeah, that Reid guy was definitely blowing smoke," Jeff notes.

Gail says, "Oh, I don't think they were bad either. I definitely made new friends. I just…I wish we could have met under other circumstances."

Jeff sits on Piers's other side. Smithy reaches across the table and pulls one of Jeff's sausages off his plate. Jeff pats the chimp's head. He asks, "So you've never seen a shadowy presence in the tower room or felt like you were being watched, Piers?"

Piers chuckles. "Heavens, no. Is that what constitutes their haunting?"

"They said it's a woman in black," Ruby says. "Lots of people over the years have seen or felt her presence."

Piers laughs again. "Good God, do they have those here, too? Next to the sheeted ghost in clanking chains, the woman in black must be the oldest trope in the book. Nearly every old house in England has one. Usually it's meant to be a disgraced or murdered nun patrolling a former abbey, or a widow in her weeds weeping over her lost love."

Tammy says, "This one is supposed to be a dead servant."

Piers says, "Ah! Well, that makes sense since ransacked abbeys are lacking on this side of the Atlantic. Yes, dark clothing could signify a servant. And what happened to the poor maid? Was she ravished by the master and buried alive under the floorboards with their illegitimate child?"

Ruby says, "Reid told us conflicting stories. The most common is that she fell—or was pushed—off the roof."

Piers throws back his head and laughs. Some pipe smoke drifts into Smithy's face, and he sneezes. Jeff reaches across the table and wipes his mouth with a napkin. Piers says, "That's priceless! I'm glad I picked such an entertaining location for our project."

Ruby says, "He also said…there have been a lot of fires here. And no one could find the cause."

Piers says, "Ruby, accidents happen. Regrettably, they can happen frequently in old houses with old wiring. What happened in the solarium was an accident. Please don't work yourself or anyone else into a state about it."

"Piers? What about the lesson?" Wanda interjects.

"I beg your pardon, my dear. These ghost stories diverted me for a moment. Now look at me, Webster." He signs, "What do you want to eat?"

Smithy points to the bacon.

Piers signs, "What is that?"

Smithy signs, "Bacon."

Piers puts a piece on his plate. Smithy eats it up and signs, "More. More bacon me."

In the background, the other researchers file out of the room with their full plates.

DIARY OF RUBY CARDINI

Piers goes back to Yale next week to start classes.

It feels strange to write that and think school will be starting soon, and for the first time in fifteen years, I won't be attending. I'm getting independent study credit for working with Smithy, but all the same, it feels like I'm on an extended vacation. If I hadn't met Piers, at this time, I'd be arranging my dorm room, checking my schedule, buying supplies, and preparing to face the usual first-day jitters. I wouldn't be on this adventure.

But I digress. While Piers is still here, he freed us for another day out. Wanda stayed behind, of course, and Gail went on a date with Miguel, while Jeff, Eric, Tammy, and I took up Fred's invitation to drop in on him and Reid and learn more about Trevor Hall. I was keen to learn more about our new home's history, but I sense Jeff was just humoring me. Eric came along so as not to be left out, and I suspect Tammy was curious to learn more about Reid, though she kept cool throughout the visit.

The boys are renting a couple of rooms in town. The house is neither very old nor very large, but it looks quaint all the same, with a clapboard front painted yellow and shutters for the windows. The roof is a type I've seen frequently here that reminds me of a bowler hat with wide, pointed edges like a brim and a high, rounded dome. Reid says it's a Dutch Colonial style.

He and Fred have the whole upper level to themselves: a large bedroom, a bathroom, and a smaller room that's fitted out like an office with a desk and a typewriter. Fred explained that the homeowners' son used that room as his study, but he's since moved and they wanted to rent it to bring in a little extra money. I glimpsed the wife in the kitchen when

Fred let us in. She looks friendly enough. Reid said she sometimes cooks for them, though most of the time she leaves them to fend for themselves. It's like an old-fashioned boarding house. I think I could be happy living that way if I didn't have Trevor Hall.

We all crowded into the little study so Reid could show us his books and photographs of Trevor Hall. He's got piles of books about Rhode Island's history, some of which are very old, but in addition to them, he keeps scrapbooks of newspaper and magazine articles he's collected. "A lot of this material came from estate sales and raiding people's refuse," he explained. "You've heard the adage about how one man's trash is another man's treasure? When people clean out their attics or basements, they often have no idea what history they're dumping. I gather up the old newspapers and render them down for useful information. I've even been able to get hard copies of newspapers or yearbooks from the library. You see, they destroy their hard copies once they transfer the information to microfilm."

Reid has files on most of the great old houses around here: Rosecliff, Kingscote, Herbert Terrace, and Marble House. A lot of the articles are society news about when the families had come back to town or announcements about soirees. We got to see one photograph of a Vanderbilt family party with everyone gathered on the lawn of Marble House. Consuelo wore tennis whites. She looked so young!

He had lots of pictures of Trevor Hall, too. We saw several pages of class photos taken from old Bradley Academy yearbooks: first, rows of young women in dark uniforms, and then mixed classes of young men and women in formal, but non-uniform, clothes. Some photos depicted students in class. The room in the unused wing below the oculus was a music room! Part of the orchestra sat on the third level, and others were on the second. We could see what the house looked like almost in its heyday. Drapes and curtains were hung, statues stood whole, and no graffiti marred the walls. When did that change?

"It would have been gradual," Reid explained. "Someone would have carved their initials small, in a place where the instructor wouldn't notice it. Then somebody else would have added to it, and so on. Maybe one student dared another to swipe an art object, or worse, to deface a statue. Over time, the little damages would have added up and inspired

greater disrespect of the environment. Ultimately, when word came down that the school was closing, the students realized they had nothing left to lose and went wild."

Reid did have a small collection on the pre-school days mansion, though not much showing the interiors. We saw a formal photograph of Curtis and Cecilia Trevor standing before the great fireplace in the solarium. Greenery decorates the mantel, so it must have been near Christmas. Another photo shows their eldest daughter, Victoria, posed in the same room on her debut. I felt embarrassed looking at those grand people living in the house where I woke up this morning, thinking of all the common ways we've used those rooms. I see myself standing with Gail in that same fireplace on Orientation and dancing to records with Smithy in the solarium, right across from where Victoria posed in her chair.

When I saw the photograph of the Trevor Hall servants gathered to celebrate Miss Victoria's wedding in 1883, I was surprised and then ashamed of myself. I'd imagined a former Southerner like Curtis Trevor would have tried to recreate the glorious Antebellum world from which he came by hiring black servants. I had always pictured Trevor Hall as a pseudo-plantation in New England. But all the faces in the photo were white. Eric was right that most of them were immigrants: Irish, Germans, Swedes.

"Nobody in the upper class would hire black servants if they could help it," Reid explained. "Black servants would have appeared low or cheap, and that would have reflected badly on the master and mistress of the house. White servants were best, even if you had to get them fresh off the boat."

At last, he pointed to a figure in the second row on the left. She was a tall woman, though it was hard to tell her age. Everyone in those days looked prematurely advanced. Her hair was pulled back and tucked under a lace cap, so I couldn't see its color, but her face looked stern, so I would put her down in her fifties at least. She was clad in a long white dress with no frills and no apron because it was a formal occasion, though I understand that she would have worn a black uniform customarily.

"That was Imogene Rockwell," Reid announced. "It's the only documented photo I have, though there are other servant pictures from *other parties that aren't labeled. I can point out who I think she is, but I can't ID her for certain."*

"Do you have any photos from the Fourth of July party where the maid died?" Eric asked.

Reid did not. "I don't even know who the maid was." He showed us the news item, and sure enough, it only refers to the poor thing as "a young housemaid of Herbert Terrace." How undignified!

Jeff studied the wedding photograph a long time. "Look at that face. Can you imagine her doing anything peacefully, let alone dying?"

"Life was tough then," Tammy argued. "You'd have a sour puss, too, if you had to spend every waking minute cleaning up after someone else and bossing a house full of underlings. You can't even handle changing a chimp's diaper; how would you have borne emptying chamber pots every morning? Ms. Rockwell would have had my job and Wanda's rolled into one."

"Missus," Reid corrected. "Upper servants were always 'Mrs. Somebody,' even if unmarried. It was an honorific."

Jeff passed me the photo, and I took my own time to study <u>Mrs. Rockwell</u>. It wasn't a very detailed likeness. Apart from her servant's garb, she looked like someone I might run into on the street; that is, she didn't look exaggerated or of the time, like so many other Victorians. She could have been an extra in a movie shot today. But she was a real person. She had lived, worked hard, and died of heart failure, or so they say. She was an average woman who had had her photograph taken on June 20, 1883, before she became the local bogeywoman.

Still, I could see why she had been picked over the nameless housemaid to star in the ghost stories. Imogene Rockwell looked like she meant business. Unlike a faceless, unknown, but sure-to-be-meek little maid swallowed by the shadows of time, <u>she</u> looked like a vengeful wraith who would stalk the site of her untimely death generations later. I wasn't sure about the lore that had her as Trevor's mistress, though. It was hard to imagine that battle-ax as anyone's lover, jealous or otherwise. I could see her going after a potential rival though.

Tammy looked at the picture over my shoulder. "Maybe she was murdered because she was too unpleasant." I could also see that happening. I passed the photo to Eric, who glanced at it, then returned it to Reid.

Reid went through the rest of the scrapbook album and showed me and Tammy the next seventy years of Trevor Hall history. Meanwhile, Jeff and Eric joined Fred to listen to a baseball game on the radio. I felt bad about keeping them; I could tell they were bored with the history lessons. If Tammy had shown signs of restlessness, I would have made an excuse and suggested we leave. However, she remained patient and attentive throughout the presentation and appeared just as curious as I was to learn more about "our" mansion.

Reid gave us the full scoop, including the death of Curtis; the marriage of the new heir, David; the birth of his twins, Robert and Reginald; the death of Cecilia; the death in WWI of David's younger brother, Walter; the sale of the house in 1922 to Thomas and Edwina Bradley; the opening of the Bradley School for the Refinement of Young Ladies in August 1923; various school functions; the opening of the school to boys in Fall 1929, and the announcement of its closure in May 1936. After that, the house was occupied by a family named Pierson who appeared to have only lived in it for a couple of years before the husband and his brother decided to go fight for England when that country went to war.

"Descendants of the Pierson family still own the house today," Reid finished. "They're distant cousins, half-English, and since they live most of the year abroad, they rent the property out. The owners haven't much to do with the house. I'm sure they don't fully realize how run-down it's become. Even if they did, I don't know that they would have the resources to do anything about it. The Preservation Society has offered to buy the house, but now that you're there, I guess they'll desist. At least until your study concludes." He looked thoughtful as he said this.

"They wouldn't sell the house out from under us," Tammy scoffed.

"I hope not. How long is your lease?" Reid asked.

"Don't know. I guess we'll have to ask Wanda and Piers when we get home."

Reid offered to show us his other collections. He has such a volume of material! He must have started researching Newport when he was a kid; otherwise, I can't imagine how he found the time to compile so much information! I would have liked to at least skim through them, but I felt like we'd spent enough time with him. I told Reid we'd stop by another time, thanked him for all his information, then we picked up the boys and went out for lunch on the waterfront.

From there, we walked to First Beach, which Jeff likes to call "the sand spit." Being a native Californian, his concept of a beach is what I gleaned from beach blanket movies growing up: surfers and palm trees and kids in bathing suits playing volleyball. First Beach is more naturalistic. It's a beautiful, peaceful place with rocks and tall grass where you can take a long walk or watch the waves come in. It may not impress Jeff, who takes the ocean for granted, but I like it. We stayed out until sunset, then walked home.

Everyone was relaxed during dinner and afterward. We played Trouble and tried to keep Smithy from hitting the bubble too often. I got so caught up in the fun that I never once stopped to think about Curtis and Victoria Trevor or the Bradley School or the Piersons, and least of all, Imogene Rockwell. All the people who'd had this house before us and how they'd used it—what must they think of us if they're watching us now from beyond?

We never did get around to asking Piers how long he's rented this house, so I still don't know how long our current reign will last. I guess I'll just have to make sure I enjoy it while it does.

DIARY OF TAMMY COHEN

July 30, 1974

I'm back from my "Big Date," as Gail called it, though Reid Bennett is no one's dreamboat. I had much less to share than her epic about going dancing with "Miguelinho." We had a simple dinner at the Crab Shack, followed by a stroll around Banister's Wharf. Reid did most of the talking, mainly about the historic import of the wharf and the various places we passed. Luckily, after a lifetime spent listening to my siblings ramble, I knew how to let him run out of steam.

When it became too cold for walking, Reid escorted me home. He looked like he desperately wanted to come in, not to put the moves on me, but so he could see what Trevor Hall looked like on the inside. Even so, he kept his curiosity to himself, walked me to the door like a gentleman, and asked if he "might call on" me again. Perhaps I'll let him.

I suspect I'm more a default than a choice. Given the way Jeff was hanging all over Ruby and the way Gail paid attention to every man but Reid, I suppose it makes sense that his attentions fell to me. No matter. He's pleasant enough and well-educated—and ambitious. It's nice to have a friend on the outside and an excuse to get out of the house from time to time. We'll see what happens.

Gail's more optimistic than me. She's already pushing for a double date this weekend. That should be entertaining…

LETTER FROM GAIL EHRLICH
TO VANESSA EHRLICH

August 3, 1974

(EXCERPT)

...I've just come back from a double date with Miguelinho and Tammy and Reid. What a bust! We saw a movie and went to dinner. The movie was kind of a downer. It took place in LA, but they never went to Hollywood or the beach or anywhere really pretty. This icky old man who was trying to steal land or water or both—it was hard to tell—had a thing for his daughter. And at the end, the hero's girl died, and the bad guy got away with everything! I hated it, but Reid wouldn't shut up about it.

In fact, he wouldn't shut up about anything. Ever! He started by going on and on about how the movie was based on a true story. By the time we got to the restaurant, he was somehow onto Newport history. I heard him mention finding someone from our house. Tammy got interested and started asking questions, and maybe I would have, too, at another time, but Miguel was already bored, and I didn't want to keep Reid going. We just sat and waited for the food to come so Reid could put something in his mouth and finally shut up.

He talked <u>all night long</u>! Miguel and I didn't care about any of it at all. Reid could have been talking to a wall instead of talking to us. Then his voice could have bounced off the wall and come back to him. I bet Reid would like that. He must love the sound of his own voice to keep going on and on so much.

I don't understand how Tammy can put up with him. Maybe she stuffs her ears with cotton, like that guy in the story we read in English last year about the sailors and the sirens, and just reads his lips. I figure she's got patience with all those sisters—but wow!

All I know is no more double dates with them for me again! And I already warned Ruby and Jeff not to double up with them either.

That's if I get another chance to go into town. Wanda thinks I should spend more time with Smithy. She acts like I don't do anything around here. Piers appreciates me though. He always thanks me for my work when he's here and says I give good descriptions of all my lessons in the journals. That will help other scientists teach their apes if anybody tries to replicate our experiment. I think Wanda's just jealous because I have a boyfriend and she doesn't...

DIARY OF RUBY CARDINI

August 5, 1974

We received some terrible news today. Shortly after breakfast, a long-distance telephone call came in for Tammy. At first, we were excited. We seldom receive calls, unless Piers is phoning in instructions. Tammy took the call in the library and after a bit, I heard crying. When I looked in on her, she was sitting on the floor in tears.

The call had come from Tammy's aunt to tell her that her grandmother had died during the night. Although her nana had lived with Tammy's aunt's family, she and Tammy had been close all her life. This has been a big blow to Tammy. They hadn't seen each other since Tammy left for school in the spring. She had been planning to visit her nana in November for the Holy Days.

I sat next to her and held her hand as she told me all of this. Smithy looked in on us and returned a few moments later with a box of Kleenex. I asked Wanda about that later, but she insists nobody gave it to him. He'd spontaneously made the offering himself. He also gave Tammy a hug. She was touched.

So Tammy will be leaving us briefly. She goes home tomorrow for her nana's funeral, but says she'll be back by the end of the week. I would have thought Tammy would want to stay on longer to be with her family and grieve or sort out the estate, but she says she doesn't want to leave our project short-staffed. Maybe she's worried Piers will replace her if she takes a longer leave, although she said he sounded supportive when she told him about her trip.

I hope she returns soon. I shouldn't be so selfish, but I enjoy her company, and she balances out Wanda. It's too quiet in the house now. None of us knows what to say or do. Smithy seems uneasy, too. Sad, sad days...

ARCHIVAL FILM FOOTAGE

Date: July 1974, Audio Commentary Recorded August 1974
Location: The Solarium

Smithy plays on the floor with large colorful stuffed blocks, unattended. Maisie sleeps in the corner behind him. Suddenly, Maisie's ears twitch. She sits up and whines, staring straight ahead. The fur on her back bristles. Maisie yelps and runs out of the room. Smithy pauses in his play and turns to look after the fleeing dog. He turns again to his blocks and continues to play for a moment, then turns to stare into thin air. Smithy shifts his body, so his back is to the doorway, and hunches protectively over his blocks. After a few seconds, he turns back again to look at the same spot by the door. This time, he signs, "Who what?" He pauses and signs, "Toys mine go out." A series of voiceovers plays over the scene.

Gail asks, "Is he talking to Maisie? She just went out."

Eric replies, "I don't think so."

In the footage, Smithy resumes playing, but squirms as if in discomfort. Again, he turns to look at the door. He signs, "No happy go out." A third time he signs, "Go out."

Jeff asks, "What do you make of this?"

Ruby says, "I've seen something like this before! Wanda wrote it up as Smithy 'was acting defiantly,' but *I* thought he was talking to an imaginary friend!"

Eric laughs and says, "No way!"

"Why not? La Fontaine reported that Osage would sometimes sign to her dolls in the absence of live people," Ruby says. "Why couldn't Smithy sign to a make-believe person?"

Gail says, "That's far out! We've got to tell Piers. He'll be thrilled! This will prove that Smithy is far more advanced than we thought. He has an imagination!"

"I'm not so sure," Jeff says.

In the film, Smithy hugs himself and rocks back and forth, whimpering. All the while, he continues to stare fixedly at the wall. He jerks his head back with a small cry and leaps up, then runs out of the room just as Maisie did before him.

The screen turns white. The audio commentary continues.

Jeff says, "Ruby's suggestion is enticing, but let's refrain from speculating about Smithy's inner life, at least until we've observed some more examples. We'll treat this as we would his use of a new sign: if we can find three to five more examples of this type of behavior—either him speaking to inanimate objects or speaking to imaginary people—within the next few weeks, then I'm all for bringing it to Piers. But we don't want to jump the gun or look foolish."

"Have you shown this to Wanda yet?" Eric asks.

Jeff says, "No. I only reviewed the footage this morning, and she had already left for the university. You're my first test audience. She'll be next, and then, depending on what she thinks, I'll show it to Piers."

"This'll blow everybody's minds if we're right!" Ruby says, excitedly.

Jeff says, "Yeah…I just wonder why he was so jumpy toward the end."

LETTER FROM GAIL EHRLICH
TO VANESSA EHRLICH

August 8, 1974

(EXCERPT)

...*It's not my fault! I swear! I don't smoke. I've never even tried a joint before. I don't know what happened, but everybody's mad at me and Piers is even saying he might have to send me home, but none of it is my fault. I didn't do anything wrong!*

I was reading in bed last night. Since Tammy's been away, it's been hard to fall asleep. I'm used to having her nearby and knowing if I need anything, I can holler. When I'm on my own, the room feels bigger and a little spooky. I know that's silly because I'm not a little girl anymore. I'm almost twenty. But that's the way it is.

Because I can't sleep as good anymore, I've been reading at night. Last night I had this big book on the anthropology of language that Wanda wanted me to read. I don't know why because Smithy can't talk, and this book is about the sounds people make when they first start learning to talk, but Wanda wanted me to learn this stuff anyway because she says Smithy's aquisition of words follows the same process as a kid who's first learning to talk. She said it would help me with my work. The book is huge with teeny tiny writing in two columns going up and down the page and it's super boring, so I figured it would be perfect for putting me to sleep. And it was.

I was reading and rereading this one page about generalization (Tammy's always talking about that but what she says makes more sense than what's in this book), and I just drifted off. I left the lamp on because I was reading. I know that.

I woke up a little while later, feeling sick to my stomach, and it was hard to breathe. It smelled really bad in the room, and it was completely dark, except for some candles at the foot of the bed. I <u>thought</u> they were candles at first anyway because I was still half asleep. Then I realized the bed was on fire!

I jumped out of bed and started screaming. I didn't know what to do! I wanted water but I didn't have a glass by my bed or anything like that. I hit the flames with Wanda's book to put them out, but they were too hot, and my hand got burned. I tried folding over the blankets to smother the flame, but I could still feel the heat through the comforter. I screamed and screamed, but I was coughing hard, too. The fire had filled my room with smoke! I kept wondering why someone didn't come, and then I remembered Tammy was away, and I felt totally abandoned.

Then I heard Maisie barking and someone knocking on the door. I yelled at them to come in, and Ruby did. She saw what I was doing and helped me pull the blankets off the bed. She rolled them on the floor, and she told me to help push the mattress off the bed. She threw it on top of the blankets and sat on it to squish the flames. Then she opened the windows to get the smoke out.

Then Wanda came in with Eric. Ruby told them about the fire, and Eric filled Tammy's rinsing glass from the bathroom and poured water over the mattress and blankets, even though they were already out.

Ruby checked me out to see if I was hurt. The back of my hand was blistering from trying to put the fire out, so she put some cream on it. Luckily, the fire was on the very corner of the bed, away from where I was sleeping. My nightgown wasn't burned, and I wasn't burned besides my hand.

Wanda wanted to know how the fire started. She accused me of smoking in bed and dropping a cigarette in my sleep, but I don't smoke. I don't even own a pack of cigarettes. I emptied my purse to prove it, but she didn't care. She told me she was going to tell Piers all about it and get me kicked out of the study for being irresponsible. She yelled at me that I could have burned the whole house down and killed everybody, even Smithy.

Ruby tried to help me out. She said it couldn't have been a big fire because the alarm didn't go off, but Wanda said that didn't matter *because the wiring is screwy anyway, and the alarm doesn't always work. That's a scary thought! What if I didn't wake up in time to put the fire out? It could have spread, and no one would have known until it was too late.*

Eric said he would check the wiring in the morning, and he'd get Jeff to help. He thought maybe something had shorted out in the room, and a spark jumped on the blankets. I wish Wanda would listen to him. I told them how I'd left the lamp on because I was reading. But the lamp was out when the fire started. Maybe the lamp shorted out.

Ruby told me I could sleep in her room for the rest of the night because my bedroom had to air out, and I'd need a new mattress and bedclothes, anyway. She had a small bed, but we both squeezed into it. I still couldn't fall asleep, though. I was lying awake all night, thinking, What caused the fire? What happened?

It's a good thing I kept the connecting door to our rooms closed. Tammy would have killed me if I'd burned up her room while she was gone. That's if I somehow started the fire. And I know I didn't! *I have no idea how it started, and I'm scared. What if it happens again?*

Piers came back today and met with me privately. He scolded me and said I should know better than to take chances in an old house, especially one with lots of other people in it. He thinks I was smoking, too, or playing with candles or something because the fire definitely started in the bed. It wasn't a wire or the lamp. I cried and told him all the same things I'd said before, but he said he didn't want to hear any excuses. He said he was giving me a warning, and if I do anything else wrong, I'm out.

It's not fair! None of this is my fault. I almost died and nobody even cares!

EXCERPT FROM LETTER BY RUBY CARDINI
TO SARAH-BETH ANDREWS

August 10, 1974

(EXCERPT)

… *Tammy has returned. She's subdued (she's even wearing full mourning attire), but she's back and seems happy to be here. Nor does she want to take it easy. Wanda offered her a reduced workload, but Tammy told her, "No, thanks. I want to get back to business as usual. The work will help take my mind off my troubles." I admire that attitude. Heaven knows I'd be a wreck for days if anything happened to someone in my family.*

There was a slight hiccup with Smithy. When Eric brought him downstairs to greet Tammy, Smithy pulled away from her when she tried to give him a hug. Tammy made a joke about it, saying, "I've been gone so long, he doesn't remember me." Still, I could tell she felt hurt, especially because Smithy had been so affectionate with her just before she left.

I don't know what his problem is. Eric said he signed that they were going to see Tammy, and according to Eric, Smithy acted happy about their pending meeting. It's not that he doesn't recognize Tammy anymore. During lessons, he responded to instructions to "Give Tammy the ball/cat/crayon." But he's skittish when he's around her. He watches her all the time, and the hair stands up on the back of his neck, as if he's afraid she'll turn and attack him.

Maybe it's some kind of separation anxiety, and he's afraid she's going to suddenly leave again. It's weird because Smithy's never behaved that way toward Piers, and he's always leaving for days at a time to go back to the university for an interview or a lecture tour.

Then again, Smithy's behavior has been unpredictable lately. Today, he managed to break out of Trevor Hall and go on a short spree!

Wanda had put him down for his nap and locked the door so he wouldn't get up too early and wander around. We also lock the windows when he's in the room by himself. Then Wanda came downstairs to discuss research issues with us. Gail got up to use the bathroom and came running back into the dining room, shouting that Smithy was loose in the backyard.

At first, no one believed her; we'd been sitting in view of the stairs, and no one had seen Smithy come down. Still, Tammy and I went to the solarium to look, and Jeff checked Smithy's room. We girls didn't see him in the yard, but Jeff called out that one window was open. Somehow that little sneak had figured out how to get all the way to the top row of unobstructed windows (without a ladder or a tall enough shelf) and open the lock. _Then_ he climbed down the side of the building and ran away!

We rushed outside to look for him. We tried calling his name. I shook the trees in case he'd decided to climb one. We were in a panic. He could have gone anywhere! Nightmare scenarios flashed through our minds. A car might have hit him, or he might have gotten scared and bitten somebody that he saw on the street, or he might have been kidnapped for the exotic pet trade...

Instead, he went next door to play. All right, Herbert Terrace isn't exactly the house next door. It's probably a quarter- to a half-mile down Bellevue Avenue, but it's the closest property to ours. It's close enough that we could hear screaming coming from the property while we were in our backyard. So we ran in search of the commotion.

At first, the locked gate to the mansion stymied us. Jeff climbed up the wall to get onto the property; Eric and Tammy followed, but Tammy stopped to unfasten the gate and let the rest of us through. We ran around to the back of the house where the Belancourts, the owners, have a beautiful garden. It's landscaped and terraced (maybe that's where the house gets its name) and so unlike our own untamed lawn with rampant roses. They have a swinging bench on the veranda, and some picnic tables with a canopy were set up on the patio. Smithy had crashed a party in progress.

Poor Smithy was held hostage up in a tree. The Belancourts have an enormous dog—some kind of mastiff, I think—and it had cornered

Smithy. Our boy was high in the branches, screaming and shaking. The dog was going crazy, barking, snarling, and jumping. I'm sure if he could have climbed, he would have gone up after our chimp. One of the child guests was crying because she was afraid the dog and Smithy were going to hurt each other. Mr. Belancourt was trying to pull the dog away and oh, was he furious!

The family was having a reunion that day. They had set up the tables for lunch but then had gone around to another part of the house to take a group photo. When the family returned to the backyard, they found Smithy rocking on their bench and chowing down on their appetizers. The out-of-towners knew nothing about a chimp in the neighborhood, and they panicked. The Belancourts know about our experiment, but of course they never expected to find Smithy at their own house. Someone had already called the police to catch and remove him when we came running up.

Mr. Belancourt finally dragged his dog back inside the house. We called out to Smithy that it was safe to come down, but he clung to his branch. Jeff had to climb up the tree and carry him down. I was afraid he was going to come crashing down and break his neck. Those branches looked so flimsy!

I kept apologizing to all the Belancourts and reassuring them Smithy wasn't dangerous. I said he was only playful and had broken out in search of some adventure. I don't think any of them really listened. Some yelled at me and weren't very polite in their choice of words.

At last, Jeff came down, cradling Smithy, both in one piece. We left Eric and Wanda to talk down the police (Eric has such a friendly, reassuring way with people, and Wanda's so organized and forceful that we knew she could explain) and took our boy home. This time, Jeff stayed in Smithy's room with him, trying to calm him down. He complained all the while about the dog and his audacity in trying to get Smithy, as if he'd completely forgotten _Smithy_ had trespassed on the dog's home territory! He even tried to give Smithy a pep talk, telling him, "You could have taken him, buddy! You could ride that dog like a pony!"

Wanda came back to tell us the police were not going to fine or arrest us, but we were under orders to keep Smithy secure. Eric went to the hardware store to get some new, stronger locks. The alternative would be to board up the windows. None of us can figure out what Smithy did to the original lock. My own hope is this excursion will have shaken him sufficiently that he doesn't try to tinker with the new locks or attempt a future break-out.

Mrs. Belancourt shares those hopes. She came to Trevor Hall later in the afternoon to give us a piece of her mind. She's a stylish lady, petite, blonde, and proper, but she's also tough. She's got a fierce temper and isn't afraid to show it. We apologized over and over and swore we would keep a closer eye on Smithy and that it wouldn't happen again. I told her how much I liked seeing her beautiful house every time I entered or left Bellevue Avenue. She smiled but remained firm. I'll do whatever I can to keep Smithy away from her home and her great big dog, too, because I don't want to incur her wrath again.

At least we're going to be getting some help soon in looking after Smithy. Believe me—we're due for a break. Even when he isn't going AWOL, he keeps us on our toes. I'm not sure what Piers told the Meyer School teachers to convince them to take Smithy, but I hope they don't regret it. He was sweet when our team started working with him, but by now, he's in his full-blown terrible twos…

DIARY OF RUBY CARDINI

August 20, 1974

The festivities are over. The dining room is still covered in streamers and whatever balloons Smithy didn't manage to pop, but we're too pooped to bother with intensive clean-up. Tonight was for celebrating.

We held a joint "birthday bash" for Gail and Wanda at the house. It was Piers's idea to celebrate them together by ordering pizza and eating in the dining room instead of going out to a restaurant or a bar. Wanda's birthday was last Friday, and Gail's is next Friday, so he picked tonight for the big event because it was smack in the middle of both dates.

Jeff thinks Piers wanted to do it this way because he's a cheapskate. I believe Piers wanted us to feel at home by doing something fun in our own space where we usually work, work, work. (Though Tammy's point that he probably didn't want us partying with the locals after they got everyone riled at my birthday is valid). I'm impressed Piers took the time off to come back to the house for the occasion. Wanda seemed pleased, too.

Gail was chagrined no friends from town could come, but I enjoyed having a party just for our gang. Though we see each other every day, it felt different to be in party mode instead of teaching or disciplining. Everyone was looser, happier. Piers was the life of the party! He distributed party hats and blowers and even put on a hat himself. More than that, he sang along with Wanda's records and told dirty jokes as the night dragged on. No wonder he's been able to get funding for this project. The man can schmooze!

Smithy was fascinated by everything he saw and heard. We put a little party hat on him, though he soon tugged it off and tried to peer through it as though it were a telescope. He loved the party blowers. I tried to tickle him with the end of mine, and he jerked back, wide-eyed, and ran and hid behind the door. But his courage soon returned, and the next time someone (Eric) blew one, Smithy tried to grab the wiggling paper end. Teasing him with the horn became a game for the rest of the night. Gail and Wanda stood on either side of him for a photo op, and Jeff snapped several shots of them blowing their party horns at Smithy simultaneously. He didn't know which to reach for first, but eventually figured he could use two hands and got to spend the rest of the evening playing with his captured prizes.

Smithy danced with us, too. First, I led him out for "Ruby Tuesday," then we switched albums, and Gail rocked out with him to "Rebel, Rebel." Wanda even twisted with Smithy a bit but danced the next two sets with Piers, who is a very smooth dancer. I'll bet he took lessons. Of course, he danced with Gail to be fair. He even invited Tammy to dance, but she shut him down with an elaborate (and hopefully fabricated) story about how she had broken her prom date's foot.

When the pizza boy arrived, we had even more fun by sending Smithy out to meet him with the money. We hid behind the stairs and almost died choking on our laughter at the sight of a little chimp in suspenders, a bowtie, and a party hat in the doorway, the way the delivery boy's eyes bulged in proportion to his widening mouth, and the spectacle they both made when the guy set the pizzas on the ground as an offering and ran back to his car with Smithy behind him, still waving a fistful of Lincolns over his head. Jeff had to chase after them to keep Smithy from escaping, and to settle our account properly. By the time he came back with our boy, we were rolling on the floor.

Wanda praised the flowers and the hair combs that I gave her for her birthday, but she seemed to prefer Jeff's gift: a dartboard. I hope she's not planning to stick any of our pictures in the bull's-eye.

I wasn't sure what to do for Gail. Our styles are so different that I wouldn't know what kind of clothes or accessories she might like. Tammy gave her a journal; I suspect that's a gift Tammy herself would enjoy. Finally, I settled on a little painting of the ocean and the Cliff Walk. This way, she can still see the ocean even with no windows facing it. Tammy promised to help Gail find a place to hang it ("I'll start by tearing down that old David Cassidy poster.")

When the time came for cake, Smithy took the initiative to blow out the candles himself. The girls didn't mind. Before cutting the cake, Piers made a grand speech. He saluted our birthday girls and spoke about how each has contributed to the study. Then he told us to look around the room at one another.

"All of you have contributed: to the study, to Webster's education, and above all, to Trevor Hall. By that, I don't mean you've become stewards of the house, though it looks better than it did when I signed the lease. I mean you've fulfilled one of the foundational requirements of the study: you've transformed Trevor Hall into a home. <u>Our</u> home. We're a family now, and I expect we'll share many more happy holidays here in the months to come."

Tammy picked up the thread, albeit satirically. "He's right," she said. "You all feel like family to me. Ruby is like my sixth sister, and Eric is my annoying little brother."

Eric objected, "I'm older than you by a year."

"But mentally, you're much younger," Tammy retorted.

Gail made her own toast. Piers had given her champagne, even though Tammy suggested sparkling water would be better. I think some of the bubbles may have gone to Gail's head, for she was certainly effusive. But her words were heartfelt. "This is the best present ever! Having you all here with me is just super! I was real nervous about being away from home for the first time, and even though Trevor Hall turned out to be a beautiful place, and all of you are beautiful people, I was bummed about having my birthday away from my family. But you came through for me, because you're my family, too! This party has been fabulous! And knowing I can lean on you, and talk to you, and learn from you is better than I can find the words to say!"

Wanda spoke more formally, first thanking us for embracing the goals of the study and stepping up to meet the demands of performance. "It's been an honor to work with each of you. We have a brilliant and dynamic team here. Together, we can make a difference in the field of human and animal psychology. I know this because of how you've made a difference here at Trevor Hall. Piers is absolutely right: you've taken an assignment and built genuine connections. You've made us into a family, and that's a result you can't make in a lab."

It made me feel good to hear them speak that way. I used to wish I had a big sister instead of a brother, even though Vincent was never really all that bad. I'd love to have Tammy as my sister, even symbolically.

Though I'm not sure I want to count Jeff as a brother. That would make our recent activities illegal...

For all that we may disagree about how best to bring up Smithy, however much we may occasionally annoy each other, we've a strong spirit of camaraderie. Living in Trevor Hall feels richer than I imagine the Trumbull dorms could have ever been. I've been estranged from my own family for so long. I'd forgotten how it feels to be surrounded by laughter, hospitality, and acceptance. To have your own place at the dinner table. Here, in my pseudo-home, I've found another family.

MEMO FROM DR. PREIS-HERALD
TO WANDA KARLEWICZ

August 21, 1974

My next presentation for the Board of Regents is set for 26th Monday. I intend to screen the film of Webster's lessons in colors, complete with a discussion of his innovation of the "black" sign. The psychological reasoning behind this development is complex enough to intrigue them. Jeff has urged me to show the "imaginary friend" dialogue also, but that involves a more tenuous assumption about Webster's inner life. If this behavior persists, we may consider it for the next round.

I should like to have some film from Webster's sessions at the Meyer School for comparison. I've spoken with Jeff, and he's agreed to sit in on classes the first week and rush the cuts over the weekend. Please notify me as soon as his footage is available; if possible, courier it to me yourself.

In addition, I recommend a longer leave of absence for Tammy. Her gloomy mood mustn't be allowed to affect Webster. He refuses to interact with her unless pressured to do so. I've urged her to return to her family, but she's stubborn. I suspect she doesn't wish to appear weak before me. Talk to her and help her see our research must take precedence over her personal determination.

I hope you saved your birthday wish for our prospects. I'll call after the meeting. Many happy returns once again!

— PPH

DIARY OF RUBY CARDINI

August 23, 1974

Tammy's officially out of mourning. I'm sure she's still sad about her nana, but the black is gone, and she's smiling again. Smithy can sense the change. He's cuddling up to her again and pulling her hair and running off with her glasses. Tammy seems glad about it. So am I.

EXCERPT FROM
SMITHY: A TWENTY-YEAR COMPENDIUM
BY REID BENNETT, PHD

CHAPTER FIVE: THINGS FALL APART

As the summer of 1974 ended, and autumn's chill took hold, the nation still reeled from Richard Nixon's unprecedented resignation and equally astounding pardon. The change of seasons was mirrored in the transfer of power and the transition to a new era.

At Trevor Hall, life was also in flux. The days shortened, and the temperatures dropped; some passions flared, while others guttered and died. As the researchers dwelled on their personal lives, none of them dreamed of the impending bombshells soon to shatter their peace and permanently alter the course of their study...

"OUTTAKE REEL" FOOTAGE

Date: August 28, 1974
Location: The hallway connecting the
kitchen with the back stairs

Jeff smiles into the camera and nods in approval. He says, "There! Ready to capture the scholar coming down for his first day of school."

Ruby, off camera, says, "We should have gotten a little bookbag for him to take."

Jeff says, "Oh, you're right. Hey, maybe I can pick one up in town and stage the 'first day' again later. Oh, well. Breakfast ready yet?"

Ruby, off-camera, says, "Just about. Is Smithy ready yet?"

Jeff says, "He was still sleeping when I last looked in on him. The cats and the dog were dozing at the foot of his bed. Postcard perfect."

"You almost hate to wake him," she remarks.

Jeff says, "Yeah, but it's gotta be done. Big day and all. Oh, Smi-*thee*!" He starts up the stairs but almost trips over Harriet as she zips down. Jeff clings to the banister. "Whoa!"

The sounds of yowling and whimpering grow louder, and both Peter and Maisie race down the stairs and run into the solarium. Ruby hurries out of the kitchen and asks, "What's happening? Is it another fire?"

Smithy charges down the stairs after the other animals, hissing and screeching. Jeff catches him and struggles to hold him. He says, "No!" He speaks and signs simultaneously. "Bad Smithy. No."

Smithy clings to him and signs, "Up hug Smithy." Jeff scoops up the chimp, and Smithy clings to him, shaking. Jeff says, "I'm going to put him back in his room for a time-out. Will you call the school and explain that we're going to be late today?"

Ruby says, "Sure, but first I'm going to check on the pets to make sure they're not injured." Ruby enters the solarium, and Jeff carries Smithy up the stairs.

Smithy begins to struggle and worms his way out of Jeff's grasp. He tries to run to the solarium. Jeff grabs him and fights to hold on. He says and signs, "No! No chase. Bad. Bad."

Smithy points up the stairs and covers his eyes.

Jeff shakes his head and signs, "No sleep." Aloud, he says, "No, you're not going back to bed. You're just going to sit in time out." He starts up the stairs again; Smithy whines and burrows his head in Jeff's neck. Jeff says, "Sorry, buddy, but you've got to learn how to behave. No bothering the other animals. You're going back to your room whether you like it or not. Oh, Ruby, can you—?" He half-turns toward the camera, then shakes his head and resumes his climb, shifting Smithy on his hip. "Never mind, I'll switch it off later."

VIDEO FOOTAGE: "20/20" INTERVIEW WITH GAIL BEVERIDGE

(CONTINUED)

Broadcast Date: April 6, 1989

Gail sits in her living room, telling her story.

After the first month or so, the excitement—and the intimidation—of teaching language to a chimp began to wear off, and we started to notice...other things.

Such as?

Lots of...mishaps. Things disappeared and then turned up in weird places or were never seen again.

She pauses.

And there were lots of fires. At first, we figured, "Well, this is an old house," and blamed the accidents on bad wiring. Nothing was ever seriously damaged, but it was spooky. You could be working in a room and suddenly, you'd smell smoke, and when you turned around—fire! They usually started in the corners, low to the ground. We seldom found any cause. It might start near an electrical outlet, or it might start on the carpet in the middle of an empty room. I remember one day, Tammy and I were trying to bake cookies with Smithy. They were a gesture of goodwill for our neighbors at Herbert Terrace. Smithy had gotten out of the house and caused some havoc over there, so we wanted to sweeten them up. Wanda suggested Tammy take them cookies because she was friendly with Mrs. Belancourt. It was partly my fault Smithy got out, so all three of us baked while Jeff filmed us...

The screen cuts to archival film footage circa August 1974.

Location: The Kitchen

Smithy sits on the counter near the sink beside a mixing bowl, watching as Tammy opens the oven door. Gail holds a tray of cookies and leans forward to put them inside. Smithy claps his hands over his eyes and an instant later, a jet of flame shoots out of the oven.

Gail's voiceover comments, "I was so scared. If I had been one second faster with that tray, my face would have burned off!"

In the film, Gail screams and jumps back, dropping the tray. She covers her face. At the same time, Tammy leaps back and kicks the oven door closed. She pulls Gail backward, and they huddle beside the sink. Jeff runs on camera with a fire extinguisher. Tammy waves an oven mitt at him. Jeff grabs it and jerks the oven door open with one hand while spraying the extinguisher at the now-roaring flames. While Tammy and Jeff consult each other about the fire, Gail turns to Smithy and signs, "OK?" Smithy looks around the kitchen with a downcast face. He covers his eyes again, and Gail hugs him.

The camera cuts back to the interview. Gail sits upright in her chair as she watches the footage play.

There! Did you see what he just did? That's his sign for "dark."

That's the second time he made that sign. Let's back that up.

The camera cuts to a slow-motion replay of the film just before the fire erupts. Smithy covers his eyes, and the flame blasts out of the oven.

There! He did that just before the fire…I can't believe I never noticed that before. I always thought he was covering his eyes so he wouldn't see me burned, but he covered them *first*. Oh, my god!

Gail laughs nervously.

What caused that fire?

We never found out. Jeff examined the oven, and we even called in a repairman. We kept Smithy in his room so the guy wouldn't freak out. He thought it might be a faulty gas line but couldn't find anything for sure. He said the oven looked good for its age. He tried to sell us a new appliance, and Tammy and I pushed for one, but Wanda and Piers said we couldn't afford it. I refused to use the oven after that, but we never had any more problems with it. And I remember this one time in the dining room, while Smithy was eating lunch with us…

ARCHIVAL FILM FOOTAGE

Date: September 2, 1974
Location: The Dining Room

Eric, Wanda, Gail, Tammy, Ruby, Smithy, and Jeff sit around the table, which is spread with a platter of sandwiches, a bowl of apples and oranges, a bowl of potato salad, a chip and dip platter, and a pitcher and glasses of punch.

Wanda looks up at the camera and smiles. "Good afternoon! We originally planned to go out for a picnic today to celebrate the holiday, but the weather had other plans. We're still having our picnic, albeit indoors."

Tammy loads food onto a plate. Gail signs, "Smithy, what do you want? An apple or an orange?" Smithy looks up at the ceiling. He whimpers, covers his eyes, and tries to jump down from his chair, but Ruby catches and seats him again. Gail says, "Smithy, an *apple* or an *orange*? He's not paying attention."

Eric says, "It's those faces again."

Tammy says, "It's because they don't move or respond to him. He used to try to sign to them, but when they didn't react, he got fussy."

Ruby suggests, "Maybe we could blindfold them, so they don't look like they're staring."

Tammy says, "Waiting for you to spill something on your blouse…"

Wanda replies, "That's not necessary; Smithy seldom spends any time in this room. Besides, I'd rather no one risked climbing a ladder tall enough to reach the ceiling unless we absolutely had to."

During their exchange, Smithy continues to squirm and hoot. Eric kneels beside him and says, "Calm down, little guy. They can't hurt you. Here, what do you want to eat?" He signs, "Eat." He says out loud, "How about a chip?" as he reaches behind him for the bag of potato chips. Smithy screeches and covers his eyes. He lowers his hands and looks up.

Ruby says to Jeff, "Now he's trying to hide from the faces. Aww…They're still there, Smithy."

Smithy rapidly covers and uncovers his face three more times. The final time, he leaves his hands over his eyes. A flash of light explodes near the ceiling. Gail screams. "Fire!"

Eric yells, "Holy smoke!"

"Everybody stay calm!" Wanda yells as she shields Smithy, holding him in place. Eric dashes from the room. Ruby crouches down at the far corner of the table with her plate over her head. Tammy circles the table, moving away from the flame but continuing to gaze up at it.

From off camera, Jeff calls out, "Everybody leave the room calmly. Don't get Smithy excited."

Eric runs back into the room, carrying a fire extinguisher. He aims it at the flames nibbling across the ceiling and calls, "Get down, everyone!"

Smithy screams. Wanda strokes his fur to calm him, and Eric releases the fire extinguisher. Ruby says, "Eric, you got it. That's it. Thank you!"

Eric says, "Don't mention it. Now we know why he was so upset. Good boy!" He squeezes Smithy's shoulder and signs, "Thank you."

Ruby says, "You think he knew this was going to happen?"

Eric says, "He could've smelled the smoke."

Tammy says, "I didn't see any smoke, only flame. Where did the fire even come from? Did a light fixture explode? I don't see any broken bulbs."

Wanda says, "Everyone, let's adjourn for now. I'll call the firefighters and have them check out this room to make sure it's safe."

"Come on, Smithy." Gail holds out her hand.

Smithy looks up and past her. He gazes up at the angel faces and signs, "Go away."

Gail says, "That's right, Smithy. We're leaving." She takes the chimp's hand, and he eagerly accompanies her out of the room.

Tammy continues to stare up at the ceiling. She says, "I can't even see a scorch mark up there this time."

"Eric must have gotten it in time," Ruby replies.

Tammy says, "Gotten what? If the wiring—"

Wanda interrupts. "Ladies, please." She takes each woman by the arm and steers them out of the room.

Tammy resists Wanda's pull and reaches toward the wall. "Wait, what's behind the curtain? Is that a mark? If the fire came out of the wall, why didn't the curtains smolder? I saw a fireball smack in the middle of the ceiling—didn't you, Ruby?"

"Maybe a jet of flame traveled down the wall?" she replies.

Wanda says, "We'll have the firemen investigate. I'm sure they'd like nothing better than to visit us again..." She propels Tammy and Ruby out the door.

Part of Tammy's speech is garbled as she exits. "...nothing flammable up there...looked pretty concentrated to me!"

VIDEO FOOTAGE: "20/20" INTERVIEW WITH GAIL BEVERIDGE

(CONTINUED)

Broadcast Date: April 6, 1989

Gail's voiceover plays over a montage of still photos.

He normally couldn't stand that room, and that blaze kept us out for a while because of the smoke smell.

Ruby stands in the dining room, holding back a curtain and pointing to a round scorch mark, approximately five inches in diameter, near the joining of the ceiling and the wall; a carved angel face is visible above her. Scorch marks on a wall measure approximately one foot above the floor and spread eighteen inches across a corner and onto the adjacent wall; tape measures show the size of the damage. Scorch marks on a tile floor are approximately eight inches wide; the claw foot of a bathtub is visible in the upper right corner of the photo.

Many nights that summer, at all hours, the alarms went off, and we'd jump out of bed and run around the house, trying to find where the fire was this time, so we could keep it from spreading. Luckily, when we did find a blaze, it was somewhere easy to spot, like the kitchen or the library. We were always thankful it wasn't in the closed-off wing, so we didn't have to go room to room opening doors. Of course, lots of times we never found anything—no smoke and no fire—so we'd write it off as a faulty alarm and creep back to bed, hoping we wouldn't burn alive because of someplace we'd overlooked.

The camera cuts back to Gail, seated.

Was Smithy always present during the fires?

You're thinking he was setting them? We considered that, too. Around the same time the fires were popping up, Smithy kept breaking out of his room. Sometimes he'd go next door, sometimes he'd just run around in our yard or explore the house. No matter what we did, he'd find a way out, either by getting the door to his room open, or by managing to get out the windows. The windows were twelve feet high and *locked!* So because he kept sneaking out when we weren't looking, we thought he could have been making fires behind our backs or when we were asleep. It never made sense to me, personally. Smithy hated when Piers smoked, and Piers always lit his pipes with matches, so why would Smithy want anything to do with matches? Besides, it was scary to think our little furry child might be trying to burn the house down around us!

I don't believe that was the right explanation, but it was easier to believe than…some of the other ideas. I still remember the first time Eric brought up the possibility and the exact words Wanda said to him: "This is just an old house. Stop trying to frighten everyone by accusing Smithy of arson. That's almost as silly as blaming your new friends' ghost." Weird, huh? Eric thought Smithy might be doing it because we were getting ready to send him to school. Not that Smithy understood what we were planning and was plotting against us, but he could pick up on our anticipation and knew *something* was about to happen. Eric figured he was trying to get attention…

LETTER FROM TAMMY COHEN
TO COHEN FAMILY

September 9, 1974

(EXCERPT)

...Our chimp has begun attending school in Providence, so we now have a "half-day" of our own for recreation, just like the servants of old. The Harvey H. Meyer School for the Deaf is a small, privately run foundation. Three of the teachers are paid faculty, and the rest are volunteers or interns, but all are fluent in sign language, which is more than I can say for myself, even after three months of heavy practice.

I drive Smithy to school, and that's given me the opportunity to meet two full-time instructors, Hope Wellborn and Simon Gagnon, and one part-time volunteer, a bright young woman named Sarah McMann. All were polite and supportive of our study goals. I think they hope to gain favorable publicity for their school through Piers's publications. He must have promised them something to persuade them to dedicate their limited time and resources to a non-paying animal.

It's hard to say how much this new schooling will contribute. In the sessions I've observed so far, Smithy's spent more time manipulating the teacher than making words. He frequently signs "dirty," even though he then doesn't use the toilet. I first wondered if this was a residual from training, when I took him to the bathroom every fifteen minutes whether he needed it or not, just to get him to associate the toilet with the need. Then I realized the threat of a mess guarantees his instructor will rush him out of the room and away from his dull lesson. This trick supports his intelligence, though not in the way Piers intended.

I think context plays a more significant role in learning than Piers has considered. Smithy has developed a relationship with us, his caretakers. *He's fond of us. He readily signs for Wanda, who is practically his surrogate mother. The Meyer classroom is an artificial setting, and the teachers are merely functional. Consequently, his investment in them and motivation to cooperate is lessened.*

While Smithy may not be getting the full benefit of his classroom time, the rest of us are appreciative. I feel more rested with extra time to myself. As you can see, I'm able to write more verbose letters. I'm spending more time with my housemates, too. Ruby and I take long walks around the wharf and the historic neighborhoods; she's fascinated by the old architecture and the ambience of the port city. Gail and I have also gone shopping. Once, she even persuaded me to come dancing at a makeshift disco in a little dive on the edge of town. When not with one of them, I'll go for a jog with Maisie, Piers's dog. The shady avenues of Newport are scenic as well as physically challenging.

Our neighbor, Christine Belancourt, met me when I returned from my latest jog and reported Smithy was bathing in her fountain. Somehow, he managed to slip the brand-new lock on his room, prompting Eric to declare that "Smithy" is really short for "locksmith." We'll have to brainstorm new ways to keep Smithy at home...

MEMO FROM TAMMY COHEN

September 10, 1974

Re: Classroom Learning v. In-Home Learning

Webster has logged nearly thirty hours of instructional time with credentialed ASL teachers over the past two weeks. However, his progress has not been concomitant with the amount or quality of instruction he's received. I believe the following causes are at fault:

1. The learning environment is artificial. The classroom is staged for top-down teaching with little flexibility, as opposed to our naturalistic home environment and give-and-take style.

2. The practice environment doesn't match the applied environment. Research suggests the environment where a student learns should resemble the environment where he performs the material. Hence, students are advised to study for a school exam in a quiet, well-lit room because the classroom where they test will be quiet and well-lit. Webster's school environment should match his home environment because he's more likely to use ASL at home than in an artificial classroom.

3. The relationship between student and teacher impacts student performance. The Meyer School teachers only have a professional relationship to Webster. He's not invested in them emotionally and lacks internal motivation to please them. Webster

might be motivated to perform better if his classroom instructors engaged him in play or grooming activities.

In conclusion, Webster's performance in school lags behind his performance at home because the classroom is too restrictive and foreign, and his instructors are too distant and formal. Changing these factors should yield more favorable results.

MEMO FROM WANDA KARLEWICZ

September 11, 1974

I respectfully disagree with Tammy's suggestions because they are impractical and burdensome.

We cannot expect the Meyer School teachers to alter their classroom practices to our liking. In the fifty years since the school first opened, eighty-five percent of graduates have gone on to pursue higher education. Their methods work.

A classroom environment does differ from the home, but an intelligent being must adapt to new circumstances. We must demonstrate Webster can learn and produce new signs with people other than ourselves; otherwise, we subject ourselves to accusations of "leading" Webster a la Clever Hans.

I believe Webster's struggles with the formality of the classroom results from the lack of discipline at Trevor Hall. I've striven to maintain an orderly schedule with regular teaching times and predictable methods, yet my attempts have been met with lackluster enthusiasm and reversion to playing and coddling.

To support the wonderful teachers at Harvey Meyer, who are generously assisting us at no extra charge, I again urge my fellow researchers to adhere to an organized, consistent, daily routine for Webster.

MEMO FROM PIERS PREIS-HERALD

September 12, 1974

After discussing some of the suggestions regarding Webster's education, Hope Wellborn and Simon Gagnon have agreed to include a "recess," loosely structured playtime to enable Webster to relax and bond with his instructor, and to allow lessons to be guided, in part, by Webster's curiosity. These reforms will be in force for a three-week trial period during which Webster's engagement and word production will be monitored.
— PPH

KITCHEN JOURNAL ENTRY
FROM ERIC KANINCHEN

September 12, 1974

Smithy continues to try our patience by slipping in and out of places he doesn't belong. When I came downstairs to make breakfast, I found him in the kitchen helping himself to two different boxes of cereal. His bedroom door was ajar, though Wanda swore she locked it when she left Smithy last night.

Even more concerning is that Smithy had opened all the cupboards— including the locked cupboard under the sink where our toxic chemicals are stored. Fortunately, he did not sample the roach poison, the Drain-O, or the stove polish. But it's just a matter of time until his curiosity pushes him to check out these hazardous chemicals.

To avoid another emergency, I've boxed up all the ones I could find from the kitchen and the bathrooms and stowed them in the gatehouse's kitchenette. Although it might be a hassle to go outside to get the Pine Sol or whatever, I'd much rather put up with this inconvenience than try to resuscitate Smithy again after finding out he's poisoned himself. Having saved his life once, I feel I need to keep protecting him.

DIARY OF RUBY CARDINI

September 13, 1974

Smithy gave Jeff and me a big scare this afternoon!

We were in the solarium filming a demonstration of how Smithy can recognize both pictures of objects and the objects themselves. Using a stack of picture books and magazines like National Geographic *with real photos, I'd point to an image and ask Smithy, "What's that?" He answered correctly, regardless of whether he was looking at a photo or an illustration. For instance, he identified "tree," "tiger," and "dog."*

When I presented a picture book showing an old lady feeding pigeons, however, Smithy readily identified "birds," having just seen a photo of a flock of migrating birds, but hesitated and squirmed before signing "woman." We continued with a photo of a beach ("water") and an illustration of a car. The latter he would not name, even though Jeff bribed him with playing with the cats. Instead, Smithy whimpered and covered his eyes.

Now the car in the illustration happened to be a police car, so "black" <u>was</u> *a partially correct answer. Jeff suggested we make sure Smithy wasn't confusing the color with the object itself. I found another example in a magazine of a car with a model posing beside it. When I showed that to Smithy, he looked away, showed his teeth, and started rocking back and forth, clearly agitated. I spoke soothingly and tried to draw his attention back to the cars in the magazine and the picture book. Smithy covered his eyes, then signed, "Woman."*

It was strange that he was getting each picture only half-right (i.e., "black" for car and "woman" beside the car). I reviewed "car" with Smithy yesterday, so I knew he knew the sign, and I was frustrated that he wouldn't produce it. Nevertheless, I demonstrated the target sign again and indicated the appropriate images. Smithy produced "car," then yelped and immediately made the sign for "black." He threw his arms around me and cowered against my chest. I could feel his fur bristling and his body trembling. Jeff came over to help comfort him, and we looked at each other in consternation. What had frightened Smithy so?

I remembered Tammy speaking about object permanence and how young children sometimes panic if their mother leaves the room; if they can't see her, they believe she's ceased to exist. I suggested that Smithy might get upset whenever he signs "black" because in covering his eyes— he can't see us temporarily.

Jeff was skeptical. "I don't know. Smithy's more advanced than a toddler. And hiding objects doesn't work on him. He's always going through my pockets or digging out things he's not supposed to have when our backs are turned. He knows they're still around."

My little brainstorm wouldn't explain Smithy's fixation on the "woman" sign either. He doesn't spontaneously sign any other random words, but he made that one again as Jeff and I were speaking: first "woman, woman" singly, then the pair "dark woman."

Suddenly, Smithy bolted for the French doors. It happened so quickly that I couldn't hold him back. Before Jeff or I realized what was happening, he'd wrenched the lock off with his bare hands and tore outside!

We chased him as soon as we came to our senses and were just in time to see him climbing the gate! I knew we'd never catch him before he got loose in the neighborhood. As luck would have it, Tammy and Eric were jogging up the drive with Maisie and intercepted him. Eric plucked Smithy right off the gate and calmed him down by letting him pet the dog. I'm afraid our boy was a bit rough with her because Maisie whimpered and looked uncomfortable. Smithy remained awfully jumpy, too. The hair stood up on his back, and he trembled as he clung to her. We hauled him back up to his room, and Jeff stayed with him the rest of the day. I'm relieved no actual harm ensued from this escape, but I'm embarrassed it happened at all, especially with Piers back for the weekend.

After Smithy was in bed, we went to the gatehouse to watch Jeff's film of the aborted lesson so we could find out what had triggered Smithy's agitation. We also wanted to show the film as a demonstration of his strength. Eric examined the lock and pronounced it "trashed." However, he insists the very violence of its destruction is an argument against Smithy escaping the house that way before.

Every other time he's gotten out, none of the locks on the doors or windows have shown any scratches or other signs of force; it's as if Smithy's gotten them to unlock themselves by magic. "Either this time, he was in an awful hurry…" Eric trailed off and frowned. "Or he didn't do the other ones." Wanda asked if he thought someone else in the house was releasing Smithy from his room, and Eric got flustered and fell quiet. That's a crazy suggestion, but no one else can explain how our chimp has become Houdini.

Piers was both fascinated and puzzled by Smithy's refusal to sign "car" and his reversion to signing "woman," especially his combining it with the other sign. We tried to figure out what he could have meant: "dark woman," "sleep woman," "Get me out of here, woman!" But just as Piers once warned us, because the eye-covering sign has come to mean multiple things, it makes Smithy's message ambiguous.

We're all concerned about what his backsliding could imply. Piers just met with the board last month and said they were pleased, but if our progress stalls, or Smithy doesn't adapt to his new school, the next meeting could shut us down.

As we fretted, Gail innocuously remarked on Smithy's appearance. "He looks like one of those little monkeys—see no evil!" That set Piers off.

"He's not a monkey! He's a chimpanzee! You know better!" Gail looked startled; I thought she was going to cry. Later, Tammy and I assured her Piers wasn't angry at her, only frustrated by Smithy's odd behavior and worried about the study.

We'll resume our lessons tomorrow, and Smithy will attend classes next week as scheduled, but we'll warn his teachers that he could try to give them the slip. I hope they won't expel him if he acts up. I also hope we don't have to deal with any more such stunts here.

DIARY OF GAIL EHRLICH

September 14, 1974

Dear Diary:

If this isn't the worst day of my life, it's definitely in the top ten. Today, Miguel ~~dumped~~ ~~broke~~ said it's over. I was shocked. I thought everything was going so well. I was happy. I thought he was happy too. He kissed me goodnight on Sunday like always. I don't understand why this is happening. It's not like he has to go back to New York or someplace now that summer's over. He lives in Fall River! I can take the bus there. Did I do something to make him mad? Did I say something wrong or dumb or mean? I hope he isn't still mad at me for double dating with Reid and Tammy that time.

Doesn't he still think I'm pretty? Haven't I always done as he's asked? I've tried to be the perfect girlfriend. What happened?

The worst thing is he dumped me at breakfast this morning. In a restaurant. Full of people. Where everyone could see us. When he said it was time to stop seeing each other, I wanted to cry, and I couldn't because <u>all those people were looking.</u> Even that waitress Trish was watching us. Why did he have to do it with an audience?

I didn't stay to finish eating because I thought I was going to be sick. I wanted to go away from people to be by myself and let all my feelings out. I tried going to the Cliff Walk, but it was so crowded. I didn't want to walk through all those people while I was crying, and I didn't want to have to climb over rocks and maybe slip and fall because I couldn't see through my tears (even though it would serve Miguel right if something bad happened to me because of what he did!) I ended up coming back to Trevor Hall, but I've spent the day dodging my roomie and anyone else who's around. The house is big enough to lose yourself in.

Wanda caught me crying in the bathroom and scolded me for spending so much time feeling sorry for myself when there's so much to do around the house. She thinks the best way to deal with my problems is to get involved in work. She says my mind will be too busy to think about my pain. She doesn't get it <u>at all</u>! I think Wanda might even be glad I got jilted. I know she didn't like me going out so much. She just wants everyone to bury themselves in work like she does, and she's always going on about how Miguel's a distraction. I'll bet Wanda's happy I got dumped. The bitch!

At least Piers understands. I was sitting in the backyard on the swing when he found me. He saw I'd been crying, but <u>he</u> was nice about it. He asked me why I was unhappy and said he was sorry about Miguel. He told me he couldn't believe anybody could cast aside such a beautiful, brilliant young woman. He also told me not to waste my tears on someone so unworthy of me because with my good looks and friendly spirit, I won't be alone for long.

Maybe Piers was just saying those things to make up for yelling at me yesterday, but I felt better after hearing them. After all, he's a famous psychologist, so he must know about people. It made me happy to hear him say I was beautiful. I hope he was telling the truth, and maybe I will find someone else. Someone better than Miguel.

I <u>will</u> find someone new. And soon.

MEMO FROM JEFF DALTON

September 16, 1974

I picked up Smithy from class today. When I arrived, the lesson was still in progress; he was having such a good time that his teacher, April Heath, extended the session. They were bouncing different colored balls to review colors with him. April was crawling on the floor with Smithy and tickling him. I almost had to pry him away from her. He didn't want to leave!

April said Smithy signed more often and more accurately in this session than ever before. He showed no anxiety when asked to identify the color black and didn't make a break for it. Maybe Ruby and I were just unlucky.

I think this new teaching style has <u>definitely</u> caught on. Way to go, Tammy!

DIARY OF TAMMY COHEN

September 17, 1974

Today marks the end of the America's Cup Race and the official end of summer. Now it's time for all summer people to vanish back to their homes.

It was a surprisingly restful day for us. I sat in on Smithy's lessons, but I had time to read during the meal break and again when I got home at the end of the day. Hope and April were out with stomach flu, and Simon taught Smithy solo, though I sat nearby, prepared to pitch in if needed.

Wanda's decided Smithy's transition to part-time student is successful enough that we can now drop the pupil off and return for him at the end of the day instead of staying to observe the sessions. She'd rather have us all at home cramming new ASL vocab. So much for the half-day off plan!

Nevertheless, I agree the Meyer team is fully capable of caring for Smithy. I'm impressed by what a turnaround the faculty has made, compared to how things stood last week! I'd even say they're doing a better job of teaching than we are because, unencumbered by distractions or favoritism, Smithy is better behaved. Now he seems more comfortable in this formal situation than at the house. He concentrates more consistently and reproduces signs at a faster rate. Moreover, he's reluctant to come home at the end of the day. Does something about the house, absent from the classroom, bother him?

I wish I could concentrate more consistently, but I've been fielding distractions ever since I started to pen this entry. Gail barged in on me, still bemoaning her newly single life. She partly blames Reid—and by extension me—for her breakup. First, she complained about the movie he chose for our last—make that first and last—double date: "Not scary enough for cuddling, even though it was a murder mystery. And that pervy old guy and his daughter? Not romantic at all!" Then she complained about Reid blathering nonstop and how "poor Miguelinho" was bored. I noticed Miguel's restlessness, too, but I chalked it up to his interest in our waitress. I didn't say so to Gail at the time; I thought it would be kinder not to tell her that her crush was a cad, especially since she was unlikely to listen to me anyway. Perhaps I did wrong.

I thought it would cheer her up to learn I'd parted ways with Reid today. He suggested we could still see each other on an occasional weekend, but I pointed out all my responsibilities to Smithy and our study. It wouldn't be fair to the others if I took off once a month to visit Boston, nor fair to Reid to require him to make the trip here. The distraction might affect his studies, and that would be unfortunate.

After Gail wandered off to mope elsewhere, Eric came looking for her so they could practice with the flashcards he'd just made for Wanda's newest list. I offered to study with him, but he made some lame excuse, so it was just a ploy to spend more time with Gail.

I feel sorry for Eric. He can do much better than Gail, but I almost wish she would go out with him just to make him happy. Eric's a nice guy.

"Too nice" is how I once described him when Gail tried to set the two of us up back when we first came to Trevor Hall, by which I meant he's too·easygoing, too eager to please, too easily led. I adore Eric, but he's like family to me. I hope my comment didn't put her off him. Ah, well. Gail is lovely to look at, but what would they ever talk about?

There, now I've succeeded in distracting myself. Enough gossip. Back to the Journal of Cognition and Development.

SMITHY'S BEDROOM JOURNAL ENTRY
FROM ERIC KANINCHEN

September 18, 1974

The day is done, and Smithy is asleep. It started out promisingly. I got Smithy ready for school. He was alert and signed rapidly of his own accord. He greeted me when I entered, signing, "Smithy school now. Now hurry hurry school." The whole time I tried to dress him, he kept on signing. "Smithy go to school now" (OK, technically, "Go Smithy school now." I understood him anyway. In German, it doesn't matter what order you put the words in.)

He was eager to see his teachers. At breakfast, he signed, "See April. See Simon. See Sarah now. Smithy wants Simon and Hope." (Well, "Give me Simon Hope now.") I was glad he was so gung ho to go to school, but I was kinda miffed, too. Smithy's never that happy to see us. I've never seen him say, "Give me Eric" or "See Jeff now," anyway. But as Tammy pointed out, the Meyer teachers can afford to be the "fun parents." They can be his buddy for a few hours and send him home at the end of the day.

I made the mistake of getting Hope's hopes up when I dropped Smithy off because I told her how eager he was to work with her again after she was out yesterday. He must've missed her lots because he jumped right out of my arms and into hers. He held on to her so tightly that he didn't even wave goodbye to me. Yet when I picked him up after running errands in Middletown, Hope looked glum.

Once I was gone, Smithy asked to play a game, which Hope had done for a warm-up, but he'd become cranky after about ten minutes and wouldn't sign in response to any prompts. Hope had put him down for a nap and almost couldn't wake him again. After about two hours, she got him sitting up, but he was still sluggish and refused to sign. Hope gave Smithy a snack to perk him up and offered him treats for every sign he made after that. She got a few words out of him that way, but Smithy soon got bored. He interacted with April when she came in about midday, but was definitely more interested in playing tickle than in doing much work. So much for that early pep he'd shown.

Some vestiges of it returned when we were driving back. Smithy started to hoot as we turned onto Bellevue Ave. and signed, "Where's Hope? See April. Smithy go school." I told him no more school until tomorrow, and he fussed and pouted. When we got home, he refused to get out of the car. I had to carry him inside. April said she took his temperature at school, and he didn't test as sick. He had a normal appetite at dinner. Maybe he is catching something, and it's not full blown yet. Let's keep an eye on the little guy.

NOTE POSTED TO BULLETIN BOARD

September 20, 1974

Thought for the day: If you want something done, do it yourself.

MEMO FROM WANDA KARLEWICZ
TO PIERS PREIS-HERALD

September 20, 1974

Re: Update: Week of September 16th

P,

Enclosed are your lecture notes for the next two weeks. I've prepped diagrams based on the preliminary analysis. Jeff spent the past week reviewing footage and screening the most relevant bits for me. We've tagged the canisters; if you want to show any film in class, Jeff can make you a print.

The biggest problem now, as always, is that because our team members don't pay their own living expenses, they act as though everything is free. I've had to push for secondary reinforcers for Webster instead of snacks to keep our grocery budget down.

Furthermore, I've posted several notices advising staff to turn off lights, radios, and other appliances every time they leave a room, but I still find lamps blazing in the library or in unoccupied bedrooms. I know they've read my notices because the papers are always torn down within a day and must be replaced. I'm tempted to hold back on paying the latest bill—let DWP cut the power for a couple of days—and see how everyone reacts. I dread what they'll do with the heating in another month.

Re: your last memo: Yes, I'll forego my stipend for another quarter. My own expenses are few since I don't have a thriving social life. Send

me whatever waivers need to be signed, or bring them on your next visit. You can make it up to me then, too.
    —WK

ARCHIVAL FILM FOOTAGE

Date: September 21, 1974
Location: The Kitchen/Hallway

Tammy appears in the full frame, smiles, and says, "We're here to record a breakthrough." She beckons Smithy from his seat at the kitchen table. He hops down from his chair and approaches the camera. Tammy says, "Ask him now, Eric."

Eric enters the frame and stands over Smithy, signing, "Smithy, what do you want to do today?"

Smithy signs, "Play cat."

Eric signs, "What cat?"

Smithy points to Peter, who is sitting on the stairs. Tammy kneels and signs to him, "Who is that?"

Smithy signs, "Peter."

Eric signs, "Smithy, tell me what you want to do."

"Smithy play cat Peter," Smithy signs.

Tammy signs, "Where play?"

"Outside," Smithy responds.

Eric signs and asks out loud, "Smithy, what do you want?"

Smithy signs, "Smithy Peter play outside. Play tickle. Smithy tickle Peter outside. Climb tree." Smithy points to Peter, then to the door. Tammy stands up, smiling.

Jeff cheers off camera. "Ya-hoooo! There you have it, folks. The first complex sentence—"

Tammy interrupts, "Practically a whole paragraph!"

Jeff finishes, "—from a chimpanzee! With minimal suggestion."

"I didn't ask, 'Do you want to play with Peter?' or 'Do you want to play outside," Eric clarifies. "Smithy generated those requests himself."

The camera zooms in on Smithy, who is walking rapidly in circles around Tammy. He looks back and forth among the humans.

Jeff, off camera, says, "You didn't see it, but at breakfast, Eric asked Smithy what he wanted to do today while the girls are out shopping, and he spontaneously said he wanted to play, then asked for Peter. Then he said he wanted to *go outside* with Peter and play."

Tammy says, "Don't get ahead of yourself. He signed, 'Smithy Peter go outside.' Then he signed 'Smithy Peter *play* outside.' At that point, we realized he was producing some unusually sophisticated messages, so Jeff got out the video camera. The rest unfolded just as you saw. I solemnly swear none of us coached him."

Smithy tugs Tammy out of the kitchen by the hand. He points to Peter and signs, "Cat play."

She says, "OK. We've got to work on your syntax some more. Get some consistency to your structure."

Eric starts up the stairs. Peter sees him and tries to run away, but Eric catches him and puts the cat in Smithy's arms. Eric says, "Here you go, buddy." Smithy grins and hugs Peter. Peter mewls as Smithy starts petting him. Eric adds, "Play nice, now."

Smithy looks up at him and signs, "Where Harriet?"

Eric puts his hands on his hips. "I thought you wanted to play with Peter. We're greedy this morning, aren't we? All right, I bet she's in Wanda's room. Here, kitty, kitty…" He runs up the stairs.

Tammy faces the camera and asks, "Is that enough? Should we run through the sequence again with Harriet? Make Smithy work to get her?"

Jeff, off camera, says, "Nah…it will look too repetitive. If he just says the same thing with a different cat as the object, it will look canned. I think this demo was effective, but it will help our cause to get more frequent—and varied—examples. That's why I'm gonna take this camera outside with us while he plays."

The image on the camera tilts as Jeff loosens the tripod. Jeff continues, "Maybe we can ask Smithy to tell us more about his games or his surroundings."

Tammy says, "Even if he's not so talkative for the rest of the day, this is a big achievement. We've elicited complex sentences after only four months of work!"

Jeff, off camera, says, "Yeah! Take that, Robert La—"

Pounding footsteps approach. Tammy spins around and pulls Smithy closer to her, protectively. Peter whines and squirms as Smithy throws him onto his shoulder as if he's burping a baby. Eric appears in the tilted frame of the camera. His face is blanched, and his mouth hangs wide open. He reaches the bend in the stairway and launches himself down the rest of the staircase. When he hits the bottom, he lands in a crouching position. Eric pushes himself up and starts to run toward the camera.

Jeff calls, "What the hell? Hey, man!" The image rolls as the camera comes to land against the wall. Jeff and Eric are still visible in the frame, Jeff struggling to restrain him.

Tammy runs to Eric and puts her hands on his shoulders, asking, "Are you OK?"

Jeff asks, "What gives?"

Tammy asks, "Where's the fire this time?"

Jeff asks, "You didn't break that leg, did you?"

"I saw it!" Eric says in a strained voice as he looks back up the stairs, shudders, and covers his face with one hand. "Jesus! I saw it! It was waiting for me!"

Tammy asks sharply, "Saw what?"

Eric says, "That thing, the ghost!"

Tammy steps back and laughs. Behind Eric, Smithy watches the proceedings intently. The cat crawls over Smithy's shoulder and runs away down the hall, but Smithy doesn't try to stop him.

"What the hell?" Jeff repeats.

Eric insists, "I swear it!" On the ground, he hugs himself tightly, shuddering. "It was standing in the doorway. The sun was shining right through it, and it cast no shadow! It *was* a shadow. It wasn't a person; it was *the ghost!*"

Smithy looks up at the stairs, covers his eyes, sits down, and starts to rock. Tammy steps closer to Eric and says evenly, "Calm down. Start again. Where were you? What did you see?"

Eric shakes his head and stands up from his crouched position. He stumbles down the hall, saying, "I've got to get out of here!"

Tammy calls, "Hold on. You might have a sprained ankle, the way you jumped over all those stairs. Take it easy."

"I'm not staying here!" he shouts.

Tammy says, "You're with friends."

"We can go to the gatehouse to talk," Jeff says, pitching his voice higher and stretching out his hand to the chimp. "Smithy, let's go outside!"

The camera frame rises and bounces gently, still capturing Eric and Tammy as they walk behind it.

Eric says, haltingly, "I went—to Wanda's room—looking for the cat. And I saw—someone—standing in the hallway. Right outside my room. I looked up. Couldn't figure out—who it could be. It—it wasn't anybody. It was just a thing. A—a—a big black shape. It looked like a person, but it had no face! Just—just a waving shadow. I couldn't see through it—into my room—but I could see—the sun—shining through the window—onto the wall—in the hallway. Right through this thing! I felt it looking at me. Oh, God, I felt so cold. And then I turned and ran the hell out of there!"

Tammy asks, "Was Harriet there?"

Eric says, "I don't know! I didn't go in Wanda's room. Once I saw that thing, I bolted. I'm not sorry. No way in hell was I going to stay and watch whatever it was about to do next."

Eric and Tammy walk outdoors into a sunny day. Tammy asks, "What do you think it was going to do?"

Eric says, "I don't know! Come at me? Suck my blood?"

Jeff, off camera, says, "That's vampires."

"Well, shit, since you know so much, why don't *you* go back there and talk to it?" Eric replies, irritated.

"I will. Could be you saw a burglar. We'll need to make a search," Jeff replies.

"Search the whole house?" Tammy asks.

"Search the second floor anyway, in your rooms. Since those are the only ones occupied, if a thief did get in, he'll look there for valuables."

Eric shakes his head and says, "It wasn't a person. Maybe it was once, but not now. I'm telling you—it wasn't solid!"

Tammy asks, "Did you see any features?"

"No."

"Anything in the profile? Do you know if it was a man or a woman?" she continues.

"A woman—I think. It was all billowy…" He flaps his arms weakly. "Like it was wearing a dress or a robe."

Jeff, still off camera, asks, "Long hair or short?"

"I couldn't tell." Eric pauses. "I did see something…rippling around its head. It could've been—long hair in a queue—or…it could have been a rope. Like a noose."

Jeff, off-camera says, "I thought Reid said the woman who died here fell off the roof. If that's the one you saw."

"Maybe he's wrong or maybe there's more than one. I don't know. I never knew anything like that could exist. I don't want to think about it right now. I don't ever want to go back there!"

Jeff unlocks a door, and they enter the gatehouse, proceeding down the hall to the recreation room. The frame stabilizes as Jeff props the camera against the wall. It focuses on a couch. Eric sits on the couch and buries his face in his hands. Jeff leads Smithy by the hand to the sofa. He says, "You don't have to. Just stay here and relax. Keep an eye on Smithy for a minute while I go back and look around."

As he talks, Smithy jumps up beside Eric and hugs him. Eric lowers his hands and smiles faintly. He signs, "thank you," and puts an arm around Smithy. Eric says, "I needed that." Smithy starts combing through Eric's hair, grooming him. Eric laughs. "Aw, thanks, little guy."

Tammy says, "I'll go, too. If it's a burglar, you can distract him while I go for help. Two is better than one."

"All right," Jeff replies.

Tammy asks, "Is there anything I can bring back for you, Eric? Maybe a beer?"

"Yeah. Maybe two or three beers."

Tammy asks, "Anything else? Something to read? A toothbrush? How about some clean underwear?"

Eric glowers at her.

"In case you end up spending the night here."

Eric nods.

Jeff says, "OK, then, we'll be back. Just take it easy." He and Tammy exit the recreation room. Eric remains slumped on the sofa, hugging Smithy and staring into space.

DIARY OF TAMMY COHEN

September 21, 1974

The ghost has finally appeared—to Eric, of all people! Or so he says. Jeff and I were in the middle of taping a session with Smithy when I heard what sounded like an elephant stampeding downstairs. The next thing I knew, Eric flew into the hallway and might have kept on running until he'd knocked a Wile-E. Coyote-shaped hole through the wall had Jeff not caught him. It took us a while to calm him down long enough to stand still and to give us anything coherent. Eric insisted he wanted to get out of Trevor Hall, so we walked him over to the gatehouse, and he's been there ever since.

He thinks he saw a shadowy figure in the hallway. Whatever it was, it scared the daylights out of him. Of course, Jeff and I went back and checked the rooms to make sure no one from outside had made their way inside, unbeknownst to us. Everything was in order. The cats were jumpy, but that's nothing new. Most likely, they were spooked by Eric's behavior. We're lucky his anxiety didn't communicate itself to Smithy. Rather, I'm lucky, since I've been Smithy's babysitter all day. Jeff has decided to keep Eric company down at the gatehouse to comfort him.

I made a care package of necessities for Eric, then took Smithy for a long walk on his leash and brought him home to read picture books and work on his signs. Right now, our boy is napping. He's been remarkably good, considering. With luck, he'll stay this way for the rest of the afternoon. He can start bouncing off the walls when the others come home from town.

I tried to kid Eric about what had happened once we'd established no one was in the house. I asked if the phantom had threatened him. Did it have glowing red eyes and tentacles that reached for him, etc.? He wasn't biting. Then I asked him to tell me in his own words what had happened. He replied, "I already did." I urged him to write an account of what he witnessed to send to Reid, as he might be aware of accounts from previous occupants to which he could compare it. Eric wasn't receptive to that suggestion either.

"You're going to use it against me," he said. "If I write something down, you'll hold on to it and use it to embarrass me in the future. Maybe when I'm applying for tenure." In other words, he's afraid the ghost sighting will come back to haunt him. I thought it was funny, but when I made the joke aloud, Eric got mad.

"I know what everybody thinks of me. I'm good old Eric, the guy you can count on. I'll go along to get along, and because I don't make a big fuss about getting recognition like some people, you can downplay me. But I won't be downplayed in this! I told you what I saw. I'm sticking to what I said. If you don't believe me, that's your problem."

I've always considered Eric one of the most level-headed people in the household. I admit, if Gail had told me she'd seen the ghost of Trevor Hall, I'd have just rolled my eyes. She's emotional and suggestible. Even Ruby would have given me pause. She has a romantic streak. I remember her coming back from one of the public mansions during our first week, rhapsodizing about how she'd been in tune with Consuelo Vanderbilt. If anybody else had reported this, I'd have blown it off. But Eric is different.

Whatever truly happened this morning, Eric believes he saw a ghost, and he's genuinely shaken. I have to respect that. What on Earth did he see?

I can't wait to talk to Ruby about this when she gets back from shopping. Moreover, I can't wait to see Wanda's reaction.

EXCERPT FROM
SMITHY: A TWENTY-YEAR COMPENDIUM
BY REID BENNETT, PHD

CHAPTER SIX: BUMPS IN THE NIGHT

The fortuitous documentation of the first human sighting of the "Dark Woman" is upheld by paranormal believers for its subtlety. Had the haunting been a hoax, they say, a more dramatic first appearance would have been staged.

Of even greater interest is the discussion among the principals captured later the same day and only recently released as part of the "outtake reels…"

OUTTAKE FOOTAGE

Date: September 21, 1974
The Gatehouse Rec Room

Eric and Jeff sit on a long sofa in a room with wall-to-wall blue shag carpeting, watching TV. Several empty beer bottles are spread on the coffee table before them. Ruby, Gail, Wanda, and Tammy enter the room, excited.

Ruby says, "Tammy said you saw the ghost! Is it true?"

Gail asks, "Where did it happen? I want to know so I can avoid that room! Were you scared?"

Ruby asks, "What was it like?"

Eric shifts, uncomfortable, and glances at Tammy, who gazes back with a teasing smile. Wanda stands back, arms folded, observing. Finally, he says, "Yeah, I saw it. Coming out of my room. Wanda, I wanted to talk to you about getting a new room. I know there are others available. I don't care how small it is—"

Wanda says, "Eric, if I open up one of the other rooms for you, what's to stop Tammy from wanting her own room, or Ruby from wanting a bigger room? Come on—what did you really see? A shadow? Your reflection in the mirror?" She looks down at the litter on the table. "How much had you been drinking? Or were you smoking?"

Eric leans forward, gesticulating. "I only did that once at Ruby's birthday! And no, I wasn't on anything. I was just looking for Harriet, and there *it* was, by the door to my room. I'm not going back in there! I'm sure as hell not sleeping there! Jeff said I can crash on this couch. I don't want to crowd him, but I'll stay here before I set foot back there again. I'll sleep on the bench outside before I use that room again!"

Jeff says, "He was completely sober when he went upstairs, Wanda. I never saw anyone so white as when he came down. I thought I was gonna have to carry him out here." He slaps Eric comfortingly on the shoulder. "You're OK now, man, and you can have the couch as long as you want."

Tammy says, "Actually, I wouldn't mind moving into Eric's room if that's an option. I'm kind of curious to see what happens there."

Wanda asks, "And you'll have him move in with Gail?"

Tammy puts her arm around Gail and says, "We can move together, right, roomie?" Gail shudders and twists away.

"What did it look like, Eric?" Ruby asks. "Was it the woman from the photo?"

"Huh? Oh, Geraldine, the old maid?" Tammy asks.

Ruby corrects her. "*Imogene*. Did she see you, too?"

"I don't know," Eric begins. "I couldn't see the eyes—nor any features. She didn't have any! Her face was just black. Everything about her was solid black. Like a silhouette come to life. More like a shadow than a person. Just a shape, a figure of a female. But it was human, for sure. Not a tree or furniture casting a shadow. It was a dark—" Eric freezes. His mouth gapes, and he twitches. "Oh shit! Oh shit, oh shit..."

Tammy sets her hand on his arm in concern. "Eric?"

Ruby looks around in alarm and asks, "What's wrong? Is it back?"

"Holy shit...I saw *a dark woman*!" Eric pauses, then signs, "dark woman" as he speaks, looking around at his friends. Ruby covers her mouth.

Silence fills the room, then everyone talks at once:

Ruby exclaims, "No way!"

Tammy says, "Oh, good grief!"

Gail says, "But that's what Smithy's been saying for months..."

Jeff says, "You can't—Are you sure?"

Tammy says, "Hold on. Are we really saying we believe in ghosts now? On what grounds?"

Eric insists, "I saw her, man, and I'm not the only one! Smithy's proof! He *told* us!"

Gail says, "*Months* ago! Even before we went to the bar, before we talked to Reid!"

Jeff covers his head in his hands and moans, "Oh maaaan! He couldn't have known..."

Wanda asks, "Are you sure? Maybe one of you tipped him off. You could have heard the story of the ghost before you came to Trevor Hall and communicated it to him somehow. Maybe it was mentioned to you in the cab—" She looks at Tammy. "—or you overheard it at the bus depot—" She looks at Ruby. "Or possibly one of the schoolteachers let slip some local gossip when you went to pick up Smithy from class." She looks from Eric to Jeff. "And you let Smithy pick up on your fears about the house and play off them."

Tammy asks, "Are you suggesting one of us has been *coaching* Smithy? And playing dumb this whole time about the ghost stories?"

"Not deliberately," Wanda says. "But you could have heard the legend and then forgotten about it. It could have stayed buried in the back of your mind without you consciously thinking about it."

"Cryptomnesia?" Ruby asks.

Wanda says, "Yes. And then when Smithy began to make signing errors, you reacted as if he meant something more, and that reaction has encouraged him to continue...misbehaving."

Tammy purses her lips and looks at Ruby, who shakes her head slightly.

Eric protests, "No! Don't you see? Smithy wasn't making mistakes or saying he was tired. He's been trying to tell us what he's been seeing using the signs he already knows, but we didn't understand!"

"How could we? Who would have thought...?" Gail says.

"The experiment isn't a failure! He really *can* communicate," Eric says. "And what's more, he's a medium! He probably doesn't know it. How would he know what a ghost is? He just knows something really weird is happening. We've all noticed it, too—we just couldn't account for it."

Jeff asks, "Isn't that worth considering, Wanda, if only to rule it out as an alternative?"

Wanda says, "No. If we go that down that road, it will never end. How do you prove the existence of life after death? People have been trying to do that for millennia with no solid results. We aren't here to test for ESP. Our job is to teach Smithy sign language and test his comprehension of it. That's an uphill battle already."

Jeff argues, "But the one could prove the other. We can test whether Smithy is making errors against the likelihood that he's perceiving something more than we see."

"He only ever makes the 'dark woman' error," Ruby adds. "He doesn't backslide into using any other words to make false identifications."

"There are a number of mundane reasons why Smithy could be doing that. Do we really want to try to persuade the scientific community Smithy is seeing ghosts?" Wanda asks. "Do we really want to drag *that* into what we're doing here? We'll have a hard enough time justifying our accomplishments in teaching Smithy language."

Eric says, "The ghost is definitely part of the study. Her presence affects Smithy's behavior. I want to talk to Piers about all this when he gets back. He should be the one to decide what we do next."

Ruby turns to Jeff. "Yes! We need to review all the footage and show him the times where Smithy signs 'dark woman.'"

Jeff nods.

"No. Piers has enough on his mind without having to listen to campfire stories. Don't pester him with this," Wanda warns.

Ruby says, "I'd like to hear what Piers thinks."

Wanda asks, "Do you think he's going to believe Smithy saw a ghost?"

Ruby sits up taller, her voice rising accordingly. "I'd like to know if he believes *Eric* saw a ghost."

Wanda addresses the room. "Listen to yourselves! You sound ridiculous! I thought we were scientists, not peasants."

"Wanda, are you afraid there could be a spirit in the house? You're protesting an awful lot," Jeff asks.

Wanda says, "Because we have so much to do for this study, and I don't want us distracted by a—wild ghost chase! What's more, I don't want us framing our research in terms of far-fetched speculation. If you assume there's a ghost in the house, you'll start attributing everything that happens, everything Smithy does, to the ghost. Any random word pairing will take on portentous meaning. Worse, if you let on to Smithy that you think there's something else in the house, he's apt to respond by giving you the reactions you want. If you ask him questions about this so-called 'dark woman,' you'll be reinforcing his errors, whereas if you stop acknowledging them, he may stop on his own. You could lead him further afield by entrenching this distraction in our study when we've worked so hard to make it stand up to scrutiny."

Wanda looks around the room. Everyone stares back at her, stone-faced. She shakes her head. "Fine. Do what you want. I'll go see about a room change for Eric." Wanda starts to exit the room, then glances into the camera and pauses. Her lips peel back in a mean smile, and she asks, "Jeff, why is this camera set up over here?"

Jeff says, "I brought that down from the hallway. I was taping when all the commotion started."

Wanda says, "That was—what—two hours ago? The record light is on; should it be?"

Jeff asks, "What?" He jumps up to examine the camera. His face fills the frame. "Aw, sh—"

The picture goes black.

EXCERPT FROM
A RARE MEDIUM
BY ARMAND STOKES, PHD

REPRINTED WITH PERMISSION FROM
OPPOSING VIEWPOINTS: THE SUPERNATURAL,
SECOND EDITION, **ED. BY WILLIAM IRISH,**
BLACKHAVEN BOOKS, 1995

...The first edition of this book featured a section titled "Can Humans Communicate with the Spirit World?" Such a narrow characterization overlooks the most famous case of spirit communication of our time and misses the larger question of whether a spirit world exists. I'm pleased to correct that oversight now.

For as long as humans have believed in communication with unseen spirits, folk wisdom has held that animals are able to see and interact with spirits, even when humans cannot. However, while animals may be able to see ghosts, none could ever describe the experience. Until Smithy. ...

MEMO FROM WANDA KARLEWICZ TO PIERS
PREIS-HERALD

September 21, 1974

P,

We've had a minor incident at the house. Eric
was spooked by something he saw in the hallway
and now is telling people he saw "the ghost."

Unfortunately, his claim has caused
consternation. Gail insists we bring somebody
in to bless the house. Eric refuses to sleep in
his room and wants to share the gatehouse with
Jeff until new accommodations can be made for
him. I asked Ruby if she would trade rooms with
Eric. I know she's complained to Tammy about not
having much space and thought she would welcome
this opportunity and spare me the trouble of
airing and furnishing a new room, but she's
also convinced Eric's room is somehow tainted,
although he says he saw his phantom floating in
the hall <u>outside</u> the room.

I then thought to shuffle Tammy into Eric's
room, move Ruby into Tammy's room, and let Eric
have Ruby's room. To my surprise, Tammy asked why
three people should have to move just because one
person wanted to move. She mentioned she's fond
of Eric but would be considerably less fond of
him if she had to uproot herself because he took
a fright. And yet, if I'd declined to move him, she
would have criticized me. Sometimes I think it's
impossible to deal with her.

Therefore, I've opened Room 217 in the back
hallway. Jeff helped me relocate Eric's bed and

furnishings, and Tammy unpacked and repacked his drawers. Eric will have more privacy and the use of the second bathroom, on condition that he maintains these facilities. Also, the room is near the servants' stairs, affording an emergency exit if one is needed.

Be advised, several members of our team want to meet with you on this issue. I did my best to dissuade them, but the majority insists on being heard. I'm sending this memo to limit the amount of time you must waste on the matter.

I've explained talk of ghosts is an inappropriate distraction and harmful to morale. Furthermore, I said any more such gossip will prompt a reevaluation of that researcher's role on the team. I meant to scare them into knocking off the silly superstitious talk, but if you think it's worth following through, I will implement said reviews.

I'm not sure what to do about Eric. I'm hoping he'll settle down, now that he has his new room. Frankly, I'm amazed he originated this ghost rumor. Ordinarily, I'd consider Eric a sound source, but his claim is too incredible to consider. However, I don't believe he's lying. It's possible he's sleep-deprived or otherwise ill.

This foolishness has overshadowed much better news I wanted to share. Jeff obtained a recording of Webster signing complex sentences (involving four or more words, including noun-verb-object combinations) on his own initiative and is editing this footage for your use. You should have it before the next donors' meeting. If you also wish to release it to any news outlets, let me know, and I'll prepare a cover letter.

— WK

DIARY OF RUBY CARDINI

September 25, 1974

Now Eric has me spooked! I was sitting in the library this evening, writing a letter to Sarah-Beth, trying to pick up our correspondence (my fault, but so much is happening). Maisie was curled up at my feet under the desk while I wrote. I felt her twitching and heard her whimper. I thought she might be having a little doggy dream. Then she sat up and looked around the room.

I asked, "How're you doing, girl?" She looked alert, edgy even, so I scratched behind her ears and spoke gently to put her at ease.

Suddenly, she jumped and spun around. The poor thing almost struck her head on the edge of the desk. Then she dropped her head low to the ground and started to growl. Her hackles rose up. She stared across the room at the fireplace, her eyes fixed on it as if it was about to attack her. But I saw nothing there!

My hair prickled, and I felt my skin grow colder. I tried to tell myself I was just reacting to Maisie's strange behavior. I called to her, asked what was wrong. She yelped twice, high and curt, like when one of the cats takes a swipe at her, or Smithy pulls her tail too hard. I kept looking from the fireplace back to her crouching in defense, realizing she could see something I couldn't.

"What is it, Maisie? What do you see?" I couldn't help asking, even though I knew she couldn't tell me. I wondered briefly, if she could talk, would I have listened to her? What has Smithy been trying to tell us all this time? Does he feel helpless when he knows something is in the room but can't make us understand the danger?

Maisie yelped once more and bolted from the room. In that moment, I feared being left alone with I-don't-know-what, so I grabbed for her. I held on to Maisie, trying to keep her between me and whatever it was. I still couldn't see a damn thing!

Maisie struggled in my grasp, but I had her by the collar so she couldn't wriggle away. But Maisie, usually so sweet and affectionate, had had enough. She twisted her head and snapped at me. I was so startled, I let go and jumped back, and Maisie shot across the room and out the door, still whimpering.

I watched her go and examined the blood on my arm. The bite hadn't started to hurt yet. I think I was too pumped with adrenaline to feel it. Not sensing the pain made the wound seem unreal. I couldn't believe Maisie had bitten me. Normally, she would never do a thing like that!

Not unless something truly terrible impelled her to it. Not unless she feared for her life.

I glanced at the fireplace again and held my breath, the better to hear any phantom voices whispering to me. But I heard nothing. The bricks glowed in the light from the fading sun, but they didn't look ominous. I looked all around, just in case some shadowy menace was about to zoom at me from an unobserved corner, but the library appeared just the way it always does. It didn't feel right, though. The air seemed disturbed, and it reminded me of that day Gail got hit by the tiles. Like a storm about to break.

I got out then, too. I didn't run like Maisie, but I walked quickly and backed out of the room so nothing could sneak up on me.

I left my letter on the desk. Luckily, I hadn't written more than the preliminaries—how are you, how you're your folks, etc.—so there was nothing sensitive for anyone else to read. It was a silly thing to do. I felt foolish and knew I was acting like a baby, but I couldn't make myself go back in to retrieve it. It would have sat there overnight if I hadn't bumped into Eric as I headed to the bathroom to wash my wound. I mentioned I'd forgotten something in the library and asked if he could please get it for me.

Eric is so sweet—he never even asked why I'd left it or didn't go back to get it myself. I didn't tell him about Maisie because it would have alarmed him, but I worried after he left that the ghost might appear to him again. Fortunately, that didn't happen. Eric brought my letter back to my room and left it on my bed as I'd asked. I haven't touched it, though; there's no way I can write to Sarah-Beth about what happened. There's no way I can lie my way through a cheery, banal catch-up missive now.

Jeff is the only person I've talked to so far. I can't even bring myself to tell Tammy. I'm afraid she'd laugh at me. I almost want to laugh at myself, but then I see the bite on my arm and the fear becomes real again. Jeff didn't laugh. He offered to take me to get a rabies shot, but Maisie didn't do more than break the skin; it looks like a long paper cut now. I did a thorough job of washing it out. I don't want to get doctors involved because I don't want Piers or Wanda to know she bit me. Then they would have to hear about the circumstances behind the attack.

Maisie isn't sleeping in the library tonight. I last saw her curled up under the dining room table. I wonder if I'll sleep tonight.

NOTE POSTED TO THE BULLETIN BOARD

September 29, 1974

*We've no warm water in any of the upstairs baths
(ours, Eric's, or Smithy's). Please call plumber
right away!*
— Tammy

P.S. The toilet downstairs won't flush either.
— Gail

AUDIO RECORDING

October 1974

Piers says, "…I was thinking of bringing you with me this time. I suspect the board is tired of seeing me every time. A pretty girl will catch their interest—and maybe bring us a bigger budget for the spring."

Wanda says, "Oh, no, Piers. You don't need me. You've always presented by yourself before and gotten the results we need. Besides, I need to stay here and keep an eye on things."

"The study will be well cared for if you step away for a couple of days," Piers insists. "The house hasn't burned down yet, has it?"

Wanda snorts and says, "Not for lack of trying… Look, I chose research over therapy because I'm more information-oriented than people-oriented, and I chose it over teaching so I wouldn't have to do so much public speaking."

"You'll have to present your findings eventually," he notes.

"I'll publish and let the findings speak for themselves." She sighs. "I don't want to be the face of the experiment. I enjoy being a supervisor, despite my complaints. I love the work, and I'm honored to have my place, but I don't like the PR part of it. I'm just no good at it."

Piers says, "Nonsense. You've a much prettier face than my mug. The public will adore you."

"It won't. No one here likes me. I don't have the personal touch. I'm an administrator, not a house mother." She laughs. "I can't sustain the social niceties people expect. I'm used to getting to the point. We're here to work, not chitchat. I know I'm supposed to pause and make small talk before I ask for something, like "How is your sister? How was your date?" but in the moment, I don't think of it. That's not really what I want to talk about, and Tammy or Gail will know that. Why dance around the subject?"

"Because people expect it, and it's part of the persuasion game, my dear. You know the rules; you just don't like to play. Odd, considering all the time you spend reminding others to follow the rules. You know how to make people like you. You've been studying psychology for five years, three of them with me. Apply what you've learned. I find you charming. Now charm the others. Eric likes you. Didn't you tell me he's flirted with you? I think that's the real reason you don't want to come to New Haven with me. You want to remain here with him to continue your mad affair."

"That was months ago," Wanda replies. "He doesn't like me anymore because I didn't change his room right away when he wanted it. Eric will go for any pretty face. He's not particular about what's behind it. He flirts with Gail, too."

Piers says, "I don't understand why you're so hard on Gail. You liked her in the beginning. She's learned a great deal in her time here and has helped Webster considerably with his vocabulary."

"She's plateaued...she's not making much more progress than in her first couple of months," Wanda explains.

"Give her the benefit of the doubt. Give her a compliment occasionally, even if it's not earned. Maybe you'll create a self-fulfilling prophecy. At the very least, you'll make her feel good about herself, and then she'll feel good about you, too. Try it. You've never let me down before, Wanda."

"I don't intend to." Wanda pauses. "Piers, I've been meaning to ask…Do you think Webster is capable of comprehending what we talk about?"

"That's what we hope this experiment will show, my dear."

Wanda says, "No, I know he can process concrete questions like, 'What color is Tammy's shirt?' or 'Where is your ball?' But do you believe he has the ability to understand abstractions like, 'Ninety years ago, a woman you never met died here?' Could he grasp an idea like that, and from it, formulate a belief that such a woman occupies the house?"

Piers says, "You mean, is he susceptible to suggestion?"

"Yes."

"Well, that's trickier. I don't believe he's vulnerable in the way you described. That is, I honestly don't know how much Webster understands in the way of intangibles. That would be a fascinating question to explore, and it's one we should investigate. Imagine being able to convey to him higher concepts like 'justice' and 'peace.' But to return to your original question, Wanda—no, I don't think Webster is able to form a belief in a haunting based on rumors he's overheard. However, I believe he does respond to the attitudes you and your cohorts have formed toward these stories. Though he likely can't process the stories themselves, he can sense your anxiety about them and your overreaction to his 'dark woman' signs. He may try to exploit that, so I need you to be sensitive to all things said about such matters. Once impressionable minds are exposed to the idea of a ghost, people will begin to perceive all sorts of normal noises and mishaps as evidence of the supernatural at work. They'll become watchful and jumpy. Webster will sense this fear and react in kind, becoming edgy himself. He may also increase his pranks or tell his teachers what he believes they want to hear. These reports about him describing a woman when none is there, or referring inexplicably to darkness—they've no significance themselves. They're errors that need to be corrected. But they're blown out of proportion to support ghostly fantasies. It's got to stop, Wanda. I'm counting on you to crack down on this nonsense, especially when I'm away."

Wanda says, "Of course, Piers. I'll see it doesn't get out of hand."

DIARY OF RUBY CARDINI

October 12, 1974

After ten days and two false victories on Jeff's part, our plumbing is finally fixed, but at an unnecessarily high cost, and I don't mean whatever Wanda had to pay the plumber. It's opened rifts in our group that didn't need to be there.

After Gail and Tammy reported the problem, Eric put up a note to suggest the plumbing issues—and maybe other problems we've had, like the fires, things in the kitchen disappearing as soon as you set them down, and the way locks seem to melt for Smithy—could be part of the haunting. He reminded us Reid mentioned similar things happened at the boarding school.

Wanda erupted. She called a meeting in which she tore down his note and ripped it up in front of us. "There. Is. No. Ghost," she emphasized. "This is an old house. Things fall apart. It's normal. If we find termites next, it won't be a sign of a biblical plague. Stop trying to scare each other, and grow up!"

We were speechless. I've seen Wanda frazzled before but not spiteful. Once upon a time, we all could have kidded about a ghost causing mischief. Now she's quick to shut down any hint of suspicion that things aren't quite normal in this house. She's been on the warpath since Piers's last visit. I wonder if they had a fight.

Then Wanda went further. "If anyone discusses this nonsense around Smithy, he or she will be off the study. We're scientists. Act like it!"

I stared at Jeff, who looked equally flummoxed, then across the room at Eric. The gag order seemed intended for him. Eric's face was red, his lips pressed together. I wonder if he will cut back on the ghost talk now. Nobody wants to leave Trevor Hall, but nobody likes to be censored either.

Now I'm glad I didn't tell Wanda or Piers about what happened in the library last week. I talked to Tammy though, when Smithy wasn't around. We met in the library, of all places. I hadn't set foot there in days, but I saw Tammy writing a letter and joined her. We were the only people on the ground floor, so I decided this was my moment to come clean.

I tried to sound her out at first. I asked her flat out, "Tammy, do you believe Smithy can see and talk to ghosts?"

Her reply, as usual, was flippant: "Only on Tuesdays and Thursdays. And Sundays, if it's an odd date of the month."

That ticked me off. Not because I thought she would laugh at me if I told her my story, but because she could be so easy about the whole thing. "I'm serious," I told her. "Do you have to turn everything into a joke? Don't you ever wonder? Can't you give me a straight answer about this at least?"

This time, she turned away from her letter to face me, and I didn't see a hint of laughter in her eyes. "I am being straight with you," she explained. "On some days, I accept completely that Smithy is communicating with a ghost; and other days, I don't. That's how I learn to see both sides of the question. Some days I think, 'Ghosts are real. There's a ghost in this house, and Smithy talks to it, and sometimes it causes trouble for the rest of us.' I think about what that means for us and how to handle it. What's it like to be a ghost? What would I say to a ghost if I saw one? Should we hold a séance with Smithy to find out more about his woman in black and what she wants?

"On other days, I think, 'This is preposterous! There are no such things as ghosts, and since there aren't, what else is going on here? What's Smithy really doing? What do his signs mean? Is he taking us for a ride? Are we taking ourselves for a ride and making a big mess of a simple and laughable situation?'"

I was impressed she could make an intellectual exercise out of it. I marveled that she wasn't scared at all, even on the days when she accepted that something otherworldly could be messing with our lives.

"Oh, I do get scared," she admitted, "but at least treating the question as an intellectual exercise keeps me from lying awake at night."

That's when I told her about the last time I was in the library. I also admitted how uneasy I'm feeling now that I see our lives at Trevor

Hall in a new context. At first, when Eric told us about seeing the Dark Woman, and we realized that's what Smithy might have been trying to describe, I was excited. It gave me a rush to think there could be a world beyond, and Smithy could reach it. But when I really considered the implications, all I could think was, 'There's a ghost in this house. This is our house, and it's haunted.'

Because Tammy's right: we do have to sleep here—and wake up to find the bedrooms on fire and our lives possibly in peril. Half the time, these things happen when we're wide awake, but we still can't see what's going on. That makes me feel helpless and weak.

What scares me most, though, is that whatever Smithy sees, he doesn't like it. What does that mean for the rest of us?

Tammy listened respectfully until I was all talked out, then gave me a hug. "You know," she said, "on Saturdays, I try not to think about it at all. I push the questions and fears out of my mind and focus on how lucky I am to be living rent-free in this beautiful place, working on a mind-blowing, groundbreaking study, living and working with amazing people like you. Maybe you should try to think of the bright side instead of dwelling on dark possibilities."

I could tell she wasn't chiding me, and I knew that whether she thought I was silly or flat out nuts, she would never scream at me like Wanda.

Having an ally feels good, even if we have to keep our voices down when discussing the Dark Woman.

SMITHY'S BEDROOM JOURNAL ENTRY
FROM WANDA KARLEWICZ

October 17, 1975

Another unproductive day for Webster has come and gone. This time, he put his head down on the desk as soon as he got into the classroom and went to sleep. He ignored all Sarah and Simon's attempts to engage him and would not be roused. After a lengthy (two-to three-hour) nap, Webster demonstrated a sullen demeanor. He signed only after extensive cajoling and would not work on any new material. At lunch, he drank chocolate milk but wouldn't touch his food.

When I picked him up, Sarah said she couldn't figure out why Webster appeared so anxious to come to school because he certainly didn't want to learn once he arrived. She remarked again on how tired and listless he's appeared in recent days and suggested his behavior may be due to not getting enough sleep at home. I offered to try an earlier bedtime, but she thinks something about the living quarters itself may be disturbing him.

Sarah volunteered to take Webster home with her for the weekend to see how he behaves in a different setting. She lives with a roommate who loves children and would be glad to try out a chimp for a couple of days. I agreed, albeit reluctantly. Sarah has demonstrated herself to be a competent and patient teacher, and I believe she's a responsible caregiver, but I have doubts about how comfortable Webster will be in an unfamiliar environment. I don't want him to think the rest of us have abandoned him. However, the attempt is worthwhile, and Webster's absence will give us a chance to change his bedding in case bedbugs are keeping him awake, or set him up in another room altogether, if necessary. Eric suggested this option some time ago, and Piers is now supportive. Sarah is to call us immediately if Webster proves to be uncontrollable, or if she has any concerns. Monday morning will tell.

SMITHY'S BEDROOM JOURNAL ENTRY
FROM ERIC KANINCHEN

How about Sarah's suggestion, Wanda? Can you think of anything at Trevor Hall that might be bugging Smithy?

MEMO FROM WANDA KARLEWICZ

October 20, 1974

P,

I just retrieved Webster from school. Sarah and Hope report that he worked well today. He was calm, responded to requests, and observed his normal routine. Moreover, he's using three new signs.

I called Sarah last night to see how their weekend was going, and she said Webster was the man of the hour. Her roommate loved playing with him. Webster asked her name when they were introduced, and was happy to sign with them both throughout the weekend, asking for food or toys, and identifying objects and pictures on TV or in books. He was a good boy all weekend and didn't mess up the house or his big boy pants. Sarah said they'd gladly host him again. I may take her up on that by scheduling a sleepaway at least once per month. It seems to be good for his socialization, and I admit, it's been nice to have a break here at Trevor Hall.

I'll continue to report on his progress.

— WK

DIARY OF RUBY CARDINI

October 23, 1974

I feel like a spy on a top-secret mission. This should be silly fun, but I'm so nervous, more so about if we succeed than if we get caught.

Tammy approached me with a proposal after Wanda had gone to the gatehouse to watch Jeff's latest cut. She smiled, almost apologetically, as if to ease the shock. "Eric isn't satisfied with leaving the issue of the ghost unexplored. He wants to hold a séance with Smithy."

I was incredulous. "That's too risky!" I was thinking of the trouble we might unleash if we tried to mess with the ghost, but Tammy thought I was referring to Wanda.

"I agree. It would be too hard to explain if we were caught. Eric doesn't think Wanda really could fire us all at once—she'd lose half the research team—but I don't want to test her definition of zero tolerance. Therefore, I've suggested the compromise of talking to Smithy instead of the ghost. We know we still need to be very careful, and we don't want to jeopardize your position in the study, but we wanted to offer you a chance to join us since you've been a witness, too. If you don't want to, no hard feelings—only please don't rat us out."

I wasn't about to do that. Like Tammy, I didn't want to call Wanda's bluff, but the idea of pursuing a resolution instead of blithely pretending nothing more is wrong than a few bad circuits appealed to me. So did the fact that Eric and Tammy were letting me (not Jeff, not Gail) in on their plot. But I didn't see how we could interrogate Smithy without leading him. "If we ask him directly if there's a ghost, we risk putting ideas into his head. Any answers we get will be suspect."

Of course, the real process was more oblique. We met in the kitchen at lunch ("Since you saw him talking to it here once," Eric said, "and because of the fires.") Eric seated Smithy next to an empty chair and sat on the other side of it as he served us. He gestured to the open place and signed, "Does your friend want some juice?" Smithy just stared at him. Eric poured a fifth glass and put it before the open chair. Smithy reached for it, but Eric shooed him away. "What's your friend's name?"

"You're presuming this thing's friendly," Tammy observed.

"All right. Smithy, what's the woman's name?"

Smithy glanced between me and Tammy, perplexed, and signed each of our names in turn, then looked to Eric for praise.

He sighed, "Who is the woman? What does she want?"

We waited for Smithy to respond, to grasp what Eric was really asking. These questions were innocuous enough, in case Wanda popped back in early, but would they be enough to help us learn what we needed? It all reminded me of a game I'd played at my cousin's baby shower, where we couldn't say the word "drink," or we'd be out. "Imbibe," "tipple," "sip" and other euphemisms made our interactions increasingly ridiculous. How could you interview a chimp about a ghost without asking about "the ghost"? How were we supposed to find out what Smithy knew if we could only talk in a circle?

"Where is she? Has she hurt you?"

I clasped my hands in my lap and held my breath. Smithy shifted and looked to me and Tammy as if for a reprieve—either because he didn't want to discuss the dark woman or because he was bored?

Eric continued down this path of abstractions, holding his frustration behind his carefully modulated teacher voice. "Is the dark woman here? Who is here? What do you see?"

Finally, Smithy responded: "Ruby," "Eric," "table," "drink," "sandwich," "sink…"

"This isn't working," Tammy declared. "Either he doesn't understand, or there's nothing to report. Either way, let's stop for the day. We can try again another time. We'll figure out a better strategy."

Eric huffed in exasperation. Smithy cocked his head and looked him up and down until Eric forced a smile and scratched Smithy behind the ears. "I'm not mad at you, pal. It's not your fault. When you tried to tell us before, we didn't listen. I don't blame you for not wanting to talk now." We finished our meal and conducted Smithy's afternoon lesson without further ado.

I feel foolish. All this secrecy, and for what? We didn't accomplish anything but sit around and play twenty questions with ourselves. Are we idiots? Are we creating a problem where none exists? If Wanda finds out what we're up to, we're in for it. Even if she doesn't sack us, she'll reprimand us. Not only are we defying her, but we could be suggesting the idea of an interloper to Smithy, hard as we're trying to avoid that very problem.

Still, it feels good to be doing <u>something</u>. I'm glad we're taking the situation into our own hands. I don't want to be ruled by Wanda's ultimatums—or by anything else.

DIARY OF GAIL EHRLICH

October 31, 1974

Wanda is such a spoilsport!

We've been excited about Halloween for weeks, and she had to ruin our fun! Jeff wanted to take Smithy trick-or-treating. He was going to put a sheet over his head and make him a ghost. Ruby and I made costumes, too, a scary witch and a good witch. Tammy put on a red rain slicker and said she'd bring Maisie, and they'd be Little Red Riding Hood and the wolf. Jeff was going to film us all.

Well, Wanda overheard us talking and put her foot down. Smithy couldn't go out with the other kids, and we absolutely could not disguise him as a ghost. She insisted we not talk about ghosts at all, not even in fun. Jeff tried to argue, but she said she was just doing what Piers would have done if he were here. Poor Smithy had to stay home. At least April and Hope gave him some candy at school today, but it's not the same thing.

Ruby, Tammy, and I still walked around to see the kids' costumes and the decorations in the storefronts. They were cute, but it wasn't the same. We're too old to go door to door. It would have been so fun if we could have taken Smithy. I would have held his hand, so he didn't get scared or run away. It would have been good practice for him, too, to ask for candy and say thank you and let the neighbors get to know him and see that he's not so strange or wild. But nooo! Now I guess we'll have to wait until next year.

Why does Wanda have to be so uptight?

EXCERPT FROM
WHY CHIMPANZEES MAKE BAD MEDIUMS AND WORSE PETS
BY HARRY DINGWALL, PHD

REPRINTED WITH PERMISSION FROM
OPPOSING VIEWPOINTS: THE SUPERNATURAL,
SECOND EDITION, **ED. BY WILLIAM IRISH,**
BLACKHAVEN BOOKS, 1995

The desire to prove life after death has led to far-fetched foolishness over the years. History is replete with fraudulent mediums and gullible scientists. Sometimes the willful desire to believe in weird things can have more dangerous consequences…

DIARY OF TAMMY COHEN

November 8, 1974

We held our second exploratory session with Smithy today. This time, we met in the library, another sighting site. As before, we spoke informally with Smithy to see if he would mention anything about the dark woman. Eric arranged the desk and wingback chairs in a circle, along with a couple of chairs swiped from the solarium, so it felt like we were having a séance. Eric spoke to the ether, inviting anything that wished to join us to take the empty chair beside Smithy.

Since we hadn't gotten anywhere by quizzing Smithy before, Eric instead spoke to the spirit, addressing the vacant seat: "What's your name? Did you used to live here? What do you want? Why did you appear to me?"

"Watch Smithy," he'd ordered us before we began. "The ghost probably can't talk to me, but maybe she'll tell him to respond. At least look to see if he reacts when it appears." But Smithy's only reaction was boredom. He fidgeted in his chair and stared quizzically at me and Ruby. I wonder what kind of weird game he thinks Eric is playing every time we gather not to practice words, but to sit and talk to thin air.

Or maybe he knows exactly what we're up to. As Eric spoke and gestured to the empty seat, Smithy looked right at me, and I'd swear his lower lip drooped into a knowing smile.

"He's toying with us," I said. Smithy blinked at Eric and yawned. He might as well have signed, "Who, me?" I said, "Even if something is here, he might not tell us. We can't know if he sees it or not."

Eric decided to bring in Maisie, claiming she'd react to any presence because "Dogs don't deceive."

While he slipped out, Ruby groomed Smithy to keep him still. She remarked, "I'd feel more secure if we could establish that he wasn't just signing to an empty chair, like if we had a baseline to show he signs only when the chair is occupied." When Eric returned with the dog, Ruby suggested he get the puppets.

He fetched one shaped like a white bird that he called Donald. Smithy's eyes sparkled when he saw Donald; at last, this session was beginning to resemble something familiar. Maisie poked her head up once, then turned in a circle and went back to sleep under the desk. Eric positioned the puppet over the empty chair, and we asked Smithy questions about it: "What's his name? What color is he? Which arm is he waving?" Smithy had no problem signing to and about a toy figure.

Then Eric pocketed Donald, and Ruby continued to question Smithy: What color is she? What's her name? Smithy scratched his chin and looked perplexed.

"Where is she?" Smithy glanced all around the room, as if seeking. He pointed to Maisie and made to jump down from the chair.

Eric restrained him. "No playing yet. Where's the woman?" He picked a tennis ball that Maisie likes to chase off the floor and threw it at the wall. "Is she here? You were testing before to see if she was real or if the toys went through her, right? Did this toy go through her just now?" He tried different locations, bouncing the ball off the shelves. Maisie barked and tried to chase it. Ruby had to hold her back.

I warned Eric he was creating a confounding variable. "We can't know if Maisie wants to play or if she senses another presence. And Smithy's had enough of sitting around watching us act like dolts. We made a good effort; it's just not working. Maybe there's nothing to find."

Ruby praised Smithy for being a good boy and led him and Maisie outside to play. I stayed behind to straighten up while Eric groused. "I'm not giving up. She appeared to me for a reason. Maybe she can find some other way to get through." He stared into space. As I replaced the desk chair, I heard him muttering, "Who are you? What do you want from us?"

It made me uneasy. I grabbed the solarium chairs, hoping he'd take a hint, and said, "Eric, come on. Enough."

"You go on. I'm going to keep trying." He remained in the wing chair, his hands lying palms up in his lap like a meditating Buddhist.

As I left the library, I could still hear him channeling. "You came to me before. Let's see you do it again."

It's one thing to test Smithy and another to play with the occult. Eric wants to prove he's right, but I don't want him to push too deeply into this spiritualism business. It won't end well...

EXCERPT FROM
SMITHY: A TWENTY-YEAR COMPENDIUM
BY REID BENNETT, PHD

CHAPTER SIX: BUMPS IN THE NIGHT

During the latter months of 1974, and the early part of 1975, reports of Smithy's aggression increased in frequency, as the following journal entries articulate:

SOLARIUM JOURNAL ENTRY
FROM RUBY CARDINI

October 9, 1974

"...After Smithy completed his drills, I allowed him to play with Maisie. He started petting and grooming her as she lay on her side. Then I noticed him massaging her more forcefully. The dog whined and tried to roll over so she could get up, but Smithy pushed her back down. I told him to be gentler and signed to him, "No." Smithy stepped back, long enough for Maisie to stand, but as she tried to exit the room, he seized her tail and pulled it hard. Poor Maisie yelped. I repeatedly (four times) signed to him to let her go. ("No," "stop," "put that down," "no tail"). I was afraid he might even break her tail, but he finally released her, and she darted off with that precious tail tucked between her legs.

I haven't witnessed him being rough with the animals before. Smithy may not always know his own strength, but Maisie was making it clear she was uncomfortable, and he still didn't stop, not even after I reprimanded him. Has anyone else noticed insubordination or hostility on Smithy's part?"

SOLARIUM JOURNAL ENTRY
FROM JEFF DALTON

October 13, 1974

"Smithy refused to go to bed at his appointed time. We washed up, put on his PJs, and I tucked him in, but when I signed to him to go to sleep, he started to screech. He threw off his covers, stood up in bed and jumped. He was extremely agitated. His fur stood up, and he signed, "No sleep" over and over. I turned off the light and sat in the chair beside him, waiting for him to calm down.

He threw a pillow at me and screamed some more but eventually tired himself out. He was quiet when I left the room. When I checked on him a couple of hours later, he appeared asleep, although his pillows and blankets had been tossed off the bed. I haven't seen a bedtime tantrum from him since he was one year old, and I've never heard him scream like that. I suggest we take him to a vet[1] to see if he might have a medical problem."

---

1   An animal clinician from Yale visited Trevor Hall over Veterans Day weekend and pronounced the chimp to be in good health.

SOLARIUM JOURNAL ENTRY
FROM TAMMY COHEN

November 6, 1974

"Smithy displayed aggression when I tried to take him upstairs for his bath. I signed, "Bath time," and he ignored me. I told him verbally to put his toys away and get up, but he ignored me again. When I attempted to take his toy car from him, he bit me. Fortunately, it was only a surface wound, but it broke the skin and caused a lot of bleeding. Equally fortunate, I got a rabies shot before I began this project. I believe Smithy's intent was to warn me instead of injure me, but I'm still troubled he chose this style of retaliation. Can we have him wear a mouth guard until he settles down?"

At times, Smithy's tantrums seemed to mirror tensions among his humans over their hardships with household utilities and frustrations with their personal lives. At others, Smithy's aggressive behavior waxed and waned with no discernible triggers. Generally, his acts consisted of low-level tantrums, property damage, or minor injuries. However, in certain memorable episodes, his violent behavior exploded in never-before-seen escalation, as revealed in the following diary entry:

DIARY OF GAIL EHRLICH

November 14, 1974

Dear Diary:

Last night was the scariest night of my life! It felt like I was in a horror movie or something. I'm still trying to figure out if I should write to Vanessa about it. It may not be safe for her to visit after all.

It all started when Smithy got out of his room again. He was fussy during his lessons. He wouldn't pay attention to our questions and kept pacing, covering his eyes and making "dark woman" signs. That scared me, but Wanda was exasperated and said he was only trying to ajitate us, and we should put him in time-out.

She took him upstairs. We heard him screeching and arguing all the way. Wanda left him there for about half an hour, then sent Jeff to get him. I thought it was kind of a dirty trick to punish Smithy and get him riled up, then make Jeff deal with him. The trick was on us though, because Jeff came running down to say Smithy wasn't there. He'd gotten out the door this time. It was closed but unlocked. All Smithy's toys were knocked off the shelves, but the door wasn't scratched up. He'd done something to the locks again.

Wanda was alarmed because the house is so big, and we had no idea where Smithy might have gone. Jeff offered to look for him outside, and Tammy suggested we call the Belancourts to warn them to stay inside with their dog, but Wanda didn't want to involve them in case it turned out to be a false alarm. Instead, she told us to split up and search the house. She even said if we didn't find him on our side of the house, she would open the sealed wing in case he found some way in there.

Wanda wanted us to close and lock all the doors behind us as we searched, so Smithy couldn't go in if he wasn't there already. Tammy said it wouldn't make any difference because he's a lock-picker, but Wanda said to do it anyway. She also asked Tammy to lock Maisie and the cats up so they wouldn't wander around, too.

For the first time, Wanda gave out skeleton keys. I always thought she and Piers must carry around a giant ring of keys to open all the different doors like you see in old prison movies, but it turns out they just have a handful of skeleton keys that can open any door. She gave one to Tammy and Ruby, one to me, and kept one for herself and Eric before the two of them went up to the third floor. She asked me to stay on the first level while the other girls searched the second floor.

I was relieved about that. The main level is where we spend most of our time, so I know it better. There aren't as many places for Smithy to hide. I did try to be thorough like Wanda had asked, but I couldn't lock the rooms behind me because most of them have no doors. I looked behind the curtains in the library and checked in the kitchen pantry to make sure he hadn't gone in there, and I even stood in the fireplace and looked up the chimney to see if Smithy had crawled up. It felt spooky to walk through the empty rooms. I wasn't used to seeing them lifeless.

Finally, I figured I'd looked everywhere I could and decided to help search upstairs instead of sitting around, waiting for Jeff to come back.

I tested the doors on some of the bedrooms, but they were locked, so I knew Tammy and Ruby had already checked them. I finally ended up at the door to the closed wing. I wasn't sure about going in since it's usually a restricted area. Finally, I pushed on the connecting door and was surprised when it opened.

It was so dark and spooky on the other side of the door! I couldn't see much farther than my feet even with the light from the hall shining behind me, and when I shut the connecting door, everything went black! I got scared and called out to Tammy and Ruby. Luckily, they were just around the next bend and came to find me. I was glad they both had flashlights. I hadn't bothered to grab one because the lights on the main level are all on. But of course, the electricity is off in the empty wing.

Tammy wanted me to get my own light for safety, but I didn't want to walk through the empty second floor, even though it wasn't as creepy as downstairs. So Ruby told me to stick close, and together we walked on. Every step we took creaked and echoed so it sounded like there were other people walking all around us. I don't remember feeling so creeped out on Orientation Day, but we had a big crowd then, and it was daytime.

We split up to check the rooms on either end when we reached the fork in the hall. I had to open every door with the skeleton key because even though they were locked, Smithy could have still climbed in the windows from outside. We'd go in a room, Ruby would shine her light around, and then we'd step around the edges of the room carefully because we didn't want to step through a rotten patch of floor.

I had chills the whole time, thinking about how Wanda always said this wing was dangerous. I wondered whether the roof might fall on our heads while we were searching. But it was kind of exciting too. I felt like we were the Three Investigators trying to solve a mystery. Those books always scared me so much that I'd hide them under the bed, but I'd go back to reading them later because part of me liked being scared. Tammy looked surprised when I told them that. Then she said she'd been thinking of us as Nancy Drew and her friends. And Ruby said the only thing missing was a storm outside with thunder and lightning. Otherwise, we had a perfect old dark house set-up.

Maybe that's what did it. I was thinking creepy thoughts already, and every time we came to a new room or turned a corner, I got nervous, wondering what we were going to see. Everything was so dark, and you could only see what was in that little ring of light moving one step at a time! It felt as if it wasn't really me walking down the hall opening doors, but as if I was watching a movie that had some other girls doing it—and I was getting ready to yell at them because the killer was about to jump out with a knife!

I called Smithy's name, so he'd come out. When we got under that octo little balcony thing, I asked Ruby if we should go upstairs and look around while Tammy finished the second floor. But Ruby didn't want to leave Tammy on her own, and Tammy said Wanda and Eric were supposed to search upstairs, so we should leave it for them.

Instead, we kept walking and went down a corridor I'd never seen before. It wasn't on our orientation tour. There weren't a lot of bedrooms here, just a few old cupboards where the servants must have stored their linens. I noticed the ceiling had skylights and thought that was funny because I knew there was another floor still on top of us. I asked why someone would put a skylight inside a house. Neither of them had any idea. I almost asked Tammy to ask Reid, but I didn't know if they still talked.

I asked Ruby to point her flashlight at the skylight, but it was so filthy and covered with cobwebs that you couldn't see through it to determine if there really was a roof above it. It looked icky. Tammy was just telling us to come back and finish searching when the most hideous face appeared in the glass! You couldn't see it very clearly because of all the grime, but that made it scarier because parts of it were blurry, like a ghost appearing. I saw glowing red eyes and sharp teeth nashing at us! The face snarled, and Ruby screamed and dropped her flashlight. Tammy pointed hers, but I was so scared by then that I didn't want to see anymore. It was the face from a nightmare, and all I could think was "This house has ghosts _and_ monsters! We've got to get out!"

Then the beast started screaming, and its voice made the walls shake. I heard a dreadful pounding, and I just knew it was coming for us, and that it would run down the stairs and get us. Ruby was trying to chase her flashlight rolling across the floor, but I grabbed her arm to pull her away so we could escape, and just then, I heard an explosion!

Tammy screamed and pushed me against the wall. I heard tinkling and felt something burn my arm. That's how I knew that whatever it was had broken through the skylight and was coming to get us! I covered my face to protect it from the glass and because I didn't want to see the monster when it finally came for me.

I heard a thump behind us, and the thing started hollering. Then I heard pounding as it ran away from us. The door slammed. Tammy yelled, "That was Smithy!" I couldn't believe it! I never saw him snarl or heard him shriek like that, and I never thought he would break glass on us. But then I thought maybe he didn't recognize us through that dirty skylight either, and maybe he was scared, too, and thought we were monsters and was trying to intimidate us, and he hadn't wanted to kill us by breaking the skylight above us.

I felt so relieved knowing it wasn't really a monster, but my body was still all jumpy. I wanted to sit because I was shaking too much to walk, but there was glass everywhere. Tammy said we had to leave because it wasn't safe and told us to step very carefully over the broken glass. She muttered something about Wanda and repair costs. I glanced up at the skylight just for a second and couldn't believe what I saw. It looked as if a bomb had gone off in the ceiling! There was a big hole in the middle, and pieces of the frame swung free above our heads. Little fragments of glass kept trickling down, too. I pulled my shirt up over my head for protection and ran faster before the rest of the ceiling could collapse onto us.

We heard Wanda and Eric ahead of us, and sure enough they were standing on the third-floor balcony. Wanda asked what all the screaming was about, and Tammy told her we'd found Smithy, but he got away again because the door to the main house was unlocked. Wanda started cussing and yelled, "Why didn't you lock up like I told you?" Ruby butted in saying it was OK because the other rooms were locked, and Smithy would have to go downstairs where we know the layout better. Eric came down to help us find him, but Wanda stayed upstairs to see the damage to the skylight.

We all went to the main hallway, and Eric called out to Smithy in a cheerful voice, so he wouldn't get scared. We heard another door slam and ran faster. Then we heard a great big BOOM like the time this big tree fell over in a hailstorm and smashed our neighbor's car. Then we heard the most awful snarling and shrieking. I said, "That's him!" and Eric just stared at me as if he couldn't believe it.

We ran to Wanda's room. Smithy had torn the door to Wanda's room right off its hinges! It was lying on the floor, and he was standing in the open doorway, grunting and growling. Harriet and Peter were perched on top of Wanda's bookcase, hissing. Their fur was sticking up, so they looked like little brillo pads. Smithy reached out for them and made the sign for hug. Harriet swiped at him. I don't blame her. He was all dirty with dust and spiderwebs from playing on the third floor, so he still looked like a monster. Plus his fur was standing up, and his teeth were showing.

Smithy got upset and signed, "Bad mad." Then he launched himself up the bookcase. He really can jump high! I guess that's how he gets out the windows. Smithy landed all the way on the third shelf and started to climb. There were only two more to go before he reached the cats.

Eric yelled at him to stop and come down, but Smithy didn't listen. So Tammy grabbed one of Wanda's shoes lying by her bed and hurled it *at him. It bounced off Smithy's shoulder, and there's no way it could have hurt him, but he got mad all the same. He paused at the fourth shelf and looked back in time to see Tammy holding the other shoe. She had it raised to throw it, but when he looked at her, she froze.*

Smithy jumped down and picked up Wanda's chair. He lifted it over his head with just one hand and swung it—the whole thing!—at Tammy. She dropped the shoe and jumped back, covering her face and head with her arms. Ruby yelled, "Run before he kills you!" I couldn't move. I couldn't think of anything to do. I couldn't believe what I was seeing. It felt like being at the movies again, only worse. I just kept hoping I could close my eyes before Smithy cracked open Tammy's head.

All this time, Eric was yelling at Smithy to stop, to put the chair down. He was so brave! He ran into the room, got right behind Smithy and grabbed the chair before he could swing it again. Smithy looked surprised. He looked up at Eric, and I swear I saw his eyes glow! He tried to pull the chair away, but Eric hung on for dear life. His feet skidded over the floor, and I saw his face turning red from the struggle.

Tammy dived away from Smithy toward the bookcase. She yelled, "Someone help me get these cats out of here!" And it was like those were magic words to break a spell. Ruby and I both ran over to help her. Ruby stretched out her hands to Peter and called to him, but he backed farther away. Tammy cursed and took a book off the shelf. She jumped up and tried to sweep the cats off the bookcase with it. I wondered if I should get some catnip to lure them down. Then I looked back to see what Smithy was doing.

Just then, Smithy flung Wanda's chair across the room <u>while Eric was still clinging to it.</u> Eric's feet left the ground, and he turned a kind of summersalt, then fell against the wall with the chair on top of him. He looked out of it. I guess he hit his head on the wall. Smithy was on him in a flash. He knocked the chair away and grabbed Eric's leg. Then he started to drag Eric across the room!

Eric came to and realized what was happening. He tried to get away, but Smithy swung him <u>around over his head</u> and threw him across the room. He let go, and Eric hit the bookcase right at our feet. Lots of Wanda's books and nick-nacks fell. The cats even started sliding off.

Tammy grabbed Peter and shoved him into my arms and yelled, "Gail, go across and open the door. Put him inside!" I backed away, holding the cat but was too afraid to walk past Smithy to get to the hall. Tammy tried to help Eric up, but Smithy grabbed him again by both feet. She tried to hold on, but Smithy pulled so hard that he tore Eric's grip loose, and Eric went rolling across Wanda's rug. All I could think of was that suitcase commercial and I wondered if Smithy was going to start jumping on Eric's back next.

Eric was trying to sign to Smithy, "Stop please. Be good." Smithy wasn't paying attention though. He was panting, and his eyes kept darting around as if he was looking for something. Then he looked right at me, and I about died! I thought he was going to come over and grab me next, like a caveman dragging his mate around by the hair.

I heard Ruby say, "Help me tip it over!" and Tammy yelled, "Gail, move!" I looked back and saw they were tugging on the bookcase. And down it went. All Wanda's things went crashing down, and Harriet yowled as she hit the floor. The bookcase fell toward Smithy, so he let go of Eric and jumped back onto Wanda's bed. Luckily, Eric still had good reflexes, and he rolled out of the way before the bookcase hit the ground. Then Ruby snatched Harriet and grabbed my arm and dragged me into the hallway.

She asked for my key and gave me Harriet to hold, while she fumbled with it to open one of the bedrooms. It was hard to hang on to the cats because they were squirming and clawing at me, but I hugged them so they wouldn't get in harm's way again.

Maisie was shut up in the room next door, barking and howling and whining. She had to know something bad was happening, even though she couldn't see any of it. She must have been crying for a long time, but I hadn't noticed with all the excitement. There was something else I hadn't noticed either until it was almost too late. But Ruby did!

Her key was in the lock and the door half-open, when she turned to me. Her face was already pale, but it got even whiter when she asked, "Do you smell smoke?" I looked at Maisie's door, and sure enough, I saw little gray clouds pouring out. And then the fire alarm howled.

Jeff came running up the stairs, shouting questions about what the hell was going on. Ruby began to tell him about Smithy attacking Eric, *but Tammy and Eric barged out of Wanda's room just then. Tammy yelled at us to lock ourselves in and take cover. She pushed me and Ruby inside and tried to shut the door behind us, but Ruby blocked it. She told her Maisie's room was on fire. Tammy's face twisted up. "Oh God! I separated the animals so they wouldn't harass each other!" she said.*

I was screaming and crying and still squeezing the cats. I told them, "We can't stay here! The fire could burn the wall and get us next! Let's go back to our room!" Ruby was back in the hall by then and trying to unlock the door of the burning room, but something was wrong. Either the key wouldn't fit, or the knob was too hot. Maisie was whimpering but it didn't sound as strong. I thought she must be dying from the smoke, or she was about to burn up.

Tammy stood in the doorway, blocking me. She asked, "How could a fire start? That room was completely empty."

Eric was leaning against the wall, trying to catch his breath and said he'd seen something dark dart across the hall ahead of him right before Smithy had ripped Wanda's door down. He said maybe Smithy went to Maisie's room first and started the fire. I wanted to know where Smithy was because I thought he might come after us. Eric said he was still on Wanda's bed, covering his ears and rocking back and forth. I guess the alarm had him freaked out.

Finally, Jeff told Ruby to find a safer room to hide, and he was going to try to get Maisie out. "How?" she asked. "Will you knock the door down? We should wait for the firemen." But Jeff said that would be too late. He ran back downstairs while Ruby called after him. Eric steered her down the hall and beckoned us to follow.

The four of us went to my and Tammy's room and locked ourselves in. Ruby went to the window to watch for the fire trucks. I heard her scream and went to see what was wrong now. I saw Jeff climbing up the fire escape. I held my breath, watching him go up and up. Those fire stairs are so rickety. I was afraid they would collapse and send Jeff tumbling down. Ruby must have thought so, too, because she clung to the curtains so hard her knuckles turned white.

Tammy opened the windows, and we stepped out on the balcony to watch. Jeff kept climbing up and up the side of the building. He didn't slow down, and the fire stairs held until he was right outside the burning room. He paused and looked through the window. Then he hopped up on the railing of the fire escape and kicked until the glass broke. Tammy whispered he shouldn't do that because the air would stir up the fire worse. That made Ruby start to cry. And just like Tammy said, a big dark cloud came billowing out of the window.

Then Eric slapped Ruby on the back and said, "Here he comes! See!"

I could see Jeff on the fire escape again. He had something big slung over his shoulders. It was Maisie! I cheered even though I didn't know if she was alive or not. That's when the fire trucks arrived. One parked underneath the fire escape as Jeff climbed down with Maisie. He dropped her but she got up, so she was still alive. Then Jeff jumped down, too, and we clapped again because he was going to be fine. The firemen put their ladder against the wall and brought the hose up to put out the fire. We ran back in the hallway to meet Jeff.

Wanda was standing there, looking completely blown away. She was holding Smithy, jiggling him up and down like a baby to calm him. It worked fast. It was like watching him shrink. He went from a big scary ape to our little Smithy again. The alarm shut off, and I heard footsteps behind us and figured it was a fireman, but when I turned around, it was Jeff. Smithy saw him, too, and let go of Wanda and ran to him. I thought Smithy was going to attack Jeff and I cried out, but he jumped up into Jeff's arms. Jeff stayed cool. He caught Smithy and hugged and talked to him like nothing had happened. "Hey now. What's up? Did you make a mess, buddy?"

Wanda freaked out. "Do you mean he did all of this?" Jeff promised Wanda he'd help clean up her room and secure her bookcase and put her door back up, but she was still wound up. "And will you replace the skylight in the East Wing, too?" she asked him. Then she turned on us and asked why we'd left Smithy alone. "Because Smithy was possessed and trying to attack us, that's why," Tammy said. Smithy acted like he heard her. His little ears perked up, and he stared at her with big sad eyes. She got nervous and said she was going to keep an eye on the cats and stay inside the rest of the night. She went back into our room and shut the door.

"And the fire—did he do that, too?" Wanda pointed to the door of the burning room. Suddenly it popped open, and we screamed, but it *was only a fireman coming out. He said the fire was out and they were looking for what had caused it. Looking for matches or something, I guess. But by the time they left us, they still hadn't found anything. At least they didn't say Smithy started it. Eric wasn't positive he'd seen him come out of that room, so we gave him a pass.*

Eric and Smithy made up. After the firemen left, he went over to Smithy and signed "friend" to him. Smithy looked at him for a long time, almost as if he didn't recognize Eric. Then he reached out and patted his head and messed up his hair, and Eric laughed. It was a relief to see Smithy calm again.

Eric admits he was stupid to struggle with Smithy when he was in a bad mood. He knows he was lucky not to get badly hurt. His legs and arms are all bruised, and he's limping, but that's it. Smithy is strong enough now that he could probably have smashed Eric completely, but he didn't. He held back.

Tammy warned me he could smash any of us. I don't think she trusts Smithy anymore. She says he's not the same. I guess she means he's more dangerous now that he's getting bigger. I hope she doesn't really think he's possessed. He looked so normal and quiet after his tantrum was over. Exausted I guess.

Maisie's going to be fine. She's coughing a lot—I can hear her from Tammy's room where she's sleeping. But the firemen said that in a couple of days, after she rests, she can run around like nothing had happened. I think it'll take longer for Maisie to warm up to Smithy.

We still don't know how he got into the locked wing. Or why he had to rip Wanda's door off, when he's usually so good at just opening any lock he wants. We'll probably never know how he escaped or what had set him off—maybe seeing us unexpectedly in that empty wing with the flashlight. He'd become territorial and broke the skylight. Then maybe he heard the animals barking and whining in the locked rooms and wanted to get to them. Maybe he got frustrated because they wouldn't play or let him pet them, so that set him off again.

Jeff took Smithy back to bed and stayed in his room while he slept. Wanda says we'll have to guard Smithy for a while now. That or tie him to his bed so he doesn't get out and cause trouble again.

I know Smithy's not normally like this. Everyone can have a bad day sometimes. Humans do, so why not apes? But I wonder if I should let Vanessa visit for Christmas Break. I know she'll be crushed if I don't let her come next month. I just don't want her to see Smithy like this. It would give her the wrong idea about him and spoil her whole trip. I guess I'll have to think about it some more. And see how Smithy does in the next few weeks.

That's enough for now. Good night, Diary.

DIARY OF RUBY CARDINI

November 14, 1974

File this under "Conversations I Never Thought I'd Have With Wanda:"

Wanda: I don't know what to make of him!

Me: Do you think he really could be?

Wanda: What?

Me: What Tammy said. Possessed.

Wanda: Possessed by what? A demon?

Me: By the Dark Woman. Or by something similar?

She hesitated, then scoffed. "That's silly."

"But what if?" I prodded. I was terribly rattled by our battle with Smithy. At that moment, it seemed crucial to consider all possibilities and try anything to get him back under control. Normally, I would never have suggested the idea aloud, and certainly not to Wanda, but I thought she seemed open to <u>considering extreme possibilities</u> now.

But Wanda still had qualms. "How would we be able to test for anything like that? Do you want to pray over him?" I thought she was being sarcastic, until she lowered her voice. "You're Catholic, too, aren't you?"

I admitted I wasn't practicing, but I still remembered the prayers. "In English, that is. I don't know if it makes a difference."

Wanda took a deep breath and stepped into the acrid room. Her nose wrinkled, and she stifled a cough. Then she lifted her hand—and drew back. "This is dumb," she muttered.

I heard myself say, "I'll do it." Somebody needed to, but I wasn't quite sure what to do. I didn't even see "The Exorcist" last year because I got scared just hearing people talk about it. I stood in the doorway and raised my right hand. I closed my eyes and thought back on all the church services I'd attended with my family as a kid—not about how bored I could get listening to the sermon, but about all the things that made church special. The smell of the candles. The glitter of the stained glass. In my head, I heard the organ playing and the swell of the choir's voices. I thought of the priest transforming the wine and the wafer. I pictured posing with my grandparents for a photo in my white Communion dress. And I began to recite the Lord's Prayer.

I spoke slowly and considered the meaning of each word as I never had before. Usually, I would jibber out the prayer automatically, like the words to "Row, Row, Row Your Boat." It's awful to admit, but when you're a kid, so much feels routine because you don't understand it. You just do what an adult tells you to do and don't really care about it. This time, I took it seriously so it would count. I wanted God to hear me and dismiss whatever chaotic force had come into our home and our lives.

Wanda stood quietly behind me, humoring me, I thought. But as I finished, she joined me in saying "Amen," and went on to recite the entire Nicene Creed. When we finished, neither of us spoke. Maybe I was expecting to hear devils screeching as they were sucked back into Hell. Maybe I thought we'd see a puff of smoke or a light bursting through the window to tell us our prayers had taken effect. Needless to say, none of that happened.

Wanda asked, "Do you feel better now?" And I did. Maybe that was the sign; not any change in the room, but a change in me. Hopefully a change in Smithy, too. I admitted as much, and Wanda smiled. "Me, too." We stood for another quiet moment, serene. Then she turned to me, serious. "Whatever you do, don't tell Tammy about this!"

I promised, and I'll keep that promise. Even if our little do-it-yourself exorcism works (and please, God, let it work!) I won't tell anyone else what transpired.

MEMO FROM WANDA KARLEWICZ
TO PIERS PREIS-HERALD

November 15, 1974

Re: Incident of November 14, 1974

P,

I herein memorialize our telephone conversation regarding the above. Webster temporarily escaped from his room, wandered into the unoccupied wing where he damaged a skylight, then made his way to my room where he tipped over a bookcase. When Eric tried to intervene, Webster resisted, knocked him off his feet, and dragged him across the room by his leg. He released Eric after less than a minute. Webster then left my room and took refuge in the kitchen. While we searched for him, a fire erupted in an unused second-floor room where Maisie was being kept. She is fine. No cause has been determined for the blaze.

Although the excitement was distressing (Gail in particular is shaken and continues to rehash the events, though as usual, she exaggerates the hazards), no irrevocable damage ensued. The wallpaper in the burned room is charred, but the walls and flooring remain sound. Eric reports bruising and soreness in his leg, but no lasting injuries. Jeff agreed to reassemble my bookcase and anchor it to the wall so it won't fall again; a few picture frames were broken, but can be easily replaced. Likewise, I've scheduled an estimate with a local glazier for the skylight repair.

Eric is installing a news series of locks on Webster's door and windows today to prevent any unauthorized exploring in the future.

I assure you I have everything in hand to prevent such a situation from recurring.

—W

DIARY OF TAMMY COHEN

November 15, 1974

We've just learned Piers isn't coming up to assess the situation or Smithy. He's confident Wanda has everything under control.

I'm not.

The damage to property and people is "superficial:" the burned room is soot-stained, not structurally impaired. Eric is battered, not beaten. How badly does a person have to be injured before Piers will step in?

Never mind. I don't want to find out.

Given how Piers micromanages so many other aspects of his study, it's a wonder he refuses to personally investigate his chimp's misbehavior. Evidently, there's no glory in removing people from danger when you've put them in its path to start.

He's made it clear how deeply invested he is in this study. Now it seems he values his research more than our well-being. I'm not satisfied Smithy simply went exploring, got spooked, and threw a tantrum when the cats wouldn't play with him. We were all "lucky" nothing worse happened. I don't want to be "lucky" again. Someone needs to own up. Something must change.

EXCERPT FROM
SMITHY: A TWENTY-YEAR COMPENDIUM
BY REID BENNETT, PHD

The arrival of the winter holidays ushered in a welcome peace to Trevor Hall. Beginning with a dual celebration of Eric Kaninchen's birthday (November 26th) and Thanksgiving, reports from the team began to reflect greater levity and less strife. Staged photos show Smithy hanging wreaths, playing in the snow, and attempting to wrap Christmas presents alongside his beaming caregivers.

Between Thanksgiving and New Year's Day, the makeup of the household fluctuated. As students returned home for Christmas or other celebrations, only Jeff and Ruby remained behind to tend to their precious charge. Skeptics have noted that the absences of other signature players coinciding with the respite from strange noises and other accidents must indicate that one or more of those team members were secretly responsible for the mayhem at Trevor Hall.

Parapsychologists have noted the same correlation but attribute it to a different cause. According to their paradigm, the particular combination of all six personalities in the house, with their attendant micro-dramas, generated a certain energy that was conducive to a haunting. When some of the personalities exited the charged setting, the effect was akin to a release valve in a nuclear power plant opening. Energy was discharged or entirely absent, hence no phenomena occurred. It is a tempting hypothesis to consider, especially regarding Karlewicz and Ehrlich. However, this conclusion is suspect, considering the events that later transpired...

LETTER FROM RUBY CARDINI
TO VINCENT CARDINI

December 17, 1974

Dear Vinny:

I hope this finds you well and happy, and that Mom and Dad are both in good shape and good spirits. By now, you'll have finished finals; congratulations. That's something I did not miss one bit this year.

I wanted to let you know I won't be returning home for Christmas. Originally, I had talked with Sarah-Beth about spending the holidays together, but I'm very happy here in Newport and want to stay on. Actually, Jeff invited me to spend the holidays with his family in California, but I have no way to pay for airfare, and I wasn't about to let him bear that expense, Christmas present or not. To my surprise, he's chosen to remain with me instead of joining his family, so we two will be "holding down the fort," as Piers says.

Tammy went home last week to celebrate Hanukkah, but she's going to stay in NYC until after New Year's because her sister Ruth's birthday is coming up on the 23rd, and since most everybody else will be away for the full holiday week, she feels justified in taking the extra time. Wanda will only be away from the 23rd to the 26th, so we won't be on our own for long. Nevertheless, it will be an adventure; it will also be our chance to see how well we get along on our own.

We'll have Smithy, of course. He'll stay with us in the gatehouse, as we'll have less space to heat and the lure of the TV. We can watch Rudolph and Frosty together. I've already learned the sign for "snowman" and can sign most of the verses. Someday, I'll show you how it works.

I'm looking forward to this Christmas. It truly feels like I've found my place to belong and room to finally grow into an adult. This is what

I wanted when I set out on this project, and now I'm seeing at least part of my ambition fulfilled. Please be happy for me.

Please don't give Mom the full details; just tell her I'm sharing Christmas in RI with a friend from the study, and we're continuing important work. Tell her I'm happy, that I miss her and love her, and that I will be thinking of her warmly when I'm listening to Christmas Eve mass. Should Dad ask about me at all, please tell him the same.

I love you, big brother, and wish you a blessed holiday. Take care of our parents. And don't open the enclosed present until the big day!

Much love,

Ruby

LETTER FROM RUBY CARDINI
TO TAMMY COHEN

December 26, 1974

Dear Tammy,

Happy Boxing Day to you, whatever that is². I heard Piers mention it before he left; I gather it's a kind of second Christmas with presents and goodwill, but not explicitly religious. Maybe that can be our official celebration next year. I miss having the whole gang together.

I wish you'd been with us for the holiday. Jeff and I staged Christmas for Smithy. We set up sleeping bags in the solarium and spent Christmas Eve in the big house. We got to enjoy the warmth from the big fireplace and the fresh smell of the pretty pine tree in the corner. I was concerned Smithy wouldn't sleep well if he wasn't in his own bed, but I discounted the nights he's spent with Sarah and underestimated his general laziness. He didn't budge as we took turns moving presents out of the gatehouse where we've been hiding them.

Jeff and I woke Smithy just after sunrise. We didn't sleep much all night from anticipation and couldn't wait to spring the surprise any longer. We expected him to be grouchy, but he popped awake, as if he'd been expecting us. Maybe he recalled holidays spent with the McKenzies. He's known something was afoot this whole time. All week long, he's been checking the stockings over the big fireplace and looking reproachfully at me when he's found them empty. As of yesterday morning, they're all full and awaiting your return.

Smithy sprang right for them when we led him into the library. He wasn't satisfied with his own sock full of candy and wanted some of yours, but Jeff is guarding them. Then we gave him his presents and

2   Modern Boxing Day is based on the Ancient Roman festival of Saturnalia, held during the winter solstice, when slaves were placed in charge for the day and enjoyed fine dining and privileges in their masters' stead.

asked him about them as he was opening them (What color is the paper, etc.). Instead of handing presents directly to each other, Jeff and I also let Smithy play Santa. He put a little cap on Smithy, and it stayed on for maybe fifteen minutes. I took this picture of the little elf handing Jeff a package (a new dress shirt for when we go out).

We'll go through the process again when everyone else comes back, and you can all take turns giving Smithy your own gifts (though Jeff warns that in future, Smithy will always expect twelve days of Christmas presents). I gave him a stuffed Big Bird, a little fire truck, and a new little Christmas sweater (big enough for him to grow into). Jeff gave him some new records (folk music this time, but stuff he can still "sing" along with—though we'll have to figure out how to sign "Puff the Magic Dragon"), a couple of kids' puzzles, and a paint set.

"Now that he's mastered the vocabulary for colors, he can practice using colors," Jeff said. Well, Smithy's first trick was to try practicing with his colors on the wall of the library! I put a quick stop to that and told Jeff that's what he can expect when he buys paint but no paper; we rectified that today, and our little Pollock is merrily dribbling away at my feet as I write.

My presents to Jeff were less exciting. Besides the shirt, I gave him more film for his still camera and a biography of Edward G. Robinson, since Jeff does his voice so often. He gave me some unmentionables and a 45 of a song I'd never heard of called "Ruby Baby." We've already danced to it, and so has Smithy.

Today Jeff, Smithy, and I slept late and lazed around in our pajamas doing a whole lot of nothing. I miss our boisterous crowd. I think Wanda is due either tonight or early tomorrow, so I'm sure we'll get back to our regular routine soon enough. That may be a good thing. I look forward to having you back with us as well.

Happy New Year!
Ruby

LETTER FROM GAIL EHRLICH
TO VANESSA EHRLICH

January 4, 1975

Dear Sis,

I'm back! Even though I was away for ten whole days, it doesn't feel like I missed a thing because so many other people were away, too. I had to take a bus from the airport this time. It dropped me off at the Visitor's Center, and Piers was there having coffee and a Danish. We got to have breakfast and drive together to Trevor Hall. I asked if you could visit for Spring Break, and he said "Maybe," but he was smiling when he said it, so I'm pretty sure he meant "Yes."

I know you were disappointed I didn't bring you back with me after Christmas like we'd planned, but I think spring will be better for you. Right now with all the snow, there's not a lot to do. It will still be cold, but most of the snow should be gone by then, and the flowers will be blooming. We'll have a lot of fun!

Here are some photos of our mansion all covered with snow. Isn't it pretty? I'm also sending you a painting Smithy made! Jeff gave him finger paints for Christmas, and he loves them! He's been making new artwork every day. None of it looks like anything. I mean, he's not painting people or houses, just swirls and dots and handprints. Alot of it looks like what a preschooler would do, but that's still cool when you realize it's a chimp doing it. And he's almost as old as a preschooler; he's going on three years old!

Smithy likes the bright colors: yellow, red, and orange. He hardly ever uses purple or blue and never black. I wonder what that means. I'll have to see if I can find a book about colors and mood. Wouldn't it be amazing if Smithy became a famous artist like Van Gogh (I saw his pictures in Ruby's book), and all his swirls and blobs really meant something deep! I've asked him to make me some paintings, and I've put them up in my room. You can see them when you visit...

EXCERPT FROM
SMITHY: A TWENTY-YEAR COMPENDIUM
BY REID BENNETT, PHD

CHAPTER SEVEN: THE WRITING'S ON THE WALL

Much has been discussed of animal-produced artwork and whether the pictures indicate a true aesthetic sense (or even an attempt at evoking an inner life) or random smudges. Greater attention would surely have focused on Smithy's expressive attempts had the unfortunate events following his receiving the fateful paint set not overshadowed his artistic output. As always, observers disagree as to what extent Smithy's artistic impulses truly may have been involved. Predictably, the division arises from what one believes really happened when the weeks of peace and quiet were irrevocably spoiled...

KITCHEN JOURNAL ENTRY
FROM ERIC KANINCHEN

January 13, 1975

We think there may be intruders in the house. Last night, Gail got the midnight munchies and crept downstairs for a snack. While she was raiding the fridge, she claims she heard voices from behind her. She thought it was someone coming in the kitchen, but no one showed up. Then, when she was walking back down the hall, she heard the voices again, louder, and "from all around." According to Gail, she couldn't make out any words, only the sound of voices mumbling or possibly speaking another language. I've asked how many voices she heard, but she wasn't sure, and though she thinks it was a man and a woman, she won't swear to it.

The voices were creepy, she said. They got loud and then soft and sounded both far away and as if they were coming from right around the corner. Gail didn't call out because she was afraid whoever it was might not be friendly. Also, she wasn't sure if they knew she was there, but didn't like to think they did. She said it felt as if the speakers were following her. She freaked out and ran back up to her room to wake Tammy, who then came and woke me for reinforcement.

We left Gail locked safely in her room with all the lights on while we investigated downstairs. I figured with all the noise Gail made in retreating and the time that had passed, if anyone <u>had</u> been in the house, they would have split. Sure enough, we didn't find anyone hiding on the ground floor, and we looked in all the rooms, under the tables, behind the drapes, and even in the pantry. I also checked the radio and turntable in case one of the devices managed to turn itself on, but both were cold.

Maisie was sleeping in the library. She lifted her head when I came in but went back to sleep. The whole time I searched, she never came to investigate what I was up to. She's a good companion but a lousy watchdog. Keeping in mind she knows me, I wonder whether any outsider entering the house would cause her to raise an alarm.

Just to be sure, I went outside and around the house to look for footprints and still didn't find anything (though, instead of a prowler, I caught a cold). The front and back doors were locked before I opened them, and neither lock looked tampered with. We didn't check the windows because there are so many, and we didn't want to wake everybody up, but I'm confident no one got through that way either. We've had a lot of rain and sleet this week, but there weren't any footprints beneath the windows. (See, Tammy, I did read my mysteries carefully).

So what happened? Gail swears she was wide awake and didn't dream or imagine hearing noises. She's adamant she heard human voices and not creaking boards, the wind, or the refrigerator running. Wanda thinks it's possible Gail heard Piers's voice traveling down the stairs and into the kitchen. He likes to dictate his notes to a tape recorder so she can type them later. He's a night owl and was working on his manuscript in the wee hours. Wanda pointed out that the architectural features of this house cause sound to travel in strange ways, like in the gallery downstairs. So maybe Gail somehow could hear Piers talking and playing back his words from his room on the third floor, even though she was all the way down on the first floor. Maybe his voice carried through some old air vents. That would explain why the voices sounded so muffled. Gail said she'd write to Reid Bennett and ask him about it because he's an expert on old houses.

As comforting as Wanda's explanation is, I'm still willing to consider there was an intruder in the house. (Or still is? One whole wing is closed off—what if someone's been hiding and living in there? What if there are secret passages we don't know about?) I recommend a night patrol and checking the unused wing before we turn in, at least for a few days. To be extra safe, I also asked Piers to change the locks, but he says that's too expensive, and I'm being ridiculous.

I mention all this here because I suspect the adventure may connect to Smithy's lock-picking abilities. If he's sneaking out at night and going around the house unlocking doors, then it would be possible for a prowler to get in.

OK, I just read that, and it sounds pretty stupid to think Smithy's in league with cat burglars. To be clear, I don't believe he's consciously working with any prowlers. I'm saying someone who's out to get us may be aware of his little quirk, maybe after overhearing me talking at the hardware store, and is taking advantage of it.

I've found no signs of forced entry, so that means whoever's doing these pranks either has a key or someone is letting them in.

Or it's someone who is already in the house.

Or it's no one, and we're all going crazy.

MEMO FROM TAMMY COHEN

January 14, 1975

Following Gail's reports of strange voices and a potential intruder, Ruby and I investigated whether Gail could have perceived natural noises or voices from another part of the house.

We focused on the ground floor, the main staircase, the servants' stairwell, and the second and third floors (first corridor). One of us stood on the first floor, alternately in the kitchen, at the foot of the servants' stairs, in the connecting hallway between the foyer and the solarium, and in the foyer, at the foot of the main staircase, while the other stood on the servants' stairs, in the hallway between the kitchen and the solarium, in the hallway between the solarium and the foyer, and at the top of the main stairs, respectively. Each took turns speaking random doggerel while the other attempted to identify what was said. We synchronized our watches and took turns speaking for one full minute every five minutes (e.g., Tammy spoke for one minute, paused for a minute, then Ruby spoke for one minute and paused for a minute, repeating this sequence every five minutes). Carrying out all the permutations took about one hour.

What we discovered is as follows:

a. It's impossible to hear anything said in the third-floor corridor (outside Piers's tower room) from the second floor, the ground floor hallway, or the kitchen. It _is_ possible to hear a voice from the landing on the servants' stairs between the second and third floors, but only if the speaker shouts at the top of her lungs.

b. When the speaker is on the main stairs between the ground and second floors, and the listener is at the foot of the stairs, the latter can clearly hear the former speaking at normal volume until the speaker ascends above the second floor. At that point, the listener hears muffled speaking. When the listener retreats further down the hallway or to the kitchen, the speaker's voice does not carry at all.

c. Likewise, when the speaker is on the servants' stairs, and the listener is in the hallway between the stairs and the kitchen or inside the kitchen, it is possible to hear some of what is said, and vice versa. For example, when Ruby was on the second-floor landing, and I stood at the foot of the stairs, I thought she was reciting Edgar Allan Poe's "The Bells"; in fact, she was chanting "She Sells Seashells." When I recited "Mary Had a Little Lamb" from the same landing, Ruby heard my voice from the kitchen, but couldn't distinguish any words. Note that in each location, even when the speech could not be identified, the listener could always identify the speaker's voice and the relative position of the speaker (e.g., Ruby knew I was on the stairs, but not necessarily how high up).

Based on these trials, I don't see how Gail possibly could have heard Piers's voice on the third floor as she moved from the kitchen to the main staircase, unless he was broadcasting into a PA system. Normal voices simply do not carry within the house that way. Some other cause must be responsible.

MEMO FROM JEFF DALTON

January 15, 1975

Inspired by Ruby and Tammy, Eric and I embarked on a similar set of trials. Instead of relying on fallible human ears (e.g., "Bells" v. "Seashells"), we left a tape recorder running while we spoke from various locations. We then played the tape for an objective audience (Tammy, Ruby, Wanda) to see if anyone could detect our voices.

We started our experiment in the ground floor corridor near the main stairs (e.g., the "echoing hallway") since we know sound <u>can</u> carry in this spot. Sure enough, the tape recorded our entire conversation. When we moved upstairs and left the tape recorder behind, it picked up nothing at all.

We moved the device around to various rooms on the first floor and different spots on each stairwell. On the stairs, you can hear muffled voices and footsteps from people going by (It's important to note that Gail reported voices, but no sounds of movement), but when you leave the recorder in the kitchen and walk down the hall or up the stairs, the tape picks up nothing but air hissing. We certainly were unable to record any speech or other sounds from as high as the third floor when the recorder was left in the kitchen.

The recordings are clearest when the speaker is within a twenty-foot radius, speaking at a normal decibel level; the device still picks up approximately eighty-five to ninety percent of speech from within a thirty- to fifty-foot radius when the speaker uses an atypically loud tone of voice (e.g., a teacher projecting her voice above a noisy class).

Tonight I plan to leave recording devices running overnight in the kitchen, in the foyer, and somewhere else to be determined on one of the two staircases. This will allow us to review any ambient noise Gail may have heard. I'll keep Maisie in the gatehouse to get her out of the way. If any of you were planning a romantic rendezvous, or if you wanted to use the landing to rehearse for your summer stock starring role, know I'll be listening!

EXCERPT FROM
SMITHY: A TWENTY-YEAR COMPENDIUM
BY REID BENNETT, PHD

CHAPTER SEVEN: THE WRITING'S ON THE WALL

The pluck and ingenuity of the researchers in testing potential explanations for the unsettling occurrences they experienced is admirable. In reading their notes and observations, we recognize this was a group of trained scientists and not the flighty frat boys and sorority girls so often mocked elsewhere in the literature.

Although no satisfactory explanation was ever identified for Ehrlich's experience on the night of January 13, 1975, her housemates effectively ruled out the possibility of sound echoing from an upper level of the Hall. Unfortunately, their scientific thirst appears to have dried up after Dalton's memo. No diaries or memos describe the outcome of his nighttime investigations. Some authors have speculated he never went through with the investigation and only issued the memo as a threat to any would-be pranksters in the house.

However, Wilbur Roland's recent acquisition of the reels from Dalton's investigation effectively thwarts any naysayers and broaches a new, chilling possibility.

Years before the Smithy study, Latvian scientist Konstantin Raudive had claimed to be able to record the voices of the dead using standard audio equipment. His own recordings of birdsong allegedly picked up the voice of his deceased mother calling his name from the Other Side. Thus, Electronic Voice Phenomena was born.

Reasonable people may dismiss such now-ubiquitous popular recordings as auditory pareidolia, the desire to find meaningful patterns in random white noise, but reports of ghosts caught on audiotape are frequent enough to draw attention and often consensus as to what is heard on tape.

Roland's team analyzes tapes believed to have captured spectral speech. In its examination of Dalton's tapes, a panel of independent judges noted the following:

- At 3 hours, 21 minutes, the kitchen recorder picked up an androgynous voice saying, "Who's there?"
- At 4 hours, 57 minutes, the main landing recorder caught approximately forty seconds of a male voice. Only fragments can be deciphered, including, "Tell them... going out... can't" and either "bye" or "why."
- At 5 hours, 13 minutes, the hallway recorder caught a female voice vocalizing: *Eeeee eeee eeee eeeeee* and laughing tonelessly at intervals lasting to the 5 hour, 25-minute mark.

Roland's team compared these snippets to samples of voice recordings by all the people then staying at Trevor Hall, as well as other related principals, including the 1974–75 school year instructors of the Harvey Meyer School, me, and Robert La Fontaine. Voices, like fingers, have a pattern that persists throughout the lifetime, and not even the most skilled celebrity impersonator can change his or her actual voice pattern though they may successfully pitch the sound of their voice differently.

None of the voices matched what was heard on the tapes.

It is easy to imagine the consternation and even fear with which the intrepid research team may have listened to their recordings the next morning. Perplexed and wary, did they make a pact never to discuss the results of this particular experiment? Or perhaps nobody at Trevor Hall wrote about the recordings because none of them knew about them. It's possible Dalton shielded his fellow housemates by hiding (though not destroying) the tapes and lying about what they contained.

Because no one left any documentation of the EVP findings, we don't even know at what time the recordings were made. By extrapolating from journals about Smithy's care and feeding, and his stated bedtime of 9:00 p.m., we can assume the recordings were made between 10:00 p.m. and 6:00 a.m.

No living member of the household at Trevor Hall will make a statement on the tapes. Did the dead?

DIARY OF TAMMY COHEN

January 16, 1975

I no longer believe Gail was imagining things the other night. Not that I ever truly did. She can be melodramatic, but she was frightened enough that I knew <u>something</u> had happened. Now I have a better idea of what she experienced, but I'll be damned if I know what it was.

As luck would have it, I woke up needing to use the bathroom at the same time as Gail. She got to our toilet first, so I went down the hall to the public toilets. On my return trip, I heard noises.

These weren't voices, but the sounds of frenetic movement. Shuffling exploded over my head, followed by loud scraping. If I had to guess, I would have said somebody on the third floor was dragging furniture around the room. However, the rooms above our floor are unoccupied.

Next, I thought Smithy had gotten out of his room again, and that he'd broken into the unused bedrooms to wreak havoc. I hesitated long enough to try to get a better feel for where he was. In that brief interval, the sound jumped down the hall and morphed into loud scratching, unlike the sound of animals' claws on hardwood flooring and more like the sound of a crowbar trying to force open a sealed door.

I started down the hall in pursuit of the noise, still trying to envision the third-floor plan; it varies significantly from the second-floor layout, and I haven't been up there often enough to form a cognitive map. At the same time, I tried to imagine how Smithy could have gotten from one room to another so quickly. The worst of my speculation involved decimated walls or exposed ductwork.

The sound of an anvil plummeting to the floor froze my stride and drove me into a defensive crouch. My first thought was the weakened floor, or the roof, of the closed wing had collapsed at last. The wall to which I clung still trembled with the reverberations. Yet Eric and Gail failed to appear and ask what was wrong. Surely one of them had to have heard—and felt—that racket. Nobody came, and the noises continued, now as running footsteps crossing just over my head. They moved toward the main staircase, so that's where I went, too, determined to intercept the little stinker and bring him to justice.

Since my floormates hadn't yet shown themselves, I didn't want to rouse them. Though I moved swiftly, I stepped on the balls of my feet at the edges of the hallway and hugged the walls to make as little noise as possible. Whoever was over my head felt no such restraints, for they had begun to pound or kick the walls rhythmically. The throbbing now emanated from the vicinity of the tower room, and my lascivious side wondered if Piers and Wanda were getting in on the action. That thought was knocked right out of my head as I rounded the staircase and almost walked into Wanda.

She looked surprised to see me and asked what I was doing. For the moment, I couldn't answer because I was so startled. She looked curious but otherwise calm; yet, if she'd just come from the third floor, why hadn't she heard and done something about the racket?

I said I thought Smithy was up to his tricks because I'd heard moving furniture, pounding, and footsteps. Wanda frowned and said, "That can't be. I just checked on him and for once, he's sound asleep and snoring like he means it. There's no way he could have gotten past me." Left dumbstruck again, I considered whether Piers might have someone else upstairs with him if Wanda was standing before me. She must have read the uncertainty in my face because she suggested we go back upstairs to look.

Wanda escorted me to Smithy's room. Sure enough, you could hear him sawing logs from halfway down the hall. She pushed the door open wide enough for me to peek in and see him splayed on his back with his teddy bear, the moon grinning through the window just like in a storybook. I agreed Smithy couldn't have been the noisemaker, but I urged her to keep investigating the third floor to ensure there was no intruder. Wanda frowned, no doubt reflecting she would have heard the kind of ruckus I'd described, but I prevailed. I wanted to be thorough, and more importantly, for my sanity, I wanted an answer for what I'd experienced.

We tiptoed down the hall to the corridor where I thought the noises had originated. Wanda used her skeleton key to unlock a couple of bedrooms; they were empty—not just of prowlers, but of furniture. The walls were intact and neither scraped nor knocked in. No moving beds, no crowbars. What the hell had I heard?

I thanked Wanda for placating me and made the first lame excuse that came to mind: I must have heard the pipes acting up. "Let's hope not," she said, coolly. "We've had more than enough of that." I said, "Amen to that," and told her I appreciated her time, then took my red face back to bed. Wanda probably thinks I was sleepwalking. I would like to believe that, too.

I don't believe in the bogeyman any more than I believe the water pipes can sound like a hippopotamus rampaging through the third floor, or that Piers's dictation machine can be heard from the kitchen. I don't believe I'm crazy, or that my senses are untrustworthy either. But Gail was already competing with Smithy for lumberjack of the night when I got back to my own room (she couldn't have been in Piers's room), and she wouldn't be sleeping so soundly if she'd heard what I'd heard. Would that I could believe Wanda was gaslighting me!

I asked Eric at breakfast if he'd heard anything odd last night, and he said no. But he looked knowingly at me when he asked why I wanted to know. I wish Ruby had slept in the main house last night; I wonder if she would have sensed anything amiss.

So what was it? And why did it only target me? Given some other things that have happened in this house, I'm glad I only heard something weird. But it's still more than I bargained for and plenty more than I'd like to experience again.

EXCERPT FROM
SMITHY: A TWENTY-YEAR COMPENDIUM
BY REID BENNETT, PHD

CHAPTER SEVEN: THE WRITING'S ON THE WALL

The new year saw more literal breakdowns recurring within the household. During January, the occupants recorded three failures of the amenities:

RECEIPT FROM "BOB THE PLUMBER"

January 3, 1975:

(3) clogged toilet/ $70 = $210

Paid Cash—received in full

TELEGRAM FROM WANDA KARLEWICZ
TO PIERS PREIS-HERALD

January 6, 1975:

Please release $300 emergency funds for repairs.
No hot water in shower and toilet has overflowed.

MEMO FROM JEFF DALTON
TO WANDA KARLEWICZ

January 8, 1975

Hey, Wanda!

What's it gonna take to get a plumber back out here? I thought I'd suddenly become popular, what with all the people dropping in, but it turns out they just want me for my bathroom. I've tinkered all I can with the pipes. It's time to call a professional. ASAP, please!

NOTE POSTED TO BULLETIN BOARD

January 16, 1975

I'm aware of the ongoing issues with the upstairs bathrooms. For now, the ground floor plumbing is holding up. We can all share this toilet.

Tammy and Eric—Many thanks for your clean-up efforts! Your contribution is greatly appreciated!

Gail—No, we cannot put Smithy back in diapers. Tammy worked hard to train him. I won't risk setting him back for untold months, just to make the day or two until we get a plumbing appointment more convenient. If worse comes to worst, use a bucket.

Please have patience. I am doing the best I can.

These inconveniences wore on nerves already thinned by fear of the unknown causes behind the nightly misadventures. What bearing they had on the timing of the next notorious incident has been hotly debated...

THE DIARY OF GAIL EHRLICH

January 20, 1975

Dear Diary,

The most disgusting thing happened last night! When Eric got up this morning to fix breakfast, he said he smelled something terrible in the hallway. He told us that at first, he thought Maisie had had an accident, but then he saw what was on the wall. He went to wake up Wanda so she could see it. Naturally, she flipped and hauled us all downstairs to look. She even called Jeff at the gatehouse and made him bring his camera to film it...

ARCHIVAL FILM FOOTAGE

Date: January 20, 1975
Location: The Hallway

Eric, Wanda, Ruby, Tammy, and Gail stand in a tight circle, whispering. Only Ruby wears jeans and a sweater; the others sport pajamas and robes. Wanda's voice rises more shrilly above the rest: *"Look at it!"*

The camera zooms in over the backs of the crowd and focuses on the wall. The wallpaper is smeared at eye level with a dark substance that loops up and down. The smears look vaguely like large crooked letters. Wanda exclaims, "Do you all see that? It didn't get there by itself!"

Eric says, calmly, "Wanda—"

Wanda's voice cracks, "It's my name! It's my damn name written in—in *shit!*" Eric raises his hands towards her, placatingly. She swats them away. "Don't touch me!" She takes a step back and wipes her face with the back of her hand. When she speaks, she sounds calm again. "Which one of you did it?"

Ruby asks, "Beg your pardon?"

Wanda says, "You heard me! Did you think it would be a fun joke?" She scans the faces of her housemates. As she talks, she glances between faces, quicker and quicker. "Were you waiting to see my face when I came downstairs? Is this supposed to intimidate me? What were you trying to prove? Is that what you think of me? That I'm a shitty person? So you decided to write my name—"

Tammy argues, "It isn't writing."

Wanda says, "No? You don't see this here?" She traces her finger in the air over the letters. "A 'W' and a lowercase 'A-N,' a capital 'D.'"

"No, I don't see it," Tammy murmurs.

"Jeff, get closer!" Wanda instructs. "Get all you can so Piers can see!"

The camera moves forward and tracks up and down each individual symbol on the wall.

Tammy insists, "It doesn't look like your name. It doesn't even look like letters. Those are just random smears and half-circles. I think you're reading too much into it—literally."

"No, I see it," Ruby says, and Wanda looks triumphantly at Tammy. Ruby continues, "They look more like the letters of Wanda's name than they do random smears." She indicates a horizontal half-circle and beside it, a diagonal line that transects a vertically oriented curve. "An 'N' and a 'D.'"

Eric nods. Gail wraps her arms around her torso and shivers.

Tammy says, "I mean, I believe *you* see it. People see shapes in the clouds all the time. To me, it just looks like lines and arcs. That thing you called a 'D' is barely connected. The stem and the…dome are at acute angles. And if you were trying to write something, why jump between upper and lowercase letters?"

Wanda says, "Maybe that was the best way to do it with whatever instrument was applied and still make it legible. What did you use, Tammy? A stick? A paintbrush?"

"Me?" Tammy says, startled.

Ruby puts her arm around Tammy's shoulder. Tammy takes a step forward, and Ruby's grip tightens, changing from supportive to restraining. She says, "No way! Tammy wouldn't do this; none of us would."

"Damn right!" Tammy yells.

Eric says, "Guys, you'll wake Smithy…"

"Why would I?" Tammy demands.

Wanda says, "Because you don't like me. You never have. You resent me or you're jealous."

"Jealous how?"

"Maybe you think you could do a better job running the study. So maybe you pulled this stunt, hoping to drive me away."

"Why me? I hate to break it to you this way, Wanda, but I'm not the only one you've abraded." Tammy regards her steadily.

Wanda says, "You had access…"

"I change his goddamn diapers when he has an accident! I don't wallow in the stuff! It's…it's… *shit*! It's foul! It smells, and it's disgusting, and the only reason I handle it is because everyone else is too squeamish to come near a dirty diaper."

Gail chimes in, talking over her: "Exactly! You see, none of us could have done it—"

Tammy says, "It has to be done, so I step up to do my part—"

Gail says, "—we'd all be too grossed out."

"—and if this is the thanks I get…" Tammy trails off.

"Then who did do it?" Wanda demands. "Huh? Did this just appear on the walls by itself, magically?" She spreads her palm over the wall to indicate the figures. "Somebody put this here, and I don't even care why anymore or what you think of me! I want to know who is vandalizing this house that Yale University, represented by Piers and by me, has taken on as a caretaker!"

Wanda steps forward, hands on hips, face livid; tears stand in her eyes, but her voice is steady and harsh. As she speaks, she looks from one person to the next. "So tell me. Come clean now, and I won't press charges. I won't call the police or report your conduct to the university.

You'll be asked to leave Trevor Hall immediately, but you can continue your studies at whatever school you came from. That's my offer. You see—I can be fair, even for an ogre."

"But Wanda, it wasn't any of us!" Ruby pleads.

"It could have been Ruby. She's dressed for it," Tammy says.

Ruby spins around. "Huh?"

Tammy gestures to her outfit and asks, "Why are you fully dressed so early this morning? Did you have something you had to get up to do?" She indicates the wall.

Ruby's mouth drops, and red spots appear on her cheeks. "Of course not! How can you say that, Tammy? You're my best friend!"

"Wanda was hard on you when you first started. You used to complain about keeping up with all her targets. And she's argued with your boyfriend almost nonstop from the start. You could have decided to sabotage Wanda so Jeff could get ahead," Tammy suggests.

"Is that what you really think of me?"

Tammy says, "Not at all. I'm just tossing out wild theories at random until we find one that sticks. Because it's ridiculous to think any of us did this. Ruby's as innocent as I am. But do you all see how easily she's willing to believe the worst of us?" Tammy points to Wanda, who's now eyeing Ruby suspiciously. Ruby crosses her arms protectively and backs away from both women, scowling. Tammy continues. "She'd rather have someone, anyone, to blame than get to the bottom of this mess."

Wanda asks, "Then who was it really, Tammy?"

Jeff, off camera, says, "Robert La Fontaine." Everyone gapes at the camera. Jeff repeats more confidently, "Robert La Fontaine. He had the motive. We're running a rival study. Our chimp is smarter than his chimp. Once our study is released in full, all the accolades and all the funding will go to Smithy, not Osage. He probably heard Piers sharing preliminary details on the radio or got wind of our progress through one of the donor's reports. Then he came here and tried to sabotage us. It wouldn't surprise me if he was behind all of the—pardon me—crap that's been going on: the fires, the unlocked doors and windows—"

Eric says, "I heard La Fontaine was lecturing somewhere in Texas this week."

Jeff, off camera, says, "OK, if not him directly, then one of his agents. He could have sent a grad assistant into town to keep tabs on us. Look at all the people who were here for the summer and the yacht race. How many did we pass on a regular basis and not notice? Or how about those guys we met at the tavern? How much do we really know about them? Could be Fred or Shaun or Miguel—"

Gail says, defensively, "Not Miguel!"

"One of them could be conspiring with La Fontaine. How about Reid?" Jeff asks.

Tammy laughs.

Jeff's voice continues, "I'm serious! He could have been in on it from the beginning. First, he tried to scare us out of the house with his ghost stories, then when that didn't work, he cozied up to Tammy and got himself into the house. Now he's seen our operation, he knows the layout. He could have told La Fontaine's people all about us and how to gain access."

Tammy shakes her head and says, "Reid Bennett is the most staid, unimaginative person I've ever met!"

Eric says, "Sure sounded like he had plenty of imagination when he was talking about the ghost."

"Anyway, he went back to Boston months ago," Tammy mentioned.

"Boston's not far away. Neither is Fall River," Jeff retorts.

"Reid's fascinated by Trevor Hall. He wouldn't dirty it like this." Tammy points to the wall.

Jeff's voice grows excited. "Then maybe he resents us for being here! A chimp is living in his precious house, possibly tearing it up worse than the Bradley students. Even more reason to crash our study and get us out!"

"Ridiculous," Tammy mutters

Wanda asks, "How would anybody get into the house? We searched before, and all the doors were locked with no signs of forced entry."

Jeff, still off camera, says, "Maybe they made a copy of one of our keys. If it was Reid or Miguel, someone dating one of the girls, they could have taken her key out of her purse when she was in the bathroom or something."

"And made a mold of it, like in a spy movie," Eric adds.

Tammy says, "That's a joke, right?"

"It could be someone else we know, maybe someone from the Meyer School," Gail suggests. Everyone looks at her. Wanda cocks her head and a thoughtful expression crosses her face. Ruby shakes her head. Gail continues. "Someone who knows Smithy! Maybe they just talked to him and asked him to let them in. He could open a door or window and shut it again behind them without us knowing. He does it all the time."

Ruby says, "No. This is getting out of hand. We're not going to start suspecting everyone we know. The Meyer teachers are our friends, and why would the locals betray us? We spend a lot of money in this town. Our study is bringing attention to Newport."

"It could have been one of them," Jeff says.

"Maybe La Fontaine made Hope and Simon a deal for them to work with Osage afterward. That would be great publicity for the school."

Tammy stares at the walls, bemused. Slowly, she says, "Will you listen to yourselves? Robert La Fontaine, a respected academic and a leader in his field—or one of his *agents*—broke into our house and smeared doo-doo on the walls?"

"It had to be him!" Jeff insists.

"Are you nuts?" Tammy asks.

"He's afraid of us. He's trying to shut us down by intimidating us. Everything that's happened has been designed to undermine our confidence and make us quit. This is the *piece de resistance.*"

"Robert La Fontaine is the closest thing to the establishment this field has. What does he have to fear from us?" Tammy asks, harshly.

"He's secure. We're the ones challenging him."

"Exactly! He's afraid of us," Jeff says.

Tammy says, "But nothing we've done has threatened him! It's not like we've overturned his life's work. We haven't even contradicted him; all we've done is found a few things he could be doing better."

Jeff's hand appears on camera, gesturing violently to the walls. "He's telling us our research is crap! That's what this is about! That's his message to us."

Tammy whistles, puts her hands on her head and walks away. She passes Ruby and says, "Your boyfriend has cracked."

"If this is a message about our study, why did he just write *Wanda's* name?" Gail asks.

Jeff, off camera, sounds uncertain. "Well, maybe he's sexist. He feels threatened because a woman is in charge of the study, so he's going after Wanda."

Tammy, now off camera, calls out, "*Piers's* name is all over this study! *His* face is all over the television. *His* voice is all over the radio."

Jeff, off camera, says quietly, "Yeah, but everyone knows Wanda's the one working the levers behind the curtain."

Wanda lifts an eyebrow and says, "Someday, you'll have to enumerate for me just who 'everyone' is."

Eric clears his throat and adds, "Tammy said we were almost attacked by the Giant Rat of Sumatra the other night."

Tammy steps back into the camera's frame and says quietly, "I heard noises, that's all. I already told Wanda about them."

Jeff asks, "What noises?"

Wanda says, "Just what are you implying, Eric? Are you saying it's a *poltergeist*? That's what you Kaninchens would call it right? That's German for a noisy ghost." She turns to Tammy. "At least that's what Reid said the last time you brought him over to the house."

Tammy says, "I don't remember that. I must have been powdering my nose."

Wanda says, "You were an awfully long time about it! And you left me to entertain him. He wanted to tell me all about the history of this house, starting from its founding and going all the way up through the ridiculous stories people have spread about things that go on here. He didn't tell you about any of that?"

Tammy looks away. "Reid talks *extensively*. I don't follow everything he says."

"Are you sure?" Wanda asks.

Tammy turns and faces Wanda coldly, stepping forward. "Are you still thinking I did this? You should know me better than that by now. If I took exception to anything you said or did, I would say so to your face. I don't have to stoop to this!" She turns to face the walls, and her face twists. "This is disgusting!"

Eric says, "Look, I never heard of a polderwhatsit, but why couldn't it be that?"

"Please. I don't have the stomach for this again." Wanda rolls her eyes.

"No, really. Why can't we talk about it?" Ruby asks. "We've listened to other possibilities; why can't we at least consider this one? Just maybe. It makes more sense than Robert La Fontaine." She looks at the camera apologetically.

Wanda deliberately averts her face from the camera and says, "When you eliminate the impossible, whatever is left, no matter how improbable—"

Ruby says, "I know. I know that one! But I also know Occam's Razor: the simplest explanation is the best. Are these contorted conspiracy theories really easier to believe in than a ghost?" She steps forward and speaks more softly. "Eric has seen things. I believe Smithy has seen things, and so have Maisie and your cats. *I've* heard and felt things. I think you have, too, Wanda, but you're afraid to admit it. It won't make you sound like less of a scientist to consider an *outré* possibility. What makes us appear ridiculous is trying to deny what the evidence of our senses suggests. It would be hard for a cabal of people to pull off all the things that have happened to us, but if it were a ghost—"

"Hey, guys! I thought of something else!" Gail shouts excitedly, and all faces turn toward her. She hops on her feet. "Maybe Smithy did it!"

Wanda scoffs, "Oh, sure!"

Eric says, carefully, "Well, he *has* done something like it before. He's smeared his bedroom walls and bathroom walls—"

Wanda stresses, "*Smeared.* He's never *written!*"

Gail says, "But we already know he can use sign language. What if he's become literate, too? All the times we've read to him and all the times we've been writing in the journals. Maybe he's been watching us and learning his letters! He could have been trying to write us a message. We've been teaching him to finger paint. Maybe…he got a little carried away."

Silence greets her remark. Tammy narrows her eyes and looks hard at Gail. Gail looks at the floor. Ruby stares at her feet. Wanda steps back to consider the writing again.

Ruby asks, "Did whoever it was leave any fingerprints in the…on the wall? Because chimps don't have fingerprints."

Wanda says, sarcastically, "I don't know. Why don't you look, Ruby?"

Jeff asks off camera, "Has anyone checked Smithy yet? Is he in his room?"

Eric says, "Yes. I checked him first thing. His door was locked, and he looked asleep. Not that that means anything."

Ruby asks, "Did you happen to see his hands?" Eric shakes his head.

Gail says, "He still could've done this and washed his hands after."

Eric surveys the wall and says, "It's too high for Smithy. This is where a human would stand to write something."

Gail says, "He could have jumped up to do it. Or stood on something. That chimp Wanda had me read about, Pasha, learned to stack up boxes to reach hanging food. If Smithy wants to do something, he'll find a way. We all know that."

"I've never seen him try to write," Jeff says, quietly. "We've painted together. I taught him how, but I never showed him letters."

Tammy looks at Eric. "Do kids ever acquire writing spontaneously?"

"I guess…I haven't seen it before, but as long as they're exposed to it and they're motivated, it could happen," Eric replies.

Gail says, "Oh, wait until Piers hears about this!"

Wanda cuts in. "Wait a minute. We're only speculating. We don't know anything."

Tammy says, "All we've done all morning is speculate!"

"But if it was him, it would be so exciting!" Gail exclaims. "We'd have a chimp who could sign *and* write! I bet Robert La Fontaine would choke on that!"

Eric asks, "But why Wanda's name?"

"Ohhh! I'm getting a headache," Tammy moans. "I'm going back to bed. Please, nobody wake me until after noon. I don't care if you catch Smithy writing the ninety-five theses on the wall next!" She exits.

Wanda shakes her head abruptly. "All right. This has gone on long enough. All we have for certain is a mess on our wall and a lot of animosity. I'm sorry for stirring that up. I—really, I was out of line. I'll apologize to Tammy when she comes back down. And to the rest of you…I'm sorry."

Eric says, "It's possible…It looks childish and crude…"

Ruby says, "*Very* crude!"

Wanda says, "I just want it gone. I'm sick of looking at it. Sick of smelling it. Let's get a couple of pictures then start scrubbing."

Gail says, "I'll get the Polaroid!"

Jeff, off camera, says, "I have my Leica in the gatehouse. I can bring that back."

Ruby says, "I'll clean up, Wanda. Why don't you lie down? You're stressed out, too—I can tell." Wanda shakes her head.

Eric asks, "Does anyone still feel like eating breakfast? Smithy's going to pitch a fit soon if there's no food when he wakes up. I might as well cook for the rest of us."

Ruby says, "No, thanks."

Jeff says, "No."

Wanda is silent, looking at the wallpaper.

Jeff comes around on camera to stand beside her and asks, "How bad do you think it is?"

"Jeff, the walls are smeared with excrement."

"So we're not going to get our security deposit back. What if we scrub down really hard with ammonia?" he asks.

Wanda shakes her head. "We'd be better off just tearing all the paper down and putting up new stuff."

"Except—look—this is antique wallpaper. It's probably a special pattern dating back to the turn of the century that we'll never be able to find."

Ruby suggests, "Talk to Reid. He can probably ID the year and the pattern. He may even be able to tell us where to find a match for it."

Jeff puts an arm around Ruby. "That's not a bad idea. Does Tammy have ol' Reid's number? I think I'll give him a call. Maybe I can send him a picture of the paper or even a sample.

"I'm not going to ask her…" Ruby says.

"So you don't believe Reid's behind this after all?"

"I'm…reconsidering."

"I'll believe whatever cause is easiest for us to stop," Wanda says. She studies the damage in silence for a moment. "Do you really think Webster could have done this?"

Jeff sighs. "We know chimps are good problem solvers when it comes to getting what they want. We know Smithy can climb, pick locks, hide food, and do several other things we wouldn't expect. If he wanted to write on this wall, he'd find a way to do it and cover his tracks after. We really don't know everything Smithy can do because we're not exploring his full range of abilities. All

we're doing is measuring his sign acquisition."
He looks at Wanda. "If we expand our focus to
investigate all the things he's capable of, in
addition—"

Wanda shakes her head. "We can't afford to break
from protocol. It would violate the terms of the
study. Our hypothesis is about sign language,
not about other ways Webster might communicate.
We've got to measure what we said we were going
to measure to prove what we want to prove. We
can't speculate about anything else. Now, if your
candid camera catches him painting something that
looks like writing, come see me." She exits the
room.

Jeff hugs Ruby. "You OK? Still mad?" She
shrugs. He turns back to the camera. The picture
goes dark.

DIARY OF TAMMY COHEN

January 20, 1975

...After I calmed down, I sat down to speculate further with Eric.

He admitted he didn't see how someone outside could have done it but couldn't believe any of us culpable. He smiled at me. "I don't really suspect <u>you.</u> You don't dislike Wanda <u>that</u> much."

"Are you sure?" I challenged. "I have every reason to resent her. Jeff does, too. They've butted heads from the start over who really has seniority. This wouldn't be the first time he's pulled a prank on her. His ridiculous accusations could have been intended to divert suspicion from himself."

Eric seemed truly aggrieved by that. "Jeff's all right. I know he's not your favorite, but he's not the type to do <u>that</u>. And he really does hate changing diapers. So do I. So even if I wanted to get back at Wanda for giving me grief about the ghost, for example, I'd find a different approach."

"Then maybe it <u>was</u> Ruby." For the sake of being thorough, I didn't hold back from putting the heat on my best friend. I pointed out that Ruby worries Wanda will fire her for being inexperienced and might want to undercut her preemptively. Wanda certainly didn't behave professionally today. Piers won't be happy to see that footage.

Eric wasn't swayed. "Ruby's too sweet to hold a grudge."

That left Gail, whom he refused to consider. "Wanda's praised Gail's work often. I can't think of any reason why Gail would want to hurt her."

I can. If Eric had any objectivity and had been paying attention in September, he'd recognize Gail's jealousy immediately.

Finally, I proposed Wanda herself. I've observed that Wanda angers easily, especially when we don't do what she wants. Staging vandalism and framing one of us would allow Wanda to boot anyone from the study who was seriously obstructing her. Eric still wasn't buying.

"I guess Smithy <u>could</u> have done it," he conceded. "I don't know why he would, but I can't understand the things he does. He can be mean." Eric rubbed the faded bruises on his ankle.

"He's your suspect then?" I pressed.

"No." His bleak tone surprised me. "I think it was the ghost. Wanda won't believe in her, so she's trying to get her attention. I don't know what she wants to say, but if that's how she goes about it, it can't be good. I don't think we've seen the last of her..."

SOLARIUM JOURNAL ENTRY
FROM JEFF DALTON

January 21, 1975

This is where I could write about Wanda going apeshit, but I'll refrain.

Instead, I'll share the results of my recent work with Smithy. Acting on Gail's hypothesis, I spent all day testing if he could replicate the wall writing, albeit with finger paints and paper.

First, I tried to get him to write her name. I demonstrated it several times, and he made some half-hearted swooshes, but wouldn't form the actual letters. I then switched to making individual letters, starting with the simplest: C, I, J, O, U, V, S, and X. Smithy showed more interest in this task and imitated my C and O, but his letters don't look as finished as mine (the O doesn't close properly, and several look more like 6s; the Cs are crooked and asymmetrical). I tried to get him to make other letters (specifically W, A, N, and D), but our boy was bored and starting to fuss. I gave him a one-hour recess to play chase and watch a cartoon on TV.

Afterward, we tried making letters again, but after a few half-hearted attempts at forming U and J, he refused to do any more writing or painting. I tried to teach Smithy the relationship between the written letter and the concept by pairing finger spelling with the pictorial letter. I think this bored him even more. Reading and writing letters doesn't have much relevance to a chimpanzee.

Smithy's apparent frustration could have been meant to distract me, like when he asks to go to the bathroom so he can get out of class, but I think he was truly disinterested in the task. Further, I note that the symbols he formed were all in response to heavy prompting after I showed him many examples.

As Eric optimistically says, "They never do it when you're watching them," meaning, when you're trying to get a kid to show off something you know he knows, he won't do it if you're watching and goading him. I suppose it's possible Smithy __did__ make the writing, and we're just never going to prove he has those skills at this rate.

Meanwhile, the walls have been scrubbed, but remain stained, and the main hallway is currently blocked off. Smithy seemed curious about the barriers and asked about them but didn't show any interest in returning to the scene of the crime (if he was even there in the first place).

JOURNAL RESPONSE
FROM TAMMY COHEN

January 21, 1975

Eric's right. When my sisters were little, I used to try to get them to show my parents they could walk, but the little brats would always freeze up and stare at me. No amount of cajoling of or threats would move them. Yet, left to their own devices, they ran around the room as much as they liked. Maybe you need to set up a hidden camera so we can see how Smithy acts when he doesn't know he's being observed.[3]

---

3 Unfortunately, no such candid footage of Smithy exists, so it appears no one followed up on this suggestion.

DIARY OF RUBY CARDINI

January 24, 1975

I'm really not a nightmare person. I can count on one hand the number of times I woke up crying or needed Mom to turn on the lights and sit with me. Yet now I'm twenty-one and lying awake at night. Since I'm not likely to fall asleep again anytime soon, I'll attempt to exorcise my fears by writing out what happened.

Firstly, I must be more upset than I realized over my argument with Tammy. Nothing else makes sense for the way my dream played out.

I was here at Trevor Hall, but it looked different, the way familiar places do in dreams. The halls had carpeting instead of bare floors, and there was an extra wall in the dining room[4] next to the French doors and an extra entry from the hall. Everything seemed shadowy, like when the bulb in a reading lamp is about to go out, even though it was daytime. I kept rubbing my eyes to clear my vision, but that didn't help. My inability to see clearly made me feel frustrated and uneasy, and that set the tone for the dream.

I was walking down the main stairs as Tammy was coming up. I'd already decided not to greet her (childish of me), but she brushed past without even looking at me. She practically elbowed me and didn't apologize. It didn't seem deliberate, just careless, as if I mattered so little that she couldn't even bother to grant me enough space to exist. I started to reprimand her, but she was already too far up the stairs.

I heard Wanda moving about the kitchen and went down the hall to complain to her. Even in my dream state, I figured she'd appreciate a chance to dish about Tammy. Wanda was cleaning the stove; it wasn't our stove but an old cast-iron job. A year was stamped into the metal: 1888.

---

4 An early floor plan shows the dining room was partitioned to create a "breakfast nook," a smaller dining space to accommodate smaller parties; in 1897, the wall was demolished and the entry to the nook plastered over, effecting the current layout.

"Why did you install that old thing?" I asked her. "Is it supposed to be safer than the other one?" Wanda ignored me and kept scrubbing away at the interior with the black brush. I joked, "Hey, did you hear me? You aren't giving me the silent treatment like Tammy, too, are you?"

Wanda still didn't answer. I tapped her on the shoulder, just in case the cast-iron blocked sound. She turned around then but didn't look in my direction. She spoke to the corner, "Smithy, keep your hands to yourself," and signed, "Don't touch." Smithy was sitting on a stool beside the sink. He stared at me, his mouth hanging open. He seemed scared, like he was afraid of getting caught at something. I wondered if he'd been instructed to have nothing to do with me, and if Tammy had poisoned the entire household against me.

I walked back down the hall. It was cluttered with end tables spilling over with sickeningly sweet flowers; they hadn't been there before. Jeff was coming toward me. I smiled and waved. He saw me and quickly averted his eyes. He kept walking and didn't respond to me. Like Tammy, he passed me, but just by a fraction of an inch. It was as if he knew I was there without consciously knowing I was there.

Baffled and hurt, I went to the library to sit and think. The fire was built up, but I couldn't feel it. Eric was making notes in the journal at the desk. He looked up when I came in, looked right at me, then turned away and shuddered. "You need a sweatshirt in this place," he grumbled. He closed the journal and started to leave.

I pleaded with him. "Wait, Eric—don't go! Please stay and tell me what's wrong." I even tried to block his exit. His turned up his nose in disgust. He looked angry, and that gave me pause. I've never seen Eric lose his temper, and I felt chastened by having him mad at me. I didn't follow when he stepped around me and into the hallway; I waited a beat instead.

This time when I exited, the hall was cluttered with luggage: not backpacks and suitcases but trunks and hatboxes. I stumbled around it all and entered the solarium where everyone had gathered around the fireplace, listening to Gail. Her hair was piled up in an elaborate coiffure like something out of the last century. Gail was chattering away, telling an animated story, but I couldn't understand it. Her voice was muffled, *like someone talking on a bad long-distance connection. It kept fading in and out, so I couldn't make out any words.*

Nobody noticed me when I came in. I walked all around the circle, trying to find a place to fit in. All my friends kept their backs to me, even when I spoke. I asked, "What's going on here, guys? What are you trying to do to me? Is this a joke? Cut it out!" It didn't feel like they were purposely ignoring me but like I didn't exist for them. Like I was a ghost...

Only Smithy acknowledged me. He didn't do it openly. He didn't wave or sign to me. But he looked at me. He squirmed and became agitated. He looked from me to the rest of the company and then looked back to see if I was still there. I signed to him and pleaded aloud. "Smithy, tell them I'm here. Make them talk to me. Please! This has gone far enough. I can't take it anymore. Look at me. Help!" I signed, "Please help" over and over as I begged.

Smithy started crying and hooting like he does when he's overtired or wants an extra dessert. His cries were so loud, overpowering my own, and naturally, everyone surrounded him. I reached into the group to grab Smithy and shake him. I wanted to make him snap out of it so he would respond to me. Smithy recoiled from my touch and signed, "Bad woman." My friends saw his message, and they turned toward me. But even though they were looking right at me, and I was yelling, "I'm here!" at the top of my lungs, I could tell by their blank stares they didn't see me.

And then I woke up with tears streaming down my face and a lump in my throat.

OK, so it's not the most dramatic nightmare. I wasn't chased by a maniac with a butcher knife. I wasn't trapped in a burning building. I was ostracized by all my friends with absolutely no explanation. And I'm still feeling sick about it now that I'm awake. Completely drained. Apprehensive. Normally after a nightmare, you should be glad to be awake. But that's not how I feel. As the sky lightens outside my window, I'm afraid to face the day. What if I go downstairs for breakfast, and everyone ignores me as they did in the dream? What if I try to speak and discover I have no voice? What if I end up trapped in a separate, parallel world?

I would cry. I would run away.

No, I would stand up for myself. I wouldn't go quietly after how hard I've worked to earn my place. If I had to, I'd stage a scene to force their attention. Tip over the table. Pull the fire alarm maybe.

"I exist. I'm here. Talk to me. Look at me." If I couldn't say it with my voice, I'd still find a way to communicate it. I'd probably terrify everyone in the process.

It felt so realistic. That's what made the dream so frightening. It could happen.

DIARY OF TAMMY COHEN

January 29, 1975

I've debated about whether and where to record the events of this afternoon. It didn't seem right to create a journal entry, given the sensitive nature of what I need to describe, so for now, I'll write about it in my diary. I may show it to Ruby, and possibly the others, later. Jeff, at least, already has an inkling of Wanda's fragility.

My description of this incident will be more detailed than usual, in part because the events made such an impression on me and because I just watched a recording of what happened. Hence, the dialogue and sequence of events is fairly accurate.

At around 4:30 p.m., I went into the kitchen to get a soda. Wanda was preparing supper with Smithy. She was trying to teach him another recipe; the camera was set up on a tripod in the corner. Things were not going well. Wanda's hair was messy, and she had a smear of flour on her cheek. I'd never seen her looking so much at loose ends. She also looked uncharacteristically happy to see me.

"Thank goodness you're here," she said. "Smithy's being a handful, and I'm out of paprika. Can you please go into the pantry and get me some more?" She phrased it not as a question.

So I went down into the pantry. We ought to have a map for it. It's on the scale of a small cellar rather than the type of "pantry" cupboard I grew up with at home. A map or labeled shelves would be an immense help in guiding people unfamiliar with what's kept where (that would apply to most of us) and would almost certainly have prevented all the trouble.

I made my first mistake by not switching on the light when I first entered. The light from the kitchen illuminated the shelves. I didn't see any paprika. The shelves were well-stocked with dry goods—cereal boxes, flour, canned food, condiment jars, gelatin mixes—but no spice jars.

I'd assumed the extra seasonings would be on a shelf close to the kitchen, because if I were organizing the pantry, I would put the things I was most likely to need near at hand. But I had no luck in my search. And Wanda was getting irritated.

"Are you still down there, Tammy? What's taking so long?" she yelled.

"I can't find it," I admitted. "Can you tell me which shelf it's on?"

I heard her curse. Then she said, "Look on the bottom shelf to your immediate left. You should see a second spice rack and canisters of salt and pepper." I did look on that shelf, but all I found were pickled fruits and vegetables. When I told her this, Wanda cursed again. I heard footsteps, her shadow filled the pantry, and then she was beside me.

"Damnit, they were <u>here</u>! Somebody's moved them!" Wanda shifted the pickle jars, as if the paprika might be hiding behind them.

I nearly told Wanda that was ridiculous since the kitchen was her domain but thought better of antagonizing her. Instead, I peeked at the shelf on the right-hand side, in case Wanda's sense of direction was flawed. I glimpsed a C&H label, then the room was plunged into darkness.

We both yelled, "Wait! Don't close that door! We're in here!" Wanda and I almost collided in the darkness trying to reach the door. She took the handle first.

"It's locked! Oh, no!" She pounded on the door and called out, "Smithy? Are you there? Let us out, please! This isn't funny! Open the door, Smithy. Open the door!" She kept repeating it, loud and slow, like she was talking to a simpleton. When the door didn't open, she grunted and cursed under her breath. "Damn, damn, damn…"

I decided we needed some light to better assess our situation. Also, listening to our disembodied voices echoing around the blackened pantry was disconcerting. I groped along the wall, blind. Finally I asked, "Is there a light anywhere in here?"

"Ah… to the left, near the door," she said.

I fumbled my way to the left, farther and farther without success, and kicked over a sack of onions; I could smell the acrid tang when they spilled over the floor.

"Your other left," Wanda corrected.

I didn't have any better luck with those directions than I'd had in trying to locate the damn paprika in the first place. I patted down the wall and fumbled in the air as my frustration built and built. "Is it a switch? A pull-chain?" I asked.

Wanda hesitated. "I don't remember."

By now I was annoyed, and I went off on her. "How can you not know? You do all the cooking. You're in here all the time."

Wanda was full of excuses. "I just don't pay attention. It's something I do automatically." Again, I bit my tongue and continued to search; this time, I knocked over a pyramid of cans. Wanda snapped at me. "Are you going to tear apart the entire pantry?"

That tipped me over the edge. "Maybe I will," I said. "The more noise we make, the more likely someone will hear us." I started beating on the door and kicked at the gap along the bottom. "Hey! Come on down! We're locked in!" I shouted.

"No one ever comes down here until dinner time," Wanda complained. "The boys will show up in an hour or so when they get hungry."

I picked a can off the ground and weighed it, half-contemplating smacking Wanda in the head with it. I couldn't get over how passive she had become. "Could you please do something helpful instead of criticizing?" I said. "You're supposed to be the leader, Wanda. Brainstorm us a way out of here!"

She retorted, "I can't think if you keep talking! Damnit, he jammed the door tight! That, or he's standing on the other side holding it closed." I could hear her jiggling the handle again. "Smithy! Smithy, can you hear me?" She banged on the door some more.

At that point, my mental wheels started turning. I had last seen Smithy sitting on a chair at the table, almost an entire room's length from the pantry. I hadn't heard him cross to the pantry the way I'd heard Wanda, and I couldn't picture him locking us up and running away when we hadn't posed any problem to him. It didn't make sense for Smithy to be our captor. "What was his problem with you anyway, and how did he get away from you?" I asked.

Wanda grumbled, "I can't watch him, make notes, cook supper, work the camera, and then come help you find paprika all at once. I'm not a superhero, Tammy!"

"You act like you are," I muttered under my breath.

"Meaning what?" Wanda demanded. I could practically see her standing there with her hands on her hips.

I tried to craft my reply carefully, since it appeared we would be trapped together for a while. "Meaning, you take charge. You always have a plan, and you're quick to tell people what to do—except in this case."

Wanda's voice took on an edge. "Do you want to be in charge instead? Because it's a lot harder than it looks. Smithy's not the only child in this household. But if you think you can do better, if you've got a plan to make everything run more smoothly, then step right up and be my—"

Wanda broke off suddenly. I thought she might have heard something, but when I started to ask, she shushed me. We stood in the dark without a sound, just the smells of the stored food and the musty pantry closing in on us. I hoped to hear footsteps or one of our friends calling out to us. But I heard nothing.

Wanda whispered, "I hear breathing, but _inside!_" We held our breath, and I held extra still so I wouldn't accidentally kick over anything else. Again, I couldn't hear a thing. Then Wanda cried out, "Who's that? Come out of there! Come out and show yourself!"

She moved in front of me. I felt her breath on my face, fast and shallow. Something had frightened her. "Wanda, what is it?" I asked.

"I hear rustling. Someone's down here with us! Behind the shelves." Then she screamed and nearly blew out my eardrum. "Something brushed me! Someone's in here!" She sounded hysterical, and Wanda never sounds like that. She's always in control, always a leader.

Hearing the terror in her voice frightened me. What also frightened me was not hearing any of the things she's claimed. I backed away from Wanda and stumbled over the fallen cans. They clattered across the floor, making a racket like a roaring animal.

"That was me! I kicked the cans," I explained so she wouldn't freak out.

I heard scraping along the floor, then a whoosh and a loud bang as Wanda hurled one of the cans across the pantry. "Hey! Announce yourself!" she shouted. Nothing happened. She threw a second can. This one smacked into some jars, which shattered into a geyser of glass. I covered my face and stumbled away, trying to avoid getting hit—either by Wanda or her debris. She yelled again, "Come out! I mean it!"

She's gone crazy, I thought. "Hey, be careful!" I told her. "I'm in here, too!"

"Did you hear them laughing at us? We'll see how funny you think this is when I get my hands on you!" Then she really went to war. Can after can clanged and smashed against walls, against shelves. Wanda screamed threats all the while.

My stomach flopped. I was honestly afraid for my safety. Wanda had never seemed unstable before. Tightly wound, yes. But now she was hearing things and growing violent. I had been mouthing off to her just before she snapped. How long would it take for her to attack me next?

I tried to slip away from her without drawing attention. Luckily for me, Wanda was making so much noise in her own attempt to destroy the pantry that the clattering cans and thudding onions I kicked aside didn't register with her. I folded myself against the wall and nearly had a heart attack when something touched my face. Before I wigged out, I realized it was that damned elusive light chain, at long last! I yanked on it as if it could pull me out of that dark place and away from that madwoman, but the bulb was out! That's when I started screaming. "Help! Get me out of here!"

Like a miracle, the pantry door swung open. Wanda and I squealed and reached for each other. The kitchen light stabbed my eyes after the pitch black, so at first, I couldn't see who had found us. Instead, I had to rely on the British voice calling, "What the devil is going on in here? Are you fighting? What are you doing in the pantry?"

Wanda pulled herself together once she knew Piers was there. She caught her breath and took a quick look around the pantry. Nobody else was in there with us. "We got locked in," she explained. "Smithy slammed the door and trapped us in here. Is he with you?"

"No, he's at the gatehouse watching game shows. Gail said she found him wandering around the ground floor unattended," Piers told us. "I came over here to find out why."

He looked cross, so I tried to explain. "We thought he was holding the door on us. Wanda tried and tried to open it from our side, but the handle was jammed."

"No, it wasn't. This door wasn't locked, and nothing was jammed against it. It was simply shut. I heard you two screaming and smashing the dickens out of this room. I couldn't imagine why."

Wanda looked like someone had punched her in the stomach. "But I tried to force open the door and couldn't! I threw myself against it. It wouldn't budge. Then I heard someone else in the pantry with us; someone was breathing heavily and laughing at me. I thought a prowler must have broken in to play another joke on us—or maybe it was two people teaming up. One moving things around in the pantry and taunting us, and the other pinning the door closed from the kitchen."

Piers stared at me as if to implicate me in this mad conspiracy. I could only shrug. "I didn't hear anything." To avoid incriminating Wanda's sanity, I added "But being stuck in the dark was disorienting."

Piers marched into the pantry and pulled the light chain. _The bulb flared on_, throwing more light onto the mess Wanda had created: toppled, dented cans and smashed preserve jars lay all over the floor at both ends of the room, mingled with trampled onions. Piers walked around, making a great show of looking behind and under shelves. Of course, no one was hiding in those tiny spaces, nor lurking in the shadows. And the only exit had been barred, we thought.

"Try the door for yourselves," he invited. We scrambled out of the pantry and watched him close the door and open it, close it and open it, the most basic of tasks. Out of curiosity, I went back inside to see if the handle might be stuck from the inside only. Yet when I gripped the handle, it popped open. I could have kicked myself for not trying it sooner. Wanda watched, growing whiter all the while. Had she been lying to me about the door being stuck? Had she honestly believed we were trapped? Maybe she hadn't twisted the handle at the proper angle or used enough strength. I decided something like that had happened with the light, too; perhaps I pulled at a bad angle and simply didn't trigger the light bulb. I didn't say anything about the light to Piers.

I tried to help Wanda by suggesting there was a draft in the pantry and what she'd heard was the distorted sound of the wind blowing through the gaps. In her distress, she could have interpreted that noise as a living person. She wasn't having it. "Don't try to humor me with a rational explanation! I know what I heard and felt!"

"Then let's _see_ for ourselves what happened," Piers proposed. When Jeff came back, Piers made him run the film for the four of us in the gatehouse. We sat through Wanda's aborted cooking session to the point when I entered the kitchen. Smithy watched me enter the pantry, then watched Wanda go after me a few moments later. Once her back was turned, he hopped down from his chair and walked out of the kitchen, heading down the hall, _away from us_. The pantry door had closed by itself (blown by wind from the draft I invented?). He never touched it.

The rest of the time, the camera showed the closed pantry door. It picked up the sounds of our voices shouting and of me crashing into food sacks and cans. And it recorded Wanda's freak out, of course.

Hearing it happen the second time around was just as scary as when it had happened in the moment, but with Jeff and Piers looking on—and Jeff shooting Wanda puzzled, concerned sidelong glances—it was also embarrassing. Wanda watched the footage stoically. No one ever entered the kitchen but Piers. No voices were heard but hers and mine.

So what had really happened in the pantry? I've been thinking about it all night and haven't settled on an explanation. I'm only glad Piers came along to let us out when he did. Has Wanda lost her mind? Could she have been hallucinating? Had she snapped after a long, tiring day of working with Smithy and a long, difficult month of household strife? I know she's been under a lot of pressure, but I never figured her for the type to break down. Faced with the evidence of the film and of Piers himself, she made no explanation or excuse for her behavior. Instead, she apologized for upsetting everyone and cleaned up the devastation in the pantry by herself.

Incidentally, we never did find the paprika that had begun all the fuss. Instead, after all that, we called out for pizza.[5]

5   Tammy's diary entry is the only record of this incident. The film of the women trapped

DIARY OF RUBY CARDINI

January 29, 1975

Looking back through my entries, I realized it's been over a month since I last wrote to Sarah-Beth. There was a time when we wouldn't have let a full week go by without exchanging at least one letter. That wasn't so long ago. Yet so much has happened to change us both and push us into different worlds that I struggle to communicate with her.

My problem is that I simply don't know what to say. I can't relate to her life and the topics she writes about, and I can't seem to put my life into words she'd understand. I can render down our scientific jargon into layman's terms if necessary, but Sarah-Beth doesn't want to read about our study, and I no longer care to write about it. Increasingly, my thoughts linger on the subtext all around us. "The ghost." Is there one? What mishaps can we lay at its spectral feet, if it is here? Are we making ourselves crazy? Nobody who hasn't lived with us in this house could fully understand what goes on here. When I try to present my case, the words lie dead on the paper. The things that frighten and provoke me make no impression on Sarah-Beth.

"So he messed up a word," she wrote back once, "so what?" Except it's not "a word." It's an aggregate of messed-up words, all some variation of "dark woman." It's the broken locks and missing measuring cups. It's the dog barking at an empty room and the apparent break-ins. That's what she doesn't understand. All these little mistakes and mysteries pile up, and when you look at them altogether in context, the pattern of something <u>darker</u> appears. Doesn't it?

Am I imagining things, looking for castles in the clouds and finding patterns that don't exist?

---

in the pantry is not included on the outtake reel, and neither Karlewicz nor Preis-Herald have issued statements about it.

Do I prefer believing in a ghost to believing all those little missed words are true mistakes?

Yes. Even though it scares me, I'd rather believe in something outlandish—that our home is infested by something otherworldly—because to believe in a ghost means to believe in Smithy and the validity of our work. If there is a "dark woman" at Trevor Hall, then we're not wrong or foolish to devote so much of our time, energy, sweat, and dreams to this fantastic goal of bridging the gap between human and animal.

Is it crazier to believe in a talking chimpanzee or to believe in the ghost of Imogene Rockwell?

What does it say about me that I'm asking these questions?

I picture Sarah-Beth reading my letters and thinking I've gone completely 'round the bend. I wonder if she tells my folks anything about me. If I could read my own letters with fresh eyes, would I laugh at me the way she does?

I don't even like to go to the bathroom in the middle of the night anymore. I don't want to walk down the lonely hallway by myself in the dark in case I run into whatever Eric saw. Instead, I lie in bed, growing increasingly uncomfortable, and wonder if Tammy would kill me if I tried to set up a cot in the suite with her and Gail. They're lucky to have each other—and a connected bath. They're not as vulnerable as I feel.

Maybe I should sneak Maisie into my room at night. She can walk with me and stand guard if I need to get up for any reason. She'd make a better bodyguard than Peter. Though he does make a nice bed warmer.

Boy! Reading over these last two paragraphs makes me see how pathetic I've become. No wonder I've lost my pen pal.

I'd hoped going away to school would broaden my mind. I had no idea how much the move would change me. When I read Sarah-Beth's gossip and her concerns about boyfriends and hairstyles, and when I think back to our lives in Scranton, where I used to share those concerns, I feel like I'm trying to watch a movie I once loved in childhood, only now the plot is insipid and makes no sense. I'm grown, and my tastes have changed.

So what kind of movie am I living in? A romance? A horror film? A mystery? Sometimes it feels like all three. I stumble along, improvising my lines, wondering how it will. . .

DIARY OF TAMMY COHEN

February 2, 1975

The shit's off the walls, and it's hitting the fan.

Smithy broke into Ruby's bedroom last night. Somehow, he got the lock off his own window again, climbed onto the roof, came down the wall to the second floor, and opened her window from the outside. Ruby swore she'd locked it (as if she would leave a window open in the middle of a New England winter), but by now I know not to be surprised by anything that happens in this house.

Ruby's screaming almost jolted me out of bed. It took a moment to understand what was happening and where the screaming had originated, followed by another two or three minutes to fumble my glasses on straight. Her screams overlapped like waves. As the first trailed off, another swelled underneath it. Over and over. I thought people only screamed like that when they were being murdered.

Naturally, I assumed that's what was happening and ran to her room, joined by Eric and Wanda. Lately, Ruby has taken to locking her door, so I couldn't open it to come to her aid. Those seconds spent fruitlessly jiggling the knob, kicking at her door, and calling to her will remain some of the most frightening of my life.

Eric wanted to kick the door down, though we both knew he'd just break his ankle. I shouted at Wanda to get the master key. Gail had stayed in bed and kept yelling, "What's happening?" as if I ought to know or could do anything other than assume the worst. I had read in some mystery novel that a locked door can be jimmied open with a charge card, so I screamed at Gail to get her purse. Though I knew it was a long shot, I simply wanted her to get involved. How dare she hang back while my best friend screamed for her life? My frustration bubbled up and nearly boiled over into panic when Ruby's screams cut off.

Little did we know what had happened: Smithy had crept in through the window while Ruby, oblivious, wrote in her diary. He jumped in the bed, right on top of her. Most likely, he only wanted to get out of the cold and seek comfort from someone he knew, but Ruby panicked, shrieking and lashing out with fists at what she thought was an attacker. Naturally, that aggravated Smithy tremendously.

He screamed back, which accounts for the bloodcurdling overlap we heard, and struck her. Ruby will have a shiner for a week at least, but she's lucky he didn't do worse. He did succeed in knocking her out of bed and out of the reach of his own wrath.

There's no telling what else he might have done if poor Peter hadn't distracted him. The cat had been dozing on Ruby's lap, and when Smithy and Ruby began their altercation, he awoke and yowled. Ruby said Smithy turned his rage on the cat. He grabbed Peter around the neck and started to pound him against the pillow. Peter was lucky the chimp didn't try the floor or the headboard.

Ruby was still stunned from his punch; when she realized what was happening, she wasn't sure what to do. Even when Smithy dragged Eric last fall, he seemed more panicked than hostile. Ruby yelled at him to stop and threw one of her books at him but was afraid to intervene more directly, lest he attack her again. By then, she could hear the rescue squad at her door and tried to let us in but couldn't unlock the door. The latch stuck in her hand. Panic? Coincidence? Or something more? She asked me later what I thought, but it being Saturday, I chose to reserve judgment.

Back in the bedroom, Peter fought back and scratched Smithy's arms and face. He managed to evade Smithy's death grip and was trying to run away with Smithy hanging on his tail. I imagine them bouncing off the walls, careening off the top of the wardrobe, back onto the bed, and up the curtains; Peter mewling and trembling, and Smithy's eyes ablaze, grasping.

Ruby's room was in shambles by the time Wanda opened her door with the master key, and Peter was half-dead from shock and his injuries. Once I saw the door swing open, I felt enormous relief. True, Ruby looked like a zombie with her fixed eyes and purpling jaw, but she was standing and in one piece.

I pulled her out of the room by her wrist while Eric went inside. He was under the impression a burglar had somehow forced his way into the house. Eric stood in a defensive crouch as if to take on the culprit. Over his shoulder, I had one swift glimpse of Smithy grabbing Peter's legs, one in each hand. He swung the cat around in a half-circle and launched him across the room. I heard the cat screech, Wanda scream, and Eric shout a reprimand all at once. Then Peter smacked into the wall and lay twitching on the floor. Gail chose that moment to creep into the hall, and when she saw the devastation, she shrieked to beat the fire alarm. As much as I wanted to check on Peter or assist Eric, I felt it was more imperative to tend to the younger girls. I steered both Gail and Ruby into our room and locked the door until Eric said it was safe to come out.

He later told me Smithy was in a state. He kept panting and gnashing his teeth. Eric could see he was on the verge of reverting into attack mode, so he quickly switched from a disapproving tone to the mellow voice he uses with schoolchildren. He both signed and spoke to Smithy, urging him to be quiet and stay still.

Smithy hopped up on Ruby's wardrobe and signed, "Go away" and "bad woman." Eric chose to interpret that to mean Smithy disapproved of Ruby's behavior, since he didn't sign "dark."

While Eric tried to calm Smithy, Wanda gathered her shattered cat and rushed him downstairs. I don't know where she found the private number for a vet, but she did, and Eric took her in the truck to meet the doctor in town. Miraculously, Peter is still alive, last I heard. He suffers from two broken legs, a sprained back, and a concussion, not to mention the trauma of having been beaten by his former playmate. I could almost believe in the adage about cats having nine lives, having seen what happened to him.

Before all of that though, Wanda called down to the gatehouse to make Jeff come and control the ape. Poor Jeff looked shell-shocked when I saw him this morning. When I asked him what he thought of Smithy's behavior, he only shook his head.

Because Jeff had just arrived on the scene, he was able to gain Smithy's confidence. It seemed the chimp believed Jeff didn't know of his transgressions. Jeff approached Smithy with smiles and asked him, "What's bad? What's wrong?" and urged him to "Come down." For his part, Smithy signed, "Sorry" and "hug?" Jeff welcomed Smithy down from the wardrobe with open arms, then took the chimp back to his room where he sat up for the rest of the night to ensure his charge didn't escape again.

Smithy has been sequestered there all afternoon. Jeff goes back and forth to feed and change him. Wanda is understandably bitter and doesn't want to see Smithy right now. She's spent a significant amount of time on the phone with Piers but hasn't said if or when he'll be returning. I wonder what he thinks about Smithy's behavior and if he told her how to handle him.

Ruby was more shaken than anything. Even the pain in her jaw has subsided with hourly applications of ice packs, though she doesn't want to go into town with a fraction of her face still black and blue. Nor does she feel safe sleeping in her room anymore. The likelihood of Smithy breaking in again is practically nil, but I suppose the trauma of what happened lingers. In fact, the idea of sleeping anywhere in the house, even with me and Gail, makes her uncomfortable. This afternoon, she packed the remnants of her things and moved them down to the gatehouse.

So now Ruby and Jeff are shacking up. I doubt they would even have gone on a date if they hadn't been thrown together in the same house day after day, but they seem happy together now, and I'm happy for Ruby; she looked more relaxed at dinner without the prospect of sleeping in a potentially haunted house dangling over her. I'm also glad she's developed the confidence to take this step, although it was certainly more a case of push than pull.

And now there's a vacant bedroom on our floor, a little worse for wear but still fit for a new occupant. However, the idea of rooming with Gail is more appealing than ever. There's strength in numbers, even if one of our number is a frightened girl. I'd feel like a heel for leaving her alone after such a scare. And honestly, I feel better having her around. I'm even going to leave my door open tonight, in case one of us has an emergency. I certainly don't want any trouble with my locks.

DIARY OF RUBY CARDINI

February 2, 1975

My last unfinished entry is staring at me, but it feels like bad luck to continue it, so I'm moving on to a new page, quite literally, and on to a fresh start.

Today has been much better. Not only did I wake up safe in my new bed, but Jeff had breakfast ready for me. The poor man was up all night with Smithy but still trekked back to the gatehouse this morning to take care of me. Sure, the bacon was a little burnt and the eggs were fried instead of scrambled, but it was still the best meal I've ever had, knowing the care that went into it. I think I'm going to like living here.

I don't know why I didn't do it before. Well, yes, I know perfectly well why. It never would have crossed my mind before. Jeff never brought it up out of consideration for my feelings. It could only have happened this way, I suppose, and that's why, despite my fear and pain and guilt and concern over Peter, I'm a teensy bit grateful to Smithy. Once again, he's brought Jeff and me together. I could wish for more romantic circumstances, but not for a happier outcome. It feels right to be with him.

Up till now, Trevor Hall has been a place for me to discover myself, a sheltered oasis from the confusion of the outer world, where we can conduct our experiment and live our ersatz, extended-family life in shabby-genteel privilege. Likewise, the gatehouse is now my refuge from the ambiguous threats of the mansion and a protected nest where I can grow my relationship and myself. Jeff and I get to be together. We've our own little house to keep however we like. In every way that counts, we're practically married now. That's a little scary and intimidating, but in this case, the unknown brings excitement rather than dread, and curiosity for what tomorrow will bring.

Tammy seems to approve of the arrangement. Of course, she could be trying to get back on my good side. She came to see me this morning, too, after Jeff returned to the big house to fix Smithy's breakfast. I was trying to make myself useful by doing the dishes, but then I lazed around, postponing going back to Trevor Hall. I think Tammy must have known I would procrastinate and came to talk me around and to check on how I was. With her prodding, I returned to face the fallout of last night.

I found Gail and Eric in the library. They were thrilled to see me up and about. Gail had been afraid I might need to go to the hospital, or that I'd be so spooked I'd want to leave the house. She's right that I'll be leaving the <u>house,</u> but I would never leave the <u>project</u>. I accepted their hugs and assured them my only problem was going to be restricting myself to soft foods for a few days because my jaw is still tender. We made small talk, but it was strained. Neither Gail nor Eric knew much about the other casualty of Smithy's attack, and discussing the incident made Gail uncomfortable. Finally, I excused myself to my old room to retrieve my clothes and toiletries and finalize my move.

At breakfast, Jeff said Smithy had slept through the night without further incident and seemed "contrite." I thought that an odd word to use to describe an animal. I do think of Smithy as an animal now, after last night. So often, he's seemed to me a changeling child, a young human mind trapped in the body of a beast, but last night I truly saw his wild self and understood for the first time how Piers could keep an emotional distance from his charge. Did he know that Smithy would behave this way one day?

Jeff has previously mentioned scrapes Smithy got into with the McKenzies, but I thought that was part of a youthful phase, like puppies chewing everything in sight because they're teething, or the result of an inconsistent upbringing. I was always sure Smithy would be fine with us. I thought we'd raise him to be his best self because we knew what to do and because Smithy cared about us. At least, I thought he trusted me.

What had he planned to do last night when he crawled into my room? Suppose he only wanted to cuddle, and instead I screamed in his face and slapped him—two things I've never done before. Perhaps the whole thing was a big misunderstanding. Perhaps I'm being unfair.

If it is my fault, then I'm truly sorry. But it's not enough to say "mea culpa" because of Peter. Wanda took him to a vet in Middletown, where she spent most of the day. I saw her briefly on my way back to the gatehouse.

I spent a considerable amount of time amid the wreckage of my room, making piles of things I'd need immediately and other things I could grab on a future trip. Jeff and I still need to work out where "my" space is. The bedroom has a closet, but it's already mostly full of extra camera equipment and Jeff's few shirts and pants. I'll have to see if I can turn an adjacent room into my dressing room/sitting room.

When I emerged with my paper bag of necessaries, Wanda's door was open. I could tell she'd been crying by her reddened eyes and the way she spoke as if she had a cold. If my pet had been attacked in such a way, I would have been beside myself, too. I told Wanda how sorry I was about Peter and apologized for not doing a better job of protecting him. Jeff says it's silly to blame myself, that I needed to look out for my own safety, and nobody could expect otherwise, but I felt I needed to say something.

Wanda thanked me and was kind enough to ask how I was feeling and whether I was going to be comfortable in the gatehouse. I said "Sore" and "Sure" in that order.

It helped that Piers came back this evening. None of us knew to expect him. Evidently, Wanda called him immediately and demanded he come back and check on his ape. He seemed annoyed; I don't know if that's because of what happened or because he had to leave New Haven before he'd finished preparing tomorrow's lecture.

He met me in the library and spoke gently about my "experience." He asked me to describe what had happened in my own words, then asked me to tell him again. He quizzed me on several points, such as Smithy's demeanor when he first appeared in my room, and whether Peter had scratched or bitten him before Smithy started to whale on him. Piers seems to think one of us provoked Smithy into assaulting us.

Piers examined my jaw and pronounced it only bruised. He joked, asking me to "open wide and say 'Ahh.'" He shined a flashlight in my mouth and asked if I'd lost any teeth, which I hadn't. He asked if I'd been to a doctor or wanted to go. Again, I said no. Finally, Piers called me a "trooper" and said he hoped we could all put this "sorry business" behind us. I think he asked about my injuries because he was afraid I might ask the university to reimburse me for my suffering.

Wanda has asked Piers to pay for Peter's treatment, but Piers's position is Peter is Wanda's pet, whom she introduced into the house of her own volition, and he's not a part of the experiment—never mind that Peter has often been used as a carrot to reinforce Smithy. Peter's injuries happened outside of any training session, so the cat is ultimately her responsibility. Wanda must be seething, poor thing! I would have expected Piers to show her more decency. Even if there's no budget in the study for vet bills, Piers has money from his books and radio appearances; why doesn't he help Wanda as a favor? She's done plenty for him!

Piers was anxious for me to "reconcile" with Smithy. He invited me up to Smithy's room, where Jeff has been watching him. "You three are old friends. Webster's always enjoyed his time with the two of you. And you trust Jeff, don't you, Ruby? He won't let anything happen to you."

I hesitated in the doorway. Smithy sat on Jeff's lap in the rocking chair as Jeff read to him from Goodnight, Moon, an odd choice, considering it was two hours before Smithy's usual bedtime. I guess Jeff was trying extra hard to mellow him out before he went to sleep. When I appeared, Jeff smiled, and both said and signed, "Hello, Ruby."

I signed back, "Hello."

Smithy looked up at me with sad eyes and signed, "Hello" back, so I came a little closer.

"Kiss and make up," Piers urged from behind us. Smithy sat calmly in Jeff's lap. He didn't whimper or threaten me as I came closer. I signed, "Friend", and Smithy signed, "Hug," so I took a chance and opened my arms. He leapt up and wrapped himself around my neck. I almost staggered back under his weight, but I felt he was enthusiastic, not aggressive, so I hugged him back and kissed the top of his head.

Jeff invited me to stay and read with them. We made an odd family tableau: I sat in Jeff's lap, Smithy curled up in mine, and I read the rest of the book, asking him to sign for the pictures he knew. Smithy was extra good. Jeff had told me Smithy signed, "Sorry" several times after I left the bedroom last night, but he didn't apologize to me during our reading. I suppose being a model student was his way of making amends.

Once we finished the book, I felt I left on good terms with Smithy. Now that I know how fast he can snap, I'll be more careful around him—but I don't believe he's malicious or intended to hurt me or Peter.

Piers seems satisfied the study is back on track. Though Wanda sulks, he expects her to come around eventually, and I think she will, too, once Peter has recovered. In the meantime, running this study will take her mind off her troubles.

I'd hoped Piers would stick around until things returned to normal, but he's going back first thing tomorrow morning. Far from leaving us empty-handed, however, he's presented us with a memo concerning new protocols for working with Smithy. Piers also talked with us about chimpanzee dominance hierarchies and displays, so we can better recognize the signs if Smithy's about to lose it. Forewarned is forearmed, so they say, but I'd rather have a real tool for ensuring this won't happen again.

Wanda voiced a similar sentiment. "What, no stun gun?" she demanded (sarcastically, I'm sure). I would never want to use a weapon on Smithy, but I wish we had a warning signal or a reliable procedure for calming him quickly. I guess we'll have to develop one ourselves, through trial and error, as we've done for everything else in this study.

Part of Piers's statement included an admonition to send the cats away. Wanda has refused to do this. Tammy suggested they could board with one of the Meyer School teachers, but Wanda rejected the idea. I understand Piers doesn't want to risk another incident, but at the same time, I sympathize with Wanda. These pets are her companions. She's been willing to share them with us; it's not fair to make her sacrifice them for the study. Wanda has had Harriet locked in her room all day and intends to keep the animals there from now on. I'm hoping this is only a temporary measure. I'll miss their comfort if she keeps them in isolation. Of course, who's to say Wanda would trust her cats with me again, considering?

The important thing is that we're gradually knitting ourselves back together. I feel hopeful.

I've got to hope. Because otherwise, what could happen to us next?

MEMO FROM PIERS PREIS-HERALD

February 2, 1975

Re: Webster: Discipline & Risks

Many of you witnessed the events of last night. Although we've taken safeguards to reduce the risk of any future incidents, it's the whole team's responsibility to reduce the risk of general injury.

1. Be mindful: Webster is no longer an infant. Upon entering adolescence, chimpanzees grow increasingly assertive. Webster's strength surpasses that of most humans, and his temper may become equally impressive. It shouldn't surprise us that he's begun trying to intimidate us. Keep in mind this is typical behavior for a young male chimpanzee and not indicative of anything unusual.

2. Do not allow Webster to steer the direction of the study. We must continue to set rules and hold Webster accountable for following them. Thus, we will maintain Webster's respect for our authority and enjoy a safe learning and working environment.

3. Going forward, instructors are to work with Webster in pairs or triads (ideally with at least one man on each team). You will rely on each other to physically control any of Webster's outbursts.

4. Henceforth, Webster is not to hold any of the house pets. Though we humans can control

how we interact with Webster, animals lack such autonomy, and we cannot predict their reactions. Small as they are, they could suffer serious harm if they become targets of Webster's frustration. Because the pets are liabilities, Maisie will return with me to New Haven; when in residence, I will keep her leashed within the house or tied in the yard overnight. Wanda, I recommend finding a new home for your cats as soon as possible.

Heed this advice, and all will be well. — **PPH**

DIARY OF TAMMY COHEN

February 3, 1975

So new guidelines are supposed to make everything better. This is the third time Smithy has lashed out at one of us. This time, he drew blood. Piers doesn't even care what set Smithy off, or how he escaped in the first place. Now that the danger's passed, he can puff away our fears with a fresh pipe. What he can't do is promise it won't happen again.

In addition to debuting his miracle-cure memo, Piers announced Wanda is taking a "vacation." I'm guessing it's an enforced leave of absence; I simply can't see that woman going on a real vacation, especially when she was away for only three days at Christmas. Heaven knows she could use time away, given all she's been through this past month. If Wanda had thrown up her hands and declared she needed to get away, I would have been mildly surprised but proud of her. That Piers is arranging it leaves me less sanguine.

I'd like to believe Piers is genuinely concerned about Wanda's welfare and wishes to give her a break, but deep down, I know he's just covering his ass. I'll bet he's uneasy about the prospect of a potential neurotic running the study.

I'm also concerned about the duration of Wanda's "vacation." Is this a temporary absence so she can refresh herself, or is Piers trying to railroad her out of the study? It would be disgraceful if he banished her because she's strained from a run of bad luck. It may be his study, but Wanda has been the engine driving it, and however much I may gripe about her positions, she is capable.

Smithy's attack on Ruby and Peter still has me in defensive mode, so perhaps I'm overreacting and overanalyzing this new announcement. I'm full of questions: How long will Wanda be away? Will she come back? Will Piers oversee us in her absence? If not, what will become of us?

Why am I still here? We need a grown-up to keep an eye on things, but I haven't made much difference. Is it worth it to continue? Will any results we obtain balance out our injuries and fear?

~~*Next time*~~ *I'll be more vigilant.*

DIARY OF GAIL EHRLICH

February 3, 1975

Dear Diary,

The most exciting thing happened today! Piers asked me to run the study while Wanda's away! She's going to take a week or two off to go home and rest after all the stress she's been through. Piers can't supervise us because he has obligations back in Coneticut.

I was sure he'd put Jeff or Tammy in charge. Jeff's been on the team the longest, and Tammy's so smart and organized. But no! He called me aside as the meeting broke up and asked if I would keep an eye on things for him. He told me he's been watching me for a long time and thinks I'm really smart and talented! Especially for my age! He said he's impressed by all the progress I've made with my language skills and by how good I am with Smithy. And he said he doesn't think people give me enough credit because I'm young, but he wants to promote me to show them what I can do.

Piers is taking me to dinner Saturday when he comes back for the weekend so we can talk more. I'm so excited! This is a BIG responsibility, and I don't want to let him down. I hope everything goes perfectly at dinner. That will be like a sign everything will go perfectly when I'm in charge, too. I'm going to wear my flowered dress. Piers told me once it was pretty, so I hope he likes it. I wonder if I should take notes when we're talking or if that would look too immature? I bet Tammy wouldn't need to take notes. She would understand everything the first time.

I can't wait to tell Mom and Dad all about this. And Vanessa! If Wanda stays away a long time, I might even still be in charge of the study when my sister visits. I'll have to talk to Piers about her coming. Saturday will be perfect because I'll have him all to myself.

Fingers crossed...

DIARY OF TAMMY COHEN

February 10, 1975

Day 1 of the new regime, and so far, everything is still standing. I was in disbelief when Piers announced <u>Gail</u> *was going to be our interim supervisor. She's the least qualified among us, and I quail to think what she must have done to get this job. However, she's definitely taken to the role. She keeps asking me how to spell words so her reports look more professional (Wanda nags her about that). I'll be getting her a dictionary/thesaurus for her next birthday.*

Actually, Gail has embraced her position too readily. This morning, as I was preparing Smithy for school, I told Gail I would see her in the afternoon. "Why this afternoon? Why are you going to be gone so long?" she asked. I explained I was planning to observe Smithy's lesson, and she informed me that wouldn't be necessary. "The Meyer teachers can take care of him. We need you back here. If you want to do extra studying, you can practice with Ruby or Eric. Or me." Wanda always frowns about me shadowing at the school, but she's never tried to interfere with it. Still, I decided not to make a big deal about it. After all, Gail is only temporarily in charge, right?

Gail wanted me back at the house to participate in a meeting about Smithy. She's designed a new schedule that builds in more playtime. For instance, when Smithy is spending a full day at Trevor Hall, he'll have a two-hour lesson after breakfast, followed by "recess," just like in a "people school." Game time will be Smithy's new reward, instead of playing with the cats (who left with Wanda) or eating junk food. It's also meant to help him expend his energy so he can come back to class reenergized.

Furthermore, Gail has decided to implement the token economy we discussed months ago. Her rationale is we need something new to motivate Smithy now that the pets are off-limits. Eric agreed to help her develop a "prize progression" and conduct training. Better them than me this time.

Gail's curriculum includes a significant amount of unstructured time, so we can simply socialize with Smithy. Real people don't sit around always pointing to things and asking, "What's that?" she says. They have conversations, and Gail believes Smithy is more likely to converse with us if we focus on topics he cares about: playing games, commenting on his paintings, or discussing TV shows. I've noticed TV time happens to be scheduled around programs Gail herself likes, such as "General Hospital." I can't imagine what Smithy is learning about the world by watching nurses and doctors perform operations and lock lips.

We're not to have any artificial vocabulary lists either. Instead of teaching Smithy bunches of new words he may never use just to build a bigger vocabulary, our goal is to get him to use his existing vocabulary more "naturally," since most people have a standard vocabulary they exercise daily. I agree that sounds reasonable. We'll get a better quality of material by charting the words Smithy opts to use in an organic context instead of documenting how he uses assigned vocabulary in scenarios designed to elicit those preselected words.

Not all changes have to do with Smithy's routines. Gail has scheduled "clean up duty" for us, a fixed period when we're to make improvements to the house. Gail thinks it's a terrible shame we're adding to the decay of Trevor Hall. We should leave the mansion in better condition than we found it, and so we're to sand banisters, polish doors, and repair any damages Smithy has caused by tearing or biting the walls. It's a nice idea; I'm curious to see how long it lasts.

Lastly, Gail has temporarily moved into Piers's third-floor quarters, taking just a few possessions with her. Since Smithy's on the third floor, it makes sense in Gail's mind to take a room closer to him. Piers went back to Yale today, so his room is presently vacant. Gail sees no reason why it shouldn't be occupied by anyone who wants to use it. Besides, she says birds nest under the eaves, and you can hear them singing so prettily in the morning. I don't like knowing she knows that.

Ergo, after months of griping, I finally have a big bedroom all to myself—and I don't really know what to do about it. I can't send for more of my things and spread out because Gail will reclaim her space *eventually. I can now sleep with the connecting door open and even sleep in Gail's big bed if I want to. I have all the peace and quiet I've ever wished for now that Gail has moved upstairs, and Ruby has moved out to the cottage. I should be happy. Right?*

I hope Wanda is enjoying her peace and quiet as I wait to see what else Gail has planned.

LIBRARY JOURNAL ENTRY
FROM GAIL EHRLICH

February 18, 1975

After one week of practicing with token rewards, Smithy finally seems to be getting it!

Eric and I started teaching him about tokens last Wednesday. First, Eric made tokens out of cardboard. They look like giant pennies with a picture of Piers on one side instead of Abe Lincoln, and a picture of Trevor Hall on the back. Ruby suggested we keep a lookout for movies and TV shows that demonstrate people buying things, so we can teach Smithy about transactions. Jeff has taught him the signs for "buy" and "money."

Then we acted out scenes where each of us took turns buying food or toys with the big tokens, so Smithy would learn they were important and could get him things he wanted. I tried to explain that if he was good, he would get a token. I signed, "Lots of tokens are good."

The next day at school, Sarah and Hope gave Smithy either a token or a treat when he performed well. We didn't want him to be stuck with just tokens yet. At home, we gave him a token every time he answered a question correctly. Eric says this is continuous reinforcement. We wanted Smithy to get used to receiving a token for a job well done, so he would know it was a reward.

After dinner, I offered him different desserts and when he told me the one he wanted, I asked him for five tokens. That wasn't a lot because he had over twenty by then. We just wanted him to know he had to trade his tokens to "buy" things he wanted. After that, whenever Smithy wanted something, like a tickle or juice, we made him buy it with his tokens. The amount we asked for didn't matter. We fixed it so at the end of the night, Smithy had no tokens left and would have to start over the next day.

I think Smithy was confused at first because we never traded with him for things before, but he didn't get mad, as I thought he might. He thinks it's a kind of game, and it's making him practice numbers, so that's good. We did continuous reinforcement with tokens for the next three days. Then we switched to intermittent reinforcement, in which he didn't always get a token or a reward. I thought that would make him mad, too, but I think it actually made him sharper. If you don't pay him his token, Smithy tries harder to get your attention the next time he signs to you. It's like he thinks you didn't reward him because you didn't see him the first time.

He wants those tokens now. But he hides them. It's like he doesn't want us to know he has them, so we won't ask for them later. Jeff found two hidden under the couch cushions in the solarium yesterday and two more behind his bookcase. We know how many Eric made, so we know if any are missing, and then we ask Smithy for them. He gets nervous when we do that. Then we go looking for them with him. It's like hide and seek. He tries to lead you away from his stash, but we catch him anyway. So although it's not what we expected, the tokens have become his reward on their own. We're all having fun, especially Smithy. I wish Wanda had let us do this a long time ago.

DIARY OF RUBY CARDINI

February 23, 1975

"It's quiet. Too quiet," Jeff jokes. He's right. I've been expecting another disaster while Wanda's away, but life with Gail in charge has been surprisingly peaceful.

It's not that she's a bad leader—it's just been hard to adjust to Gail's program after nine months of Wanda's vastly different style. Thank goodness she comes back tomorrow! Gail isn't much of an administrator (we've all been going along to humor her) or an innovator (that token system is Eric's baby, not hers). She does have the magic touch with Smithy, though.

It's like he's back to his old self. When he smiles at me, I almost have to pinch myself to remember this is the same ape that trashed my room and thrashed Peter within an inch of his life. His personality has shifted 180 degrees. Maybe he needed Gail to sweeten him up. And I mean this literally: she hands him a treat every time he waves a token at her. We'll have to script a chimp exercise program if Wanda extends her vacation.

I know our progress won't be enough to make Wanda happy, but at least she can't say <u>we've</u> been taking a vacation. We're on track again, and I hope everything can go back to normal now.

VIDEO FOOTAGE: "20/20" INTERVIEW WITH TAMMY STEINMETZ

Broadcast Date: April 6, 1989
Location: Inside an Office

Tammy sits behind a desk, hands folded. She wears silver glasses, a white blouse, a light-blue vest, and a blue and purple paisley shawl knotted like a scarf around her neck. Her hair is shoulder-length and gathered back in a clip. She addresses the camera.

At the end of March, Gail's sister, Vanessa, finally came to visit. Gail had dangled that visit to Trevor Hall in front of her ever since Memorial Day, but it was never the right time. This wasn't the right time either, but it was Vanessa's spring break. I think her visit was Gail's reward for running the study in Wanda's absence.

Wanda wasn't happy about it. She complained to Piers about bringing in outsiders and the liability of the study if anything happened to Vanessa. I think she was afraid I might want to invite all my sisters to Newport to balance things out.

Tammy laughs.

Piers told her it would be good for Smithy to meet new people and for us to observe his interactions with outsiders other than his teachers. He emphasized that Vanessa was visiting Gail, not Smithy, as if any harm that might befall her would become Gail's sole responsibility.

I wasn't looking forward to her visit either, although Vanessa surprised me. She looked just like a smaller Gail, blonde and pixieish, with shorter, curlier hair, but she was quieter. Shy. She was just as dazzled by everything Newport had to offer, though. And she was thrilled to meet Smithy.

We'd waited to introduce them until after Smithy's nap, so he would be well-rested. It was the first time we'd brought a stranger to the house for Smithy to meet, and none of us had any idea how he would react. I could only imagine Smithy at his worst. Vanessa was such a young thing. She must have been about fifteen, but she looked twelve. He could have picked her up and swung her over his head if he wanted.

Wanda must have prepped Smithy somehow because when he walked downstairs, he looked interested, not alarmed. He spotted Vanessa, and his eyes lit up. He let go of Wanda's hand and ran right over to her. Vanessa knelt at eye-level with him, and my stomach dropped. I'd always heard you're not supposed to lower yourself to a dog's level because it indicates you're subservient to them, and I imagined it would send the same signal to a chimpanzee. I panicked. I wanted to push Vanessa behind me to protect her, but by then it was too late. Smithy reached out his hand—

What did he do?

He touched her hair. He always liked playing with Gail's blond hair. I was tense, thinking he might yank on it and scalp her, but he was very gentle. Oh, he was absolutely charming. He signed a greeting and asked Vanessa her name. Gail had already taught her a name sign that he picked up right away. On his own initiative, Smithy tried to engage Vanessa in conversation. She got flustered because she didn't understand him and couldn't respond, but Gail translated, explaining what Smithy was expressing, then asking for Vanessa's reply and modeling the signs for her to copy. Even

Wanda was pleased to watch Smithy interacting so nicely—and coherently—with an outsider.

So her visit went well?

Yes…but I didn't expect it to at the time. All week long, I was anxious. I tried to stay near Vanessa through all her excursions. Gail was determined to repeat all the activities we did during our first week in Newport, from visiting the Breakers to taking a harbor cruise, even though the wind was icy and the waves that time of year bounced our boat up and down. I was so sick after that trip that I had to go home and lie down, but I felt guilty doing so. I worried if I wasn't around to watch Vanessa, something awful would happen to her.

That's what the entire year was like: we'd brace ourselves for a tantrum, a fire, or some other nasty surprise, and it wouldn't come. Then as soon as we'd let our guard down and decide we were imagining things, or that Smithy had outgrown his outbursts, *bang*, another attack. Vanessa's visit was a microcosm. I didn't trust Smithy around her, knowing what he'd done in the past. My big-sister eyes kept looking for things that could go wrong with her around, but nothing did. Vanessa had lots of fun and when she went home, she told her parents and all her friends that she'd talked to a chimp. Piers called her our unofficial spokeswoman and bragged to Wanda about the great word-of-mouth she would bring our study. Smithy's success with Vanessa encouraged Piers to introduce him to more new people. He saw her visit as a great victory, but I saw it as dodging a bullet.

You still expected disaster?

Oh, yes. By then, Smithy was no longer the chimp we'd started with. He didn't look like himself anymore because he was growing up. His little face had lengthened, and his muscles were more defined, but he also had a—a *canny* look in his eyes. At times, I'd swear they glinted red. It was an illusion, of course. Chimps' eyes have no whites like humans' do, so they look entirely brown. The change in Smithy's attitude and personality made the animal in him stand out. It became harder to think of that new creature as "Smithy." Our Smithy was cute and impetuous but sensitive. This new ape was just shy of menacing. I started referring to him more often as "Webster" in my conversations, which took Wanda by surprise, considering I had been part of the faction that pushed for him to take a nickname. He had the potential to become Mr. Hyde, but I'm grateful he didn't while Vanessa was around. He was saving up his ire for someone else.

 Tammy pauses.

 They both were.

DIARY OF RUBY CARDINI

April 8, 1975

After several quiet months, we've had another sighting. This time, Gail had the honor (or the misfortune) of spotting the ghost.

Whereas Eric had seen his phantom in the afternoon, in broad daylight, in a well-lit hallway, Gail's encounter took place in the evening, in the shadowy stairwell. Wanda's reaction was predictably derisive.

Gail was alone when it happened because we were scattered throughout the house preparing for visitors. Simon and Hope were bringing Smithy back from a long weekend sleepover, and to thank them for keeping him, we offered them dinner. But the whole thing was a setup. Piers wanted to pick the teachers' brains about Smithy's progress. I think he's trying to get a grant renewed (though I thought he just got funding approved through the spring) and wants more supporting evidence in his favor. Luckily for us, they were excited about coming to Trevor Hall. Jeff and I were curious to see how Smithy would behave at dinner with new additions at the table. Would he take directions from his teachers outside the classroom? Would he sign with them? How well does his behavior translate from one context to another?

I mention these details to better set the stage and explain what we were thinking and worrying about before the storm broke. Suffice to say, we all were in a heightened emotional state: nervous about hosting guests, nervous about having to be on our best behavior when we're normally so casual at meals, nervous about how Smithy would act, and above all, nervous about whether Piers would get what he needed to allow us to remain here. I imagine Gail was anxious, too, though she's usually the most upbeat of the group.

She dressed for dinner while I set the dining room table. Tammy helped Wanda with meal preparations, so Gail was alone in her room—

alone on the entire floor. Yet she says she heard someone in the hallway calling to her.

She thought it was Tammy. Gail called back to her, "I'm here, come on in!" but of course, Tammy didn't appear. Gail assumed her roommate couldn't hear her, so she stepped out in the hall and called to Tammy again. She received no reply and saw no one in the corridor. Then, though the voice had sounded feminine, Gail decided it could have belonged to Eric. She didn't know Eric was helping Jeff set up his cameras and projection screen in the library, so she wandered down to his room and knocked on his door. Eric didn't answer.

Undeterred, Gail surmised whoever had called her had gone back downstairs, and since dinner was to start soon, she made her way to the ground floor via the servants' staircase. It was only an unfortunate chance she chose to do that; it only happened because she had gone to look for Eric and those stairs were closest to his room. I doubt Gail had ever used them at any other time in her stay here. They're narrow and gloomy. ("Just right for an overactive imagination," grumbled Wanda). I heard a scream rip through the house, tearing through the tension and releasing our collective anxieties in a panic storm. Tammy almost dropped a roasting pan on her foot. Sound from the servants' stairs does carry clearly to the kitchen. Wanda says Gail just had to be dramatic, but I think she was genuinely frightened. She was crying when we found her. As Gail made her way downstairs, she had reached the last turn in the stairwell, when she suddenly sensed someone above her and thought Eric or Tammy had finally come to look for her. Instead, on the landing above her hovered a dark figure, faceless, but nevertheless watching her.

When Gail screamed, everyone heard it and ran to her. Tammy said Eric was so scared of the specter he practically flew out of the house, but Gail's fear paralyzed her. When we found her, she was clinging to the banister, rigid and crying so hard her makeup was already staining her face.

"What's wrong?" Wanda demanded. "Are you hurt?"

Gail blinked up at her through caked and dripping lashes, whimpering but unable to speak. Tammy stepped forward to help her, and with Gail's arm slung over her shoulder, she started to guide her back up to their shared room. Instantly, Gail came back to life, protesting,

"No, no, no, no!" Tammy turned her right around and took her into the kitchen. As Gail sank into a chair, she sobbed, "I saw it! I saw the ghost!"

Wanda's face wrenched from concern into disgust. "Oh, Good Lord. This is not happening!"

"Better her than me," I heard Eric mutter behind me. "If I ran into that thing again…" His pause left us to imagine him dying of fright or losing his mind. "It better not have been looking for me! Those stairs go right up to my room!"

"Stop it!" Wanda snapped. "We can't afford this right now! I don't need you carrying on, too. And if you think I'm going to find you yet another room, you can move into a hotel instead!"

She was twisting her hair and biting her lower lip, just like on the day the writing had appeared on the walls. Gail had resumed crying and wouldn't respond to any of Tammy's questions. Wanda stood over them, glaring and tapping her foot. "We can't have this!" she repeated, now devoid of all sympathy. "Our guests will be here any minute! We have important things to discuss, and these childish fantasies aren't allowed!"

"I want Piers!" Gail screamed. "He'll listen to me! You're mean! Where is he? I wanna talk to him!" She did sound awfully childish then, but I felt so sorry for her. I'd never seen anyone look so terrified.

"He's busy getting ready for tonight. He's probably in the shower, and with any luck, he didn't hear your caterwauling. In any case, you certainly aren't going to bother him with this story before dinner." Wanda turned on Tammy, who was shooting her dirty looks but wisely keeping silent. "See if you can get her cleaned up and calmed down. Piers wanted all of us present, but if she stays in this condition, I'll tell Hope that Gail has the flu—no, that makes us sound contagious—I'll say she has a headache. Or cramps!" I could see the wheels spinning in Wanda's brain as she tried to salvage the situation.

"Do I have cramps, too?" Tammy asked.

"Of course not!" Wanda looked like she wanted to spit.

"Because I'm not going to be present for dinner either if it means leaving Gail behind," Tammy continued.

Catching on to the thread of the conversation, Gail seized Tammy's arm. "No, don't leave me all alone! Please don't! What if she comes back?"

"Look at her! Can you imagine if 'she' comes back and Gail starts screaming in the middle of dinner? Wouldn't *that* disturb our guests?" Tammy's eyes were glittering, and I thought she was enjoying the stand-off too much. Wanda *was* being cold, but I thought she spoke from worry, not sadism. This dinner was a bigger deal than I had suspected.

I felt I had to step in, so I offered, "Why don't we take Gail to the gatehouse? She can freshen up there." I felt bad for talking over Gail as if she couldn't hear me and reached out to squeeze the hand that wasn't clutching Tammy's elbow in a death grip. "The ghost has never been seen in the gatehouse. I feel perfectly safe out there, and you will, too, even if you're by yourself."

Wanda breathed out more steadily. "That's a good idea. Even if she freaks out again, nobody will be able to hear her from out there."

The boys had been shuffling behind me all this time, but Jeff looked happy we'd reached a decision. "Good thinking, Ruby! Gail, you'll be fine. There're plenty of snacks if you get hungry, and you can watch the Oscars on TV. Maybe somebody will streak again." At least he was trying to help lighten the mood. I don't think Gail understood anything Jeff said, but she did seem to get that she wasn't going to be abandoned in her room for the ghost to find.

Jeff kissed my cheek and whispered, "Help her get settled in and then come back here." Tammy and I each took one of Gail's arms and half-carried her the distance to the gatehouse. She sniffled all the way, but the sharp outdoor air seemed to perk her up. By the time I got her to the bathroom so we could clean the mess off her face, she was ready to talk again.

"Thank you both so much for taking care of me." Gail reached out to squeeze our hands, blocking Tammy from wiping her face. "I'm sorry I made such a fuss, but you don't know how scared I was. You can't imagine what it was like! Suddenly, she was right there! She just rose up out of the dark as if the shadows gave birth to her!" And therein lay the problem that would later develop: for Wanda keeps insisting that Gail saw a shadow and let her imagination do the rest.

Part of me thought talking about it could help Gail. "What did you see?" I asked.

Gail closed her eyes and shuddered. "A horror! Something demonic!" Her lip trembled and she didn't go on—until prompted.

"Did it have glowing red eyes and horns?" Tammy asked in a monotone. Gail took her seriously and paused as if trying to recall.

"No. It was just black. All solid black. _Evil_ black. _Cold_ black. I could feel all the darkness pouring from her into the stairwell. I thought I would die!"

Tammy pressed, "Was it a big mound then?"

"No, it looked like somebody. I thought it could have been _you_ at first. It was a woman. I could tell…" But Gail didn't elaborate on how she could tell.

"Did it have _any_ distinctive features?" Tammy asked.

Again, Gail was quiet for a moment, thinking. During the pause, I was able to wipe away the snot that had pooled under her nose and framed her mouth. At that point, I realized I believed her. Gail, always cute and conscious of her appearance, would never let herself look so frightful—unless something had badly rattled her.

"I couldn't see her face," she said. "She didn't have one. I saw her from the waist up." She closed her eyes, the better to see again. "Her arms…they were at her side…like she was holding the railing. Oh! Something else was moving…She had this long, trailing shadow floating around her face, kind of like that veil Arabian women wear, or like a scarf, or maybe a rope."

I saw Tammy start and her eyes widen when Gail said that, but when I asked her what was wrong, she said it was nothing. I didn't believe her then, and I still don't.

"She spoke to me," Gail whispered. Again, her glistening eyes fixated on a void. "She knew my name! Eric didn't have to put up with that."

I decided to lead Gail away from the subject of the ghost by asking if she wanted to lie down. Instead, Gail decided she would like to watch TV after all. I left her in the rec room with a glass of warm milk, and Tammy and I scooted back to the main house. Wanda greeted us with a strained smile. "Please, please don't say anything about this to Piers until after dinner. Preferably not until tomorrow."

She didn't ask about Gail. Tammy prompted her by asking, "Is there anything else?"

Relief washed Wanda's face. "No, I think we're set now. The roast didn't even burn; wasn't that lucky?"

Not ten minutes later, Simon and Hope showed up, fawning over the house, just like I had on my first day. Piers breezed down the main stairs in a dinner jacket, looking very much the lord of the manor, and gave them a tour of "the ground floor." Wanda morphed into a smiling debutante and was positively charming all night. The rest of us followed them, making awkward comments behind stiff smiles. Our guests were too starry-eyed to notice.

Only Smithy saw through the deception, and he called our bluff by taking liberties he normally wouldn't dare. He didn't wait to be served but took meat directly off the serving platter and reached right into the circulating bowl of mashed potatoes. Hope and Simon laughed it off, and Piers archly made a joke about Smithy devolving. When eating, he stuffed his mouth with food, only reaching for his utensils when Wanda told him for the third time to "Eat with a fork."

"He's too excited by his visitors to remember his manners," Piers excused.

Fortunately, Smithy remembered his signs and responded appropriately to Hope's inquiries about what he was eating and if it was good. That pleased Piers and Wanda, for it indicated he would converse with his teachers outside the classroom. Smithy's was virtually the only conversation. Tammy was unusually quiet for the rest of the evening. Piers had counted on her to lead a discussion on pedagogy, but he had to keep prodding her to ask our guests questions, which she did in a distracted manner. She also kept trying to catch Eric's eye at dinner. I assume she wanted to compare notes with him about Gail's sighting. Eric and Jeff chatted awkwardly with Simon about baseball, and I concentrated on simply chewing and swallowing my food, first wondering if Gail was OK at the gatehouse and then wondering what it was she had really seen to put her into such a state. Throughout dinner, Smithy watched us intently with his head cocked knowingly, as if listening in on our thoughts.

Our guests praised us for the food and gushed to Piers about what a bright pupil Smithy has been all the way out to the car. Piers was so satisfied to hear of this progress that he didn't even chafe at the nickname, though he and Wanda had both referred to him as "Webster" throughout the course of the night. We all should have been elated, but as soon as the eyes of the outsiders were off us, we deflated. Tammy immediately cornered Eric, but she still won't tell me what they talked about. That bothers me terribly. She's always confided in me before.

Ironically, Gail probably had the best evening of all of us, resting in peaceful solitude. She was sound asleep on the couch when Jeff and I got back, and she hasn't budged since. Tomorrow, of course, she'll want to tell Piers what she saw. I sure hope the afterglow of the dinner sticks with him.

What did you see, Gail? Are you and Eric both visionaries? And Smithy, too? What does Tammy know about what's going on?

What will we face next?

NOTE FROM PIERS PREIS-HERALD
TO WANDA KARLEWICZ

April 9, 1975

My dear,

Last night went swimmingly! I'm confident the Meyer School will provide us third-party validation. Thank you for planning and executing a lovely dinner. I know you dislike socializing, but you were perfectly charming. You sparkled against the rest of the team.

Incidentally, I think I interrupted some post-prandial celebrating. While making my rounds of the ground floor, I heard noises in the pantry. On investigating, I saw Eric and Tammy exiting. They seemed embarrassed to be discovered, though I played cool. Eric stammered an excuse about wanting a celebratory drink. Tammy had one wine glass but no bottle with her. Eric was trying to hide something behind his back that appeared to be flashcards. After they left, I inspected the pantry but instead of libations, I found only candle wax and a spent match on the floor.

You know I'm no puritan, but I generally disapprove of colleagues fraternizing for professional reasons. I had misgivings when Ruby and Jeff started dating, though they seem to get along well. I advise you to ensure these two don't cause any distractions to our study, as our prospects are not yet fully secured. — **PPH**

DIARY OF GAIL EHRLICH

April 13, 1975

Wanda is such a bitch!

We were working with Smithy in the Solarium, and she wanted to reward him by reading him a story. I thought we should use tokens instead. We haven't played with those much since Wanda came back. I thought she'd be excited about them because they proved Smithy can understand how money works, but she only read my reports and said our demonstration was interesting. I think she was jealous because I taught him the token system, and she didn't, so she acted like she didn't care.

Instead, Wanda told me to get a storybook so we could read and sign about the pictures. I went toward the main stairs, and she called out, "Why not take the servant stairs? Their closer." I told her I was too afraid to use those, and she got mad.

"What's your problem?" she said. "You don't really think your going to see anything, do you? You let your imagination get the better of you last time." Then she said, "I can't believe you ran this study two months ago, and now your cringeing at shadows. Your better then this. It's time to grow up, Gail."

Well that made me furious! First, she doesn't believe me about the ghost, then she has the nerve to lecture me. I've given alot to this study! I deserve better then this! She can't be the boss of everyone!

I could tell her a thing or two about who's really boss. Better yet, I wish Piers was still here. Then I could <u>show</u> her!

I'd love to wipe the smirk off her face.

DIARY OF RUBY CARDINI

April 14, 1975

I managed a rare day off and visited the Elms, another historic mansion open to the public. It's more sedate than Marble House or the Breakers. The house is still huge (three floors, like ours) but far surpasses ours in elegance. What made it stand out was the spaciousness and beauty of its grounds. The estate is huge with sweeping lawns, fountains, statuary, and trees. It was peaceful to sit beside the fountain and admire the view. I wished Jeff had been along to see it with me like when we went to Breakers, but he's been locked up editing footage for Piers.

Being a free agent prompted me to do something I wouldn't have if Jeff had joined me.

The tour guide was a charming elderly woman, Mrs. Harding. She's been a volunteer with the Newport Preservation Society since her husband died three years ago. She said being around new people and lovely things lifted her spirits. She spoke with a British accent, so I figured she wasn't local, but when I inquired after the tour had ended, she said she's been in the area "nigh on thirty-five years." I know a lot of British aristocrats married wealthy American heiresses whose families summered in Newport, and I wondered if Mrs. Harding might have a connection. When I tentatively asked if she was related to anyone from the area, she chuckled and seemed to know just what I meant.

"No, dear, I'm no distant cousin to the Vanderbilts. But when I was a girl, I knew of the fine ladies and duchesses who had come from America after meeting their husbands in Newport. Newport sounded like a fairy story land where all the houses were grand, all the women were beautiful, and Prince Charming was bound to find you. I wanted to see it for myself. I was lucky my parents supported my wish to go to school in America. Rumors of another war were beginning to rumble,

and doubtlessly they supposed I would be safer across the Atlantic. They were right." She looked wistful then, and I felt bad for upsetting her. I wanted to change the subject and decided to ask the question that was really on my mind.

I explained I was from Trevor Hall. Mrs. Harding's eyebrows went up, but she didn't comment. She'd obviously heard of us, though I don't know exactly what she'd heard. I asked if she knew any details about our house. "I understand a woman died there," I added.

Mrs. Harding nodded. "A young lady fell off the rooftop. And she wasn't the first."

I was shocked to hear her alluding to multiple deaths. Had there been a mass slaughter at Trevor Hall no one told us about? My mouth must have dropped open because I saw Mrs. Harding's expression soften.

"Many people have lived in Trevor Hall over the years. Death is part of life. People died in that house, just as they die in most houses," she added, gently. "Until recently, people died at home and were laid out in the parlor for a wake. Hospitals and funeral parlors are innovations of the twentieth century. My husband died in our home, in our bed, after a long convalescence. Does that surprise you? Does it frighten you?"

I shook my head. "No, it's just that I understood foul play was involved with this girl." I repeated the name I'd heard Trish say at the Black Pearl: "Imogene Rockwell."

To my surprise, Mrs. Harding chuckled. "Oh, poor Mrs. Rockwell died in her bed when she was past my age. That happened in…1890, if I recall. The young lady who fell to her death did so years later. Yes, I'm almost sure it was during a New Year's celebration for the start of the new century. I don't know how she's come to be associated with Mrs. Rockwell's death, but I've heard their stories combined."

That threw me, but I'd only had Reid's lectures to go off. "Oh. I heard she was mixed up with the master of the house, and she jumped because of the scandal…" I trailed away because Mrs. Harding was shaking her head.

"Mr. Trevor was an infirm old man, not up to hijinks with the servants or any other woman. He couldn't even ride his thoroughbred stallions anymore. He sold them to his neighbor, Damon Herbert, in 1887. I've seen the bill of sale in our records. He died at Trevor Hall in

1892. Mrs. Trevor died at their New York home five years later. Curtis Trevor was mostly bedridden toward the end of his life. We've pictures of him in his bath chair—his wheelchair—being pushed by his nurse in our archives, too."

"Could she have been the servant who fell off the roof?" I asked. Reid had claimed the dead woman was from Herbert Terrace, but local legend must have associated her with Trevor Hall's master for a reason.

"_He_ was a conscientious objector in your Civil War—a Quaker, I think, and a surgeon's assistant whom Mr. Trevor knew in those days and later employed as nurse."

I felt more foolish every minute. Mrs. Herbert's eyes still twinkled, and if she thought I was an idiot or a ghoul, she was polite enough not to say so. "I'm just trying to find out something about the tragedy. We were told about it shortly after we moved in, and we're all curious. Do you at least know the name of the woman who died?"

Mrs. Harding shook her head. "I've seen the obituary, but her name wasn't given." That, at least, tallied with what Reid had said.

"Isn't that strange?" I asked. "Do you suppose someone was trying to cover up her death for some reason?"

"I suspect her name was omitted to spare the poor girl's family," Mrs. Harding answered. "They would have to be notified of her death, and it would have been cruel to let them find out by reading the newspapers." That made sense.

Mrs. Harding took further pity on me. "People like to tell stories. It's how they bond. Having a local haunted house is exciting. I'm not surprised this poor lady's tragedy has become a story. Rather, I'm surprised hers is the only one. As I recall, a workman was killed during construction of the tower, but I'm not aware of any stories concerning his ghost. Two years after the house opened, Mrs. Trevor delivered a premature child who died, but I've never heard reports of any disembodied crying. I hope you and your friends enjoy your stay at Trevor Hall and don't worry about silly rumors." I didn't tell her what Eric and Gail had seen. Instead, I thanked her for her help and finally let her collect her next tour group.

The man selling tickets at the front followed me outside. When I was on the bottom step, he called out: "It's not the servant you should be looking at—it's the teacher."

I didn't know he'd been eavesdropping. He had been sitting at his desk while I had what I thought was a quiet, private conversation. I asked what he meant.

He pointed back toward Mrs. Harding. "She wouldn't know about it because her focus is on the Gilded Age, the 1880s and '90s. In the 1920s, when Trevor Hall was a boarding school, one of the teachers hanged herself up in the attic or somewhere. She'd been having an affair with another teacher and was depressed because he wouldn't marry her. She was expecting."

I had to fight not to flinch when he mentioned hanging. Gail had referred to a rope or a scarf on her phantom. And Tammy had noticed. I wondered if she knew this story already.

"How do you know?" I asked. "You're too young to remember that happening." The guy looked like he was in his thirties.

He smiled condescendingly. "My parents were around when the school was operating."

"Did they attend the Bradley School?"

"No, but I had an aunt who worked in the kitchen."

"And how did you hear about it?" I doubted his aunt had told him about the suicide as a bedtime story when he was a kid.

"My aunt worked in the kitchen," he repeated slowly. If he'd felt inclined to help me out before, he wasn't forthcoming now. His upper lip curled slightly. "You're suspicious."

"I'm sorry. Some people have tried to scare us with different stories. It's hard to know what to believe." I tried a different tactic. "If I wanted to verify the teacher's death in the newspapers, what year would I need?"

He shook his head. "It was bad publicity. It would have been hushed up."

"But there must be a death certificate! A police report?" I was growing frustrated. I wondered if I could look up a list of teachers at the school. There couldn't have been many instructors, and I could trace what had happened to them more easily than I could locate all the servants who had passed through Trevor Hall or Herbert Terrace. "Would the historical society have copies of the yearbooks? Or the library?"

He shook his head. "That stuff wouldn't have much value. An annual might turn up at an estate sale, or you could check the junk shops. I could put out word that you're looking, if you'd like."

I thanked him, then I finally left the house and made another tour of the grounds. Instead of meditating on the beauty around me, I sat by the fountain and considered all the new, conflicting information I'd just picked up. Everybody in town knows so much more than we do about Trevor Hall. Or claims to. It's hard to know what to believe.

Sitting here now, I'm still confused.

DIARY OF TAMMY COHEN

April 16, 1975

The plot thickens! After dinner, as Ruby and I washed dishes, she confided some news she's learned about Trevor Hall: We may have a second ghost. Apart from the maid who fell off the roof, a teacher from the boarding school supposedly hanged herself. That's consistent with Eric and Gail's descriptions of the spirit. I'm astounded Reid never mentioned it, even if it were only a rumor. He acted like he knew everything worth knowing (and a lot that was inconsequential) about Trevor Hall. The story is sketchy, but it came to her through a volunteer at the historical society, so I'm willing to credit it.

Ruby is determined to trace the instructor. She plans to review old newspapers from the years the Bradley School operated on her next day off. I've volunteered to help. If there is a ghost, knowing who she is might help us to coexist with her more smoothly, or even help her to rest. Isn't that what ghosts always want in the movies?

I asked Ruby why she thinks the ghost is appearing to us. She answered, "She's probably mad at us for messing up the house she had to work so hard to clean in life. She wants to derail the experiment and drive us out."

That doesn't make any sense to me. If we assume the ghost is the maid who fell off the roof, then she came from Herbert Terrace and had no responsibility for Trevor Hall. When I asked Eric why he thought the maid might be haunting the house, he pointed out that the servants used to gather at Trevor Hall for parties. "Maybe she had good memories of the place and stayed because it used to be fun." Is she trying to have fun with us now? That could account for playful pranks like hiding our utensils and setting Smithy loose.

If, on the other hand, the ghost is a suicidal teacher, then presumably she had no fondness for the house. She may not care much for students either. That would account for the more malicious acts, like starting fires and frightening Eric.

It sure would be nice to know something concrete. I'll tackle the historical society while Ruby looks at the newspapers. Between us, we're bound to find something eventually.

DIARY OF RUBY CARDINI

April 16, 1975

I've got reinforcements now! Both Tammy and Eric have agreed to help me investigate the origins of the ghost. Eric was particularly excited about the prospect of getting some explanation for what he experienced. He plans to seek additional information from the locals: Trish and Jess are still in town and probably would be happy to talk. Meanwhile, Tammy and I will investigate the archives of the historical society and the library.

Tammy says Reid thought he'd identified the maid who died, at least by her first name. This came up months ago, during their double-date with Gail and Miguel, but the link was so tenuous that Tammy didn't mention it at the time. Reid said he'd discovered a letter written from a housemaid of Herbert Terrace to her sister, who later worked at Kingscote, among a pack of old papers. It was a simple account of her days, but according to Tammy, "She specifically complained that her workload was heavier 'ever since Tessie has been gone.' Reid fixated on that. He was convinced 'Tessie' could have been the unknown maid." Tammy thought it was more likely that "Tessie" had simply quit or left to get married; maids came and went all the time. Still, it's something to go on. Now, when one of us visits the historical society, we can look through the rolls for a servant named Tessie.

Unless, as Eric suggested, "Tessie" was a nickname or a middle name.

At Tammy's request, we've agreed to keep Gail out of our investigation. Tammy's concerned any open discussion of the possible haunting might upset her further. "I've tried asking her more questions about what she saw and heard, but she becomes hysterical and keeps accusing me of doubting her. She acts like it's too traumatizing to recall. Perhaps it is."

I asked Eric again what he'd seen and felt. His description was enthralling, yet chilling: "The figure was flat. It had no dimension or substance, but at the same time, it was solid enough that I couldn't see through it. It reminded me of seeing a film projection, but I knew Jeff's equipment wasn't anywhere nearby. It was a shadow blocking everything else. It was real, not an optical illusion, I mean; it wasn't really part of this world."

I asked if he thought it was a shadow, an echo of some sort, or if it was a sentient spirit. Eric said, "It saw me. I understood that. I don't know if it was looking for me, or if I surprised it, but it definitely noticed me."

"Did it recognize you?" Tammy asked. "Did it know you were Eric, or that you were a living person?" Eric wasn't sure about that, but he insisted the shadow had been aware of him.

Now I'll lie awake at night imagining the dark woman spying on us . . .

MEMO FROM PIERS PREIS-HERALD
TO WANDA KARLEWICZ

April 17, 1975

W,

Success! Though we didn't obtain as large an allotment as I'd hoped, we're approved for six additional months of study. The testimonials Hope and Simon wrote were most persuasive. Please give them my thanks when you next take Webster to school.

We're still operating over budget due to the repairs necessitated at the start of the year. I've applied to Tom Burton for reimbursement. As the property's owner, upkeep of the estate is his responsibility; we're merely tenants. I haven't high hopes for prompt payment, but I promise to compensate you for your deferred stipend.

As always, your contributions are warmly appreciated. — PPH

DIARY OF RUBY CARDINI

April 19, 1975

Tammy completed her first round of research at the historical society today. She had no luck finding any news about a dead teacher, nor any further details about the servant. "It was the same information Reid showed us," she said. "All the clippings were about society functions. Nothing was ever reported about the help. They didn't count."

Not only didn't they count, but they were interchangeable. I read a bit about Lizzie Borden after the Teixeira twins mentioned her. The Bordens had a new servant (an Irish girl, like Eric guessed our ghost might be) whose name was Bridget, but everyone in the family called her Maggie, the name of the last servant they'd had. They couldn't bother to see her as an individual. She wasn't a person, just a "Maggie" to them. Even the obituary Reid cited didn't mention the fallen servant's name, and I don't think that was to preserve her privacy as Mrs. Harding suggested. I suspect nobody bothered enough to want to know who she was or to remember her.

To Eric, our inability to find any additional information about the maid suggests more than just a lack of status. He thinks there's a sinister conspiracy afoot to cover up the circumstances of what really happened. "Maybe the ghost talk is bringing down property values around here. Maybe people want to keep us from digging up the messy details and spreading the stories further."

For one thing, he's bothered by the discrepancy in the maid's date of death, something we haven't been able to clear up yet. To be on the safe side, Tammy and I will search articles from January through July of each year from 1890 to 1910, casting a wide net to be sure we can locate the original obituary Reid showed us (none of us remembers seeing the publication date).

Eric was also perturbed when I reported that my own visit to the library to find articles about the school only yielded tidbits about spelling bees and parents' weekends. I found one story about a fire, but the blaze had been controlled easily, and no one had gotten hurt. Later, there were stories about the school preparing to close, but nowhere was any death mentioned. Eric insisted the local reporters must have covered up the suicide to avoid bad publicity, especially with a previous infamous death in the house's background.

I'm not sure what to think yet, other than I'm starting to feel glad I didn't major in history, after all. The research process is more grueling—and disheartening—than I anticipated. I'm not sure what to make of the conflicting rumors and the lack of factual information. How do historians sort through all the data, determine what's real, and fill in blanks? I wish I had first-hand witnesses to interview, but the Bradleys are long gone. My contact's aunt now lives in Arizona, so I can't even go to the source of the teacher story. I need to find the names of all the schoolteachers and where they went after the school closed, assuming their whereabouts were recorded. I feel tired just thinking about the work ahead.

I'm glad not to be on my own in this.

DIARY OF TAMMY COHEN

April 29, 1975

Five fruitless hours later, my hands still smell of musty paper and newsprint. I'm tired and frustrated, but at least I kept my promise to Ruby.

The historical society has its information compartmentalized and cross-referenced; when I asked for information about Trevor Hall and Herbert Terrace, the volunteers showed me designated collections and scrapbooks. The library, however, is not so organized, and when I made my request, the librarian showed me to the archives and offered me oversized volumes of bound periodicals dating from the Victorian era. When Ruby went looking for information on the boarding school, the articles were on microfilm. Instead, I got to slap on gloves that still allowed the smell of the old paper to permeate through to my skin, even as they kept the oils of my hands from staining the pages. I also got to squint at the small print as I searched for. . .anything.

It's all the same nonsense about the local big wigs: balls and dinners, concerts and cotillions, visiting dignitaries, yet another Vanderbilt arrived for the season. I'm not a great admirer of television. Piers calls it the idiot box (in view of some of the things Smithy likes to watch, I'd agree), but if reading the society pages constituted entertainment back in the day, I'd rather watch "Hee Haw" and "Let's Make a Deal" any time and gladly.

Again, no details were ever published about the servants' lives, but I did find the notice of the nameless maid's death—in July 1896. So much for Mrs. Harding's reliability. This article places the accident well past the date of housekeeper Rockwell's death, so why did their stories become linked? Was Rockwell just a more forceful personality? Did she have a reason to want to haunt the house? Why would anybody want to haunt a house?

I'm on my way to finding that out, too, for as I was finally leaving the library, I bumped into Eric at the checkout. Unable to learn anything of value from the locals, he decided to pursue a different line of inquiry. He showed me the book he'd found, <u>Ghost Hunt</u> by Klaus Kleiner. Eric said he saw the guy on TV once, and he was very convincing. I asked if Kleiner was the guy who bends spoons, and Eric got annoyed, insisting that Kleiner is a respected authority on the paranormal who has visited many haunted sites and "cleansed" them. Obviously, we wouldn't be able to bring an exorcist or a medium to Trevor Hall, but Eric thought learning something about the nature of hauntings could help us help ourselves.

Of course, that presupposed his smuggling such contraband into the house under Wanda's nose. I walked Eric to the fiction section and finally found a copy of <u>Lolita</u> that was the same size as his book. I showed him how we could peel off the dust jacket and transform a provocative book about ghost hunting into a still-provocative yet, in these circumstances, less risqué book about a perverted professor that he can read openly without Wanda being any wiser. Instead of thanking me, Eric grew flustered and complained, "If she sees me reading it, she'll think I'm a creep. So will Gail."

So I've ended up reading the book myself. Nobody's questioned me or given me any dirty looks. I've promised to give Eric a summary once I've finished, though I'm not sure I'll have anything useful for him either.

Kleiner's exploits all read similarly. His M.O. is to visit a haunted place with one medium from his stable and have her establish contact with the spirit. Often, that spirit is someone famous: Benedict Arnold, Marilyn Monroe, Abraham and Mary Lincoln. Clearly, those spirits have a lot of baggage. Others who, like Wanda's poltergeists, make noises, turn lights on and off, flush toilets, and sometimes, even start small fires, are average Joes who seem not to know they're dead and are playing with their new reality. Famous or humble, all these lost souls can be persuaded to move on to the Other Side via persistent (though garbled) conversation.

I will admit that the halting and repetitive communications Kleiner alleges to have transcribed from his ghosts do remind me of Webster in their *simplicity and ambiguity. Lincoln and Arnold read as far less eloquent after death. (Or does the curtain of the ether muffle transmission?) I see Kleiner reading elaborate meaning into these bits and pieces, and I think it's all a crock.*

But then that might mean our work is also a crock.

I don't think Kleiner's book is helpful, exactly, but I do see its appeal. That makes it dangerous. People who want to believe in ghosts will see what they want to see, just like Wanda warned us. Without anything to back up those ghosts, however—without proof that Washington slept here, for instance—it all sounds ridiculous.

"Tessie" Doe? Imogene Rockwell? Miss Schoolteacher? Alva Vanderbilt, perhaps? I still have no idea who our ghost could be. I'm inclined to think that where there's smoke, there's smoke. Even Ruby's decided the hanging teacher probably isn't real. She says the story is too like the plot of Turn of the Screw; *it's probably made up, but who knows why or how it caught on?*

Will we ever understand what's happening here?

DIARY OF RUBY CARDINI

April 30, 1975

Tammy's birthday is coming up in a little over one week. I've no idea what to get her! She loves to read, but any time she wants a book, she buys it for herself. Maybe she'd appreciate something homemade, like a friendship bracelet, kitschy as that sounds?

I've wanted to brainstorm with Gail, but she was out most of yesterday getting her hair permed. Now her head looks like a giant pom-pom with tiny golden curls popping out of it. Smithy digs the way those curls bounce. He doesn't take his eyes off Gail when she's in the room, and he keeps tugging on her curls when he's near her. It reminds me of the way he used to pet the cats.

Piers observed Smithy playing with Gail's hair and cautioned her not to let him do it. "He's older now and doesn't know his own strength. He's liable to yank your pretty hair out entirely without realizing it."

We'll order take-out and serve cake on Tammy's big night. That's a school day for Smithy, so he should be tired, and we'll have more time to sit up together without having to watch out for him and his newfound strength. I pushed to have the party in the gatehouse for more privacy, but Wanda pointed out there's more room to move around (and maybe dance) at Trevor Hall.

OK, Ruby: thinking cap. Got to find a nice present for your best friend...

DIARY OF TAMMY COHEN,

May 8, 1975

My 24ʰ birthday bash has come to a close. And what a lucrative day it was!

Eric and Jeff collaborated on a homemade coupon book like the one I'd made once for my parents in Girls Scouts. It contains favors like "A ride into town: good for day or night," or "IOU $5," or "Will cook breakfast and wash the dishes afterward." That's only fitting, considering I've done the most obnoxious chore for them already.

Gail gave me "the cutest little purse," which I expect she secretly wants for herself and will ask to borrow within a week. Well, it's the thought that counts.

"Thoughtful" certainly describes Ruby's gift. I've no idea where she found the time to work on it. It's a scrapbook, still in progress, of our time at Trevor Hall. She's begun to fill it with photos of our excursions to the beach and the mansions, as well as snapshots of Webster. She's even inserted copies of newspaper articles about our study and underlined all our names. We can both add to it in time. What a wonderful treasure this will be someday, when we're looking back!

A treasure is the last thing I expected from Wanda. I thought she might give me a decent vintage, but she went beyond and gifted me with a lovely silk shawl in a purple paisley print. It's colorful, vivacious, and just the sort of accessory I'd love to wear but couldn't afford on my own. I'd never have expected her to recognize that. I guess Wanda must like me more than I thought.

Or it's a bribe of some kind. If she expects me to teach Webster table manners so he can mingle in high society now that I've finally gotten him out of diapers, I may strangle her with my pretty new shawl.

Webster was generous, too. He brought me a pink balloon, a green and yellow abstract for my wall, and a bowl of ice cream.

As we feasted on sugar, we realized Webster is the only one of us who hasn't yet celebrated a birthday. We felt ashamed and remiss. According to Jeff, we ought to have done something for him at the end of September. As it is, we've agreed to observe Webster's birthday on May 24th, the day he moved into Trevor Hall, though we may have to shift the timing to accommodate Piers's attendance.

We spent the rest of the evening planning how to celebrate. Gail made pie-in-the-sky suggestions about hiring a magician and renting a pony. Ruby was more pragmatic, asking if the party should be for ourselves, or if we ought to include Sarah, April, and the rest of Webster's friends from school. Piers called to wish me many happy returns, and Wanda got on the line to tell him of our idea. Piers was supportive; he's probably planning to invite reporters to cover the milestone.

Even though I know Webster couldn't really follow our conversation, he looked from one of us to another, as if he was tracking a bouncing ball, and his little eyes widened so hopefully that he must have known we were talking about him, if not exactly what we were saying. I'm sure he understands that a birthday is a day when you get sweets and presents, and everybody fusses over you. Jeff said he would have seen plenty of birthdays in the McKenzie family, though he isn't sure if they ever celebrated Webster's. This next party is sure to be one for the books.

UNCUT VIDEO FOOTAGE,
COURTESY OF WCVB

Date: May 18, 1975
Location: The Backyard of Trevor Hall

Ambient conversation and music from a loudspeaker fills the background. A crowd mills around a buffet lunch spread over three picnic tables on the brick-lined terrace at the foot of the tower. Eric works over a large BBQ grill at the head of the table, serving hot dogs and burgers to the guests. The camera turns to face the house. A clown stands outside the solarium, twisting balloons into shapes. Piers holds Smithy, who watches the clown. Another camera crew films their interaction. A dark-haired male reporter enters the frame. He gestures and says, "Todd, three o'clock!"

The camera turns from the clown and focuses on Tammy, gingerly carrying a tray loaded with cups of lemonade as she navigates through the crowd. The reporter runs to her and says, "Pardon me, miss! Are you one of the chimp's teachers?"

Tammy says, "No, I'm just a serving wench."

Wanda crosses the yard into the camera frame and says, "Nonsense! Tammy Cohen—that's C-O-H-E-N—is one of our most valuable contributors. She's a graduate student at Columbia. What's your major, Tammy?

Tammy says, "It's psychology with an emphasis on education, and this study has certainly been an education. Will you excuse me? I need to water the troops."

She walks toward a group of cameramen assembled in a loose circle under the tree with the tire swing. A voice calls her name insistently, growing louder as a young bespectacled man approaches her. Tammy exclaims, "Reid!" However, Wanda turns away from Tammy and doesn't see them meet.

Wanda laughs and says, "She's very focused. It's an excellent quality in a researcher, but it makes her tough to interview."

The reporter asks, "What's your name, and what role do you play here, miss?"

Wanda says, "My name is Wanda Karlewicz, K-A-R-L-E-W-I-C-Z. I do whatever needs to be done. Officially, I'm Dr. Preis-Herald's assistant. I worked with him at Yale before he invited me to Newport to help manage this project. In his absence, I maintain the household, oversee the other student assistants, and set the agenda for Webster's educational goals. I'm fluent in the sign language we're teaching him."

The reporter asks, "Are you surprised by the turnout today, Miss Kar…Karlson?"

Wanda smiles, but her eyes narrow. She answers, "Yes and no. I knew any news featuring Webster would be of interest to the media, but I didn't expect such an enthusiastic response on such short notice. This party began as a whim. We usually celebrate staff members' birthdays with a small party at home. Dr. Preis-Herald extended feelers to see if anybody in the general public might like to share in a celebration for Webster, and indeed, people did. It's truly gratifying to see how much others love Webster just as we do. He is a member of the family—not a pet—and not much like an animal at all once you get to know him. I'm sure if you can catch a moment with him, he'll also tell you how glad he is to have you here."

The reporter says, "Thank you, Miss Karlweiss. I hope we can do just that."

Wanda's eyebrows pucker. She says, *"Wits. Karl-wits."*

EXCERPT FROM
"BIRTHDAY FOR BONZO:
YALE'S SIGNING CHIMP GRADUATES FROM
TERRIBLE TWO'S IN STYLE"
BY LOGAN SWANSON

THE NEWPORT DAILY NEWS
MAY 19, 1975

Image and caption: "Cake and Candles for Webster's Special Day." L to R: Ruby Cardini, Jeffrey Dalton, Eric Kaninchen, Piers Preis-Herald, Webster, Wanda Karlewicz, Gail Ehrlich.

Newport gained its reputation for gala events at the turn of the century. However, the biggest social event of the current season is an unconventional birthday party for an unusual toddler. His name is Webster, and he's a chimpanzee.

For the past year, Webster and his entourage of graduate students have lived at Trevor Hall, engaged in the study of American Sign Language. Under the auspices of Yale University and renowned psychologist Piers Preis-Herald, the team is working to prove some animals can master language.

Preis-Herald first gained acclaim through research on persuasion and affiliation. His practical work on how trends develop and how information and opinions are adopted fed a deeper general interest in communication. Believing communication can be learned by anyone, he set out to prove it by using an ape as his subject.

The world has followed his team's progress diligently. Early results have been promising. At last count, Webster could use 72 signs, almost twice as many signs as Osage, Robert La Fontaine's simian prodigy at McGill University, has displayed.

Webster was born September 22, 1972. Why celebrate in May? "He is technically two years and eight months old," Preis-Herald acknowledges. "We're crediting him with the full three years now because Webster has never celebrated his birthday before. This party is intended to compensate for that oversight. Moreover, we're celebrating Webster's achievements of the past year and honoring the efforts of our research team on the anniversary of the study's commencement."

Ruby Cardini, 21, of Yale is one of Webster's tutors. "It's amazing to see how he's grown in the short time I've known him. When I look back at my photos from those early days, he looks like another chimp; he's so tiny. He's grown intellectually, too. He seems more confident in his signing and will talk to you without waiting for you to draw him out."

Team filmographer, Jeff Dalton, 25, agrees. "I was the first student to join the project. I've captured most of Webster's life and education on film. I love him like a son! This party isn't just for his birthday. It's to celebrate everything that he's accomplished and everything he has to teach the world."

Preis-Herald emphasizes the team's closeness as a major strength. "In our year here, we've truly become a family. Everyone dotes on Webster. As a sign of their regard, they've even bestowed on him a nickname: 'Smithy' for 'wordsmith.'"

"[Webster] is a bright student," says Hope Wellborn, 32, a senior faculty member of the Meyer School for the Deaf in Providence, where the chimp receives supplemental instruction. "When you examine his rate of word acquisition and the speed with which he uses a sign after seeing and practicing it, he compares favorably to a child of three or four. He certainly shares the curiosity of a child."

Likewise, Webster displayed a child's delight in the day's festivities, dancing to his favorite tunes, requesting balloon animals by name from the party clown, and meeting his visitors. The birthday chimp invited his guests on a tour of the premises, showing the rooms where he has his lessons and identifying some of his prized possessions. He also demonstrated how he washes and dresses in the morning and helps around the house by setting the table or putting away the dishes.

Though eager to learn the names of all the new people who came to pay their respects, Webster was shy about conversing with them. That is, until Regis Philbin showed him the steadily accumulating pile of gifts and asked the chimp what he hoped they might be. "Candy," "Jell-O," "color/paint," and "toy" topped the list. Then Webster became distracted by Philbin's wristwatch, which he called "pretty."

When cake was served and Philbin asked Webster if he would share a piece, the furry wordsmith astutely replied, "Share cake, share pretty." A bargain was struck: the loan of the watch for a slice of cake. Thus, the Yale team has shown that the language of deal-making is understood in the Animal Kingdom.

EXCERPT FROM
SMITHY: A TWENTY-YEAR COMPENDIUM
BY REID BENNETT, PHD

CHAPTER EIGHT: IN FREE FALL

Smithy's third birthday received voluminous press coverage. Correspondents from CBS, ABC, NBC, PBS, and the BBC found places on the guest list. Likewise, reporters from *The New York Times* and *Time Magazine* produced accounts like those featured locally in *The Providence Journal* and *The Newport Daily News*. Even representatives from Columbia, Yale, and Harvard student newspapers, including this humble author, were present.

Given the profusion of unfamiliar faces and peculiar stimuli (e.g., lights, cameras, balloon animals), Smithy remained remarkably demure, hiding the infamous temper of which his caregivers had gradually become wary. Indeed, he played the genteel host, leading Geraldo Rivera on a tour of Trevor Hall and showing off his toys to Barbara Walters. He gamely interacted with the hired clown; the resulting photographs engendered many circus jokes. However, his unusual reserve swiftly melted when it came time to open his gifts. Smithy's joy and wonder, for both paper and presents, is palpable in the film footage and photos of the day.

Most of the public's fondest memories of Smithy derive from his birthday footage. The reel of Regis Philbin "interviewing" the chimpanzee about his birthday wish list immediately impressed itself on the popular consciousness and likewise landed under the microscope of linguists and animal behaviorists, who scrutinized it for evidence of the chimp's communication skills.

The most indelible image remains the crowd serenading the animal with a chorus of "Happy Birthday;" at the moment the song concludes, Smithy blows out his candles with no prompting, stimulating a round of "For He's a Jolly Good Fellow" as Wanda cuts, and Gail serves, the cake.

The spectacle was a grand success, popularly and professionally, for Preis-Herald. Clearly, the research team members enjoyed themselves tremendously.

None of them guessed it was the last happy time they would share together.

HANDWRITTEN STATEMENT OF JEFF DALTON

May 22, 1975

The events I relate herein occurred this afternoon at Trevor Hall at approximately 5:15 p.m.

My fellow researcher, Ruby Cardini, had developed a severe headache and allergies earlier in the day and was resting in her bedroom in the gatehouse on the property. Two others, Tammy Cohen and Gail Ehrlich, had taken our communal vehicle to go shopping. Eric Kaninchen was in the house in his room on the second floor. Wanda and I were the only people with Smithy.

Smithy and I had been playing outside, throwing a Frisbee and chasing each other. We wanted him to be tired so he would nap before his evening lessons and dinner. When I decided he had exerted himself, I brought him back into the house.

Wanda was fixing dinner, and I took Smithy to say good night to her, which he did willingly. Then I signed it was time for bed. He protested by pouting, hooting, and sagging his posture. I tried to lead him up the rear stairs, but he was uncooperative. His body went slack, so I dragged him out of the kitchen by one hand, sliding him down the hall on the seat of his pants toward the main stairs that led up to his bedroom on the third floor. Along the way, Smithy used his free hand to untie my shoelaces. I let go of him to tie them back up, and he ran away.

I tackled him and carried him under my arm. However, he continued to struggle and grab at doorknobs and furniture. Wanda came out of the kitchen to watch us. I thought she looked exasperated with us both. She finally told me to give Smithy to her, and she'd take him up the servants' stairs, which is what we called the staircase that ran up from the kitchen. They were closer to where Smithy was then having his tantrum, but farther from his bedroom.

Wanda waited on the stairs for me to bring Smithy to her. She signed to him, "Be good" and "No cry" to admonish him to behave better. Smithy held tightly to me. At the time, I thought he was merely resistant to going to bed. Like many small children, he sometimes fusses about this. It's annoying, but we never had any special concern about his tantrums.

I told Smithy to go to Wanda, but he still clung to me. We decided to do a body-to-body transfer, in which one of us peels Smithy off another researcher by slipping an arm under his arm and around his torso, then pulling while the other person turns in a circle in the opposite direction to break the hold. Wanda got hold of Smithy, and I rolled away. He was forced to let go of me and attached himself to her right side.

Wanda stood on the second or third step with her back to the staircase, facing me and looking down at Smithy. She jiggled him a little to balance him on her hip, and while she did this, she signed to him with her free hand. I've been asked specifically whether she signed "Bed" or "Sleep" to him. Earlier, I couldn't remember, but now I do recall: she signed, "Go up" and "bed" and pointed upstairs. Smithy signed, "No" and "please." Wanda didn't respond. She started to walk up the stairs. She held on to Smithy with both hands and not the banister. When they reached the first landing, I saw Smithy sink his teeth into the right side of Wanda's face.

Blood sprayed out, and Wanda doubled over screaming, but Smithy was completely quiet and still attached to her. He didn't growl or vocalize before the attack either. It felt casual and sudden. For a split second, I was frozen with indecision as I saw what was happening. My instinct was to run upstairs and pull Smithy off Wanda, but I feared he might increase his attack on her or turn on me. Instead, I chose a distraction.

Earlier this morning, my housemate Eric had brought home a box of donuts from town. Several donuts were left over. I popped into the kitchen to get them, then dashed back to the stairwell and called, "Hey, Smithy, want a donut?" I deliberately kept my tone cheerful and didn't acknowledge what he was doing to Wanda. I didn't want to reference her at all, lest he intensify his violence. I *only wanted to shift his attention to the donuts. Just as I'd hoped, Smithy turned his head to look at me, and I threw a donut to him. It landed on the stairs, and he let go of Wanda to jump down and grab it. I kept one eye on him and one eye on Wanda.*

I saw her sink to her knees and clutch at her face. Blood gushed all over her bare hand and jaw and down her neck and shoulder. I had expected to see loose tissue from her damaged cheek dangling, but all I saw was the red of her blood and her gums and something flailing inside of her mouth, which I realized was her tongue and then I realized...(illegible)... ingested it.

I pulled off my T-shirt, balled it up and threw it to her. I called to her to hold it against her cheek, but I think she was too in shock to listen because she didn't catch the shirt. I knew Wanda was severely injured, but I realized I had to remove Smithy from the scene before I could attend to her.

I called to him in a pleasant and steady voice to come have another donut. I backed into the hallway and dropped more donuts to make a trail. Smithy followed me, grabbing and gobbling up the donuts as I backed into the kitchen. I saw the walk-in pantry was open. It has a sturdy door that I've been warned sometimes sticks. A couple of months ago, the girls accidentally got stuck in there. I threw the box into the pantry, and when Smithy went after it, I slammed the door on him and locked it. I immediately grabbed a handful of kitchen towels and went back to Wanda.

Since our only car was out, I decided to send for the fire department to help Wanda. We've always had a prompt response from them when our alarms are triggered, and I knew firemen can do first aid, so I manually triggered the alarm in the kitchen as I went out.

By then, Wanda had my shirt pressed against her wound, but it wasn't doing much good. My white shirt was practically black from all the gore oozing out of her face. Wanda was shaking and pale against the deep red of her blood. I tried to swap the towels for the shirt, but she wouldn't let go, so I just pressed the towels over her hand and held them there myself with as much pressure as I could apply. I noticed her right eye was rolling and glassy. It seemed to me like she was holding the shirt in place to keep her eye from falling out. That's when I realized the extent of her injury stretched from her eye to her chin, nearly the entire right side of her face. Wanda couldn't speak but she could still sign, and she signed to me, "Help" and "hurt," over and over.

Eric rushed downstairs then, drawn by the screaming, and I called him to help me carry Wanda but didn't tell him what had happened. Wanda clutched at me and signed, "No." I couldn't understand at first, but I realized she didn't want Eric to see her. I told him instead to call the firehouse and ask for paramedics, then stay in the kitchen and keep an eye on the pantry. However, I warned him <u>NOT</u> to approach Smithy under any circumstances, and if Smithy should get the pantry door open, to run away. I didn't want Smithy to attack anybody else. I also told Eric not to tell Ruby what had happened if she woke up and came to the house. I wanted to break the news to her myself.

I led Wanda outside so we could meet the fire trucks. I had to carry her. She was shaking and clammy. I knew she was losing blood, and I was fearful, but I tried to hide my concern and encourage her. She dropped one of the towels outside. It was sodden with blood. Her hair was loose and sticking in her blood, too. I didn't want Wanda to get an infection from things touching her wound, so I pulled her hair back. I even tried to braid it for her to keep it back, but my hands got too sticky.

She was growing heavier, so I told her to kneel and tried to prop her up while we waited. The emergency trucks came soon after. I didn't look at my watch once, but I estimate the whole sequence of events from the moment of the attack to their arrival took between five to ten minutes.

The paramedics were distressed when they saw Wanda. I could see disgust and fear in their faces before they composed themselves. I refrained from asking if she was going to live, but I could see by their expressions that she was in very bad shape. They put her on a stretcher and wrapped her face. Then they put her in an ambulance and asked if I wanted to come. I was afraid she might die if I took my eyes off her, so I jumped in for the ride.

On the way, the EMTs gave Wanda plasma, Type O transfusions, and various shots. They didn't talk to me, and I didn't talk to them. Most of what they said to each other was technical. I caught a reference to maxillofacial plastic surgery. Mostly I tried to keep calm for Wanda's sake. I signed to her, "Safe" to let her know she would be OK because I hoped she would be, but I don't know if she noticed. She only stared into space in shock.

We finally got to the hospital in Providence, and the paramedics rushed Wanda away for emergency treatment. The nurses assumed I was her boyfriend, and I let them think so because I figured that way, I could get updates on her condition. I called Piers Preis-Herald at the university and told him what had happened. He sounded flabbergasted and kept asking me to repeat certain points of my account, like what had actually been signed, but he said he would come right up to the hospital. He told me to write down everything I could remember while it was fresh in my mind because he'd need to review it. He said the police would have to get involved, and they would need my account, too.

Next, I called the mansion. Tammy picked up, and I told her everything. She took it calmly because she's tough. Then I got her to put Ruby on the phone and gave her a condensed version. Ruby cried a little but listened and asked good questions I couldn't answer. I asked about Smithy, and she said he'd been quiet. They think he fell asleep in the pantry. I told them to leave him in there until Piers arrives. He's got plenty of food to last until morning if he needs it.

The doctor just reported Wanda will pull through, but she'll need lots of help and lots of work. She's sedated now, which is for the best. He asked how to contact her folks. I know they're in Michigan, but I don't know their number. I told them our faculty advisor is coming, and he'll have all those details. The doctor wanted to know how she was injured. I admitted the culprit was a chimp but explained he's never bitten anyone severely before. The doctor has called the primate keeper at the Roger Williams Zoo to investigate. It sounded like they're plotting to take Smithy away from us.

I'm still waiting for Piers to arrive or the doctor to come back with an update. I don't know anything else currently.

EXCERPT FROM
WHY CHIMPANZEES MAKE BAD MEDIUMS AND WORSE PETS
BY HARRY DINGWALL, PHD

REPRINTED WITH PERMISSION FROM
OPPOSING VIEWPOINTS: THE SUPERNATURAL,
SECOND EDITION,
ED. BY WILLIAM IRISH, BLACKHAVEN BOOKS, 1995

The fiasco of the Smithy study, which at first blush had offered intriguing possibilities to believers in the supernatural, quickly becomes obvious. An undisciplined wild animal forced into a domestic setting with a group of naïve, untrained, unprepared twenty-somethings clearly looks, in hindsight, like a recipe for disaster.

It's worth remembering, however, that regulation of exotic animal ownership was laxer in the 1970s. The gruesome recent headlines of attacks by escaped chimpanzees were then unknown. Beguiled by their resemblance to humans and misled by popular Hollywood films, many potential owners sought apes because they were cute or entertaining. Consequently, high-maintenance, high-risk animals landed in the hands of people who were ignorant of their new pets' needs and how to deal with them. Although the Smithy study started with true scientific ambitions, the young researchers fell into the same trap of anthropomorphizing their charge, much to their sorrow...

DIARY OF RUBY CARDINI

May 23, 1975

The house is weirdly silent for once but so full of tension and fear that I want to scream and shatter that silence just to make something happen. I'm so sick and tired of waiting.

All I've done since yesterday is wait, from the moment the screeching sirens jarred me out of bed to this moment, sitting at the desk. I thought at first, we were having another fire or a false alarm. When I went to Trevor Hall to find out what was happening, I found a shell-shocked Eric sitting in the kitchen staring at the pantry, and Smithy crying from the other side of the door. Eric told me Wanda had had an accident involving Smithy and had to go to the hospital. I couldn't imagine what had happened, or why Jeff had ordered him to keep Smithy locked up. When Jeff finally called and gave a full explanation, I was in disbelief.

God knows Smithy has had tantrums, and of course, I remember those awful nights he lashed out at Peter and at Eric, but those were always after something had provoked him: I slapped him, the cats snarled at him, Eric struggled with him. Jeff said Wanda was only carrying him upstairs, a thing we've each done a hundred times before. She didn't hit or scold him or do anything to hurt him. And yet he tore one side of her face off.

I feel like vomiting just looking at what I've written. Jeff was there and said that's what happened, but he didn't get a clear look because Wanda kept her face covered to stanch the bleeding, and he admits he was terrified out of his wits, and that he could be exaggerating.

Piers and Jeff came back to Trevor Hall close to midnight, but we were all still awake. Piers was cross and wanted to know why we were all sitting around. He demanded to see Smithy, so Eric opened the pantry. Smithy was curled up in a ball on the top step, sucking his thumb. He'd messed up his pants, and he'd eaten a couple of apples and a box of cereal, but he hadn't wrought any of the destruction I'd imagined, given the circumstances. Piers took Smithy up to bed and stayed in his room overnight.

I took Jeff back to the gatehouse. He was completely wiped out. I filled up the bath and made him soak while I rubbed his back to help him relax. He didn't talk much, and I didn't ask questions. I wanted him to sleep late to make up for all he went through last night, but Piers wanted us at the house early for a meeting.

Eric made pancakes, but no one was hungry. We sat around the dining table, which heightened the formality and wrongness of what was happening, and we listened to Piers interrogate Jeff.

First, Piers slapped some notebook paper on the table. It was a report about the attack Jeff had written out at the hospital last night. Piers started reading the account and asked us to verify the details. Tammy and Gail were visiting Middletown when it had happened, and I wasn't in the house. Eric said he'd heard screaming downstairs and thought at first someone else had seen the ghost. He admits that gave him pause, but he came down even so, in time to see Wanda collapsed on the stairs and Jeff, shirtless, hunched over her. Eric hadn't seen the actual attack.

Piers was relentless. He kept asking Jeff what they'd done, what they'd said, how Smithy had acted. He got Smithy's Big Bird and made Jeff demonstrate (with me) how they'd transferred Smithy. I think that's what sickened Jeff the most: recalling that prelude to the bloodshed and having to reenact it with me.

"And he just bit her for no reason?"

"That's right," Jeff repeated.

"Webster didn't hiss, didn't cry, didn't sign anything? Didn't show any reluctance to have Wanda hold him? He didn't try to get back down?"

"No, sir. She took him from me, and he put his arms around her like a normal hold. She signed, 'Upstairs bed' and started to walk upstairs, and it was only after about three or four steps that he leaned in just like he was gonna put his head on her shoulder and take a nap. But the next thing I knew, Wanda was screaming bloody murder and blood was pouring down her face."

Gail refused to believe any of it had happened. She folded and unfolded her napkin and kept shaking her head while they talked. "No, he couldn't have done it. It's impossible! Smithy wouldn't hurt anybody, not for any reason! Wanda must have pinched him or scared him when she took him, so he bit her. Maybe he was protecting himself. She did something to him!"

Eric sat beside me, and I heard him mutter, "Oh, _she_ did something all right." The skin on my arms prickled because I knew he wasn't talking about Wanda.

Piers scrutinized Jeff's account. I know he was upset when he wrote it, so it must have been hard for Piers to read. Jeff's scrawl is nearly indecipherable under more auspicious circumstances. "Now when you saw Webster bite her…I assume you tried to intercede?"

"No," Jeff admitted. "I was too stunned, and I didn't want to aggravate the situation. I ducked into the kitchen—"

"You ran away," Piers cut him off. "You abandoned Wanda."

"I came right back," Jeff protested, "and lured him away from her with donuts."

Piers's face turned a ruddy purple. "Terrific! That was bloody brilliant, Jeff! You _rewarded_ him with food! You reinforced his bad behavior! Now every time he wants a donut, he'll chomp on somebody's face. That's perfect!"

Jeff flushed and tensed under the accusations. "I'm sorry! I panicked—I didn't know what else to do. I saw him biting her, and I wanted to make him let go as soon as possible. I was afraid if I tried to pry him off Wanda, he'd rip her up even worse. I thought distracting him with food would be a better way to make him let go. If I'd had a baseball bat or some other weapon, I guess I could have attacked him back, but I didn't. So I tried to outsmart him instead—and it worked! He dropped off her."

Piers continued to glower. "Wonderful! That was great thinking, Jeff! I ought to sack you. You've put all of us at risk now!"

"Excuse me," Tammy cut in. "Piers, are you really saying we're going to keep working with Webster now—after what he did?"

"That's my intention," he said coldly. "If Jeff's account is true, this was a fluke—a horrific accident, but not a malicious attack. Webster *is not violent by nature. If Wanda is ever able to give us her side of the story, we may get some clarity. For now, I must assume something passed between them that Jeff failed to observe."*

Tammy's eyebrows went up. "So you're blaming Wanda?"

"'Blame' is harsh, Tammy," Piers said in a strained voice. "I agree with Gail that something must have triggered Webster's defenses. At present, we don't know what."

Tammy changed tactics. "Have you <u>seen</u> Wanda?"

That was the only time I'd ever seen Piers not confident or bombastic. He blanched. His fingers tightened against the table surface. "Briefly. She was still under sedation, so we didn't speak."

"How is she?" I asked him.

He shook his head. "She looked frail. She was heavily wrapped and surrounded by machines. I didn't stay long. Technically, visiting hours hadn't begun, but as I'm the party responsible for her welfare, the doctors were willing to meet with me and let me have a moment with her."

(Later, Tammy railed to me privately about what she thought of Piers as a "responsible" party. Smithy bit Wanda, but Tammy has pegged Piers as the culprit. She thinks he didn't prepare us well enough for Smithy's potential aggression. She complains about his frequent absences. "The least he can do, if he's going to put us in the way of a destructive ape, is be on hand to witness the consequences. This is <u>his</u> study! If he wants the credit, he's got to take the blame, too!")

Piers forced cheer into his voice. "They say she <u>can</u> recover...but it will be a long road."

"She won't be back for a while then?" Gail asked.

"No—and that's if there's a study to come back to," Piers announced. He scanned our faces, still grim. "The hospital notified the authorities— the ASPCA and the local zoo. Today we're going to have a 'well-check' to determine if this environment is safe, and if Webster is stable enough to remain with us. That's why I've gathered you all here so early. A zoo veterinarian is due to meet with me, Webster, and possibly some of you at ten sharp. He may wish to take Webster for testing and observation. If the authorities agree that the attack on Wanda was an accident, we may continue our study, with new safeguards in place. If they believe he's a threat, we may need to disband."

That news sent us further down into a spiral. Nobody moved or protested or asked questions. I felt so tired from worrying and grieving for Wanda and even for Smithy that I couldn't even mourn the possible end of our project. Piers didn't grill Jeff any further after dropping his bombshell. We went through the motions of picking at breakfast but then dismissed ourselves to the solarium to sit and wait for the outcome. Jeff was required to sit in on the examination—likely so the zoo expert could quiz him, too—so he stayed behind.

I heard someone come to the door and Piers greet him. I heard them go upstairs. Then we sat and waited and _waited_ for news.

I had a book but couldn't focus on it, so it stayed in my lap. Tammy had crossword puzzles, but she stared into space often. Gail started the record player to fill the ponderous silence, but I can't remember which record it was. I don't think Gail even cared about the record. She sat in the window seat, muttering imprecations against Wanda for upsetting Smithy and putting him in this predicament—as if _he_ were the one lying in a hospital right now! I do pity him, but that pity is wound up with fear and wariness, too.

Tammy articulated it best: "It's not really any better if Webster did this by accident. If he did it because he was angry, well, it reflects poorly on him, but it's something we can understand. Animals can be bad-tempered; mean dogs bite. If he did it without reason, we'll never know when he'll decide to do it again, and one of us could be next."

Gail stared at her. "But it's our Smithy! How can you say that? We've taken care of him and taught him. He's our baby. He loves us. He's not a monster." I'd had her same reaction—at first. But Tammy's words had sowed doubts in my mind—and Eric had to go and fertilize them!

"I read an article by Jane Goodall," he began, almost dreamily. "You know she lived in the wild and studied chimpanzees. She once saw a group of three chimpanzees ambush another one from a different tribe or group or whatever you want to call it. They beat him to death and then ate him. So you know, they _can_ be violent by nature."

We all stared at him, fighting off visions of Smithy sneaking into our rooms at night with a blunt object, ready to bash our heads in and feast on our remains. "If thinking out loud is your idea of helping, Eric, maybe you should go in another room," Tammy suggested. Finally, I heard footsteps on the stairs and the front door shut. Piers came in and reported that Smithy will stay with us. Not only did the zoo rep decide he wasn't a raving maniac, but he was impressed by Smithy's desire to interact and his signing. Apparently, Smithy was calm and eager to please. No trace of aggression whatsoever. I suppose that's good news, but I can't fight the streak of anxiety beneath my relief.

Jeff went directly back to the gatehouse afterward, and I imagine he collapsed back on the waterbed and drifted into a dream more pleasant than reality. I didn't want to bother him, so I've stayed away. I thought by writing this entry, I could gather my thoughts and sort through my emotions, but it isn't helping. Reliving it all in memory has made me feel more restless and anxious. I've got to get out of this house!

DIARY OF RUBY CARDINI

May 24, 1975

I went back to the hospital today. I first went yesterday to see Wanda. When I asked after her at the front desk, the nurse stared at me for a long time. I could see so much pity in her eyes, and I had a terrible thought that Wanda had died of her injuries, and this nurse was trying to figure out how to break it to me. Then she asked if I was related to the patient. I almost said I was her sister, but I hesitated too long and knew that would expose my lie. So I told her we were good friends, and the nurse nodded solemnly and gave me the room number in the <u>critical ward</u>. She told me to prepare myself and try not to let my reaction show. She warned that Wanda's face would be bandaged, and it would be hard to understand her speaking voice. She has to get her nutrition through tubes down her throat because she can't chew. It sounded horrific.

The nurse needn't have bothered with the lecture. When I got to Wanda's room, another nurse was coming out. She gave me the whole spiel again: Who was I? How was I related to the patient? When I gave my information, she told me to wait and ducked back inside. A minute later, she emerged and told me the patient didn't want visitors. I pleaded with her, but she was immobile. No visitors. Wanda's own rule.

By then, I was overwrought. Not being able to see Wanda myself and hearing how everyone talked about her scared me deeply. I kept envisioning all sorts of horrors. I tried to go in the room, but the nurse held me back. I called out to Wanda and begged her to let me talk with her, but Nurse Nazi told me I was disturbing the other patients on the ward, and she'd have to call security if I persisted. So I left. I'd behaved stupidly, and I don't blame that nurse for throwing me out. I told myself Wanda might have taken some meds and was maybe too sleepy to handle visitors. So I made up my mind to arrive at the hospital this morning for the first visiting session to avoid any conflicts.

I arrived about fifteen minutes early and sat quietly in the waiting room, although I was too jumpy to read the magazine I'd picked up. I said hello to the nurse at the front desk and even saw the same nurse who had blocked my entry walking down the hall. I apologized for my rudeness, explaining I was anxious about my friend because we had heard so many distressing things, but no one could confirm anything about her condition. She was more understanding than I probably deserved, and she told me she would call up to Wanda to let her know I had come to see her.

She called from the front desk, and though I couldn't hear the nurse's side of the conversation, I saw she looked surprised and a little befuddled. She took her time after hanging up to come over to me, and then she was super solicitous. They must teach that tone of voice in nursing school. She said she was sorry, but my friend was firm about not wanting any visitors—not today or tomorrow—and would I please stay away from the hospital and tell our other friends not to come either?

It was the last thing I'd expected, and I didn't know what to do. I looked down at my hands so I wouldn't have to see the pity in the nurse's face. From the corner of my eye, I could see the desk nurse watching me, too. It must have been a slow day, or maybe she just likes drama. And of course, right then I could feel tears pricking the corners of my eyes, and I knew I had to get out before I made a scene for all the nurses to dissect in the days to come.

I mumbled something, but I can't remember what. "Yes, I understand. I'm sorry for bothering her. I'll go now, and please tell her I hope she feels better." What rot! "Feel better soon!" How do you feel better when you've had your face ripped off? Poor Wanda! I can't imagine the pain she's feeling or the pain that lies ahead of her, what with surgery and recovery. We may not have been the best of friends, but I still care about what happens to her.

How she must hate us! No wonder she sent me away. She probably wishes I had been at the house instead to hold Smithy when he went berserk. I bet she never wants to see or hear from any of us again. We'd remind her of what happened at Trevor Hall and everything she's lost. In her place, who's to say I would do any differently?

EXCERPT FROM
"THE LATEST WORD ON 'SMITHY'?"

TIME MAGAZINE
OCTOBER 9, 1978

...When asked about the sharp difference between their experience teaching Smithy and the Yale team's, both Wellborn and Gagnon fall silent and exchange glances. Gagnon is the first to break the silence of three years.

"Theirs was a toxic environment. It was full of tension. Wanda [Karlewicz] and the professor always liked to say they were all family, and maybe that was true. But families can be dysfunctional. There are jealousies. Rivalries. Misunderstandings."

Wellborn cited specific sources of tension. "They had money troubles. Wanda confided in me about how hard she and Piers had to work to keep the study funded. She didn't want any of the others to know, lest it hurt morale. I oversaw the school's finances, and she would ask me, 'How do you do it? How do you make a dollar stretch in these times?' They constantly had to make repairs at the house. Electricians for wiring. New locks and windows to replace the ones Smithy broke. And then the plumbing broke down five times in one month."

Gagnon speculates the infamous incident of the feces on the wall may have been in protest of the living conditions at that low point in Trevor Hall's tenancy.

Wellborn says Karlewicz also fretted about Preis-Herald's philandering. "She would say, 'I don't expect him to tie himself to me. I'm a modern woman. I just want him to be honest about what he does. It's an insult to my intelligence to carry on like that.'"

Gagnon defends Karlewicz's contributions. "People scoff that she was only in charge because she was dating the boss. They completely dismiss her accomplishments. Wanda was in charge because she deserved to be. She and [Preis-Herald] were intellectual equals. They shared a vision. He trusted her to implement it. Gail, on the other hand, was no Wanda…"

DIARY OF TAMMY COHEN

May 30, 1975

Our first anniversary at Trevor Hall has come and gone, and I feel more trepidation than gratitude about all that has happened during the year. With Wanda gone, everything feels off-kilter. I was convinced the study would end with her departure. For one thing, she was the engine driving this study, and for another, Webster's violence toward her represents a serious transgression.

Gail says we can't blame Webster because he didn't act out of malice. He's an animal, young and confused, and unaware of his full power.

First, I'm not sure we can rule out malice. Second, the concept of Webster unthinkingly lashing out and almost killing Wanda is akin to a three-year-old child running through a crowded house with a loaded gun; he may have no idea of the power he's got, but he's still capable of doing tremendous harm.

Yet the study soldiers on with Gail in command. Her brief reign in February impressed Piers, and he's made her the de facto head of operations. We proceed now in much the same vein as then. Gail has instituted new guidelines to make Webster's environment less aggravating. For example, we have no more vocabulary lists or weekly word quotas. She thinks the pressure of trying to learn so much sent Webster into a frenzy and disposed him to attack Wanda.

Also, Gail has eliminated formal teaching. She's pulled him from the Meyer School, with Piers's consent; he's afraid Webster might assault one of the instructors there, but he doesn't show the same level of concern for us. We don't sit down for formal lessons at the house anymore, either.

As before, Gail emphasizes the importance of using all the words Webster already knows to keep him from losing signs and to prove he's capable of building new ideas from an existing supply of words. All signing now occurs in the normal context of a day's typical events or through a special activity Gail has appointed. She reminds us this is what Piers always intended: that Webster would adopt his own place within a human family and become "one of us."

Much of our time now is spent either doing chores, such as washing dishes and scrubbing the floor; sprucing up the house by sanding down walls or polishing the banister; or performing basic leisure activities, such as allowing Webster free play with his toys or the opportunity to paint. Webster engages readily in everything, even the grunt work. Gail ensures Webster gets his share of exercise by taking him outside at "recess time" so he can run, climb, and burn off some of his boundless energy. We all play along with him to maintain a sense of group identity.

We also spend long stretches of time with Webster at the gatehouse, eating snacks and watching TV, so he can glimpse a bit of the wider world. Gail and Webster are always popping in to commandeer the recreation room, regardless of what Ruby and Jeff have planned for the day. They remain good sports about it though; I think Jeff appreciates having easy access to Webster, and Ruby is loath to rock the ship any further. Personally, I think Gail's trying to curb Webster's aggression by turning him into a couch potato. I could feel he's put on weight when I helped him dress this morning—too much snacking and sitting and not enough "recess."

Surprisingly, Piers agrees to all of this, though I'm not sure he knows how much TV the chimp is consuming. He calls it "the new phase" of the project, a high-flying euphemism for "We're traveling by the seat of our pants and doing whatever seems to work." If he continues to get results from Webster and no one else ends up in the hospital, I believe he'll go on this way indefinitely.

The rest of us have qualms about changing tactics and have resolved to continue building an ASL vocabulary amongst ourselves. I found Wanda's notebook containing outlines and word lists (about two years' worth!) in the trash. Who threw it away? I can't believe all the work Wanda put into this curriculum; that deserves to be honored. Ruby, Eric, and I have been meeting for at least an hour each day to practice with one another. We want to build more fluency, so that <u>when</u> we become

Webster's teachers again instead of simply his buddies, we can offer him something.

No one wants to confront Gail yet. She definitely feels her power, and perhaps rightly so. Webster seems content with the schedule she's created and is as fond of her as ever. He follows Gail <u>everywhere</u>; I think she even takes him into the bathroom with her. Webster clings to her hand possessively. He doesn't take his eyes off her. Eric suspects this is the result of separation anxiety—that Webster misses Wanda and doesn't want to lose Gail, too—but I haven't seen him ask where Wanda is or express any remorse for what he did to her. Webster has always had a bit of a crush on Gail, and now he's free to indulge it.

I'm hopeful we can persuade Gail to re-enroll Webster at the Meyer School in time for the next term. Surely, she—or he—will tire of this new program and want to return to a more structured lifestyle, or Piers will need more data for his next presentation and want to scale up productivity. Of course, getting Webster back into school will be contingent on his not running amok again. One can only hope...

DIARY OF RUBY CARDINI

At last, I have some clarity about what happened last week. Unexpectedly today, I got a letter from Wanda. At first, I just stared at the names on the envelope, hers and mine. Then I looked at the postmark with the half-formed idea she had written to me for some reason before her accident. But it was postmarked on Wednesday, well after the last time I'd gone to the hospital.

I was slow in opening it, and Tammy and Jeff kept asking what was wrong. I ended up going outside to read it. I'm not sure why I was so secretive. Maybe I was afraid of what she was going to say—accusations, name-calling—and of how I might react to it. Overall, it was a decent letter. First, Wanda thanked me for coming to see her. She even apologized for sending me away. She appreciated my thoughtfulness but is too upset to face any visitors. She says she doesn't want any of us to see the way she looks now, all wrapped up like a mummy or a "freak." Talking is hard because her lips are gone. (She didn't suggest we try to sign to each other; maybe it reminds her too much of Smithy). Also, she's in so much pain—she stays on morphine throughout the day and falls in and out of consciousness.

Even when she's awake, nothing makes much sense to her.

"Even if I could pronounce my words," she writes, "they would probably just be gibberish left over from drug dreams." She said it took her almost three days to compose a coherent note to me, and she apologized for its condition. I don't know what she has to be contrite about when she's been through so much.

Wanda wants us to respect her privacy and not come back to the hospital. Once she's released, she said she'll go home to "put myself and my life back together." Piers will pack her things and bring them back to Yale so her father can pick them up. (It sounds like she doesn't want to see Piers either). She wrote a special thank you to Jeff for "saving my life and taking such good care of me on the way to the hospital" and wishes us well with our futures.

And that's all. "Warm regards, Wanda." Nothing about Smithy. She didn't ask about him or worry about him or curse him out or express any thought of him. So maybe she has a grudge, or at least some lingering fear. I wonder if she's written separately to Piers.

So far, he continues to act as if everything is normal. (To keep us calm? Or to calm Smithy?) He's pitching in more now that we're short-handed. Gail is stepping up more than I expected she would, especially with Smithy's teaching and feedings. She seems not to even consider the likelihood he might lash out again. You would think by their own demeanor that both Piers and Gail have decided to let bygones be bygones.

Even Smithy seems to have amnesia. He never signs about what he did; not "sorry" or "bad Smithy." He never asks about Wanda either, which is weird, considering she was a part of almost every minute of his life. He should be completely freaking out that she's absent. Instead, he's abnormally calm and well-behaved. Is he in denial and repressing what happened, even about the fact of her existence? Is he hoping if he doesn't mention Wanda, we can forget all about what he did?

He seems like the good old Smithy we all know and love, but when I have the chance to interact with him, I'm reluctant. I haven't held him or bathed him or done any drills with him since it happened. Jeff and Eric, or Jeff and Piers, or Eric and Piers have been teaming up most often to work with him. When Smithy sees me, he signs, "Play," and I sign back, "Later." Smithy doesn't fuss, but can he tell I'm giving him the brush off? Is he going to punish me somewhere down the line?

Jeff says I should start with a clean slate. Forgive Smithy and approach him with a fresh attitude, because he may not even realize the magnitude of what he's done. I know that's true of dogs; it does no good to punish them for something they did because they can't make connections going back that far. However, I thought apes, as higher mammals, were more sophisticated. My readings indicate chimps have long and detailed memories, almost like elephants. But without Wanda before him as a *living memory of the damage he's done, perhaps she doesn't seem real for Smithy.*

If that's the case, I should stop judging him by human standards. I should make friends with him like I did after he broke into my room. After all, he hasn't threatened me since that night. Except now that I know what he's capable of doing, and I see what could have happened to me, I feel like screaming instead of hugging him.

If Wanda were here, would she be willing to reconcile with Smithy? I never expected she would come back to the study after the accident, but I thought she'd at least say goodbye in person, after all we've been through. Instead, all I have to mark her exit is this letter. I'm relieved she doesn't hate me, and I truly do hope she can recover and move on with her life.

I hope we can all recover.

SMITHY'S BEDROOM JOURNAL ENTRY
FROM GAIL EHRLICH

June 4, 1975

This was the fifth night in a row of Smithy screaming and waking everyone. I remember he had night terrors last year around this time, too. Could the weather be setting him off?

This time, instead of jumping from his bed to his bookcase, as if he was trying to get out, Smithy huddled on the bed and covered his eyes as if trying to hide from something. I reassured him nothing bad would happen, but he refused to sleep. He kept signing, "No sleep. Sleep bad." They must be awful dreams.

I wish we knew an animal shrink who could find out what's going on. Since we don't, we'll have to figure things out for ourselves. I can't stand getting woken up like this every night. Also, Smithy's so hard to wake the next morning, and then he's sluggish during the day.

SMITHY'S BEDROOM JOURNAL ENTRY
FROM ERIC KANINCHEN

June 4, 1975

Gail, are you sure Smithy was signing, "No sleep" and not "No dark woman"? Remember how much the signs look alike. I think we should consider that it's a possibility.

DIARY OF TAMMY COHEN

June 7, 1975

Chris Belancourt called the police again last night. Apparently, she told them we were all being murdered in our beds. I might have done the same thing in her place. I know how frightful Webster's tantrums sound when under the same roof with him. I can only imagine how mysterious and awful they must sound to bystanders. These days, I find myself ruing the peace and quiet of Newport streets. If Bellevue Avenue had more traffic and an L-train or two, Webster's caterwauling would never carry to the neighbors.

The police gave us a warning and told us if we can't control our ape's behavior, they'll fine us and possibly file a report with the ASPCA. I suppose it's only logical to conclude we might be torturing Webster to make him cry so consistently.

We're all stumped about what to do for him. Even with Jeff sleeping in the room with him now, Webster still wakes during the night in a panic. Jeff says he's tried <u>not</u> falling asleep, so he can see what happens in the room to disturb Webster. Even so, when his attention wanders slightly, Webster suddenly wakes up shrieking. This time, he pulled things off the shelves and threw them at the bedroom door. Jeff swears he didn't see a thing there, not even a spider.

Eric is still floating the idea that the ghost could be responsible. He told me this morning he wanted to try another séance, but this time I objected. I thought it would do more harm than good—not from the spirit's perspective but from Gail's. Now that she's running the show, she's renounced all talk of ghosts. If you ask her about what she saw a couple of months ago, she'll clam up and walk away or change the subject. I'm sure she's trying to put on a mature front for Piers. I'm still not sure I believe in a ghost, but it makes as much sense as anything else for explaining Webster's behavior.

Poor Ruby lives like a widow these days. She's invited me for a sleepover tonight, and I'm going to take her up on it. Having a great big room of one's own isn't all it's cracked up to be. At the least, the screaming should sound a little softer from the gatehouse.

I shouldn't complain so much. At least the problem now is violent sleep instead of violent days.

SMITHY'S BEDROOM JOURNAL ENTRY
FROM JEFF DALTON

June 8, 1975

Smithy's tantrum started this morning at 1:23 a.m. The timing is always a little different, but it's always between midnight and four in the morning.

This time, I was awake and reading and happened to be looking down at the page instead of at Smithy when he woke up. He'd started whimpering about an hour before waking. I came over and patted his hand, and that soothed him enough that he stayed asleep. However, he later sprung up, howling, and I rushed over immediately. I offered to groom him, but he avoided me and paced up and down the length of the room, signing, "Bad sleep" (or "Bad dark," if you prefer).

When I asked him, "What happened? What's wrong?" he signed, "Mad" over and over. He would not respond to, "Why?" I figure he must have had a dream that upset him, because nothing else was in the room, and no noise or weather-related effects could have contributed.

Instead of trying to quiet him and putting him back to bed, I invited him to go walking with me. We held hands and went up and down the hall about seven times. Then he agreed to go back to his room. We read "The Gingerbread Man," and he signed "Man," "cookie," "dog," and "water," but refused the prompt for "woman." After the story, he went to sleep and stayed asleep.

Now I'm going to sleep.

SMITHY'S BEDROOM JOURNAL ENTRY
FROM ERIC KANINCHEN

June 9, 1975

It occurs to me, while we've taught Smithy the words for "happy," "sad," "mad," and "tired," we've never bothered to teach him "scared." It's kind of strange when you think about it, since Ekman has named fear as one of the basic universal emotions. I wonder, if Smithy had access to that word, would he still be saying "mad" and "sad" so often. Perhaps we're misreading his experience and his intentions. I wonder what else he would tell us if we taught him to say more.

SMITHY'S BEDROOM JOURNAL ENTRY
FROM GAIL EHRLICH

June 9, 1975

I don't think that's a good idea. If we teach him the word "scared," he might think we want him to be scared. We might end up creating a problem that doesn't exist. Besides, there isn't any reason for him to be scared. He's got us to take care of him. We just have to try harder to get through to him and get him to confide in us.

SOLARIUM JOURNAL ENTRY
FROM GAIL EHRLICH

June 13, 1975

Jeff and I are now taking turns sleeping in Smithy's room. We've noticed that on the nights when he's with me, he calms down faster because he comes running to me for hugs and comfort. But when he's with Jeff, he signs more often. (Always "mad" or "bad" and "no sleep." I think he's mad because he's having bad sleep, or bad dreams or whatever. I'm cranky, too, when I don't get any sleep).

I've looked at Smithy's paintings for signs about what's going on in his head, but they don't look like anything. He layers lots of colors on top of each other and makes swirls all over the page. Tammy says that's because he likes to play with as many colors as possible, that he likes the way they look, but I think it means something. Vincent Van Gogh used lots of colors in his paintings and made the stars and flowers look like swirls. Some people said he was crazy, but others say he was just sensitive. I think Smithy is the same way. If I can encourage him to get all his feelings onto paper, maybe then he won't feel like he has to wake up screaming and throwing things at night.

But even when he can't sleep, his mind is still sharp. He came up with a new word all by himself today! I put on my sweater before we went out to play because it was gloomy, and Smithy saw that some of the thread at the bottom was loose. He started pulling on it as he made a sign I'd never seen before. I called Ruby to come look, and she said it looked like he was signing, "String." She showed me her Dictionary of ASL, and it was the actual sign for "string"! Smithy just came up with it by himself, and it was the right one. He's so smart! Ruby was so impressed, she was speechless.

I can't wait to see Piers's reaction! He's going to be so excited...

DIARY OF TAMMY COHEN

June 14, 1975

Our secret study strategy has developed complications. Eric succeeded in teaching Webster a new word, which he used yesterday, to Gail's astonishment. Instead of coming clean and explaining that he was surreptitiously training Webster, Eric allowed to her to think Webster had spontaneously acquired a new sign. I took him aside and explained this could have serious implications for the future of the study. Suppose Piers were to write an article claiming Webster magically developed a vocabulary word all by himself? That's tantamount to scientific perjury. Eric agreed not to engage in any future deception, but he still refuses tell Gail what really happened. I don't get it; is he afraid of her reaction?

I think I'll have to tell Gail I "discovered" April had previously taught Webster the sign for "string" in class, and that he's spontaneously <u>recovered</u> *it instead of inventing it. That won't correct the record fully, but it should stop an outrageous claim from snowballing. Gail will have to send Piers a retraction, but if I talk to her away from the crowd, it should soften the blow a little. Considering his "new word," I did broach the idea of Webster resuming classes. I spoke of Webster's lively mind, hungry to continue learning, and said we should act while he's receptive. She resisted; not permanently, but for the present. Gail believes Webster deserves an extended break, like kids getting summers off from school. She thinks it would be counterproductive to continue working Webster as hard as we've done this past year. She quoted to me some information about education and development she probably heard on TV about how young children need periods of free play so their brains can consolidate all they've learned before learning afresh.*

That Gail is considering sending Webster back to school in fall eases my mind. I hadn't realized before how much I'd come to depend on our regular routine. I'm tempted to argue Webster's broken nights are due to his broken structure, but I have no evidence of that. Despite how often I complained about Wanda the martinet, I see now how smoothly she kept everything running, and I regret her absence even more.

Nevertheless, I do admire Gail's gumption in taking the reins. God knows I wouldn't want the job. Perhaps I should show more support and ask how I can help her in her goals.

Except, Gail doesn't seem to need my help or advice anymore. When we were researchers, she looked up to me. Now that she's our leader, she seems almost patronizing toward me, toward Ruby, toward everyone but Piers. Ruby says eventually something unexpected will knock her off-balance, and then she'll want my help again. I don't care about that; I just want to know where this Gail came from. And where will she take us in the coming year?

DIARY OF RUBY CARDINI

June 27, 1975

Today has been a fabulous day! First, it's the end of Smithy's first full week without any nocturnal terrors. Jeff and Gail have agreed to let him sleep on his own again. We're all relieved, but Jeff and I are especially happy. It is aggravating, though, not to know what was upsetting Smithy.

Perhaps Eric was right that his behavior had to do with Wanda: the trauma of injuring her and her leaving. Maybe that all manifested in nightmares; such nightmares would certainly be sad, scary, and anger-inducing. It's been over a month since she left. Is that long enough to grieve?

In addition to our relief from Smithy's sleeping issues, the weather was gorgeous for the first time in weeks. We saw no clouds, and the air was warm. Gail suggested we go on a picnic. She initially proposed taking Smithy to the beach, but the rest of us talked her out of that because too many other people might be about. Gail didn't take our suggestion as criticism or us ganging up on her; she agreed to keep Smithy away from strangers by picnicking in the backyard.

Throughout the meal, Smithy behaved well, though he drank his Kool-Aid straight from the thermos instead of waiting for a cup, and he pounced on the Jell-O we were saving for dessert. He played for a little while in the tall tree, then climbed down and walked around, looking bereft. He signed, "Cat where cat?" Telling him, "No cat. Cat gone away" was the only blot on the day. I was afraid Smithy might throw a tantrum, but he just looked downcast. His little shoulders slumped, and his mouth turned down. Jeff started to tickle him, and that got him cooing again. We all played "tickle," and Smithy cheered up for the rest of the day. He even helped us clean up afterward by folding up the picnic blanket and washing the cups and plates.

Finally, Jeff told me he has a surprise for me for next week. He's calling it "an early birthday present." I can't imagine what it is. (It couldn't be a ring!) I'm excited to have him "home" again at night; that's enough of a present for me. I hope Smithy sleeps peacefully from here on. It feels so good to have everything back to normal.

UNEDITED INTERVIEW WITH TAMMY (COHEN) STEINMETZ, COURTESY OF "UNSOLVED MYSTERIES"

Broadcast Date: January 31, 1997

Tammy perches on a beige sofa. She wears a navy-blue long-sleeved dress, with a purple paisley shawl wound around one shoulder. Her hair is cut in a pixie style and curled. She wears large-framed silver glasses. An interviewer sits off camera.

We're ready to begin now. Just look into the camera and talk freely about what you remember. Say as much as you like. We can always edit this down. For now, please tell us what happened on the night of the accident.

OK.

Tammy draws a deep breath.

On the night of the accident, Gail Ehrlich, Eric Kaninchen, and I were alone at Trevor Hall. Wanda had left by then. Dr. Preis-Herald—Piers—was in New Haven attending a faculty function. Jeff Dalton and Ruby Cardini were out on a date. Jeff was taking her to dinner and then on a night-time harbor cruise to watch the fireworks. I remember joking with Ruby while she was getting ready by saying I would babysit for her this time, but she would have to cover me for the Bicentennial. You see, we still had every expectation of staying on at Trevor Hall for another year, or perhaps indefinitely.

It was a quiet evening. Smithy was behaving well, given that he could see we were short-handed. Eric and I gave him his bath, Gail fixed him dinner and then made him popcorn, and we all watched TV at the gatehouse until it got dark. Once the sun set, Gail urged us to go up on the roof so we could see the fireworks. Trevor Hall has a kind of widow's walk that you can access from the old servants' quarters, and it offers a gorgeous view of the surrounding homes, the water, the boats—

Was this the walk where…

Yes. It was from this walk that legend says a servant fell to her death.

She pauses.

We weren't supposed to be up there. Wanda and Piers were always cautioning us about weak spots in the roof, telling us it wasn't safe. But the view was so lovely that we often escaped to the top for special occasions. All six of us had watched the fireworks from this spot the year before with Smithy.

Anyway, the sun had just set, and we trooped up to the widow's walk again. The sky still held a tinge of red when we emerged onto the roof. I remember thinking we were too early, and Smithy would never have patience to wait until it got dark enough for fireworks. But the clouds rolled over the sun soon enough, and the spectacle began.

We had a perfect view of the fireworks over the harbor. They looked like little glowing dandelions blooming and blowing away in the sky. Smithy was entranced. He tried to catch them. None of us knew the sign for "fireworks." I just called them "light flowers." It was faster than finger spelling a new word. Eric was carrying him, against protocol, but it was a special occasion, and we were careless. He had to hold on tight, because after every new explosion, Smithy would lunge forward to grasp it. He didn't seem to mind that he never succeeded. It was a game. Gail and I would point and say, "Look! Look, there's another one!" We could also see people on their lawns and along Bellevue Avenue, waving flags or sparklers. It was a warm night, and there was a breeze—but not strong enough to make any of us lose our balance.

We must have stayed on the roof for an hour, maybe a little longer. Some of the neighbors—I don't know from which house—were singing patriotic anthems. Gail was singing along. I was getting tired. We'd had some champagne earlier—just a couple of glasses to toast the nation's birthday. Drinking makes me drowsy. I asked the others how much longer they were going to stay out. The harbor show was over, but now and then, you could see a burst of color from a private display on the ground. Eric said not much longer because his arms were getting tired. Smithy kept squirming and signing "down," so Eric lowered him. I watched him for a minute to make sure he didn't try to hop the railing, but he just stood next to Eric. Finally, I said good night.

I had just turned my back on my friends. I had opened the door leading back into the house, and I had just one foot on the stair when I heard Gail scream. That scream froze my blood. She was a jumpy girl, but this wasn't a dramatic squeal. She sounded terrified. I spun around, thinking something must have happened to Smithy.

And I couldn't see Gail! She wasn't where she had just been standing. It took me a moment to spot Eric; it had grown so dark by then. He was running toward the edge of the roof. Something was hunched over the railing. I heard Gail scream again, and I ran toward the sound.

Gail was hanging off the roof! Her little fingers were hooked over the parapet, but her body was dangling in the air. Her legs were kicking but there was nothing under her! No window ledge, no tree branches. Smithy was perched above her, growling. I saw him make a fist and *punch down* on Gail's hand!

Eric hesitated when he was a couple of feet from Smithy and said, "Help me, Tammy! Distract him!" I was aghast! I was sure I was about to watch Gail fall to her death. I was afraid Smithy would attack Eric next, and I knew I wasn't strong enough to pull both of them up by myself, let alone one of them. I thought if I got too close, Smithy could assault me, too.

All I could think to do was call him. I crouched down and sang out, "Smithy, come here!" He turned to look at me, and I signed, "Come, hurry." I told him it was cold and signed, "Inside." And wonder of wonders, he came toward me. I held out my hand and took his instead of picking him up. And I led him to the door.

All the while, Gail was crying and screaming; Eric told her to hold on, and he edged his way to where she was hanging and knelt down to pull her up. It's a miracle he could do that. His arms must have been ready to fall off after holding Smithy through the fireworks show. I deliberately tried not to look at them. I didn't want to draw Smithy's attention to the rescue effort. I tried to stay calm so I wouldn't upset Smithy, but inside, I was a maelstrom.

Smithy and I approached the door. I scooped him up under his arms, and with all my might, I threw him down the stairwell. He hit the bottom of the stairs and screeched, and I slammed the door. My only thought then was to keep him away from Gail, to keep him separate from the rest of us. It was a stupid plan because I was trapping myself, Eric, and Gail on the roof. In the interests of expediency though, all I wanted was to put *something* between us.

Smithy rattled the doorknob, trying to open it. Then the door popped out abruptly, and I knew he was trying to ram it open. I pressed my back against the door and braced my feet on either side of the frame to provide resistance. Now, I know this is going to sound strange…

Go on.

I know how hysteria works. I know I was panicked during the attack, but I'm sure I didn't imagine this. No matter how I try to rationalize it though, I can't make it work.

I could feel every blow against my back through the door. Smithy was pounding it with both fists, making the door dance in its frame. It was like he was playing a drum. The doorknob jiggled again. I watched it turn from side to side; I heard it rattle. At the same time, I felt another blow on the door from right behind my head, even as the other two were still going strong lower, behind my hips.

Tammy hesitates.

There were too many hands, you see. I tried to figure out how Smithy could bang on the door at those heights and turn the knob at the same time. Chimps have prehensile toes, yes, but he'd have had to be holding the knob with one hand—balancing on it really—and trying to beat down the door with his other three hands at the same time. I just can't picture that configuration, but he must have done it that way. Or he had someone else with him. Or I was wigging out.

I could hear him hooting, too—only, it wasn't the same call he made when he was frustrated because the cats wouldn't play with him, or he wanted to stay up past his bedtime. It was the way he screamed at night when he had bad dreams and was frightened.

All these silly observations went through my mind at once. I couldn't shut them off; I'd grown so used to recording my observations over that past year. But I remained fully aware of our danger. I kept looking around for something else that might brace the door shut, but of course that kind of convenience only exists in movies. I screamed for help, on the off-chance someone passing below would hear, but with our isolated position and fireworks still going off, nobody noticed.

The next thing I knew, Eric was beside me, supporting Gail. She looked like she was about to pass out. Her face was blank, and she was slumped over him. I was so glad to see them both safe. Eric said to me, "Tammy, we need you to go for help. I'll stay with Gail and hold the door."

I was incredulous. I said back, "Are you kidding? How will I get down from here? How will you brace the door?" I could barely keep Smithy back, and Eric was already tired, strained and holding Gail. I couldn't leave them to Smithy.

He said, "You have to bring back help. Gail's in shock. You and I won't be able to fend Smithy off by ourselves, and it won't be long before he gets through that door. Please hurry! Use the fire escape."

The fire escape must have gone back to 1924, to the days when the Bradley School occupied Trevor Hall. It was a rickety, rusty old ladder. The highest it went was to a window on the third floor; it didn't reach all the way to the roof. Jeff had to use it once when a bedroom caught fire, but he'd only gone to the second floor. I was concerned about the integrity of the scaffold. But it was our best chance.

I wished Eric luck. In my last glimpse of him, he was squatting with his shoulder pressed against the door. Gail was stretched out on the roof a few feet away, and she looked unconscious as Eric shielded her. I took a deep breath and jumped off the roof.

It was maybe a four- or five-foot drop. I
landed with both feet on the fire escape. I can
still remember the shock jarring up to my knees
and my legs buckling. But once I ascertained
that the ladder would hold my weight, I started
scrambling down it. I was never the best athlete
in school, but I think I would have given the
Russian gymnastics team a run for the gold that
night. I jumped over some steps and slid down
others until at last, I touched the ground.

At once, I started running for the Belancourts'
house. They were our nearest neighbors, and though
we'd had some run-ins with them over Smithy,
I knew they wouldn't turn me away. I sprinted
down our long, long drive and then down Bellevue
Avenue, all the while thinking, "Hurry, Tammy!
Hurry! They're going to be killed." A couple of
times, I fell. Tripped over a tree root, or a
flagstone. But I jumped right back up and kept
running.

I made it to Herbert Terrace. The gate was open,
thank goodness! I pounded on the front door, but
nobody came, and I feared the Belancourts might
have gone out to celebrate. I ran around the
house in a panic, screaming for help. I didn't
see any lights on anywhere inside. I sprinted
around to the back, down into the sunken garden.
I didn't even think about what I'd do if that dog
of theirs was out. I was frantic. If nobody was
home, I would have to go farther for help, and I
knew my friends were running out of time.

Nobody was in the garden, but I could see a
weak light on across the veranda. I got closer,
and through a window, I saw they were having a
party in a little ballroom at the back of the
house. I shouted and rapped on the glass, but
they were playing music, and no one could hear
me. So I pulled up a stone from the garden and

used it to break the window. That got everyone's attention.

I don't remember exactly what I said.

"Help me! Please help! He's going to kill them. Our chimp has gone crazy. My friends are trapped on the roof, and he's going to kill them. Hurry!"

That sounds about right.

Could you restate...?

Of course. I screamed, "Please help! He's going to kill them! My friends are trapped. Hurry!" Fortunately, they believed me. Christine Belancourt called emergency services while a group of male guests ran back to Trevor Hall with me. One of the guests had a gun that he'd been firing off to celebrate, and he swore that when he saw Smithy, he was going to shoot him.

I didn't know what I'd find back at the house. Deep down, I was certain we would be too late, and I'd just find pieces of Gail and Eric scattered over the roof. When we approached the house, I called for Eric and I heard him yell back. Then I knew he and Gail were still alive.

The men started scaling the fire escape. Denis Belancourt was an athletic man, almost a bodybuilder. When he reached the top of the fire ladder, he swung himself up the side of the house the rest of the way. A few moments later, he came back carrying Gail. He brought her all the way down himself. She was in a bad state, almost catatonic. She was so limp that at first, I was afraid she was dead. A couple of the other men helped Eric climb down. They said Smithy had broken the door—it was hanging off one hinge. But for some reason, instead of attacking Gail and Eric, he'd retreated.

We searched the house for him. I was worried the Belancourts' guest might actually kill Smithy. Even though he had threatened us, I didn't want that. We didn't find him in the kitchen or the solarium, nor on the stairs, so we went back up to his room. And sure enough, he was lying in his bed as though nothing had happened!

He sat up when we came in and just looked at us. It was as if he'd been expecting us. He didn't make any threatening moves, but he didn't pretend to be asleep or act surprised to see us—that, more than anything else, convinced me Smithy knew exactly what he had done. Normally, if he got in trouble, Smithy would play innocent. He would stare at you with a wounded expression when you told him he was bad or about to be punished, and he'd whine or protest in some way. He did this unless he was caught in the act and knew the jig was up. That's the sense I got from him that night.

We quickly slammed the bedroom door, and Eric locked it to contain him. Smithy didn't try to come after us or break the door down. Again, I think he knew he had done something wrong, and he was getting off lightly with a "time-out." We hurried back downstairs—even the guy who was armed.

Mr. Belancourt asked where Piers was. I said he was out of town, attending a party. He told me I needed to notify him about what had happened. I had the number of the house where the party was, so I called. It was noisy on the other end, and I had to keep asking for Piers to come to the phone. I remember repeating different iterations of his name over and over. Finally, he picked up—sounding tipsy and annoyed. I told him, "He's done it again! Smithy's tried to kill Gail!"

He said, "Damnation" and "I'm on my way" and hung up.

About that time, the ambulances and the police arrived. Ruby and Jeff came back, too. I saw them running up the driveway, looking frightened. What a homecoming that must have been after their date! Eric met them outside and explained, to them and the emergency personnel, what had happened. I was exhausted. My adrenaline had crashed, and I was ready to drop from all the running and fear. I remember telling Chris Belancourt I would pay for the window, but she told me not to worry about it, that I'd been through enough.

After the emergency vehicles left, with Ruby and Jeff riding to the hospital with Gail and Eric, I went back to the gatehouse. There was no way I was going to stay in the mansion after all that. Smithy was gone by then; the police had summoned someone from Animal Control to tranquilize him and take him into custody for observation. Piers would get him out eventually. But just the same, I had a bad feeling about the house. I went to Jeff and Ruby's room, lay down on their waterbed, and fell asleep instantly. I never even took off my shoes or glasses.

When I woke up in the morning, someone had covered me with a blanket. Jeff was making coffee, toast, and eggs. He and Eric were both in the kitchenette eating when I joined them. They explained Ruby had stayed overnight at the hospital to keep an eye on Gail, but that she'd phoned to say she was catching the bus back, and Gail was going to be fine. Piers was also in town and had gone to the pound to retrieve Smithy. He was going to take him back to New Haven for further observation.

Once she was released from the hospital, Gail decided she wanted to go home to Missouri. I don't think she ever set foot in Trevor Hall again. Piers cleared out her room, just like he had with Wanda's. He even tore down Smithy's paintings she had tacked up on the wall. I found the pieces in the garbage bin.

She pauses.

I didn't see Smithy attack Gail. Eric always said he just snapped and leapt at her. Suddenly, without warning. Just as he had to Wanda. But even if I don't know exactly what did happen, I know what *didn't*. Gail wasn't drunk; she didn't stumble or fall off the roof. The wind didn't blow her off either; we had a *breeze*, not a hurricane. I know some people have speculated the wind blew a spark or some ash into Smithy's eye and provoked him. That's a slim possibility. The largest fireworks show was far enough from Trevor Hall that I don't think any of its byproducts could have reached us. In all honesty, I don't spend much time thinking about an explanation. It's too upsetting.

Tammy pauses again.

That's my story of what happened on July 4th, 1975.

ARCHIVAL FILM FOOTAGE

Date: June 1974
Location: The Bathroom

Wanda, Gail, Tammy, and Ruby stand around Smithy's bathroom sink, wearing pajamas and bathrobes. Wanda's hair is in curlers. They hold toothbrushes and sing together, "This is the way we brush our teeth, brush our teeth, brush our teeth…"

As they sing, the girls pantomime brushing their teeth. Tammy squeezes toothpaste onto her brush, then Ruby's and Gail's. After brushing, Ruby takes a sip of water and gargles. Some water goes down at the wrong angle and she coughs and sputters, spraying water onto her robe instead of into the sink. Gail turns away and covers her face to obscure her giggling. Tammy continues singing, louder, and pats Ruby strongly on the back. Wanda circles with her finger, motioning to keep the camera going. Ruby regains equilibrium and finishes the song, scarlet-faced:

"This is the way we brush our teeth, when we get ready in the morning!"

DIARY OF RUBY CARDINI

And then there were four. Wanda has gone. Now Gail's gone, too. Another victim of Smithy's. Which of us will be next?

I didn't even get to say goodbye. I stayed all night with her in the hospital, until I knew she was just in shock and not injured. I came home because I was so bone-tired that I could feel my body collapsing any time I tried to sit down. But I intended to go back! Instead, I ended up sleeping through most of the day, and when I woke up, I was in such a funk that I didn't want to do anything except curl up next to Jeff.

I also thought Gail would come home when the hospital released her. But Gail was discharged sometime Saturday night and went to a motel until she could get a flight back to her real home and her family. I didn't know it until yesterday morning, when I went up to the house and met Piers, carrying a stack of boxes out to his car. That's when he told me he was shipping her things back to her because Gail was leaving. She didn't call us. She didn't even tell Tammy.

All morning, I've been looking through photos. I even asked Jeff to set up the projector and tortured myself by watching our film of "Smithy Street." We were so happy then! We had so many plans. We were working together and acting silly. It's a shame we never got to make another film. After Piers couldn't get the show on TV, Wanda said we couldn't justify investing the time to do any more. I wonder if she would have acted differently if she had known how much those happy days would come to mean later. How those films would capture her and Gail and all of us at our best and most innocent.

They both look so pretty in that movie. Like real actresses. I wonder if Wanda ever wanted to be an actress instead of a scientist. She would have been better off if she had. She was the kind of person who would have excelled at anything she tried.

There I go writing about Wanda in the past tense! Bad, bad habit!

It's funny; in the days right after she left, I missed Peter and Harriet more than I missed her. Now, I can't stop thinking about Wanda or Gail, and I wish so much that they were here and whole. They were part of my family, too. My little Trevor Hall family has scattered to the winds.

We've even lost Smithy. He's still under observation at the Animal Control facility. In animal jail. Jeff tried to see him today and got turned away. I don't know how long they intend to keep him. Surely, they can't mean to euthanize him! Nothing he's done could justify that!

Jeff's convinced he'll be released sooner or later, but he believes Piers will take him back to Yale whenever that happens. Maybe to observe him in confined quarters. Maybe to keep him away from us.

I don't know what's going to happen to us next. With Smithy away, will all this crap finally stop?

Is this how a condemned prisoner feels, awaiting sentencing?

How did we get here? No matter how many photos or movies I see, I just can't figure it out.

ARCHIVAL FILM FOOTAGE

Date: July 17, 1975
Location: The Library

Jeff, Ruby, Tammy, and Eric are seated in chairs, forming a circle before the empty fireplace. They look downcast and anxious.

Ruby asks, "So…now what?"

Jeff says, "That's what this meeting will determine, and since it definitely has bearing on the experiment, we're filming it for our records." He nods toward the camera. "Piers has given me some discretion as the senior-most member of the team. We can't continue the experiment with just the four of us. Smithy requires more attention than we can provide, especially these days. Now, we do have a pool of standbys who didn't quite make the cut the first time around—people who would appreciate the opportunity and would do well on our team. I could recruit two or three of them—"

Ruby shakes her head before he finishes speaking and says, "We can't bring more people into this house! We can't risk exposing anyone else."

Eric asks, "Could we move the study back to Yale?"

Jeff says, "The school lacks the facilities we need. A lab isn't an appropriate place to keep Smithy. He needs space to move around instead of spending his days locked in a cage."

Ruby says, "Maybe we could rent housing off-campus. An apartment or a small house wouldn't be that different from his living situation when he was with the McKenzies, and with the four of us pitching in with rent and chores, and maybe getting some other volunteers to come by every couple of days, we could make it work!" She looks around the circle, hopeful.

Tammy says, "It would be a step down from this place. I don't know how Smithy would adjust. We can't predict anything he'll do next. Besides, he was a baby when he lived in the McKenzies' cottage. He's much bigger now...and stronger...and more aggressive. I think he'd need more space."

Jeff says, "Before we discuss issues like housing, I need to ask: are we all committed to remaining in the study?"

"Pardon me, Jeff," Tammy cuts in. "But I think the question you really need to ask is whether it's right to continue the study."

Jeff, defensive, asks, "What do you mean?"

"Is it safe for us, and is it best for Smithy to keep going? We can't pretend the injuries—the horrific injuries—our friends have suffered were mere accidents. We can't brush aside Wanda's face or the way Gail almost died," Tammy says.

Ruby asks, anxiously, "How is she anyway? Has anyone talked to her?"

"I called her. She was my roomie, after all."

Ruby leans forward. "And?"

Tammy stares down at her fingernails. "At first, she sounded OK, but formal, as if we were strangers on an interview. But when I asked her about that night, she turned hysterical. She couldn't say what had happened and wouldn't even mention Smithy's name. Finally, I told her I was thinking of her and wished her well and hung up. She'll survive this. She won't even have any scars. But for now, I don't think she's ready to process it."

"Did she ask about any of us?" Ruby asks.

Tammy shakes her head, "No. She didn't even mention Eric, and he surely deserves credit for saving her life." She looks across the circle at Eric. Eric shrugs.

Ruby asks, "Eric, what happened up there? Why do you think Smithy jumped her?"

"She made him do it," Eric says, solemnly.

Tammy, astonished, asks, "Gail?"

Eric points upward vaguely and says, "No. *Her.* She's been behind all the weirdness in this house."

"The ghost had an affair with the master of the house when she was alive…Piers is running the study, so right now, he's the master of the house," Jeff chimes in.

"Well, technically, I think *Smithy's* the master of the house," Eric says. "Everything revolves around him."

"We all know Piers was sleeping with Wanda and Gail…The ghost must have gotten jealous, so she went after the people who were closest to him," Jeff offers.

"Y'know, looking back…in the days before the Fourth, when Smithy and Gail spent all their time together, I kind of had the feeling Smithy was keeping an eye on her," Eric says. "Like he wanted to protect her. Maybe he knew something was going to happen to her."

Tammy says, "*Smithy* happened to her."

Eric shakes his head. "Nah. He wouldn't have hurt her voluntarily."

"Eric, do you really think a ghost was involved?" Ruby asks.

Eric spreads his hands and speaks slowly. "It's easier to believe than Smithy's gone over the edge. What kind of alternative is that?"

Ruby measures her words. "So if you're right, then if we only took him away from here, he should be OK. Why don't we just tell Piers we need to find a new place to live?"

Tammy asks, "Ruby, are you going to gamble your safety on a simple move? Or the rest of our lives and limbs?" She glowers into the empty space in the center of the circle, speaking angrily. "Are we going to jeopardize our own health and welfare to put Piers's name in another journal? Is the fame worth all that? Are we going to keep pushing that chimp into more destructive rages to keep this study going?"

Jeff says, irritated, "You talk like Smithy is on a rampage or out to get us. You've helped raise him. You know him, Tammy! He's been going through a rough time, but like Ruby says—"

Tammy interrupts. "He's out of control. I can't imagine what could have pushed Smithy to aggress against Wanda or Gail. He adored them both! Even knowing he's developed a temper over the last few months, I never suspected this would happen. If he could attack them, then he could do worse to us! I don't know if it's deliberate or if he just snaps, but I don't care to find out for certain."

Ruby says, "Tammy, what are you saying?"

Tammy says, "I'm sorry, everyone, but I'm not willing to put myself at risk. I can no longer continue with this study."

Silence ensues. Finally, Jeff says, "Fair enough. But I'm sorry to lose you, Tammy." He reaches out to squeeze her hand.

Ruby, tearful, asks, "What will you do instead?"

Tammy says, "I'll go back to Columbia, finish my degree, and move on. But for the immediate future, I'm going to pack my bags and see if I can find a hotel room near town that won't cost me much. I really don't want to spend another night here."

"You could take the gatehouse. Nothing's ever happened there," Jeff offers.

"Thank you, but no. I'd rather get away from the property altogether." She stands; so does

Ruby. The women look at each other, and Ruby gives her a hug. Tammy says, softly, "I'm sorry."

Eric rises and extends his hand. "Good luck, Tammy."

Tammy shakes his hand and then hugs him. She turns and hugs Jeff. Everybody starts sniffling. Tammy says, "I guess I'd better hurry. I want to leave before dark."

"How will you get there?" Ruby asks.

"I'll call a cab. One brought me here; one can take me away." Tammy hesitates, then leaves the room, crying quietly. The other three return to their seats and remain silent for several moments.

Jeff says, "Well, that's that."

Ruby asks, "Eric, are you still in?"

Jeff shakes his head and says, "We can't continue with just three people."

Ruby says, "You said you'd recruit more."

Jeff looks stricken. "Piers told me he would only authorize me to recruit with the caveat that all four of *us* had to continue. I couldn't tell you that at the start of the meeting because I didn't want to unduly influence anyone's decision. He thinks if a founding member were to quit because she felt threatened…well, that it could deter other people, give us a bad rap. Tammy's leaving hurts our credibility. So no, we can't go on. I'm so sorry, Ruby."

Eric looks pained. Ruby stares at the ground, blinking rapidly. Her face is devoid of expression as she says, "So I repeat, what now? What's going to happen to Smithy without us?"

Jeff says, "Piers wants to sell him. He's got a couple of prospective buyers in mind already. Primate researchers. But not linguistics researchers."

Eric stands. "I'm still in if you want me, for whatever that's worth. Y'know, I'm trying not to think the worst of her, whoever she is. That must sound weird coming from me, when you know she scared the bejesus out of me. But maybe she doesn't know what effect she had on me, or on Smithy. Maybe she's not very good at communicating her intentions. A lot of my students weren't. I choose not to remember what I saw or what Smithy did. Instead, I remember the night Smithy almost choked to death. I always had a hard time believing he was able to trigger the fire alarm by himself while struggling for air. Maybe…maybe *she* did it because she saw he was in trouble and wanted to help. And if that's the case, then she can't be all that bad, right?" He looks from Jeff to Ruby. "Maybe we're misjudging her. Maybe something's happening here we don't understand yet, just as we didn't understand what Smithy meant when he was signing, 'Dark woman' for all those months."

Jeff says, "Well, we're not likely to figure out the answer in the time we have left here. But thanks anyway for your support, buddy."

The men backslap and hug each other. Eric and Ruby clasp hands. Eric steps back, awkwardly, then puts his hands in his pockets. "Well…I'll be in my room packing. Knock on my door if you want to watch a movie or something or…" He looks at the floor and exits without finishing his thought.

Ruby hugs herself and says, "And so it ends. Not with a bang, but a whimper." Jeff takes her hand. Ruby looks up at him and asks, "What are you going to do now?"

"Don't know. I hadn't thought about it. Don't want to think about it. I kept resisting the possibility the study would dissolve. But also, I've been worrying more about what's going to happen to Smithy than what will happen to me. I don't trust Piers to do right by him. He's angry about the way things have turned out. All the bad publicity. Piers wants to unload Smithy toot sweet, and my fear is he'll dump him in the first hellhole he can find, then wash his hands of the whole mess. I can't let that happen, Ruby! I can't leave him! I brought Smithy here. I carried him into this house myself." Jeff wipes his nose and tries to regain his equilibrium. "What about you? Where will you go next?"

"That depends," she replies.

Jeff asks, "On what?"

"On just how hellish Smithy's new hellhole turns out to be." Ruby offers Jeff a tentative smile. He gives her a long hug, then crosses to the camera. The picture goes black.

EXCERPT FROM
A RARE MEDIUM
BY ARMAND STOKES, PHD

REPRINTED WITH PERMISSION FROM
OPPOSING VIEWPOINTS: THE SUPERNATURAL,
SECOND EDITION, **ED. BY WILLIAM IRISH,**
BLACKHAVEN BOOKS, 1995

...As described by Lyle Ohrbach, animals possess a different range of sensory sensitivity than humans, allowing them to perceive stimuli that people cannot. A dog's sense of smell surpasses a human's. So does an eagle's sight or a bat's hearing. If ghosts exist on a different plane than what we call "reality," then it's entirely possible for animals to sense spirits.

Electromagnetic field (EMF) detectors often register the presence of strong energy in areas known to be haunted, including battlefields and haunted houses. Infrared sensors have also recorded abnormal levels of coldness in haunted spots. These findings suggest that a ghost is composed of energies that cannot be detected by (most) humans. On the other hand, these energies could fall within the sensory range of non-human animals. Therefore, when a dog barks at "nothing" or a cat stares into space, they could be reacting to the presence of an entity a human cannot perceive...

...Considering the testimony supporting a warm relationship between Smithy and his caregivers, it's plausible that the two notable exceptions when Smithy assaulted his female caregivers were not true attacks. Rather, Smithy may have been attempting to repel something else none of his caregivers were able to see...

EXCERPT FROM
"WHY CHIMPANZEES MAKE BAD MEDIUMS
AND WORSE PETS"
BY HARRY DINGWALL, PHD

REPRINTED WITH PERMISSION FROM
OPPOSING VIEWPOINTS: THE SUPERNATURAL,
SECOND EDITION, **ED. BY WILLIAM IRISH,**
BLACKHAVEN BOOKS, 1995

...No matter how much they may resemble us, no matter how charming they may look in human clothes, animals are not humans. They cannot be reasoned with. Their behavior is unpredictable. In the case of chimpanzees, their strength dramatically exceeds a human's, making them particularly dangerous when they lash out. Animals can and do attack without provocation. This is what happened to Wanda Karlewicz and Gail Ehrlich. Any wishful attempt to dismiss the chimpanzee's violent behavior as a reaction to ghostly activity is irresponsible and should be dismissed out of hand.

EXCERPT FROM
"THE LATEST WORD ON 'SMITHY'?"

TIME MAGAZINE
OCTOBER 9, 1978

"…Their people came from a cross-section, academically and age-wise," Gagnon muses. "A couple of the girls had never even been away from home before. Then they're thrown into a spooky, imposing old mansion that's falling apart around them and put in charge of a chimp. They were bound to be jumpy.

"At the same time, the seasoned grad students were making up the framework for the study as they went along and arguing about techniques. My impression was they never had a shared philosophy or plan of action on which everyone agreed. They were good people, and certain of them were quite idealistic, but at the end of the day, each strove more for credit for himself or herself rather than for what was best for Smithy."

Gagnon clarifies that the Yale students weren't at each other's throats constantly, but adds, "They weren't the Brady Bunch. Smithy picked up on all of that. He didn't like being at Trevor Hall. He'd ask his people when he could come back to our school. Here, he wasn't treated like a pawn. We had rules, and we didn't let him run amok, but we treated him with respect. While he was here, he was as well-behaved as a chimp could be. After a while, Sarah [McMann] started taking him home on weekends to give their team a break. She said Smithy was a good houseguest. He didn't escape, and he didn't start fires."

"Environment," Wellborn stresses, "can make all the difference to a child. We know that children from resource-deprived or broken homes struggle and sometimes stumble into lives of violence. Why should we be surprised that a human-like animal could become aggressive when chronically immersed in a stressful atmosphere?"

Was Trevor Hall haunted by the specters of ego and discord?

Wellborn remains philosophical on this point. "I understand the conditions are much worse at CSAM. I'm not surprised the ghosts followed them there…"

YALE UNIVERSITY PSYCHOLOGY DEPARTMENT
INTERNAL MEMO

It is herein resolved by unanimous vote of this Department that Research Animal #710642, a Chimpanzee, shall be transferred to the Center for the Scientific Advancement of Man, care of Manfred Teague, in exchange for the sum of $6,500. The Chimpanzee shall be used in exploratory studies involving, but not limited, to medical and psychological research.

One-half of the purchase price ($3,250) shall be paid on deposit immediately, to be placed into the Trust account. The balance ($3,250) shall be paid upon receipt of the Chimpanzee. Research Animal #710642 shall be surrendered in person by Piers Preis-Herald no later than August 15th, 1975.

Approved this 30th day of July 1975.

GRAND PATRONS

Phil Myers

INKSHARES

INKSHARES is a reader-driven publisher and producer based in Oakland, California. Our books are selected not by a group of editors, but by readers worldwide.

While we've published books by established writers like *Big Fish* author Daniel Wallace and *Star Wars: Rogue One* scribe Gary Whitta, our aim remains surfacing and developing the new author voices of tomorrow.

Previously unknown Inkshares authors have received starred reviews and been featured in the *New York Times*. Their books are on the front tables of Barnes & Noble and hundreds of independents nationwide, and many have been licensed by publishers in other major markets. They are also being adapted by Oscar-winning screenwriters at the biggest studios and networks.

Interested in making your own story a reality? Visit Inkshares.com to start your own project or find other great books.